BOOK 1 IN house of the living sky

constellations in the skin

J.D. GIGGY

Publishing Coordinator – Sharon Kizziah-Holmes

Paperback-Press
an imprint of A & S Publishing
A & S Holmes, Inc.

ISBN -13: 978-1-956806-36-6

DEDICATION

To all the creators, thinkers and innovators throughout our history that have left us their thoughts and accomplishments. They are the foundation of our cumulative knowledge, giving each of us the gift of inspiration and limitless possibility.

ACKNOWLEDGMENTS

Special thanks to my mother Nancy, without whose guidance in the editing and development of this story it would never have reached paper.

PROLOGUE: AN ACT OF WAR

Made of pure desire was the world when unborn
Nurtured by its longing until fated by its scorn
From Vaeba to the inmost veil, the cradle now is naught
In which the silent maker watches children she forgot
Murder, come in mercy, for her absent eyes are fair to me
Her songs of pain and passion are a darklight in soliloquy
I bid the mortal breaths of mortal kind to come and mesh
Now tell the endless story of the lonesome light and Manyflesh

It begins with humble heroes, the mighty but contrite
Most godlike of the mortals and so honorbound to fight
"Slaughter, end our hunger, that the mighty will survive.
Born to prey on predators and nourished by their lives.
Mercy rest, give way to power! Righteous passion rise.
Every soul that soars on wings, in righteous duty dies."
A truer word was never uttered by one of the serpent's sky
Lusting for the bitter taste of how he is meant to die
Depart from thought, pain and rue, as all their lights awaken
Return when he has fallen, and his father's star is taken
The end draws near upon his heels, a love that drowns in gloom
When every soul that soars on wings shares righteous duty's doom

From fallen thrones and wounded heart, buried in the sea
See the scattered pieces of its keeper breaking free
First a sister, then a mother, then a child pure and brave
Sharing in the ocean's blood and joining in its grave
Another, full of fire and hate, yet yearning to be held
Will suffer from their malice until waking mortal hell
For generations always fall, not by the pointed blade
But from the power left behind to children they have made

A shadow in my favored child emerges from a love sublime
Which, at the death of darkenspawn, will be his greatest crime
The culmination of his loss and eternal quest for a soul
Though for him, unknowingly, his family is the toll
That which raises dead from death, which only he could coerce
Brings with it the Son of Teeth and his immortal curse
Thence upon the darkest place where water loves the land
A soul without a soul emerges from the underhand.
She alone will know the way, by word and touch of Mother
Given light to pierce the path of Sister, Brother and Brother.
When Living Sky becomes the grave where Silence will decay
Those destroyed will be a guiding light to mother's way
Set free by her eulogy, her eyes of hunger call to me
The Merchant of Stars will manifest and take with it the will
Of Dying Wish's blight, keeping Sister Silence still
But ever then the Commanding Voice, resounding, will ordain
No rest for wicked children. Their forever ends with pain
No rest for any godlike and none for those in graves
When the endless join in emptiness to sing a prayer of blades

Heed this knowledge as I have. Depart from all your hate
Or come and end me now, my son, and send me to my mate

Hateful indeed was the thunder that pounded upon the airless void of that most distant of places from the red clay and flesh of earthplane. The radiance of creation's uppermost limit shone throughout the ineffable source of all light, immaterial refuge that it was from the world of land and sea below.

Filled with light, it was light and only light, this highest of the twenty-three veils. Infinite and singular, existing without time or depth, its pinnacle was close enough to touch the gateway beyond creation that could not open from within. Silken and plain, a rippling wall of power formed what was conceivably the very edge of existence. This was called the Far Edge by its creator and sole inhabitant. It opened at the maker's command, moved by its will, yet illuminated nothing beyond, for its keeper was greedy to keep the light as his own. Churning in the hue of luminous gold, ethereal and without substance, the purpose of the vast Far Edge was to draw all light across the veils into itself. It was born of here and lost far away. One drop at a time it was called home to be once more with its owner.

Unwitnessed for time beyond measure, a serpent with twenty-three bodies, many coiled as one, drifted inside this demi-world. Az'Rech was day. All daylight was his child, his armor and his grave. His form was as a river of mirrors with flares shimmering on every surface. Writhing, he reflected eternity without and power within. Crowned with wafting horns like ribbons of white flame, his twenty-three faces joined with such intricacy that one could not be seen without seeing all. Their features emoted nothing but behind his ever-changing eyes was a deep inner conflict of remorse and acceptance. They stared unblinking, no matter how he moved, at the shuddering entrance to his sanctuary. The thunder grew louder. His enemy had come.

The light within was no longer his own. There was a wound upon him, a darkness which did not belong there. He had reached out into the world, seeking to know it as he knew himself, and in so doing had found the thing he longed to touch most of all. He did not understand her, yet he knew her well, perhaps from a life unlived or a story unheard. She had felt his presence just as he had felt hers, reached out as he did. Their coming upon one another had led not to a joining but to a rejecting. He had touched her and broken her with his light. His punishment was how her darkness now clung to him, like a parasite slowly chewing through the only form he had. It would take time to consume him, but time no longer concerned him. It was a precious thing soon to be stolen from him.

Slithering over himself in an endless circle, one of his tails settled against the barrier as if to sense what lay beyond. The roar sounded distant, like the rumble of a conflagration deeply buried, and its vigor coursed through him. Despite the sure knowledge of his imminent demise, he remained steadfast, for he was the decider of law and understood little of fear or any other passion. In this moment they were new to his consciousness. Order, constancy; these would not protect him. This he knew. After so long apart, Az'Rech's son had returned, a father's life to claim and his power to wrench away. The age of quiet and contemplative existence had ended, now to be replaced by the age of savage passions.

Light was the vessel of the soul and the fabric of its weaving. Souls such as those of the Maengir, the world beneath the Far Edge where flesh and soul were as one, had illuminated the dark earthplane so that the living might remain living. In this way, each mortal season was counted as forty darknesses that each ended with a dawn. Maengir had survived nearly one hundred seventy-three thousand such seasons. He considered it his gift to them, unintended though it was. To be party to the upwelling of a new form of life had been his great privilege. However, it had required sacrifice. The world below was as much a part of his great antithesis, Escharka, as it was of him. His light was the soul of creation, and her flesh was its body, the world begotten by the cataclysm of their meeting.

He dwelt greatly on that nexus of his world and hers; Maengir, the mortal veil, a strange place between their domains where soul and flesh were as one. He was allowed only the briefest glimpse of it before being driven back into hiding, though he was content to have seen something so alien, so unlike himself, turning his light into something new. Desirable to him though it was, that world of the material mated to the immaterial could not last forever, though it had lasted long enough to resist its own end. Even the endless like himself were not truly endless. Death was the inevitable consequence of borrowed life, whether born of flesh, light, or something in between. The serpent had accepted this and found reason in it, before drawing his thoughts back to the present as the rumble from beyond the Veil grew to its climax. This was his final moment and he would accept death gratefully. His final words were whispered through that skin of the Far Edge that his errant offspring might hear his farewell and suffer with the knowledge of all that was soon to come. For events to unfold as he believed they would, they must begin with his fall.

Thetrulengo speaks,

It is a wondrous thing to realize that you exist. I could not comprehend this until the moment I perceived living things crawling up from the earthplane, born of darkness and light as the two collided and manifested a world so unlike either of them. Yet, it united them. I saw that they existed and had the epiphany that I, too, existed. Moreover, that I always had, for time beyond my own imagining. What had my existence been before I was aware of it? This is the question the greater portion of my consciousness has sought to answer. What can truly exist, without the ability to see beyond itself? If a part has no greater whole or other related parts, then it is not a part but the whole itself, forever oblivious to its own being...forever desolate. Indeed, if all that exists was of a single mind, unable to see its own beautiful pieces, it would surely weep from loneliness.

I learnt my present undertaking, the inscribed illustration of thoughts, from watching those that walk on the world below. I am compelled to imitate their rituals. They have written and so I will write. Truly, the very idea of language I also gleaned from those beneath. I have surmised that they record their experiences so that when their transient lives are ended the remnants they create from interrelations may acquire quickly that knowledge which their predecessors had taken a lifetime to learn, thus improving their state and advancing their kind as a whole.

Knowledge has become a source of power and, for a time, some possessing it grew beyond ordinary life, enough even to separate themselves from the material world the rest were bound to. One by one they amassed control of other beings and built a great deal of mystique around themselves, pretending themselves as masters of all. I was amused at their childish squabbling only to the point at which they started destroying one another. In recognizing their being, they sought to become the only one of their kind, hastening the end of their already impermanent existence. Is it a prized thing to die, I wonder? Perhaps I was wrong to assume that the value of life was intrinsic. After all, they were made impermanent, so why should their lives be eternal? Why might they be aggrieved by its loss? I have found longevity to be tedious at best, yet those who drank from the light became the light, postponing their death. In the discovery of stealing it from one another they had found their calling; eternal life by taking life, and in so doing crowned themselves gods.

For all their vainglory, eventually their flesh died in such a way that they were unable to recreate bodies for themselves. As it was, so their light transformed them into the stars that interrupt the darkness of night. They everlastingly look down upon creation as they are pulled back to their birthplace in the Far Edge, some with love for their beloved Maengir, others with malice. The history of these elder gods is a tangled web of betrayal and pain, ending in the death of all, but their power was not to be controlled by death. All have been swept away, yet six rule from beyond the grave: Zeniquorer the Savage, Miohaelia the Virgin, Ephielipax the Warlord, Quetzuaul the Deceiver, Ethulsula the Observer, and Oorghunak the Lover.

I write out of hope. I do not wish to be alone. I wish to be heard so that others might know what disorderly beauty I have seen in this mortal plane called the Maengir; the balancing point, the midplane.

Foremost, I disclose that this seemingly unique environment is composed of many particulate spirits that react to one another and form amalgams, which then comprise the greater world. These are held in common configurations by decaying energy that connects all corners of the Maengir in a single instance. The creatures these amalgams comprise understand this and have called it the Veil. The twenty-one intermediate aspects of the complete Veil are, beneath its energetic and material populations, a void. Void: that which is nothing, yet capable of being occupied by a thing. This definition of something that has no substance until occupied by something else is marvelous! Truly, it defines the emptiness I drifted in for...presumably longer than I have been coherent. It is what I was without the Maengir. It is with certainty that I speak the one great truth of all things pertaining to emptiness, much like the valley between two great mountains: A material world without awareness is as barren as a void without the material. A life without a definite purpose is, I infer, equally barren. By raising my finger and writing upon the face of the Maengir I have given myself purpose.

Have I merely adopted the meaning I see in mortality, the legacy of recorded thought? Is then any purpose that is not entirely unique worthwhile at all? I feel. I feel purpose. To feel something so strongly must mean it has value, yes?

I suspect all matters both physical and material are of far greater importance to the living than I, but I have tried to advance on their miniscule discoveries as to how all this existence is kept whole. I have learned many things of interest.

Despite a constant force that pushes all things inward against the two faces of earthplane, there seem to be distortions which allow things of great mass to remain suspended very high in the aetherplane, while the greatest of landmasses emerge in part from borderless waters far below. Columns of earth hold some of the smaller masses up, while others just sit idly in the sky with nothing at all to sustain them! Out of curiosity, I pushed one of them a bit, and as it moved it began to fall, crashing down. Great fun to see, though I discovered I had extinguished many smaller lives in the process.

That was on one of my very first days of this new knowledge of existence, what the creatures below call life. I had wanted to play more with the world but was readily distracted by the fleshy things I'd destroyed. They did not seem to notice the losses. Instead, they replenished, seeded one another and grew. And multiplied. I sat and watched as they created creeds and castes amongst themselves, ostensibly to determine how they would try to control and harness the resources Maengir offered. They are hungry.

My surmise is that my life is not made valued by its length, but by my own occupations. It would be presumptuous to assume that all living things must value themselves as I do. As they choose to be, so they shall be. Likewise, as I have chosen to value my own life, I must concede that I am likely incorrect. If a mind can change, then can it ever be reliably correct?

The mind fairly boggles when it considers what the mortal had been before they knew what they were. Perhaps this is why I have such an interest in them; they remind me so very much of myself.

Completely unaware for so long, though for them the memories lost are ones of horror and revulsion. It stirs strange and ambivalent feelings in me when I remember the beginning of all life, how they were created and, of course, how many times they were destroyed by...that strange darkness that created them. Father seems indifferent, while Mother decimates them, and only once has there ever been a change in the cycle of history. That is inconsequential at the moment. Today they live, and tomorrow they may die.

The most mundane concepts confuse and enthrall them. Things completely irrelevant to their lives they will scrutinize in a tireless effort to understand what they cannot control. 'Sharp tongue raised!', or so they say, for it seems that, in this aspect, I am closer to being like them with every passing day. Why this would be the case, and why it excites me, I do not yet know. The only conclusion I can draw is that I am a fool. My temperament is subject to what I observe in this world, and my conscious is obviously formed entirely by my observations. The end to which that leads is beyond me, for each coming moment I have not yet lived remains a mystery. I can command any piece of this fragile shell of life to do as I see fit. I must not condemn lesser beings for striving toward the same end. However, their days of progress will always be limited.

Ah, day! Day is still an oddity to me, far from my grasp and exclusive to this mortal Maengir. In the Far Edge, the luminous reach of Az'Rech's domain, there is no darkness. Though he is one of the creators apparent, I find his abode quite grating. It is harsh, his world filled entirely with blinding light. Once I looked on it and wondered what made it so. I suppose I have not always had either eyes or sight, but I choose to, so I do. Such has always been natural to me.

Escharka's black pit is no better. The Dark Edge is a place where not one ray of light shines, but in looking upon its fringes I was able to see in the same way I felt. With my nerves and heart, I knew every contour and hue of the flesh goddess who made it her home. The relationship between night and day do not exist in either distant realm. Leastwise in any way I can discern. One is one, and the other its foe. Considering each is essential in defining the other. Perhaps this is the root of the light cycle in Maengir; it is the world caught between these two extremes. Day and night are for mortality alone, and for me of course.

Though it was Escharka whose flesh became the Maengir, Az'Rech drowned it in his own light. A pact in natural creation between these two furies is what made them mindful, made them be. When they died, the remains of that spirit, their light, drew closer to Az'Rech, while their flesh was consumed by the dark earthplane. They yearn to be home with their father as their bodies return to the mother. It is haunting, really. A sea of spirits overhead, struggling for eternity to return to their origin, lighting the night sky when the day's Laesis burns out.

At any rate, the mortal seem blissfully unaware of how this came to pass. They understand the spiritual nature of the stars, praise them as Nhi'Thaun, north spirits. They believe the dead look down on them from above. How right they are.

The ether that covers the broad earthplane seems to ripple and shimmer on its surface, from the place of oceans to the place of mountains and bends the radiant energies of these stars into a sluggish wave of intense light and heat that repeats in due time. This they call Laesis, and it is day. Some days can last quite a bit longer than others, but that seems to have only a marginal effect on any given life.

There is another light that comes when Laesis has faded into the mountains, and this is the very last of the stars' energy, trapped beneath the clouds as earthen Maengir reflects it. They call it Lindu, the white-black. I imagine this is a sort of...poem, if I'm using the word correctly.

Most peculiar about this phenomenon is that the crest of Laesis – the breathing air having no color of its own – seems to assimilate the color of one of six extremely powerful souls that strain especially hard against the draw of the Far Edge to return to their old seats of power on earthplane. Their essence is discolored, misshapen, so full of energies molded after their liking that they are nothing akin to the peoples they left behind. They rise and fall in like fashion with the day-fire, but in much longer timeframes. This has become what the Maengir call the six seasons, some bountiful and known as the bearing, others harsh and called the passing:

The Sanguine Star, Nhi'Thaun Vaevul, is the soul remnant of the conflicted god Ephielipax, whom fate and the revelations of even higher beings turned from a terrifying warlord to a wise thinker. He had, in the best of his seasons, tried to guide his peers rather than subjugate and annihilate them. Even in death that desire lives on. As he falls from the sky, eager to lead Maengir again, he brings a cool blue Laesis that nurtures the living things and makes them strong. Even the men and animals grow faster. It is a comfort to welcome a new cycle, the first of the six seasons. Others of the firmament are less forgiving.

The Longhand Star, Nhi'Thaun Khonsael, is the lost soul of the god Oorghunak: more peaceable than Ephielipax but far more powerful. So great was his essence that he was forced to actively retreat from the residual energies of Az'Rech and prevent himself from growing, lest he, in his vast power, destroy himself and everything he encountered. While his fellow elder gods squabbled and vied for one another's provinces, he struggled to control his own passions and to stay alive. He was the strongest of all, but also the most lonely and full of longing. It was for love of another Nhi'Thaun that he unwisely unleashed his awesome power, and in doing so ripped his own corporeal form to pieces. His love momentarily defended, he yet would die with no offspring. Thus, he traversed the Veil and slipped into the sky with a whispered oath that he would see justice visited against all cruel gods, no matter their dominion. This he would do by blessing mortality, granting the boon of a white sky with the warm resplendence that is best, not for the beasts, but for the plant foods they need. Incongruous it is that such power would bless with soft winds and soothing rain.

The Windsong Star, Nhi'Thaun Buid'tskephae is the reflection of the lovely Miohaelia, the virginal goddess who seeded the oceans with kindly creatures that would accompany her through life. Though the very sight of gods and other monsters tearing at each other's throats weighed heavily upon her heart, her spirit remained sweet, and into the endless march of time her voice sang softly to ease the pain of the world. Such loveliness is rare in this universe and alas, some sought to take advantage of her goodness. One in particular was obsessed with not only abusing her purity but wholly corrupting it.

Her adversary was a rapacious god whose lustful eye never left her, and who eventually forcibly took her body and abused it often as the cruel fancy took him. Her simple joys were stripped away by his loathing but the last of it was decimated when his seed took root in her and became two ill-sired daughters. It was their birth that took her life, and all that remains of her tortured spirit is fear and uncertainty that manifests in her descent on the land. Her rising is accompanied by a blinding white sky, scorching wind and a dryness that parches the plains. She comes with a warning that the last bearing will come and go soon, serving as a reminder to conserve what is possessed and be mindful of what may happen to a land not well tended when the fields are dry and the rains don't come. Her message repeats: without love and care, the fruitful and wondrous will perish.

The Mirage Star, Nhi'Thaun Minthareb, is the last respite forewarned of. It is a chance to recover from Windsong and prepare for two subsequent passing seasons that will break the unprepared. It has a temperament not unlike its originator, the soul of Ethulsula the seeing god. Always lurking and scheming he was, but never violent, only an intelligent mind filled with curiosity. For this I admire him and consider him a being of my own kind. Like an animal in cover, he comes close to earthplane only to watch. His presence causes a bleak grey sky, and a cool dry that has an uncomfortable feeling. However, the plants seem to benefit from his sight. I think perhaps their silent and steady nature makes them closer to him than the fauna, and the fervor with which they grow during Mirage season is proof.

The Bone Star, Nhi'Thaun Thoeg comes with a cold violet sky, the reeking power of Zeniquorer the greedy god. If any elder god has a likeness to the ancient Escharka, mother goddess of flesh and earth, it is Zeniquorer. His lust was insatiable and his hate undiminished by the suffering of others. It was he who hunted Miohaelia to her bed each night and, like a ghost, he would come and go when she was most vulnerable, taking from her all the virtue she held dear. He was a god who thought of theft and murder as games, until Miohaelia became with child by him, then he swelled with cruelty. He came to take her again and to finally kill her and her two unborn children as penalty for their disruption of his game, but when he appeared and Miohaelia retreated into the abyss of the sea, one of the greatest miracles of the godly era was performed: The continents divided, east from west, and Oorghunak surged up from his protective cocoon. His pincers whirled, slithering body lashing out, binding Zeniquorer and smashing him with such overwhelming force that the mountains beneath the sea cracked to swallow them whole, and took all Miohaelia's Jiaiakhaadi with it. Oorghunak's dying breath professed his love for Miohaelia, but Zeniquorer burned with his loathing of her. Existing still as Nhi'Thaun, his madness is ever unleashed on the earth to freeze it, parch it of rain and blister the ground with lightning storms. When the Bone Star is closest to earth it is as though you can hear the sick cackling of the ignorant god, and the weeping of poor Miohaelia.

The cycle concludes with the fall and rise of Nhi'Thaun Malpael, the Mercy Star. Named so, this season is a cruel joke by the mortals, a misnomer of its original title, the Bleeding Heart Star. The Mercy Star is a spinning blade of amber light bejeweling a red sky, the mighty aftersoul of Quetzuaul the Deceiver. She was a goddess of the mind, able to dominate any creature through sheer force of will and responsible for the deaths of countless gods and mortals, until she soaked up their energies and became ruler of all she could see. As much power as her limitless desires had gained her, her own soul was her doom. Nothing could conquer her.

Only Ephielipax had fended her off briefly, yet he fell to her in the end. However, he fell not in battle but in love. His weakness was faith that he could make peace with her, a mistake he paid for with his life and dominion. In getting close enough to capture him she did join with him, thereby begetting him the son he had always hoped for. Sadly, the father would not live to see him born. Ironically, after she had finally taken his land and half of the known world with it, it was the son that killed her. So full of their souls was he that in the very moment he was born he turned upon her and devoured her, assuming supreme dominance of the aetherplane through the powers of both the mind and the sky.

From beyond her ethereal grave, Quetzuaul's vengeance stifles the advancement of life, killing the wind so that stillness swallows the world and not a drop of rain falls. It is a time hard suffered by mortals, for at its arrival the masses cower in their homes and wait for it to end before emerging again to the comforts of her victim's

Sanguine Season. Mercy in name, they speak it as if, by the mere speaking, it will yield to their pleas. Yet, though all other souls in the aetherplane may hear and mourn for them, Quetzuaul will not.

These phantasms of legend have governed the nature of the Maengir since the fall, when the mother flesh and father soul did clash and destroy each other. Even in death that which they were has resulted in this present world. Their nature is to be apart. Should even one return it will draw out the other, and just as before their meeting would destroy all.

Long has silence reigned. But one must wonder...Escharka and Az'Rech...where have they gone? They are outside the Maengir now, out of balance. Unable to be more than the single essence over which they have dominion, they are condemned to exist beyond the world they have created, yearning for it each with an insatiable need beyond compare.

~Chronicle of Wonders, Calendar of Souls

CHAPTER 1: FAR FALLEN SEED

Creamy white with mottled caerulean, soft like wax, the adaptive skin of a Mantichaena man began to flake and discolor in the abusive heat of a humid day. The restless sands were baked hard while thick vapor stifled the air as the stars changed and the season called Mercy transformed to that of Sanguine. That is to say, the star of Quetzuaul rose too high in the firmament for its light to reach Maengir and that of the sovereign Ephielipax fell closer to touch it. Red skies became blue, dry became wet, and the cycle began anew with the season of growth and goodness to sustain the living world.

The Mantichaena toiling beneath this changing sky was one of a particularly gentle brood; the Mearnum. Attuned to the lifestyle of the creatures whose form he was likened to, his rounded ears and seeking nose twitched at every sound and smell. A narrow face and a downy coat of grey fur accented his gentle nature, but he was not entirely animal, for he was not born so. This land had changed his people. The tribe had once been called Galaila, and they had been of a single kind. Their displacement to this land had resulted in irrevocable changes as their bodies and souls had united with those of other living things they encountered, flora and fauna alike. Manti was home now, the Island of "Skin", and its gifts were accepted and called beautiful. The Galaila had forsaken their birthname, embracing the power of Manti and taking the name Mantichaena, Children of Skin.

The Galaila had originated from the great land of Ellel across the sea, where cities thrived on the bustle of millions kept safe by strong walls. Generations of prosperity and progress had made life easy back home, and they had reveled in their peace under the benevolence of their god, Loi, sovereign of the sky. But that life had ended abruptly with the arrival of the evil Ferraro, a goddess and conjurer of stone and fire who reduced their proud civilization to ash. Their god had done nothing, had apparently forsaken them. And so, as one, the people had fled from Ellel in the hope that undiscovered lands would afford them safety where Loi had failed.

The Galaila had washed ashore on the stony beaches of Manti only a few short seasons ago, dismantling their ships for supply as they migrated inland. Unaccustomed to the degree of exposure on this ostensibly uninhabited land, they strove to triumph over mere discomfort so that a new home could be born. To their woe, their trials had not ended at the shoreline, nor when they were fed and sheltered in the hills beyond. Once more, as if by the wrath of yet another goddess, they were being displaced, fleeing for their lives from a foe that could not be slain; disease.

Mearnum were not known for their endurance, but urgency made this one strong and his bushy tail gave him exceptional agility as he traversed the dangerously rocky parts of the landscape. His eyes were keenly employed to find a refuge, along with several others of his brood scattered to the trackless sea of scrub-mottled dunes and cracking hills of stone. Heaving wounded breaths, he paused at the crest of such a heap of rock, down low on his paws and shielding his eyes against the wind as he studied the unseen lands all around. There was only sky to the south, a hypnotic expanse of shifting clouds over a flat desolation. In stark contrast, the north was stone, all mountains that crawled toward the aetherplane against the law that stone must fall. Too far to reach on foot, shards of the land were lifted by some ancient and godly power as they hung like a stairway to the stars. Unscalable, he thought. Even the strongest Mantichaena could not mount their dizzying heights, nor the most nimble leap the gaps between them. The higher earthplane, as they had named it when seen from afar, was untouched by even those with wings. There would be no reaching it in time. Not today.

To the west were the also impassable cliffs Taultolm, whose ancient bastion had formed where two of the undersea continents of Miohaelia's domain collided and rose above the landscape in a wall of shear faces and broken edges. Long had the winged Mantichaena spoken of this cliff, wary of what they might find above or beyond it, until they had just a few days prior been sent to investigate the other side. Reluctantly, deeply fearful, the Mearnum's gaze returned to the East at his back. Like the south, stone desert stretched to the distant horizon, though now choked by smoke and destruction. What few groves of fungal thi'zech had sheltered their survivors were now ablaze, and there was nothing to be gained by looking that direction, only a reminder of what should befall them if he failed. They were trapped now, whether by stone or sheer distance made no difference.

Under the mournful watch of the departing Mercy star, his people had only just adapted to their new ways of life, learning not just to survive but to thrive without the shelters of stone and metal erected by their ancestors back on the mother-island. Though cunning and crafty, they took no solace in the coming of Sanguine season. Its pleasant temperature and frequent showers would be little appreciated by a people still recovering from the loss of their cozy indoor lives as craftsmen, poets, clergy, and artists.

Tired, dusty, bloodied but undeterred, the Mearnum's bones ached as he desperately pressed onward, pursuing Laesis' rise in the West and the breaking of dawn beyond the cliffs. Clawing his way over yet another gravelly hilltop, he was struck by a sticky wind that threatened to knock him tip over tail back the way he had come. Bracing against the grit that flew against him, his hazy pupils dilated, and his tail thrashed in excitement at the sight beyond the curtains of debris: a canyon lay before him, a single passable avenue through the otherwise impregnable bluffs. He calmed for an instant and allowed the sense of accomplishment to course through him. From north to south, the icy Thaun to the black Dhai, this lithic wall had warned against any attempt to pass, but he and he alone had found a route of exodus. Not Govan, not Keimas, but he. His elation lasted for only a moment before his curved ears flattened against his head at a distant scream echoing from the trail behind. There was no time to lose, elsewise more lives would be lost. He tumbled gracelessly backward and scrambled up the opposing slope, dreading to look beyond, but steeling himself to give the news of deliverance.

Flailing his arms and crying out in a raspy voice, he hailed the handful of his kind – and more of other broods, for the forms of the Mantichaena were many – who fought across the rough terrain below.

"Hawth elein! Bethe Hai, h'etain pohs!" he howled. "Toward my way! See the west, the high is open!

Even as he announced the discovery, his spirit withered, and his features drooped as he swallowed the sight before him. His tribe fled not only the horrifying scourge, but one another as well, spread across the rolling wastes and evading contact with members of their own families. Panic caused them to recoil from any touch, be it of flesh, weed or stone. Nothing and no one was safe. At his call he witnessed an abrupt convergence as the forerunners took note and called others to attend the signal and pursue it. The others followed like a spooked herd, moved by instinct, fleeing the crashing tide of decay and death.

The infection had spread ravenously, reaching from host to victim as suddenly as it had appeared, and within a single day his people had been forced to flee their ramshackle encampment without even time to gather food or water. It had come from the ground, from the springs and from the roots of the thi, climbing through any permeable substance or source of water as if hunting for them. Their clothes moldered, their stores turned fetid, and nearly three thousand strong had been reduced to a few hundred. Naked and afraid, certain that they too would soon die, the people left what little they had and ran for their lives. So recently had they watched their elders, children, countrymen burned alive on Ellel. They wept and wailed at the sight of hundreds more rotting from the inside, driven to crazed violence by the plague until their blackened skin burst into flame at the touch of daylight. Flora behind them visibly withered, infested, and overcome by slithering trails of bubbling ooze that burned as it passed. Those who stopped to stare in horror would say it moved as if it was alive, but could not survive outside a dark hiding place. Even the sand darkened as the disease moved across the land. The air was choked by billowing smoke from its incineration, and a withering army of those already contaminated pursued the healthy, belching and bleeding the infection as their skin perforated and sluffed off.

Possessed by a blind rage, the infected seemed compelled to kill anything in their path until, one by one, they crumbled; loved ones overcome, claimed by an outbreak of such grotesqueness the likes of which had never before been seen. The pestilence was not a mortal hatred or some insatiable hunger: It had not appeared to even be a sickening will of the victims. This thing possessed, rendered the host incapable of resisting its need to spread. Any attempt to treat the sick had only infected the caregivers, and after only a few moments of seizure and vomit made them its own. Even death did not bring them release. The dead were part of it.

The Mearnum scout shook himself free of his paralysis as an archon of the tribe finally reached his position on the hill. Trembling, gasping for air, the father of temple Alchuneb gripped the scout's arm and gaped over his shoulder. His curling white horns flashed in the light, and when he finally stood to full height his broad chest rose over the smaller man's head. Grimy claws tipping his fingers released their grasp, and he gestured amazedly to the welcome sight.

"A pass...an escape!" He huffed.

As much to convince himself as the Patriarch, the scout stammered in reply "*Utan* Novun...we're going to make it."

Novun cast a frantic glance to his back, swung about and roared for his many beleaguered houses not to let their strength falter. Where their backs had been against a true and literal wall, that wall had seemingly split itself to give them hope.

Catastrophic as their situation was, most of those that yet lived were well ahead of the carnage. They had the advantage of distance now, and hearing that there was imminent protection in the stone ahead revived their aching hearts. The fathers and mothers of the other temples echoed Novun's mighty call and directed the people. The journey had felt eternal, but after thousands of seasons upon this earthplane, this would not be where their species met its end. They had endured and survived wars both corporeal and celestial, and they would survive this.

The elders waited at that crest as the tribe stampeded past, watching warily for any who fell behind. There would be none of the healthy who fell, for one of their best, a peerless champion, followed in the wake of the mob and collected those who succumbed to fatigue: Dace of temple Bpestaeda, created only in part by a beast, and the rest by the mountains. As Novun was tall beside his rodential scout, so was Dace uniquely titanic in comparison to all other Mantichaena. He was a Bakul, the first of his kind, towering at nineteen feet, stout with muscle and protected by a tough mineral shell and spikes. Thick tusks weighed heavily in his maw, and similar protrusions of brassic stone budded down his back, shoulders and legs. Dauntless when riled, Dace used his great strength to rescue his precious kin, hauling the slowest from the ground and piling them upon his back, easily hefting the weight of fifteen bodies without losing speed. Fearless in his heart and tireless in his charge, he was inappropriately positive, grinning greatly as he roared across the sands *"Hawth inhai!* None more will fall today!" A gentleman brute and jovial warrior, the great Bakul wasted no focus on lamenting those already dead. That time would come. For now he must be strong and save the lives he could.

The gathered archons of the various temples bowed exhaustedly as the highest among them crested the mount. The Primarch was of the Kuolt brood. His sinewy arms and legs were covered with thick brown fur, and sharp bone protruded at each joint, finger and toe. He was no hunter as most Kuolt had chosen to be, rather a governor, revered as the one chosen by the divine skies and their patron Loi to reign as supreme authority of the tribe. His name, in that honorary capacity, was Primarch Sky.

Resting briefly, he glanced about at the sixteen assembled Utanaia, the exalted men and women of the tribe's council. This place had changed them all, working its terrible blessings since their inauspicious arrival. He gazed at the various forms his people had taken. Some had horns, built to endure. Others had claws, built for predation. Some were meek and ingenious, and others still were dexterous and sly. Becoming Mantichaena, their bodies and minds were shaped anew and ever-changing, but each retained the nebulous skin and slitted eyes of the Galaila they had once been. They were becoming stronger, and each held a valued place in the society they were building, one where the brood that transformed one defined one's function.

A tremendous shriek shattered the air, and the thunder of

19

wingbeats thrust back the stench of sickness and ash as four great flyers, two men and two monsters, soared down from the North sky. Yet another brood of the Mantichaena, this one stood alone as the most dangerous of all. The Kutu were the protectors of the people, and their hunts were the kutliku from whom their wings were stolen. Transformed into the image of the massive reptilian birds of prey they had found unlikely companionship with, theirs was a life of liberating flight, the most exalted of all Mantichaena. Govan and his hunter-killers. With great talons on their feet, razor claws and teeth, barbed wings that cast the ground into darkness, there was no creature on Manti that would challenge a Kutu. They plunged to the rocky hilltop, landing in a cloud of dust and sand, and called with purpose to one of the weary archons. The speaker was just a boy, his wings barely beyond fledging, but alongside his large and mature mentor he was considered an equal.

"Father Aroch!" Young Keimas cried, aghast at the wretched sight before him, "What has gone on? What is this black fire? Is Lemalie alright!?"

Aroch, one of the spiral-horned Kubernu and being of great stature, seized him by the wrist and led him toward the canyon wall.

"Thereto, Keimas!" He assured the lad. "She is there, leading the people! Go and see what tasks she may have for you!"

Keimas launched from the hilltop in a whirlwind, made for the shaded crevasse in search of the girl that owned his heart.

Govan, the first Kutu and founder of the order, remained with the two hunts. These were the flying kutliku that shared their captors' lives and duties; Sotoatna'thane and Bogh'thane. Long and lustrous feathers bloomed from all their flesh except for a scaled neck and belly, ruffling out as they loomed on folded wings like living statues, darkening the gathering with their awesome presence as they awaited further command. Their eyes were restless at the still echoing cries of the distressed Mantichaena, yet they attended Govan obediently as he addressed the Primarch.

"*Utan*...by the blood of Loi..."

Sky's gaze never wavered from the scene before him. He took Govan's hand tightly and imbued him with purpose.

"*Udai*, tell me quickly, is the Westland in such a state of death?"

"N...no, father," the Kutu sputtered, still disbelieving what he was seeing. "It is as we first brought word; lush and bountiful." He looked up at the vast gap in the cliffs, ashamed that such a road had eluded him. "And it's just beyond this chasm."

As the last of the stragglers gained the high entrance to the gorge, they were met with furious activity as their fellow tribesmen surged around them, mounding stone upon stone, slowly blocking the mouth in a vain effort to shield against the onslaught of disease.

"Heave to!" Novun bellowed at the gasping workmen. "Tightly lay and leave no crack!" He sprinted back and forth across the wide opening, he himself hauling boulders to build the wall with little hope of success. Some had begun to collapse as fatigue overtook them and were hefted and carried away while others toiled on. This most desperate day was not over yet.

Standing amidst the frenzy was a brittle old man, Raru, his body transformed by the sap and frond of the thi'tskreol. One of the Mantichaena Thiwa, lignified vines grew in and among his muscles, bark across his skin, and in the short time he had stood stationary his feet were already taking root in the ground. Though his kind worked at common tasks their communion with the flora made them privy to secrets unknown to his brethren. His newly developed command of growing things combined with a lifetime of study in the art of classical mancy, the manipulation of the material world, had made him one of the most accomplished enchanters of his generation. The depth of his great power was about to make a rare appearance. Shaking the dust from his leaf-woven hair Raru growled through the haze at the enemy rising over the hills. Then with a sharp whistle he beckoned to those few who had committed to studying under his tutelage. Only four joined him, but they were enough; enough power to make a stand. The last of the tribe were through the rising wall now, but the wall was unfinished. The Thiwa Archon held a brief conference with his students, explaining and instructing quickly. At his war cry, the laborers closing the gap fell back as his chosen few aligned themselves near the opening and began incanting a powerful bond with their master, drawing ornate floating glyphs in the air, while Raru vaulted over the hastily built barricade and back out into the waste. Cries of alarm and protest followed as he ran past, but he would not be deterred. He shouted a single word as he stood against the horde: "*Bathleshauan!* Close the gate!". The students raised their hands and nearly invisible trickles of amber energy crackled along their curious scripts. The master layed an intricate inscription into the ground with a single stroke of his hand, joined them in lifting his arms, and repeated "*Bathleshauan!*"

As one, the students flexed and shouted, drawing their open palms inward, as though pulling against an invisible force. The earth shuddered and debris flew from cracks in the cliffs as their combined efforts ripped great sheets of rock away and dragged them over the wide mouth of the canyon. A flurry of concerned hands and voices tried to reach through toward Raru, but they were quickly recalled as the stones previously piled were bullied out of the way by the closing walls.

With no time to lose, Raru's fingers fluttered and twisted the ground around him as he set his own writing alight and summoned the living essence of the sand, rock, plant and air through it. He waited while rotting Mantichaena and tendrils of ruinous muck clambered through the hummocks toward him, their foul stench arriving in advance. Without a word or sound, he arched his back, thrust his fists down and sent the summation of his power into the ground. It buckled and thrust upward, rolling over itself and plowing forward in a surge that repelled and drowned the forefront of the infection. Thrice he landed the same blow and each time it drove back the dunes themselves, reshaping the ground into a slope as the unliving enemy was thrown back in a storm of stone. A stunned silence gripped the Mantichaena. Rumors of Raru's study had not prepared them for what he could do when his soul's accumulated essence was poured into a single miracle.

Still they screamed for him to save himself as the last glimpse of him grew more and more obscured by the barrier and, in the final moment before its sealing, they were knocked to the ground as the master enchanter hurled himself through the gap, its sundering edges nearly catching his legs as they slammed shut.

The good people returned to the task of piling stones in earnest but there was no more that need be done. Enchanter superior Raru gathered his class and together they ushered the last of the laborers away. Sky and a few other archons lingered, along with Govan and some of the foremen among masons. They appraised the work with unresolved concern, doubting the usefulness of stone in the face of a death that swam through its cracks like water. Quite unafraid, Raru gestured sharply to the enchanters once more, putting them to task and turning to Sky.

"Father, go and give the people a home. I will seal these gates forever and hang them high."

After a moment's pause, Sky affirmed the promise with a trusting nod. All departed heavily, finally calming enough that the sheer enervation of their ordeal finally caught up with them. They had faith in Raru, for his works had gained wide renown even before this spectacle. Though now he seemed more leaf and branch than man, his demonstration had proven he had lost none of his former glory, was in fact more gifted than they could have dreamed.

Raru's students approached the sturdy door and began a long night's work of writing a soul into it. Bit by painstaking bit, they would weave intricate enchantments into it and give it a mind of its own, a blessing that would purge any uncleanliness that dared draw near. Earth interwoven with Minpaxa, the veil of purity, could not be breached, not even by this inestimable corruption. Every time a level of enchantment was complete, they joined together over their carvings and their power coursed into it, driving the foundation upward to expose untouched rock and raise it ever higher, repeating this labor until two hundred feet of gleaming spellwork sealed them forever on this side of extinction.

What a different day this might have been, Raru dourly considered when his task was complete, imagining if he had attempted such an achievement in anticipation of this unforeseeable affair. *Never again*, he vowed as his fingertips caressed the glyphs upon his gate. He would build his school stronger and with it all schools and all practices that could defeat this evil. Never again would it pose a threat to them. Not while he drew breath. The schools of Classical, Romantic and Gothic mancy needed new blood. Their Enchanters, Sanctifiers and Witchcrafters respectively needed to train like never before. This 'Thuell', this corruption, would surely come again. They would be ready for it.

23

Thetrulengo speaks,

Though the Mantichaena have shed their natural form, Galaila no more, there are still remnant manifestations of who they once were. Whether Kutu or Ennedeghe, no Mantichaena appears entirely unlike their old bodies. I enjoy that sentiment, that no matter what changes any one thing experiences, a piece of its origin will always be with it.

Galaila were, by all accounts, a feeble race. They valued intellect and ingenuity, and were bred for such, not for battle, so blessed with adept senses as they were. Their skin, a soft material with a blueish spotting, functions similarly to the bark of the thi. The discoloration doesn't appear in the same patterns from one person to the next, but serves the same function. It enables them to absorb unusual amounts of light as though it were sustenance. As they mature, these darker patches shrink, and the body grows proportionately slower. I do infer that their paler skin does not react as well to light, for the elderly lose this mottling and become almost entirely white.

Their frame, just as their skin, has no standard of form that I can establish. One may be twice as tall as another of the same age. Elderly and youthful alike may be immense or diminutive. While some are slight and boney, their brother or sister is vast and muscled. Ephielipax put little effort into consistency when he divined the form his children would take.

In their original form, Galaila ears have a rounded point, sloping down toward the back of the neck. After being 'taken' by Manti, that basic shape is altered based on their K'hizu brood, with almost entirely unique results. The eyes alone have been constant, however. There is a lateral slit of pupil surrounded by a muscular tissue that can flatten or open it as needed. Embedded over this colorful iris is another layer of milky white fibers that can change shape to cover more of the eye. Its function would appear similar to their eyelid, but it has many moving pieces rather than one. If it serves a purpose, I do not know what it is, though I suspect it allows them to reduce the light entering their eyes while *still able to see, much like their variable pupil.*

Their noses are shallow, smooth from the crest of their brow to just above the lips, typically thin, but once more it can change as they are reshaped by the K'hizu. Alongside this organ are two more at the base of the forehead; flexing orifices that flare or tighten in the presence of not only scent, but sound and heat as well. As I understand, they do no more than combine the purpose of skin, ear and nose, but to what end? I have noted similar organs on some breeds of K'hizu, though not always in the same place, but Galaila are not born to be predators. A closer inspection yields the theory that while their individual organs serve a more general, defensive purpose, these amalgamated sensory pits are directional, used for sensing what is directly in front of them. Perhaps this is why Mantichaena, as well as K'hizu, move their heads about erratically when perceiving their surroundings? It fascinates me that this could allow them to hear and smell much better in a chosen direction.

They interest me, but dedicating so much time to them may be foolish. They were beasts long before their evolution in this land. To argue that they have become anything they were not previously would lack sense. An animal is an animal, after all.

~ Chronicle of Wonders, Figures of Animation

Dawn broke over the band of refugees, as did the weary revelation that the plague had indeed been stopped at the wall. Few but the very young, or very old, had slept, despite overwhelming exhaustion, as they waited to see if the horror would yet reappear. Even the most stalwart struggled against despondency. Manti had seemed a godsend in their flight from the destruction of their homeland, but it remained a great mystery, and they knew nothing of what waited ahead. And this, this tragedy weighed heavily on every heart.

Manti, 'Skin' in the ancestral Ell'hgan, was the demesne of a new goddess yet unknown to those by whom it was named, far removed from the westmost horizons. It was an untamed land, or so believed the weary refugees. Destined unintentionally for its eastern shore, the errant flotilla had fled the greater lands of Ellel and endured a full season of storm and suffering before being cast upon Manti's shores. Starvation had followed them, for their flight from home had been without benefit of supplies. For so many mouths to feed, netting of seabeasts had been insufficient, and many were as bone tented with skin when they had at last washed ashore. It had no more been a fond farewell to a prosperous life than what they had just escaped. The similarities were as painful as they were numerous, and so many despaired that that which had destroyed their home had followed them here: nemesis among divines come to their homeland, fire belched from the shattered ground as fragments of a dark goddess fell to strike the land.

Ellel had been just as the beaches of Manti, a ruined world laid low by the wrath of their enemy of legend; Ferraro, Mistress of Night and the Deep Earthplane. She remained forever the foe of their beloved benefactor, Loi of the Open Sky. Without the intervention of their deity, revered for the breadth of an era, the nation had been devastated. Where had Loi been when fire fell from his Jioukaadi? The protection they thought indubitable after lifetimes of worship was absent as the blue sky turned darkly vermillion, like day's end turning to blood. The red night had fallen as thousands had fled their homes, entire cities collapsing into the ground as it shook and opened. Even still, the memory of their homeland was a savory dream kept in the hearts of those who had escaped; The coastal settlements, ports of reasonable affluence that had barely begun to open trade by sea across the island. They had spread to the limits of the continent, but never beyond. Life had been good for hundreds of generations. Perhaps it was Loi's plan that they should move on to a new life. If it were so, then they could not be sure this was where they were meant to be. Manti might have become a thriving port of trade in another, more gentle reality. On these high mountains and forested valleys, where the land itself had transformed them, they had had such potential for a new life. They had long been a visionary people that dreamed of art and culture. But today dreams seemed far away.

They stood tall, alive, at the western mouth of the canyon where their eyes beheld proof that they were watched over by munificent Loi. The cliffs at the opposite side shot down for a thousand feet, sweeping out and disappearing under a limitless sea of towering thi, a tangle of fronds, petals and fungus that blanketed the mountainside. Beyond, lush hills seemingly rolled all the way to the horizon; bursting with life, overflowing with water. Dangerous, surely, but today they were alive. They had a fortress in this canyon and hope stirred that Manti might yet allow them to live.

CHAPTER 2: VIOLENCE OF NATURE

The Division Age – A Historic Record
Article 11
Island of Manti: Initial Measurements

I *have requested finer quarters from Raru. If you have read this in pleasure, please harass him about allowing me something more than a closet in which to conduct my research.*

These first measurements are for record. Blessed is the next who refines them.

Our traverse of the Nemhai took us eighty-two days. Maintaining a cutting speed of 5.2 knots, I estimate that we are approximately 3,300 and 3,500 leagues from Manti. With nothing but Laesis to guide us I expect we journeyed the lower estimate, and more may be added due to a horrific storm that blew us on a southerly arc. Cisiveo, our premier resident physic, thinks it's closer to 22,000 and that the storm helped us along. She may be right. I differ, but perhaps only because I am perturbed to think any good came of a whirlwind that sent two of our gondolas to the bowels of Nemhai. We are fortunate to have made it with the 28 we did, burdened as they were by our numbers.

The measured distance between Nhi'Thaun Buid'Tskephae and

Nhi'Thaun Khonsael is shorter here by approximately one eighth. We have tried to tune our instruments to account for this, but we no longer have the same landmarks to relate them to. There is no guarantee that our terrestrial measurements are correct. Nonetheless, we have made attempts. From the clifftops, we have begun using the aviary tips as well as the edges of the higher earthplane in the Thaun to calibrate our equipment, and I believe we are very close. Employing historic methods, we have determined distances only to what we can see.

From the East edge of the city to the shore where we landed is, at most, 120 leagues.

From mountain to sea, its North-South breadth is much less on the East side; cut to 82.4 leagues.

The plateau of Hanging Gate and the canyon itself is, from East to West, exactly 1.8 leagues.

We cannot begin to estimate the distances across the vast Ni'ivitnem forests in the west. The horizon consumes it in all directions. To the furthest points we can see, the stars have helped us measure 180 leagues. I have no confidence that we will ever see the far side of the island. Even on the clearest day we cannot see its end, but the Kutu have not yet explored far. Someday our descendants may see that shore, but only through many days of flight. The forest floor is far too dangerous to attempt so long a journey on foot. The predators of its tangled and soggy ground are many, and always hungry.

Article 12
An Exposition on K'hizu Mantiilt: The Kutu

Creativity is not my strength. I suffer through Raru's tasking me with an official record of the K'hizu of the island and the alterations they cause in us. I have been instructed to begin with the Kutu and I must protest it. No one seems to care about our Mearnum in this city, so I will include them after this completion.

There are, at the present Longhand season's twelfth day, four of the kutliku pride. It is necessary in most cases to capture the creature one chooses to be taken by. Otherwise, it is a matter of fate and chance for every Galaila at one time or another. No one escapes the change, so most prefer to be near a K'hizu of their

29

choosing. Of course, as we see from Utan Dace, the island sometimes has its own plans for us. Many of us have surmised that our choice has nothing to do with the making of our caste, rather than the island knows our hearts better than we, choosing what we are destined for. I am inclined to agree, for the goddess of this place does not seem a lover of free will. I digress.

Govan, first of the pride, is the biggest, with a wingspan of twenty-one feet and two hands. He was the first to capture one of the curious kutliku, and in so doing brought the kutliku superior Boa to us. There will be further records on this 'Canimperium' their kind hail from, if we ever find it. Govan's hunt is Bogh'thane, murder of clouds.

Allende, second of the pride. He was third to be taken, but Govan decided Keimas was too young to really be considered a hunter-killer at the time, so Allende was ranked first. His hunt is Ghrainegal, stormthroat.

Miriena, third of the pride. Wife of Allende, she drew the attention of the sister to Allende's hunt. Soon after Ghrainegal, then came her beloved hunt-to-be, Shisi, sharptooth.

Keimas, fourth of the pride. When he matured, he became a hunter-killer. He took his hunt when she came looking for her older brother Bogh'thane. Sotoatna'thane she is called, raincloud. He calls her Soto, the quiet rain that comes after the storm has settled. I think...I believe he did this because he loved her just as he loves our young Lemalie. He always calls her his rain. I suppose that's what she is now, in every sense of the word, what with her...unusual remaking.

I do not disregard the hunter-killers' exceptional abilities in combat, but I feel that the council places too much authority on them, feeling that they are more than our elite defenders but the heart and soul of our survival. One caste should not be elevated above the rest in this way. They even have a mantra engraved in each of their homes to remind themselves of their own vanity:

Slaughter, end our hunger, that the mighty will survive,
Born to prey on predators and nourished by their lives.
Mercy rest, give way to power! Righteous passion rise!
Every soul that soars on wings, in righteous duty dies.
Sever mortal coils binding living to the earth.

A feast of flesh and blood is the burden of our birth.
Stone and storm, bound together until the day we die.
With every life we lay to rest we rule the living sky.

Utan Raru, if you are proofing this, can I please go back to field
expeditions? I cannot stand being locked in the library every
minute of every day. This tedious khainanor is what bookish
academics like Cisiveo are for. I haven't even touched a thi'tskreol
in almost a season.

~Ms'egol Udai Siddoh

Hauan Etain, the city of Hanging Gate, had become the single great stronghold in all of Manti, a citadel beyond compare and a testament to the achievements of the reborn Mantichaena. The surrounding canyon walls, reaching above low-hanging clouds, had been their salvation as they had fled the eastern desolation of Thonsfa Tau thirty-three seasons ago. Driven first from their homeland on Ellel, then from the coastal haven they had discovered here on Manti, the lofty massif had become their latest. From the icy landforms in Nikhaadi Gao, the uninhabitable north lands of ice, down to the smoking gray warrens of Nikhaadi Ansax in the south, the mountains Taultolm that had once kept them locked to the east were now the center of their ever-expanding dominion.

Though the mountains stretched and flattened into a plateau to the south, and most notably where the canyon of Hanging Gate crossed their breadth, the northwest corner of the island was entirely dominated by landmasses most rare and mysterious. Here were islands held aloft by columns of the perplexingly resilient mineral cerrubite, dazzling in its metallic sheen and everlasting in its suspension of a fragmented 'higher earthplane' overhead. Some of these marvels, smaller and more reasonable to climb, rose from the cliffs on either side of the Mantichaena enclave, and were home to the illustrious Kutu hunts. Only one such tower was altered by hand, its pinnacle excavated to cover and conceal new Kutliku nesting grounds, and its oblong tip refined with tile and

31

battlement. It was a sacred birthplace, a testing ground where fledglings born to bonded kutliku were brought to be judged by their imposing sovereign. Boa, greatest and most terrible of all the kutliku was unbending in his judgement of the young. Kutliku were mighty from birth, immediately capable of flight, and of defending themselves shortly after. Even for those who were born here in the city of Mantichaena, he would sense the coming of a new child, and fly to see it for himself. The monstrous Jiou Boa would accept no less than perfection. If the newborn took wing from this landing, they would follow their lord to their homeland, where they would become part of the Canimperium deep in the hidden valleys. If it could not, it would perish by its own parent's jaws. Such was the pride and ruthlessness of great Boa and his kind. It was a matter of survival. A parent must not suffer the indignity of bearing young unable to fly, unable to contend with the wildlands of Ni'ivitnem. Better to die from the merciful stroke laid to it by its mother than to be torn apart by other creatures, especially in defense of their home. The Canimperium had particular enemies in the wild. The notion that their brood was flawless was necessary to keep opposition at bay, and when the enemy did come a single vulnerable target could not be afforded.

At the height of the aviary keep, on a more dismal day of Sanguine's wind and heavy rain, a stoic Kutu man and his young betrothed stood in silence. The lady was Nesh Aia Lemalie, 'Guide woman of still water'. Though she had matured into a powerful Mantichaena, she was a rarity in that she yet appeared as a Galaila. Born unlike any other, from the roaring sea and gentle river, her skin had unnatural silken toughness and her hair had changed through her life to become as blue as the darkest parts of her skin. There was more within her, hidden abilities not yet revealed to all, but beauty was her fame. To compliment her starlight features, she favored a color of dress to match her hair, in a revealing style that clung to her curves, accentuating her femininity and exposing one leg to mid-thigh. All of her united by the color of her ocean, those who looked upon her saw only the embodiment of waves and rapids.

Her husband-to-be held her securely in shared excitement, clasping her hand within his larger, more brutish one, though he took care not to unduly grip her. Exceptional as a Kutu and second only to the famous Govan, he was Nesh Udai Keimas, 'Guide Man of Bright Light.' Shoulder length dirty brown hair framed a face featuring stern, intense russet eyes, menacing even when his spirits were high. Symbolic of his kind, his garb was an ornate sarong, tied at the waist with a cable of spun metal. It was his only clothing, allowing freedom for his upper body to control and counterbalance immense and cumbersome wings. In love, battle and all myriad obligations he was as all other Kutu; consumed by conviction and the steely drive of his function within the tribe, trained into them every day in order to make a useful asset out of the insatiable bloodlust of their kind. He had already spent his younger life contending with a troubled past and dire thoughts, and when the blood of the kutliku had met his own passionate nature the result was havoc. He thought himself a true warrior, but it was not this taste for death that drew his betrothed to him. She saw his inner beauty, his hidden tenderness, the depths and complexities of his appetites. In her she had seen who he could be, what he was meant to be, and in becoming that man had finally earned her affections. All things he felt could be shared securely with her. He was his true self in the presence of only one creature other than her, and it was his titan of a hunt and lifelong companion, Sotoatna'thane. Second only to Lemalie in his love, it was Soto who had come to this skyward bastion in the dead of night to present her baby to the father of the kutliku, and to judge it according to his will.

Lemalie tightly gripped the hands that held her, not drawing strength from them, but sharing her own with the man who truly needed it. To Keimas, the new fledgling would be as a grandchild, firstborn of the other being he shared his life with. He needed Lemalie most now, when what should have been a moment of beauty turned to one of heartbreak and horror. While her face twisted in inconsolable dismay, Keimas' gave away nothing of his inmost thoughts that tore him in half. One wing, brilliantly hued in likeness with Soto's colors, curled around his love as they endured together the sight of a mother murdering her child.

Unbloodied as she yet was, Soto's feathered back and scaled belly were adorned with streaks of orange and indigo among deep and woody green, like wildfires tearing through Ni'ivitnem woodlands in the night. Her folded feathers were of such length and heft that, while she was grounded, they would drag behind her as her master's did. Among the hunter-killers there was a comic saying: 'like wings beat together, like hearts beat together, but never minds.' It was a reminder that, for a Kutu and his hunt, loyalty and individual ability were natural. The most critical function of their shared lifestyle was to learn one another and slowly come to act as one, as a single mind. Without that uniformity, they were mere animals. Keimas repeated this to himself, though under his breath, as he watched Soto pace to and fro across the parapets of the aviary's landing. Just as he knew what was in her heart, he knew the turmoil of her thoughts: Jiou Boa would be watching her, and there was no escaping him. Even the intimate and all-important moment of her child's birth was Boa's property. She and Keimas both sensed his approach, his flight far overhead, where the clouds and lifted lands were far below. His scaled eyes would see her young, make certain that his word was obeyed, and that weakness did not mar his immaculate species nor propagate a lesser bloodline.

Having only just shaken off the trauma of birth, the squawking infant born to Soto had trembled and flailed about in its attempts to take wing. At the crook of its wings, the bones were misshapen and fused, unable to extend and catch the wind. It was a cruel trick of nature to punish such a gifted predator as Soto with young who would never be more than prey, crueler still that it was doomed for the inability to perform this one act that ultimately defined its worth.

In the noisome and rainy darkness, Soto's narrow, bone-sheathed jaw descended with a chilling shriek and power that echoed through the canyon. Though obscured from any onlooker by her wings, the muffled cries of her baby skipped across the cobble and rained down into the citadel of Hanging Gate. Soto's firstborn lay prostrate before her, a lagoon of blood mingling with the mounting pools of the deluge in the broader depressions, soaking into the mussed feathers of the tiny kutliku.

Sharing her husband's tender heart, Lemalie whimpered almost imperceptibly, then froze to her core as the small sound triggered Keimas' arms to rigidity around her. Such pity was offensive to the kutliku and Soto, proud monster that she was. She swung her long neck around to face Lemalie, eyes afire with fury and wounded ego. In her grief, she did not distinguish friend and foe. Her gaze bored into Lemalie's until the water-born Mantichaena's delicate body trembled violently and shrank into Keimas'. Closing her eyes, she waited for death from Soto's murderous talons, but controlling the kutliku's wrath was a skill finely tuned in Keimas. Equally monstrous himself now, he ruffled his wings to show he would not let go and matched his beast's gaze, spread them wide and bared his teeth in an expression of dominance. The kutliku colossus snorted her disdain but acquiesced and whirled back to her battered young. Steam billowed from her jaw, gaping and bloody with thin scales caught between teeth that retracted into her mandible. With a last roar, she beat her mighty wings and blazed across the keep's roof, spiraling down to where vestibules in its rounded face allowed passage for the Kutu and their hunts into the nesting grounds.

The sire of Soto's frightful brood waited and glowered. Boa's red-ebony feathers and silent glide together made him a phantom that haunted the living sky, completely obscured from eye against the clouded night though his inky pupils were centered unwaveringly on the unfortunate death below him. He made no sound, hovered, then plunged like an ashen bolide westward into the airspace above his sovereignty. Pride for this daughter swelled in him that she had so easily dispatched the embarrassment of a child. She was his favorite child, his lost heir. In his primal heart he reveled that she had been companioned with a Mantichaena killer as excellent as herself, one whose company would make both of them stronger. Compared to that assurance, the loss of another child meant nothing to him. With a last, dismissive glance, Boa turned and soared back to the high reaches of Ni'ivitnem, secure in the knowledge that the bloodline was intact.

Silence stretched across stone as Boa disappeared. Lemalie at last broke down into pitiful weeping, she breaking free of him and kneeling with one hand in the slow, cold crimson flow that had meandered toward them. Keimas joined her in silent heartbreak and held her neck with one hand, trembling and staring blankly at the fallen baby.

"Why him?" Lemalie's voice quivered. "Why would Loi take his flight from him?"

Keimas swallowed hard and pulled at her shoulder, lifted her up and led her away from the horrible place, gently scrubbing the blood from her fingers with his own. This was not something he could easily abide. Although he had built a life on his communion with Soto he would never understand why this had become their way. With chagrin he accepted that it was not his place to judge this older species, only to honor her custom as her father honored that of the lowly Mantichaena encroaching on his land. Slowly the two made their way back to the city, wondering if Soto would even birth another. For a time she would be inconsolable.

It was quiet after they left, save for the whisper of the rain. Then, like a furtive specter, Soto's head and neck slunk over the edge of the tower. Slyly she had clawed her way up the craggy wall to surmount the platform again and, with determined poise, she approached her fallen offspring. Blood dripped from two wounds in her chest, her scales spread and torn away. They bore the unmistakable serration of her own beak, silent evidence of the true source of the blood in which her baby lay motionless. Gently she poked at the body and it immediately stirred and gave a musical chirp as it met its mother's face. She returned the happy sound, though burdened with a hidden sadness. Prodding him again until he stood with some difficulty on his stubby appendages, she turned and led him. Together they crawled to the edge of the tower, where a shadowy figure with claws of his own was latched onto the rocks. Purposely hidden in the dark rain, its clicking, needle-like fangs were those of a creature with a taste for flesh, its silhouette made more terrifying by its gnarled and spiny abdomen that glinted like oil in the starlight. Yet for all its terrible countenance, its hissing voice was as gentle as could be when it spoke to the mother. It was its heart that Soto heard when it whispered to her and its heart that had brought him to her now.

"Tsssssssk…you are beaudtiful ssstpirit Sssstoto. I ssstwear, your lit-t-tle wingling will be ssstafe in ssstecret-t-t place."

Soto pushed the infant out into the monster's crackling arms with a soft sound of encouragement and he went with relative ease. He did not understand but trusted nonetheless. Flexing her jaw and struggling to speak intelligibly, Soto uttered a single word to the monster: "Hk'khopa". In reply, the ominous rescuer nodded, smiled a jagged smile at the baby.

"Hk'khopa? Issst a beaudtiful name. He will grow up ssstafe, far from badt Boa," he promised. Soto bowed her head slightly and turned to wing away to her nest. Fierce hope filled her and gave strength to each wingbeat as she thrust higher and higher, taking flight to sooth her aguish at parting with a child she would never know. Perhaps her boy would find a way to survive somewhere far away, perhaps not. Whatever came, it would be its own life, not Boa's.

CHAPTER 3: TRADITIONS OF BEAUTY

Flushed with exuberance, Lemalie twirled in front of a polished metal mirror in her room, admiring the radiant beauty of her own figure adorned in her finest dress. The elegant blue gown had been tailored and embellished by the gifted Matriarch Sebashni, and flowed long and gracefully, swirling down to her dainty feet. It had been painstakingly stitched with a lacy design of delicate wings wrapping about her waist between curling waves, immortalizing in iridescent thread the imminent union of her spirit with Keimas'. She stopped and tilted her head to let her soft, sea hued hair drape over her eyes, stretched out one leg from the open side of her dress and rested it on a chair, ran her hand along it to her foot. In a burst of pent-up excitement, she bounced up and down giddily and seized her hair, pressing it against her lips to muffle a girlish squeal. Despite self-admonition against vanity, a charge prompted by others' incessant acclamation of her loveliness, she allowed herself one brief moment of bubbling pride and exultation. She felt so much love in her and, at long last, she could let that love run free.

The object of her delight was her betrothed, beautiful beyond measure in the way of a man for whose touch she had longed since childhood. Every image of him, from their first meeting, could be recounted without fail and her heart warmed to imagine more tender seasons ahead with him forever by her side.

She danced to the window, regarded the cerulean dusk of Sanguine and watched the revelers gathering below at the gates of Nesh Hall. Pausing briefly, she rested her arms on the windowsill and leaned out, letting the cool night air caress her face as she listened closely for the restless murmur of the river below, unable to distinguish it from the distant rumble of its sire, the waterfall that spouted from high up the northwest corner of the city just before the first window of the westernmost hall of Gazan. Her blood had made the river her home, and it had always given her a calm unlike any other. Implications by close friends were numerous that she would find equal calm in the love of a husband, and she supposed now that she would learn if it was true. She didn't love him because he gave her comfort but because he was equivalent to her in honor and aspiration. Together they had fought back creatures of the wilderness, faced the ravages of plague, drought, come together after all of it, not as survivors but as providers and conquerors. She was the warrior of his heart as much as he was hers, and both of them dreamed of a Hanging Gate even grander than the one they knew. In love thus far they had not been bound, for there was always a battle to be fought. At last she felt it was time to surrender her warrior status and prepare to be mother.

A sharp knock at her door broke her reverie and immediately her face burned with color. Forcing a respectably demure smile she sashayed slowly to the door, taking the handle and pulling it open slowly to prolong the moment of revelation.

The door swung wide and revealed Tault Udai Maurus posed outside, feet apart, hands locked in front of him and the thick claws on his shoulders curled over his chest. Lemalie quivered excitedly, delighted at the sight of Keimas' adoptive brother, so often dressed in naught but rags soiled by countless days toiling in the mines, now elegant in the customary dress and role of the occasion. Short, rye-brown hair flowed upward and away from his broad face and his bulky figure filled her view of the hallway outside, his features deep and knotted like bark. He wore Tault's ceremonial vestments reserved for its archons, or for those who would go to great purpose in the council's name. Wrapped around his shoulders and unfurling into a cloak that fed into a thick skirt, was a loguai pelt, perfectly brushed and stained in grayscale colors so that he fairly looked like one of the beasts himself. Lemalie curtsied meekly, not out of necessity, but to show that she had more respect for him than what ceremony demanded. Though Maurus made no motion, he spoke deliberately.

"I have come from the halls of Tault seeking a lady who is of love to my family's son."

Lemalie bit her lip, tempering a lowly squeal, and folded her hands behind her back. "I have this love," she said, as demurely as she could. "It is I whom you seek." She offered Maurus her hand, which he took with care and led her from the room. She barely contained a little wiggle as they started down the hall. The greatest adventure of her life was about to begin.

Thetrulengo speaks,

The Lugu, morphed by the blood of the K'hizu loguai, are a breed of Mantichaena that present with a duality of the mind. They are very socially dependent and good natured, but they spend almost their entire lives in isolation underground. The loguai are dangerous animals if provoked, deep digging earth dwellers with tough skin and boney shoulder-mounted claws for smashing and moving huge amounts of rock. Territorial and temperamental, herbivorous tendencies will not stay them from killing anything that encroaches on their nests, which results in making them one of the more difficult beasts to assimilate with. However, the attitude integrated into the mind of a Lugu is that of when they were yet pure: amiable, focused, full of curiosity though their K'hizu cousins are seldom seen in such a relaxed state. Maurus is a fine example of his brood, though I do not believe this the sole source of his kindness and loyalty.

For on the very day Ellel was destroyed he and his family adopted the infant Keimas: the day his mother died. Maurus had been too young to really know the woman, but his parents had told him stories. She had been poor and plain. They had never seen her with a man, but while she carried Keimas the woman confessed to having been of love to a man greater than any other. They never knew her name, and only by her child's infant screams did they realize she was dead and rescue Keimas while their home burned. He has been with them ever since, wholly devoted to their honor and never dignifying bitterness by dwelling on his loss. Keimas has always looked up to his big brother Maurus. I admire both for their constancy.

~*Chronicle of Wonders, Mantichaena Rokhaadi and Brother*

The journey to the atrium seemed never ending though it was only a few hallways and a flight of stairs. The torch lit passages were painted to look like the sea and the shore and mountains of fire and ice with all manner of creatures amongst them, an artist's depiction of how Manti appeared in the imagination. Lemalie lost herself in the murals, imagining in her exuberance that they all danced alongside her, celebrating with her. The hallway was otherwise empty but fairly sang with her energy, enlivened by the soul of love that traversed them. Infected by her excitement, Maurus rubbed the back of Lemalie's hand with his thumb and grinned broadly.

Before long they approached a threshold without a door, which they crossed with an irreverent eagerness reflected in both speed and bounce of step, and immediately stood upon a terrace overlooking the vast atrium of Nesh, and the vast congregation therein. This chamber was for all ceremony, all things proudly recognized by both council and citizenry; war orders, prayers, marriages. Built to acommodate general assembly, it was as finely painted as the halls, decorated with the most sumptuous of foods and brilliant of earthly treasures, all lit entirely by a gargantuan fire burning in an alcove behind a raised alter opposite the primary ingress. As Gazan was the city's arena, and Voddace its tomb, Nesh was their temple.

No sooner had Lemalie appeared than thunderous cheers rose from the crowd, arms waving enthusiastically and feet stomping the ground beneath them producing a rhythmic thrum. The arriving duo careened down a triplet of crisscrossing ramps that swept them to ground level. Streaking through the parting assembly, they arrived at the altar, where Maurus grabbed a breathless Lemalie about the waist and thrust her up onto the platform, following immediately. Standing suddenly face to face with Keimas, and an arm's reach from him, Lemalie thought her heart might burst. His massive wings stood erect, twitching nervously and belying the confidence in his face. His eyes reflected the firelight like crystal, glittering with the faintest sheen of joyful tears, a subtle witness to the great excitement that welled up in him. Lemalie's eyes tracked beyond him to the older Kubernu waiting beyond; Patriarch Aroch, her father. The three shared one brief look of shared joy before the Patriarch lifted his face to address the congregation and so begin the ceremony.

The thundering rhythm ceased as the bride and groom faced the archon. Aroch's curling horns glowed in the firelight, as did the claws on his fingers and toes. It enveloped him, giving him an aura that highlighted his authority. In combination with his thick chest and black robe, he posed a frightening figure, especially to the young warrior he would give to his daughter. He arched his bushy eyebrows as the pair turned to climb higher up the altar, lips upturned in a smile nestled in a ragged black beard.

Maurus came alongside Lemalie and took her hand, stretched it out to Keimas.

"*Einla,* brother!" Maurus' voice rang through the hall, reciting the traditional words for all to hear. "I have gone to the chamber you have sent me to, and as you said she waited within." Then, turning about to the crowd, he proclaimed "It is she!" He lowered his voice and gave Aroch his full attention. "*La,* I have returned with her hand, and I say she is worthy of him. Father of this hall and her family, I bid you on behalf of Tault Udai Mahat'tsk Aia Odense that, as I present a daughter who is of love to him, you take them together unto you." He gave Lemalie forth to the vacant space before the fire pit and Aroch bowed slightly to Maurus with a sly wink, lifted his hands and acknowledged him in kind.

"*Ein,* your word is solid, and that of your mother and father, and of your house. I say you, remain with us." He then took hold of Keimas' hand and lifted it towards Lemalie. "My daughter, I have passed beyond these walls to the place where champions nest among the clouds. There I felt the presence you have felt, the presence of love, and in this man it dwelt. I say he is worthy of you. On behalf of Nesh Udai Aroch and the spirit of your mother that, as I present a son who is of love to you, you take and watch over him." He released Keimas' hand and it remained raised, reaching out to Lemalie's. Maurus and Aroch stepped back, allowing the wedded pair to come together and lock hands. They stood facing each other while the two escorts moved between them and the fireplace. Maurus spoke first, his baritone filling the chamber like a flood.

"Nesh Aia Lemalie, Guide Woman of Serene Waters and daughter to our elder, so wise and beautiful, will you give wife to my brother and allow him to fight on your behalf? Will you watch over him and all who come after?" There was a moment of silence and Lemalie's quavering voice shimmered across the hall.

"*Eism'einla.*"

She closed her eyes and her hand relaxed in Keimas'. Aroch turned to Keimas and addressed him similarly.

"Nesh Udai Keimas, Guide Man of Bright Light, brother of my fellow tribesman, so learned and strong, will you give husband to my daughter and upon your shoulders take all burdens asked? Will you watch over her and all who come after her?"

Keimas' eyes never left Lemalie's and his affirmation resonated in her quivering heart as it did in his own.

"*Eism'einla.*"

With that simple expression the marriage was complete. Lemalie released Keimas' hand, stepped to the edge of the platform, tossed her hair over her shoulder and looked back at her husband, eyes full of love and voice rich with conviction.

"I am yours, soldier of the gate." she recited, "Come and find me." With another coquettish sweep of her hair, she turned and leaped into the crowd.

Keimas followed her to the platform's edge, laughingly accepting the challenge.

"And I am yours, lady. Where you lead I shall follow!" He launched himself into the audience, only a few feet behind his bride. As he struck the ground the two were surrounded by a tumult of cheering friends who lifted them over their heads, passing them along from person to person until they were at opposite ends of the room. Each was carefully lowered to the ground and allowed some space to move. Silence fell briefly, before the crowd threw up their hands and jumped in the air, landing simultaneously, once again setting to their thundering stomp, dancing in numerous choreographed rings around the center of the floor.

Keimas and Lemalie each flew into their own dance, following the same steps while agilely slipping between circles to progress steadily toward the center of the room where a space was preserved for the two to come together, a last symbolic reminder of the lonely struggle to find one another in the chaos of life. Keimas moved with precision, instinctively weaving between flailing appendages and flying bodies while Lemalie bent her body like a leaf in the wind, either skipping alongside the next row of obstructors or flipping deftly over them when they stooped. Sooner than either anticipated they rejoined in the center, Lemalie's hands against her husband's chest and his upon her hips. They were motionless for a moment, and with eerily uniform timing the crowd fell silent once more.

Marked only by shuffling feet as everyone found their partner, a couples' dance began and was kept in time by an ambient flute-like keen produced by the women that rose and fell in pitch, backed by a low and constant guttural hum from every man. It represented the quiet at the end of the day, the sweet music of night creatures and a time for rest. It was the end of troubles and the beginning of peace. The celebrants spun around in their partners' arms, a humble reflection on how each wedding was a celebration of all that had come before.

Keimas and Lemalie quietly held each other, following the dance but with much slower, fluid steps. Lemalie rested her head against Keimas and he let his down atop hers. Sliding one hand up from her waist and higher on her back, Keimas turned her abruptly to his side and let her fall against his arm. The world stood still all around while she peered up at him, his face framed by the haunting shadows of the fire lit ceiling, and hers against the red tiled floor. He lifted her off her feet and into his cradling arms, and carried her across the room, through the masses. The dance continued uninterrupted, parting flawlessly to let the lovers pass on their way to their new home.

Rising above the vibrating floor and out of the echoing music, they climbed the three ramps, passed through the heavy doors and traversed the very same halls through which Lemalie had arrived, then beyond them to the highest level of Nesh. At the end of this uppermost hall there was a row of four ornate archways, doors belonging to the four hunter-killer Kutu. The endmost opened into Keimas' chambers, already prepared to accommodate two. Drawing attention foremost among the furnishings was an enormous circular bed, carved into a slab of solid rock, like a well, and lined along the bottom and edges with multicolored feathers from Soto's wings as well as his own. It was a picture of true intimacy, a haven for lovers wrapped within protective wings. This room and this bed were part of Keimas, and now, so was Lemalie. He stepped over the edge and knelt in the heart of the bed, laying her down with reverent care. She grabbed his hand in hers and kissed it, holding it lightly and resting it on her stomach. Keimas lowered himself until his face hovered beside hers and pressed a kiss lovingly to her cheek. She draped an arm around his neck, pressed her head to his, breathing slowly and running her hands over his back. Completely in tune with her, he laid one hand on her exposed thigh and whispered in her ear.

"Forever, I live in your love."

Lemalie took a deep breath and held her hand to his face

"And I in yours."

Thetrulengo speaks,

Ancients unknown, whatever unfamiliar brethren that may have lived and been closest in kind to my own heart, see me plunged into the void never to be seen again if I continue this ceaseless prattling upon the pages of nothing! I am undone without her; a lie! I am undone that I pine for the momentary glimpses into happiness I see in these creatures. Is there any other than her that has drawn this sensation from me? I still cannot see her...where is she?

I took a moment and I...feel better. I am increasingly shaken when I resume this reflection. The idea that I should suffer within for the plight of mortality perturbs me. Long have I been removed from their trivial concerns, but somehow propinquity has torn down what walls in me prevented a deeper interest. Now, guised as one of their own, I do walk among them, all the while feigning meekness as I toil in their fields. I live their lives, listening to them. In the moment I wanted to assess whether it was menial labor that made them happy...which I still cannot say. I feel nothing gained by sowing seed or cutting down its growth. I want to know more about where they come from, more about their dreams and aspirations. Such dismally frail beasts cannot truly be complex...can they?

My latest discovery is the strange way they've managed to keep order among themselves. So many houses, each with so many occupations and ruled by such an array of evolutionary marvels. There's the Thiwa, not unlike our...THEIR lady Lemalie. While most have merged with the fauna, they've merged with the living flesh of a blade of grass, a humble bush or a towering thi. I think that they have been granted the greatest longevity of any Mantichaena as they are able to refresh their bodies and slow or undo the troubles of age simply by drinking water. They look a bit strange, vines and bark covering most of their skin, which can become lignified as they mature like an ancestral vine. Of all the various broods they are one of the most diverse in physical development, many of which experience an elongation of limbs, stretching of the body, even gain or loss of some body parts.

They are well thought of for their intelligence, or at least their tolerance for long silence, which I myself have seen to result in improved cognition. They would seem to do nothing but ponder the wonders of life and the intricacies of the mind, frequently succumbing to a sort of sleep for days on end. They appear at peace to live so...monotonously. I know all too well how tiresome it can be to be trapped by your own thoughts. I wish I could simply sleep and wake refreshed. I have tried. I don't know how. Perhaps it is something that cannot be imitated. Like eating...I haven't mastered eating.

The Kulo and Kubernu castes, born of the K'hizu kuolt and K'hizu imberuc respectively, are cousins in the wheel of life. In common, they have some sharpening of the teeth when begotten, and heavy, rain-resilient coats grow down their neck, arms and back. They both enjoy the extra balance of a prehensile tail, but the Kubernu's is as much a weapon as their claws. It's just as furry and comfortable as the rest of them, but far thicker and heavier

46

than that of a Kulo. In a clash of heads, the Kubernu will always win with the advantage of horns. They are rounded and do not stab, but are unbreakably dense and heavy. A Kulo's advantage is speed and numbers; pack hunters that can bring down brak with a little luck. These natural advantages are exploited just as much in the ranks of Hanging Gate as they are in the wild. I can understand why a people that has had a singular identity for so long would invent such words as 'Mantichaena' to hold them together, but they habitually identify themselves more by their K'hizu brood than by house or nation.

Though similar in design, Kulo and Kubernu are deceptively different from one another in attitude. The Kulo are often reckless, light-hearted and undisciplined scoundrels, all heat and impatience wrapped up in a rambunctious brown-furred body. They will fall to all fours when on the hunt and provide a good deal of the city's meat from the underbrush of Sekhaadi Ni'ivitnem. The Kubernu are their ultimate contrast, eternally patient and mindful of their surroundings. Even the feral imberuc, like the Kubernu, prefer to set ambushes and lure their prey. They will only turn to scrapping when there is no other course left to them.

Hunting parties are in constant demand, but these are not assigned duties. Instead, hunters are drafted in groups from the militia in Gazan. What better way to hone one's skills in battle than on those one fights alongside? I surmise it to be a matter of where their focus lies. The Kulo condition themselves for speed and maneuvering to disorient prey, while the standing Kubernu attempt a different sort of deception, doing everything possible to seem small, distracted and afraid until their prey becomes overconfident and attacks. Ein! I heard it said by a young boy watching the games in Gazan just yesterday: 'When a Kubernu cowers and you cannot see his claws, he has found your weakness and is ready to sieze on it.'

There's so much more, an eternity of description that I lack the presence of mind to impart, made more unreachable by poor understanding. I still have not come to terms with why I feel anything but indifference for the architects of my curiosity. I find myself speaking in like fashion, smiling when they smile... fearing... fearing my own misfortunes past. Certainly not to the same paralytic degree as they, but...we all have our burdens.

Abiding among them has taught me that some mistakes are meant to cling to us. Fear of repeating them guides us toward something better.

~Chronicle of Wonders, Method of Beasts

CHAPTER 4: HIS MUSIC

*H*er grace is unparalleled, her poise divine. Her body moves like the sea, her hair like the wind from where the water is deep, born inside it. She is the roil and the tide. Daughter of the seaplane, bride of the sky when they meet on the horizon. Her might is wisdom, this I say. To love her is to bring unity to the sea and sky, the firmament and the abyss, bound together in a bed of the earth. Oneness of flesh begins with oneness of its elements. Her love is sweet to the lips and soft to the touch, crashing waves in every kiss, and the setting of Laesis across the glittering horizon is in her eyes.

Her breast heaves like the swell as it greets my shore with ecstasy, caressing me, refreshing the parched roots of my inmost light. I swim in the sea and drift in consuming darkness, surrounded by her love and only her love. The surface and the waves are but beauty alone, I cast them aside, bearing for its own pleasure the savage storm that is her heart, and the drowning depths that are what lies beneath. I cry out for strength, and all my power becomes that of the sea, to give it comfort and pleasure, I give it my soul, all that I am.

The sand is softened by the waves, given structure, refined unto purity. So does my love wash me clean of my evils, refining me that I may become the son of the earthplane, solid and sure where the *wind and sea defeat the stone.*

My wings remain furled, for I will not hunt in her presence. She keeps me safe. She sustains me and keeps destruction far from me, for this there is no recompense. I stand on the timber without fear that I must fly. Though the skies are as clear as the crystal waters, I will not take flight, for she will bear me across the sea, across her breast to my home in her heart.

I see her walk beside her brothers, the rivers and streams. She dips her feet in their hands and speaks to them, though what she says I do not know. Her body is strong when she leaves them. Their comforting touch gives her remembrance, the touch of her family. Her only family. In the old day I have seen her pass beside her mother, walking in her footsteps and looking out across her skin, wishing in her heart to return to the womb deep below. This is what my love for her must be.

Her body fills me with joy. In seeing her from afar I dance with such revelry that she is fair. The gods themselves have tried to steal her from me, but she clings ever to life that we may be together yet. I am mirthful because she is mirthful, that she is the pride of beauty's creation fills her with great song, and I rejoice with her. In her eternal happiness she offers her grace to me, she rests at my touch, and together we celebrate her magnificence. Surely there is nothing finer than to come together as lovers and celebrate, for our love is in the likeness of rain that puts all creatures to sleep.

Her mind is full of great dreams. In her sleep I hear her whisper secrets, things of adoration and pleasure for her family, for her birthplace and for her husband. I feel her blood rush when she dreams of the man she loves, her body twists with the remembrance of ecstasy, and her lips cradle a smile when he has satisfied her. She is lover to romance, servant to the servant, her husband. He waits on her with praise and tends to her needs as they arise, and she finds love in her heart for him. In union they are content. Her body becomes his temple. She is thankful to receive his worship, and he never ceases to give it.

Listen well, and you will hear the laughter of the sea. From her breath there comes always a wise joy. Its revelation goads her husband. In her mirth he finds purpose, so he strives onward to her and her voice grows louder. Together they dance and sing in the storm, the revelry of the sea and sky, the union of the realms come to be by the will of love and subjugated by it. The smiting forces of existence find solace in one another, and the gods are calmed. In love calamity becomes compassion. In the house of the husband and wife depravity becomes glory, blindness becomes purpose, from disarray comes order. For her to laugh I give all I have. To honor her I bear all turmoil. I live forever in her perfection, for as strong as the tide she may be, beautiful though she is, the rain upon me is her wisdom. I kneel to her will, for her mind is illustrious and I will follow it into any storm.

Keimas stood and flapped his wings exultantly. Tossing aside the rock he had been scribbling with, he whirled across the stone and dust of the aviary in an uncharacteristic burst of exuberance. His fellow warriors would not have recognized him from such a robust display. All around him the spires rose around the aviary foundations, and below him was the belly of Hanging Gate. This nexus between the two living places would be where his testament to his marriage remained, immortalized in the rock for all time. His deft ears caught a faint cry, and his heart leapt to think that his wife called to him from where she still slept on this early morn, in his bed a thousand feet below. His ears twitched as he recognized the repeated cry as that of one of his closest friends. Nesh Udai Allende, brother Kutu, shrieked in challenge, shocking Keimas' love-addled brain back into action mode as he bolted downward from the aviaries, laughing all the way.

"Keimas! Govan says I have gotten slower since I married. *Uein*, I am enfeebled by soft touch it seems. But I fear I will shame you in a race so soft are you!"

Keimas hooted in response and raced to the edge of the cliffs, unhesitatingly taking the breathtaking plunge into the canyon in acceptance of Allende's challenge. Speed was the greatest weapon a Kutu wielded, and to race was to sharpen one's skills. The way he was feeling this morning, Allende stood no chance of besting him.

Despite the apparent failure of their god to protect them, the

Galaila had steadfastly retained their religion as they had crossed the sea. Many carried it as their last tie to home, while others had no room in their hearts for faith in silent gods. Yet, even for these, faith clung to their culture like an involuntary reflex. And like all cultures, they sought to rebuild not just their habitat, but their soul as a people, including the temples where they had once praised.

After being driven from the coast of Manti and into the cliffs, the people had found abundance, a bountiful world rich in raw materials and ripe for harvest. Once shelters had been constructed it was not long before their hearts turned to rejoicing and thus to worship: They required a place of worship. But there was dissent among some of the ruling council, many of the archons felt that Loi no longer belonged. Aroch and others felt differently. Hoping to rekindle their god's attention, archons Aroch, Sebashni, Saketsu and Mani oversaw a solution that placated both views. A temple was indeed built, but beyond the West mouth of the canyon, down the rugged paths and nestled in the Ni'ivitnem woodlands. It was a relatively safe journey due to its proximity, if well-guarded, but the greatest threat had not been from a hungering predator, but from a goddess who hated Loi more than any other.

Many seasons prior to the present, on the arrival of Mirage season when Keimas and Lemalie were still young and the council still strong, they had met with their beast.

"F... father..." a small and troubled Lemalie whispered with urgency.

Pious and proper, Aroch gave a fatherly grunt as his tutelage, droning even to the adults, was interrupted. He nearly tripped on an exposed root as he turned to face his adolescent daughter. Her face, framed by a head of brown hair only slightly tinted by emergent streaks of blue, was fixed uncomfortably ahead. His gaze followed the finger she raised to see what disturbed her.

They had arrived at their destination, a hastily erected temple in the depths of the forest, as high as the thi, wrought from wood and stone for the worship of Loi before they had even begun constructing their halls. Aroch froze and his eyes filled with rage as the others in their entourage raced forward to get a closer look at what seemed to be an act of sacrilege. Aroch's fists tightened, and he followed the others with Lemalie in tow. The thick doors of the structure were half-open as always, a constant welcome to any who came to praise their god, yet their faces were sullied with scorch marks, like fire had been set at their center. Aroch stopped at the entrance and roared his outrage.

"Who has done this? Who DARES to desecrate our house of holy honor!? Does anyone know the culprit!?"

The faithful exchanged bewildered stares, disbelieving it could have been vandalism, while a few intrepid souls ran to the doors and heaved them closed. As the two sides met, seemingly scattered marks formed words etched into the char.

False father
False god

The crowd gaped in silence. Just as Aroch opened his mouth in fury once again, a rush of wind tore through the thi, whirling about them and slowly pushing the doors fully open once more. Lemalie pushed her hair out of her face and dropped to the ground.

"Father, what's happening!?" she cried. He didn't know, could not explain. The rising gale seemed to pull them towards the opening with unnatural force.

"I don't...get back!" Aroch bellowed. "Everyone, RUN!"

Faithful acolytes grasped desperately at any sapling or shrub they could reach to keep from being dragged into the eye of the storm, until with a final clashing roar the wind abruptly stopped and all became chillingly silent. Aroch shook himself free of loose debris and stood, searched all around, one arm shielding his girl against his form.

"Are any wounded? Are we alright?"

Confused rumblings sounded that there were no serious injuries. But the Mantichaena were slow to stand as they searched around themselves for anything not of their own people. Aroch bent to help young Lemalie up, pausing when the resounding creak of wood against stone drew everyone's attention to the doors once again. The mighty portal closed as a figure emerged to confront the awed onlookers. Dust and foliage were drawn together, and tightly bound in a silent whirlwind that surrounded a small female. It passed through her, apparently created a vaguely familiar body within it. She was naked, spectrally translucent, and with every delicate footstep the grass and weeds all around her seemed to burst to life and grow taller in a flash. Her white hair flickered out of sight as it was tossed, made of the wind itself, and barely shielded her face as radiant, unblinking green eyes surveyed the frightened group. She turned further and boldly drew closer to them, her voice firm with righteous arrogance.

"*Anamaeis*, Mantichaena. Begotten of my father you are brothers and sisters to me. For this reason alone, I have allowed you to live, to invade my lands and kill my creations for your consumption. I have allowed it, but you are not of this place as I am. You exist only by my grace, and I will not ignore this…vile insult."

With utmost caution Aroch stepped forward, bowing deep, though his eyes scrutinized her closely.

"My lady…might we know your name that we…"

For the briefest of moments, like the shimmer of a mirage, the figure's visage wavered, the pale flesh of her face and right arm briefly giving way to the image of wafting fields of grain and thi-tops churning with life.

"I AM GODDESS TO YOU!" she bellowed, once again settling into the form more palatable to the Mantichaena.

The crowd cowered before her booming voice and dropped to their knees silently as she swept her hands before them and proclaimed her dominion. "I am Anama, daughter of Loi and mother of all that lives and grows here. And you…you have stolen from me."

Aroch spread his arms and bowed his head even further.

"Forgive us our terrible slights, your holiness! We thought this world unprotected. If we had known so luminous a goddess ruled here…"

Anama set her hand on his shoulder, spoke quietly and took hold of his chin to raise his face. Her touch was so warm, feeling to him as a sunlit bough of a leafy thi, yet her tone was menacing.

"What would you have done? Would you have cowed and begged as you do now?" Releasing him she raised her voice to be heard by all, "As well you should. I am far more deserving than my father, and I know how you prostrated yourselves to him. Now you will know the price of loving him; the fiend, fiend no less petty and foolish than you small creatures..."

Her listeners said nothing, not yet ready to genuinely submit to this self-impressed being.

"However, your sins are born of ignorance, innocence even. I will not harm any of you," she declared, looking around at each of them. "In truth, I will take you into my lands and bestow my clemency upon you if you will swear fealty to me and obey only two commandments."

The people waited to see how their leader would respond. Feeling the weight of that responsibility, Aroch's mind struggled with the risks of abandoning their elder god in exchange for this lesser one with no more reason than her own words. However, in light of her claim to the land, and with no home beyond Hanging Gate to go back to, what choice was there? Loi had not presented himself for their scrutiny as this one did. Nor had he protected his own temple. It was Aroch's duty, his place as one of the highest Patriarchs, to invest in the tribe's future. If this truly was the goddess of the island, then this was the way things must be, and so it would be.

"I am Nesh Udai Aroch, representative of the Council of Archons that guides our city, oh stupendous *Nhi'Maeng*. I may speak for our kind. *Ein*, you are most kind to offer us such sweet life. We are humbled by your generosity and will accept your offer and whatever terms you require."

Anama smiled, satisfied, looked up at the overcast and stale sky of the Mirage passing.

"I will savor your obedience and reward it. However," she sang to herself, turning back to the crowd before her, "I do demand two things. Firstly, know that far to the Hai lies a great valley, the Cradle of Thorns, my home. Therein my most precious children live in peace and therein you shall never enter." As bows and sounds of acquiescence indicated acceptance she turned back to the temple and grimaced. "All else I insist is that this insufferable testament to my father you will be forbidden to attend from this day forward. Let it crumble and fall as he did. You need not worship me...but worship him and I will bring all the gnashing mouths of these wilds against you."

Aroch clasped his hands solemnly.

"My divine woman, I will convey your message to our people, and we will revere you as our true provider. *Eina enta*, your home will be sacred and untouched as commanded." Despite himself, his heart silently rebelled even as he spoke. Regardless of what fate she could bring upon them he knew the faithful among his people would not readily forsake their worship of Loi. He himself could not stomach the thought.

Without looking back at him she stirred the wind again and slowly faded into it, her flesh dispersing into wafting leaves until she would be no more.

"You are wise, Mantichaena *Utan* Aroch. Remain true to your word and my offspring will not take root in your fallen corpses."

Thetrulengo speaks,

Foolishly do these people continue to revere their 'Elder gods' so fervently. They know nothing of them. All that is understood of these monsters is what their so-called prophets have passed on. The Galaila were there on Ellel. They watched as their nation was destroyed by the wrath of a god and... they're so oblivious. They cannot conceive of how misguided their faith is.

I recall standing and warming myself in Laesis' lovely course. Below me was the very first founding of a united people under any form of rulership. It was during the first era, when mortals were learning to build power inside themselves by drawing on Az'Rech's essence from within the Veil. All were unaware it was slowly turning them into what they would soon call gods. The most powerful of them were the first divisors, the supreme rulers of each great land, and they tried to rule over their lesser kind. The lingering essence of Az'Rech was all but claimed, and as less and less remained for those newly born only the oldest and cruelest had the power to dominate. Eventually, they turned their mortal armies against one another. I must reexamine how exactly the great nations of Maengir came unraveled:

Ephielipax may have become the Galaila's god of love and peace in the new age, but these are nothing but faults when you are doomed to war. He was offered peace by Quetzuaul the Desolate, and he accepted, so caught up in newfound hope of harmony and entranced by her devious smile that he was blind to her deceit. Ellel could not see their god anymore as he consorted with their enemy, then their son was born. Loi of the Siege, Jiouna of the sky. He was born to the father of the Galaila people and, yearning for glory equal to his mother's conquest he hoped to win his own.

What I don't understand is why he never took command of his mother's armies. The Hischates, like many of the immortals' dregs, cannot survive without a god's fingers inside their mind. When Loi destroyed their mother, her nation was undone, leaving her creatures stood vacantly in place until, one by one, they laid down and died. As the kutliku fled and abandoned their Galaila brethren, Loi did the same to the Hischates. Hence the two great powers of the first war slowly dissolved.

Where has he gone for so long? In times past I caught glimpses of this monstrous god of sky travelling the breadth of Maengir, like he was searching for something. I did not mind him as I should have, did not know his intent until he emerged with schemes already in motion only to be confronted by his peers.

~Chronicle of Wonders, The Advance of Potentates

CHAPTER 5: PRIDE OF A HUNTER

Keimas had lost focus, given himself to savage speed without caution as he pitted his wings against those of Nesh Udai Allende. The race was special not just to Kutu but to all Mantichaena, though less restricted in execution than a mere contest of speed. It was open combat, a display of physical abilities that allowed for all manner of bloody tricks. Keimas and Allende were well matched, similarly schooled in the art of flight. Allende, however, deviated today from his pattern of complete reliance on speed so as to dash his war-brother against the rocks in the hopes that he might win a race for once against the strongest hunter-killer of Hanging Gate. Capitalizing on Keimas' assumption that he would not dare attack unprovoked, Allende suddenly stalled midair, spinning and catching Keimas across the jaw with his heel from above, so blindingly fast that there was no anticipating it.

Dazed and losing altitude, Keimas could barely notice a jagged outcrop approaching as he veered off course, until it exploded under the impact from his shoulder and flank. The sandstone was softer than brassic, though still thick and baked dry, a painful obstacle at such speeds. Allende, tired of hearing frequent jests about his inferiority to Keimas, beat his wings furiously in a desperate attempt to gain ground before his rival could recover. He suppressed the feeling that it would be in vain, knowing Keimas' stronger and broader wings would bring them together in a flash unless he exerted himself to his limits.

Keimas wiped blood from his ribs and tightened the leather strap that now replaced the more decorative accessory he normally wore around his waist. His ears rang from the impact as he stood, arched his back, kicked off the broken stone and took flight. His unfurled wings struck down just once and raised a tornado of dust in the wake of an explosive ascent that echoed along the cliffs and warned Allende of his approach.

Allende looked back over his shoulder and breathlessly taunted his opponent: "Don't let pride rule you, friend! If that little bump has weakened you, then by all means take your rest!"

Keimas narrowed his eyes and smirked. This, like any and all other contests, brought out the most reckless will to win in him. He had already nearly closed the distance between them, threshing the air powerfully to gain the final arm's reach his adversary maintained over him.

Allende laughed and pointed ahead. "Look, *Utan*! The mouth draws near! This game is mine!" Allende accompanied the taunt with a powerful thrust of his wings, revealing hidden strength and broadening his lead.

Ahead, the canyon walls tapered gently inward, closing at the top as if a weight hung from the cliffs, drawing them together. The great egress of Hanging Gate loomed before them, though this was not the final marker. The game was to be first to touch the ground of Ni'ivitnem below, a fall of almost four hundred feet. During this deadly dive was when speed was guaranteed, leaving one's strength to be spent on trying to push the other back. Claws would flash and wings would roar, likely sending one of them home on foot until their injuries healed.

Allende's triumphant mockery was the stuff of hubris. Equal to Keimas' one was the young man's need for victory but, even with such a spirited change in tactics, he could not match his comrade's brute strength. Allende had too often forgotten that a blind, wild anger was the source of Keimas' ferocity. He was unbeatable not because he was larger or cleverer but because his vision blurred in the face of defeat, his mind dulled, his body burned with the heat of pride and fueled him to overcome or destroy anything that stood between him and victory.

With a thunderous rush and a cry of determination, Keimas swept up and over Allende, his last burst of speed catching him up to hover directly over the younger Kutu.

"Not now!" Keimas crowed. "Not now nor ever!" Haughtily offering Allende one moment to prepare, Keimas collapsed his wings and viciously dove at him just as they came upon the arch of the cliffs. His own wings were immense compared to Allende's, their bulk providing him less freedom of movement. Therein lay the only advantage Allende had when Keimas' temper took hold. Allende felt the rush of air, saw the shadow closing in on the ground below and reacted instinctively, curling in his left wing and hurling himself to the side. Narrowly avoiding the attack, he kept his pace and far outdistanced a frantic Keimas. Many seasons of lost fights had taught him all of Keimas' tactics, his weaknesses. Today he was ready to show how equal they were.

Raging and scrambling to recover, Keimas unfurled once again and skimmed along the ground, watching with bruised ego as Allende dropped out of the canyon and into the valley beyond. This was unprecedented, inconceivable. His mind was so clouded at the impossibility of his first loss and his eyes so fixed on Allende that he ignored how fast he raced among the jagged rocks. One, slightly longer than he realized, barely caught his knee and ignited every nerve in his body. Falling even lower, had to thrust again to rise above a stone that would have cut him in half. The pain gripped him so tightly that he barely noticed a creeping sensation on his back, burning and holding him. He tried to ascend and could not, tried to turn and failed, feeling his spine burn hotter and panic strangling his mind in the last instant before colliding with the cliffs. He fought back, struggled to take back control and with a burst of strength managed to push himself to the side. What he felt was brassic, uneroded by wind or rain and strong enough to beat him fairly. His life saved as his weight glanced off, he still felt his left wing catch the full power of the impact, once more dazed by pain, yet he did not fall.

The air vibrated with a savage roar, the boiling grip on his back tightening and jerking him around in a rapid circle before sending him reeling out over the forest in a spiral of debris and blood. Waking in the cloud he saw cliffs rising higher and higher above as he floundered to balance on one wing. He could do nothing to save himself from the plunge. Unable to make sense of anything else, the only vision in his delirious mind was that of Allende besting him by a shameful distance.

As Allende landed with expert alacrity and plenty of time to spare, he wiped his brow and looked upward with a smile, just in time to see Keimas' limp form dragging a wake of dust. Teeth turning to a sneer, he was unrepentantly pleased to have won by such an overwhelming distance, without a scratch on him no less. With increasing worry he watched his friend's descent for only a moment, not comprehending at first how gravely he was injured. Quickly that changed, instinct turning his vanity to fear as he vaulted from the raised pathway behind him and back to the sky.

"Keimas! No!" He gasped, arching over the canopy to intercept his fall. "KeimaaaAAAS!"

"STOP."

Allende halted in midair, his body erect and his head aching from the sudden shout. He glanced around briefly, momentarily paralyzed by the force of the unseen voice. Hovering warily further over the forest he ignored the oddity, refocused and tracked Keimas as he fell into the fruiting bodies of the towering fungi and tore a path through them. Again, the voice came, this time barely a whisper in his ear.

"He is not yours anymore."

Allende had no response. He saw no one and so could not rationalize the voice except as a manifestation of his own weary mind. Then, he felt a burning chill in his flesh as if a hot wind blew straight through him. It was fast, angry, heading directly toward Keimas' fall. He didn't need to understand. He needed to save his friend, and so dove with desperate haste into the depths of Ni'ivitnem.

Allende landed on a high branch just under the densely interwoven fronds and fruits, his sharp eyes flicking across the clearing below where Keimas certainly fell. He knew this place well; an old place where worship of Loi was once held. Directly below was the ruined courtyard of their first chapel they had built on Manti, now cursed and forbidden. He pulled his wings in, arms tense and ready at his sides as he crouched warily, appraising the structure. Creeping vines held its moldering skeleton of brick and mortar together even as they gnawed through it, entwining its ridge with nearby thi branches. Its walls buckled as the tendrils squeezed them relentlessly. Nearly all the roof shingles had been stripped away by time and the occasional Kutliku that had rested too heavily thereupon. Nature had not simply reclaimed this place. It was attacking it.

This he had seen before from a distance, knew it well after so many seasons passing it by on patrol. There was, however, one detail which was blatantly out of place: the wide, rugged hole Keimas had just punched through its ceiling.

Thetrulengo speaks,

Gholahn Eph'linthrake was what they called it, 'Temple of Undarkened Sky', in remembrance of their homeland and honor of their godking, that he might protect them in this foreign land.

Mortality is obsessed with the idea that the dominion of each god is far reaching and devoted to their good health. They willingly go thronging into the fire from blind obedience, certain that their sacrifice is for the good and offering it with a smile.

Enough of that. Instead let us know and remember these other lives that go unappreciated by beings unaware of their great spirits; the thi. These fungal structures grow without end, in all manner of hues and textures as they touch and mend to others of infinite variety. The result is a web of interwoven flora that includes thi, thi'tskreol, thi'zech, cha'tskthi and even the Thigolaia. Existing above and below ground, spanning all of Manti and providing nourishment to every living thing in a glorious pageant of Anama's nurturing power. There's nothing like this on any other land, no constancy of sustenance that guarantees the continuation of life down to the darkest caverns. This rich food is the foundation on which the tiniest K'hizu feed, many so small they cannot be seen by the larger. Greater and greater becomes the scope of living things as each is required to devour prey, and be devoured in turn so that the essence of dark flesh and luminous soul may be passed along from one to the next, and at all levels of the predatory sequence the corporeal and spiritual remains of the deceased salt the living earth and are reborn as food for those that come after them.

The factions of life that go unnoticed I would hazard to be more inspiring than the complexity of greater K'hizu and even the assorted chaena. However, I do not profess to be of the same school of thought as the mortal philosophers who believe that beauty is defined by that which consists of parts all intrinsically alike. That which is symmetrical is considered loveliest of all to them, conformity of color and texture. In opposition, I believe that beauty is in what separates an essence from others that can be considered its kind. The flesh that became the elder gods was not all alike, nor did they appear alike when made. Neither had their immediate brethren after them. The elder gods were entirely unique, and only when they cultivated the growth of worshippers in the image they chose most pleasing was there such thing as a uniform species. Uniformity, conformity to the whole and bastardization of individual image was not the innate definition of the Galaila or any other breed, but rather their creation as a master's slaves. Anama knew this, fought against it. She was the goddess who would set things in motion for Loi's inherited children to be freed from his grasp by giving them the gifts of new home and new flesh.

~Chronicle of Wonders, Thi, Beast and Redeemer

A strange odor permeated the sickly breeze rolling out of the ancient construct, a blanket that overwhelmed Allende's senses as if it consciously breathed disease upon him. He flinched at the sound of clay shingles sliding from where Keimas struck and falling to shatter below. With an uneasy stare he scanned the shaded grove. There were no young Kutliku in the thi, no Kuolt amid their trunks, not a single sound of nature to be heard though he strained to detect one. Searching behind him he half expected to hear the great voice again, yet all was silent. He swallowed hard and stepped back.

"Who am I" He growled rhetorically to himself "To cower from this ill specter that shudders my bones, in the face of my brother's mortal peril?" From deep inside the structure, he heard a bloodcurdling scream, coupled with the echoing crash of wood and stone. He gasped and lunged forward. Without fear his rallying cry sounded as he charged into the darkened vestibule, thrusting the creaking, rotten doors inward. No sooner had he gained entrance another poisonous gust engulfed him, dragging him to the ground and choking him.

"**BACK!**" thundered the sinister air.

Clutching his throat and wheezing, Allende dug his toes into the dirt and pressed forward. The taint stung his eyes and burned his skin but he blindly pressed on and into the dark, an oppressive shadow growing around him as he followed the intermittent sounds of despair that were Keimas' labored voice. Scrabbling past crumbling columns and musty furnishings, Allende could barely make out Keimas' struggle within the gloom. Terror struck his heart to see his friend, wings dragging on the ground, fingers clawing at his own face, launching himself into walls and collapsing onto the floor. Allende reached out, shielding his face with one hand, stumbled as his footing was lost when the floor became slippery. Leveraging himself off raised edges in the uneven floor, he seized the writhing Keimas' wrist, dragging him into an embrace and trapping his flailing limbs.

"*Gazeim*...I have you...hang on," he panted, one arm holding Keimas' convulsing form. With his free hand he dug his fingers between tiles and dragged them both towards the light. Despite his failing consciousness, he was ever aware of the cloak of gloom encroaching on them and the stench of an awful waxy liquid seeping into the chamber from the ground.

"**NOOOOO!**" The voice pounded again, this time jarring the walls so that blocks came tumbling down around the desperate pair.

Allende cringed at the protesting force, seizing as he sensed the voice was very near to him, nearly by his side. Again, Keimas screamed and with eyes tight shut could only grasp helplessly as he was torn away and thrown into the black. Allende willed his mind to clear and spun over onto his chest to grope after Keimas, led now by the deep red glow of a small, boney hand that clasped Keimas' side and held him down.

"No! Release him *vaeachae* demon! Release him NOW!" he demanded.

Keimas' body went stiff and expressionless, shuddered as a discoloration crept over his skin and turned it ashen gray. He opened his mouth and, with a powerful voice not his own, proclaimed, **"No! I am not...I am not a demon!"**

An unspeakable roar shook the ground as Keimas jerked to and fro against the voice, its presence weakening as if wounded by Allende's insult. Finally, the shadows churned and exploded out from the temple, taking with them the toxic air. Keimas' now limp body collapsed onto a heap of fallen stone and light at last flooded into the enclosure through breaks in the ancient ceiling, beaming through swirls of airborne must. Breathing great gasps of fresh air, Allende felt unburdened at last and crawled frantically to Keimas' side.

"Keimas! *evaleim,* can you..."

Keimas was unresponsive, dead to his friend's voice, though his chest rose and fell and abated the worst of his concern. Allende stood slowly, searching all around for whatever evil they had crossed but felt no sinister spirit nor the previous weight of fear. In that moment the chambers felt safe, if only long enough to escape. He grabbed Keimas and slung him over his shoulder, trudging wearily but with all the haste he could muster.

"Hear me if you can, *Utan.* I have you. Don't you give up now. I know you'll not breath your last while there's a rematch to be had."

As they emerged from the cold structure, Allende's gaze turned up, panning through the trunks of thi to find the footpath up the cliffs. He could not remember the last time he had been forced to climb something, let alone with another Kutu across his shoulders. It would not be an easy return home but to escape from what haunted their steps he entertained no feelings of exhaustion, blocked them out and stomped resolutely toward Tau and Hanging Gate. His chin quivered at the memory of the ominous hand; the words spoken. It had not been in his head. It was a real voice from a real tongue, no doubt lingering and watching them even now. He wondered, however, why it had fled so suddenly. It was angry before, yet the last of its anger sounded so...indignant, even hurt.

CHAPTER 6: HER MUSIC

*N*one know power as he does. His tongue speaks and the earth trembles. At his touch the hearts of the wicked wither and die, and the voices of the righteous exalt him. His wings rend the earth and air. Material and spiritual, from the underland to the vastness of the sky, in his name I command you to kneel in awe, for the fate he would visit upon you would match the hands of god. His flesh is a stone, he is the son and brother of the stone, unharmed by blade and bludgeon. Armies may rage against him, but his power grows with savage anger. No victory is too great for him and never has forfeiture been his experience. The color of his plume and the black iron of his claw are the marks of the predator, the hunter killer, the wrath of gal'tskhizu. He becomes them, and they are legion within him. Knowing his majesty, were he to dote on a woman with gentleness and sweet romance, she would surely be blessed beyond imagining. This blessing is upon me. His arms too, are stone. A refuge for a lady. A stronghold against malice and malcontent. In his arms my body takes its rest, and in his heart, my own power is tenfold. Am I so lovely to merit his affection? Impossible. Though the sea may dwell in my flesh, it cannot be so fair as to deserve the adoration of the sky.

The clouds are his dark skin, Laesis and Lindu his eyes. His left *eye is Lindu, amorous and sweet, loving me no less than his lips. His right is Laesis, an indescribable light that dominates the heart as it does the sky. His hands are powerful, cradling me as though I were a babe, worshipping my strength as though I were his deity. To feel a softer caress no woman could ever hope.*

Storms come in due time. Water and fire cascade from overhead, but by his side I am safe. From all chaotic forces I am sheltered in the shadow of his wings. At his feet he feels the sea as it spreads beneath him, a pool of desire, romancing him even as he makes his war. In it he washes the blood from his hands, the tears from his face, and behold, he is the lover once again.

Let me dance in him! Foolishness and fame together in exposition of every nuance I can present him of my innermost self. Let me sing in him! May the beauty of my skin and voice be torn away and creation will still witness his continued love for me. I am unbound by all suffering and caution. Now to rest in him I am given freedom to be as my soul would dictate and know that my burden is love eternal.

To think that nature's Jioukhaadim should be joined so graciously, water and wind, the sea and the sky, the bosom of the deep and the battleground of the firmament, peace and war, cruelty and kindness, the arms of the gods themselves clasped harmoniously in matrimony. Apart we were elementary. Together we became as nature's fury. In marriage we are a hurricane.

~Nesh Aia Lemalie

Lemalie drifted slowly away from the riverbed rock she had been scribbling on. Letting the current carry her, she breathed the cool water deep and pushed off the silt bed. Her head popped up from the water and as she floated gently in the river's surface her father stood with crossed arms and an indulgent smile, towering over her like a mountain.

"Finished, are we? That was neither as hasty nor as lengthy as I would have expected." He reached one colossal arm down and took his girl's hand, lifting her from the water and releasing her as her feet settled on the bank. She leaned against the impressive creature and giggled as she wrung the wetness out of her hair.

"*La*, it is what I feel that I have written without hesitation. Why would it be so brief, or lengthy?"

Aroch snuggled her and laughed. "I am caught. I had ungrounded thoughts that perhaps you were at a loss for words; that you did not know him as deeply as you've proven to. Otherwise, if there was a conciseness to how you defined your love you might profess it in the simplest terms so that your immortal affections were not tarnished by excessive wordage." He paused as she giggled again and tightened his grip on her arm as they started back to Nesh Hall.

"My girl, I have been wishing to tell you I could not be happier with you. You've lived well, married well, and have not once in all your life disappointed your old father."

Lemalie bounced up and planted a kiss on his cheek, causing him to blush. "Thank you for saying so, and never have I been wanting for love before coming to join my husband. Without you I would not have learned to see the love in him." There was a short silence as two kindred hearts felt the uncomfortable tug of remorse at a shared thought.

"It is a sad thing that Keimas should be deprived of the same belonging from birth," Lemalie sighed at last.

"*Aiana*, it is true. He is too good a man to be born to loss and grief," Aroch lamented. "I wish I had known his father, so that I might bury him with a single blow for abandoning a wife and..." He hesitated, rubbed Lemalie's shoulder and felt warmth coming back to skin, previously chilled by the cool stream. "...But no matter. We are his family now, and a fine family we make." She patted his chest and skipped ahead a few steps, hardly able to restrain her joy as she spun around to face him, prattling on aloud.

"*Einla!* The best family!"

Lemalie's boisterous demeanor was famous among the young and lighthearted girls of the Gate, but the unexpected arrival of Allende would strip it from her in ways she could not have prepared for. Her husband's race against Allende had been on a whim, unannounced and lightly witnessed since few had even noticed its commencement, but the length of their absence raised some concern among Nesh. For some, concern matured into anger.

Principally so for Miriena, the lover Allende had parted from to tend the hunts while she yet slept that morning. Just as dangerous as her wrath was that of Govan, commandant of the hunter-killers, who growled his displeasure when it came time to practice combat formations and two of his warriors were nowhere to be found. Both tempers flared when the missing Kutu arrived.

At first there was only a slight hubbub among the spectators lining the cliff terraces, but it swelled into a frenzy as the burdened Allende emerged on the westerly Hai, and many ran out to lighten his load.

The assembly clutching Keimas' limp body was the first Lemalie had seen of him that day. In her heart, fear of the absolute worst turned her sanguine spirit to one of despondency. For one brief moment she saw in the theater of her mind the remainder of her life, painfully absent her Keimas.

Thetrulengo speaks,

The methods of mortality in sorting the aspects of Maengir are elegant, especially so when it is revealed that they greatly (though not fully) comprehend the extramaterial planes of Vaeba and Aurba.

Foremost, I examine how the first of them, during the elder gods' generation, stood upon the highest peaks of Apos and saw that there was a world beyond its shores. To the icy wastes closest to the stars he did look, and he called the path from him to them Tau and Thaun, the left and right hands of the North horizon. At his back from this vantage point was that which he called Dhai and Hai, the similarly halved South horizon. He founded these two principal directions on the presence of land, but also devised names for the open sea, like a river between these two masses. Colloquially they are still considered the western horizon of Hai and the eastern horizon of Tau, but this is a misunderstanding of the true 'Wheel of Everyplace' as it was enacted by the seeing god Ethulsula. Verily, there is no name for the horizons upon which there is no land.

The wheel also contains two symbols at its heart which

represent the principal directions of the ethereal plane which Maengir calls Vaeba, the 'other within', and Aurba, the 'other beyond.' In terms considered modern by the poetic Galaila and similar creatures, these divisions are the inward and the outward layers of space in the variable dimensions occupied by a single soul.

To travel Aurba is to venture outside one's own being and attempt to see the world through the eyes of others, or the eyes of nothing. Meanwhile, travelling Vaeba is to expel thoughts of all other life and become wholly consumed with oneself. Both are beautiful in mortal eyes, considered the two halves of the soul. Aurba is the essence of empathy, compassion and understanding, while Vaeba is the discipline of knowing the self, believing that only by understanding this being can one begin to understand others of its kind. Incidentally Vaeba is also the mortal's title for their many undesirable, painful afterlives. This stems from their almost universal dogma that to be entirely devoted to the journey Aurba will serve the world at the cost of one's own advantage – not entirely righteous as it only serves kindness and lacks inner reflection – but to journey only toward Vaeba's self-obsessive form of enlightenment is the ultimate injustice, treason against the world which is one's home and mother.

Essentially, Galaila teach that to give wholly of oneself is foolish but noble, while serving only oneself is practical but unforgiveable. In summation, perfection is found in balance. To understand oneself opens the path to understanding the world, but one cannot truly know oneself until after experiencing the world.

~Chronicle of Wonders, Life's Regiment and Toll

CHAPTER 7: KNOWING THEMSELVES

D ays passed and the sky grew dark and light with Laesis'
rhythm. People went about their business in peace with
little word of what ill had befallen Keimas, save that he
was injured yet alive. Allende informed the Council of Archons as
to what he had witnessed and cautioned that he and Keimas both
should be kept sealed in Voddace's 'retention and observation
quarters' – fancy nomenclature for a prison – until they proved to
be free of infection or otherworldly influence. Allende's claims
seemed so preposterous that no one could truly fathom, making
separation a vital precaution to Keimas' safety, and that of the
people, until answers were found. Despite the absence of burning
to ash, so similar was his derangement to thuell infection that no
defense seemed too extreme in preventing his contact with others.
Allende was kept in the holding cell adjacent to Keimas', and all
through their recovery both were kept under the watchful eye of
Ms'egol's alchemists and sanctifiers.

No heads of the city nor any persons not directly charged with
Keimas' care were allowed visitation, but from down the hall that
skirted the circular arrangement of dungeons came a constant
stream of well-wishers, offering words of comfort to Allende as
they passed on their way to the atrium just above, where they
would kneel and entreat Anama for Keimas' recovery. Amidst the

one-sided meetings forced on him, Allende's hands wrought the bars that kept the world away and his eyes ever set themselves on Keimas through a narrow window in the partition wall separating them. His own health was of no consequence to him, and he could not understand its importance to others; while he felt fit and whole a brother may be dying not ten feet from him.

Across the river and up the face of Nesh, Lemalie sat on a short stack of books by the window of her room and stared vacantly into the city below as she waited for the resin and powdered bark she had applied to a nearby table to dry, after nearly turning it to kindling when she was told she could not see her husband. The complete crack through its center had almost certainly rendered the finest of their furniture unusable, but it felt good to use the chore's tedium to direct her thoughts away from the unbearable thought of Keimas in a dank cell without hope of being near him. She did not pray as the others did. She did not believe in the protection of either Loi or Anama, worshipped no god though she pretended in the presence of her father. Despite her departure from faith in gods she subconsciously bargained for Keimas' life with them, wondered if they would make demands of her for sparing him. In that thought, she chose to conclude that it would not be she who yielded first and fell to begging. She was too proud to pray for immortal mercy, even if Keimas lived. Too many had already gone unprotected by the gods for her to act like only Keimas was worthy of her prayer. He was, truly, but all love aside she felt it was an insult to the dead to only pray for one man's life, and an insult to all living things that deities would choose whom to spare.

Her joy on the first morning of her new marriage had been intoxicating. After consummating the love of her life, she had bounded to the river, her heart full as Laesis emerged in the Hai and she reverently carved into stone the words her heart had sung for Keimas for as long as she could remember. Then had come the numbing sight of his battered body hauled back to her, possibly near death. It was too much to bear, but nothing compared to being forcibly removed from his side so the healers could work. For her own protection? Damning the circumstances, she wept bitterly.

She slammed her mind shut at the prodding thought that the old plague of Manti had come to claim the land again. Primarch Sky had reassured the people countless times that the thuell had perished in the Thonsfa wasteland, unable to reach them through the enchanted Hanging Gate as they burned away to ash. Keimas had never bought a word of it. Nonetheless, a loyal soldier and Kutu to the very edge of reason, he had diligently enforced the law barring all from nearing the sacred barricade. Due more to caution than reason he had always supposed the thuell were still alive somewhere in the east in some horrid new form. If he was right, then Lemalie's worst fears could have been realized. They knew the thuell could travel through soil, water, even solid rock. A single gate should have been little deterrent to them unless they were indeed dispatched by its purifying mancy. It was presumed that a disease had not the awareness to circumvent their bulwark, but they would never know for sure unless it appeared once more.

A knock roused her from her reflections, and she whirled to her feet, beating back her pain and forcing a halfhearted smile.

"Please, come," she invited.

The door slid open and revealed her father, poor in posture but with an expression that conveyed cautious optimism. Lemalie took a deep breath and a step toward him, her hands tying and retying themselves in knots until his lips drew into a smile. He waited, speechless as he saw her face light up, and he gave her a small nod of assurance.

The news had spread so quickly that even those who had no knowledge of Keimas' injury discovered it by hearing of his improvement. They all, in particular those who loved him, were vivified at once to hear he was healing, infinitely more so upon seeing his wife racing across the city fields, her dress streaming in the wind and tears of joy on her face. No citizen dared hinder her, each relieved to see her in high spirits.

She arrived, breathless and shaking, at the lower level of Voddace and not deigning to present herself to the Ms'egol sanctifiers that stood brooding over her lord.

"*Seauwekt*, be gone! Now!" Her demand echoed through the detention area and the observers obeyed with their heads down. She stood silently and gazed long at the sleeping Keimas. He looked sane enough, lying on his side with wings neatly pleated against the far wall. His breathing was even, and his claws did not scratch or twitch but curled into his chest. She neared, outstretched fingers finding their home among his and interlocking with them as she sat. Bending to kiss the sewn scars in his forehead she hoped for a reaction, but he did not move. Disdaining any distinction between the slab on which he lay and their shared bed at home she laid herself down within his arms and closed her eyes. It was enough to be where she belonged. In this musty and poorly lit dungeon she was again in the paradise of her choosing.

A rumbling grunt heralded Keimas' awakening. Lemalie's passion was rekindled by the compression of his embrace. Savoring it, she drew him in with sweet words.

"I thought you would sleep forever."

His eyes remained closed, and instead of his usual fanged smile he grimaced under a furrowed brow.

"I haven't slept. Even when I am out of mind I cannot sleep. I lay in darkness until I am restored to life by the touch of my woman. She alone draws me away from my terrible thoughts. *Minein*, how long has it been? Six days?"

Lemalie wiped a tear from her eye, "Seven my treasure, one of them a long day."

Keimas' frown deepened, "How long?"

"Two and a half times. The gardens suffered."

"*Aia*...It seems the Sanguine may end sooner than expected. I will need more time hunting if we are to be ready for the passing by Longhand's end."

Lemalie took his hand and kissed it. "No, *uta*, you have not strength enough and we have food aplenty. All that is needed is you if only by she who adores you." She leaned in and kissed him lightly, before resting back again on his chest. He pulled himself upright against the rock edge and rubbed her shoulder, his voice quiet but smoldering with indecision.

"Sadly, you are not alone in this. There are thousands...thousands more who feel as you."

"*La?* In my need?" She inquired, sliding down to rest her head in his lap with tense arms around his back and across one knee.

He scratched absently at his temples, his eyes still sealed and his fangs grinding noisily. "There's just...god's blood, there's too many. None of our routine matters. None of this matters, only what we've lost. Everything it took from us!"

Lemalie tried to hold him, insulted as he pushed her hands back and stood erect. His wings burst from his sides, filling the room and inadvertently pushing her even further away.

"Keimas, why anger? What's wrong!?" Her plea was both indignant and confused as his snorting sounded more like a crazed animal than the Kutu she loved.

"Only that I know the truth! I have seen it now. We've been blind for so long...I cannot stay here. Please, don't try to stop me." He made to escape, but Lemalie stormed after him. Keimas struggled to pass through the outermost doors as Lemalie seized his wings and held tight. Passion for him, mixed with anger at his apparent abandonment, aroused an unfaltering strength within her.

"Keimas, STOP!" she demanded. "*Prostas,* what drives you from your wife!? You would run from me without a word!?"

Keimas relented for a brief moment, pulling her tight to his chest and squeezing tears from her as he whispered in her ear, "Not you...this place. These people. I'm...*eina malpael,* I'm so sorry, I just...I MUST go. He's there. Somewhere out there he's...waiting for me." He withdrew slowly and held her face in his hands, his own contorted with feelings his muddled mind could not give voice to. "Please forgive me, and know that only for the gravest purpose would I leave you like this, but leave you I must. I have seen his face, heard his voice; a spirit that has shown me a good world, a new world, not just for me but for all of us."

Lemalie forced herself to remain in control of her bristling feelings and spoke in a deliberate tone, accompanied by a disarming caress.

"Husband. Believe in me. In this moment I live but to be your strength. Tell me what happened."

Though his blurred mind resisted, her touch did sooth his mania.

"I...I saw the thuell. I saw the faces of a thousand dead...at her feet."

Lemalie balefully inquired "Her? Whom?"

"I could not tell," He replied direly. "And then a voice cried out to me, filled my mind with visions of the East, calling me there into the Thonsfa Tau to where it waits for me. I think...I believe it wants to show me something; something that could change the world for the better, or be the end of us."

"What is 'IT'?"

"I don't...I don't know. It was a man, I think. Surrounded by shadows, he was hard to see, though I know it was his voice and...his eyes; a creature with so many unblinking eyes that darkly glowed like poisoned stars."

Lemalie stared into him, seeking the husband and lover that she knew but seeing only the warrior, and the warrior was fixated on his fight. Seeing the unspoken determination in the lines of Keimas' face, Lemalie at last looked down and pushed her husband away from her.

"Go then," she said bitterly.

"My love..." he fumbled, feeling the stab of remorse.

With a thrust of her palm knocking him aside, Lemalie spun around and quit the hall ahead of him.

"Say no more to me! I chose a champion, so let him fly and follow his heart if your own does not object. Go and be a champion."

For Keimas, a brute with the hard head of one, his wife's cold perspicacity was confusing. He was not blind but wholly devoted to two lives which now diverged. Though this devotion was a quality they shared, she would likely never choose a path that left his own. She was the source of his only depth and though she inspired the best in him he still struggled with the worst. Yet, this was not merely the rebellious conviction of a man who wished for her to cow to his words and support his every decision. He knew full well the patience and understanding that made her his better, married her for them, but he could not find it in himself to imitate them this time. Fear of what was to come had taken him back to younger years, darker places and a less disciplined mind.

His heart stung as he silently trailed behind her as if to speak while she went out of Voddace and departed across the grassy fields, ignoring his presence in her wake. Her command, bitter though it was, he considered to be her blessing, earnest even if begrudged. If remaining with her meant ignoring a danger to his people, then he saw no virtue in it. With a last glance at her stiffly retreating form, he turned Tau and an upwelling of conviction silenced the conflict within. He was compelled by the nameless voice that revealed so much. Clenching his face and turning it aside he resisted love, resisted vulnerability to the one person who could sway him. With a great thrust of his wings, he shot up into the air, quickly veering away from the city so as to avoid notice, rising higher and higher toward the high cliffs and leaving his whole world behind with only the most obfuscating of explanations.

Keimas' great wings rose and fell with the landscape as he soared eastward, eyes narrow and unwaveringly frontward, wings thrust confidently behind, gliding silently on high and hidden by the early morning fog beneath him. At length he came to land in the narrow avenue that separated Hanging Gate from the east side of the plateaus, a winding path that wove between great statues carved long ago into the opposing cliffs. Never since the founding of the city had any Mantichaena dared walk this road.

Thetrulengo speaks,

During the struggle for power between elder gods it was not uncommon to mark one's province with monuments. Most often, as in the case of Quetzuaul and Ephielipax, it was the many lesser beings underfoot that toiled in their name to erect such landmarks. Of course, some such as Zeniquorer and Oorghunak never lowered themselves to such vanity; Zeniquorer being too distracted by his vices and Oorghunak not given to meaningless pomp. Ethulsula inspired the most loyal; religious worshippers that gave their lives building for him, but very little remains of his domain now, even in the form of decaying ruins. Ferraro, his only child, did what she could to keep his Apochaena thriving, but she was restless and preoccupied, as many ascendants were. She worked to keep Loi from his goals for many seasons, returning rarely to her ancestral home. Soon there came a time when none even remembered the name Ethulsula, and Ferraro was revered only in shrines and prayers, never in the flesh.

The way from Thonsfa through Hanging Gate, which the Mantichaena call the Guardians' Road, was not their creation. Rather, it was Anama's attempt to claim the glory granted to her ancestors. Since her exile to this desolate patch she has labored inexhaustibly to transform it into a paradise, marking her territory by having her servants carve elaborate statues into the silent canyon which would reflect the forms of all those creatures whose birthright it was to live therein. When the Galaila invaded her eastern shoreline she lead her K'hizu into the west, whilst she studied the remnants of her father's people and determined what should be done with them. Despite her hatred for her father, she allowed them room to grow while ensuring the safety of her most beloved creations, the thi-born K'hizu creasle. These had created the gallery of crude images on cliff faces of the lone safe passage across the island: savage kutliku, giant brak, steadfast imberuc, humble loguai, thronging kuolt, watchful deghni, timid ibor and sensible sumear. By the time the Galaila discovered the statues they already knew the creatures represented, had begun to assimilate with them and so were undeterred. Even Anama was surprised at how drastically her mancy which gave life to the island affected the flimsy flesh of Loi's Galaila. Their bodies transformed without harm and so, when they found themselves on sacred ground guarded by the spirits of Anama's creation, she was not intimidated but rather embraced them as a sign of Loi's blessing. They erroneously held that their haven from the plague of thuell was safeguarded by the K'hizu, who shared their land for living and their flesh for sustenance. Ein, mortals can convince themselves of anything. Fortunately for them and their children Anama would sooner leave her own home than begin another war. Though she touts herself as indomitable, she is heir to Ephielipax, not Quetzuaul, predestined to be a lover of peace and a slave to the ideals of the Sanguine Star.

I noticed one other oddity in the way the statues were erected. They are at various heights, seemingly without order, but their faces all uniformly point inward and downward, towards the innermost canyon floor. I have postulated much about their purpose but...there seems some secreted reason for their making that I missed. If only I were blessed with omniscience and had no need to choose what to observe and what to ignore.

~Chronicle of Wonders, K'hizu Stronghold

Drawing up sharply, Keimas perched on the cracking hand of an imberuc figure, resting one hand on a downturned claw and staring, unmoving, down the remainder of the ever-tightening chasm. Every five or so wing beats ahead stood staggered figures not unlike his current perch, each of a different K'hizu breed. The morning mist filtered through this shady domain, drifting over its floor and refracting the waxing dawn, contributing a dreamlike quality to the sentinels and making them appear as though alive.

Keimas hopped from the great stone hand and glided down to the ground, alighting at the base of the carved form of a loguai, seemingly emerging boldly from the ground. He strode solemnly until the last statue was at his back, still with another hundred feet of bald escarpments between him and where two faces met either side of the 'door' to Thonsfa. The portal itself was a great slab of buffed rock, adorned with glowing glyphs and standing almost half the height of the cliffs at several hundred feet. Erected and adorned by Ms'egol's sanctifiers to destroy all impurity that neared it, the gargantuan seal and its power had never failed in the forty seasons since they had made their escape from the Tau. It was the very same mancy the sanctifiers used to treat the sick, and had, very rarely, cleansed the thuell from infected hosts. Even as he approached it now Keimas felt all weariness and lingering weakness flow out of him.

Keimas sat, contemplating the glyphs, recalling the incidents that had set him on this path. To continue would mean leaving behind what he had spent almost his entire life protecting, and the people who had shared the journey with him, all at the behest of a compelling force he could not see. Though he could discern no firm reason to fear these apparitions, neither did he understand their purpose. One vital image had plagued him throughout his illness: Anama's pale form standing over thousands of dead.

And what of Lemalie? How quickly he had abandoned her after finally attaining her. Keimas wrestled with the conflicting pulls as he sat before the sparkling bulwark, debating his next choice. Should he pursue the phantasmal guide, possibly into further nightmares, or return to the world he knew and risk the nightmares manifesting and swallowing it whole? His desires warred but the visions warned a price if he ignored the urge to press on. Why east? Who was this creature of many eyes?

CHAPTER 8: RECOVERING LOST THINGS

Lemalie's return to her bedchamber was grave, the world around her bleak and uninteresting. She ignored the attempts of friends to gain her attention, avoided their eyes, lost in her own mind. As a guide of Nesh her heart was relieved that Keimas' recovery had set the city at ease, but oh, as a woman her heart was broken. She, whom he had worshipped above all else since first they had met, was now second to this mysterious obsession. Deep in reflection, she did not notice the daring approach of a shy Mearnum, a maiden of youthful countenance, though none knew her exact age, Ms'egol Aia Raphenie.

Raphenie was a unique specimen of the fair sex who might have been the great fantasy of many a man had she not been predisposed to isolate herself. She was not watchfully introverted by choice but frightened by the stress of interpersonal connection. In stark contrast to Lemalie, the idol of whom the maiden stood in awe, she felt always beneath the notice of even the lowest in the social order. No one knew her. No one who worked alongside her in Ms'egol's alchemical division paid her any mind. But this day her silence would be broken as it had on only the rarest of occasions. Wringing her bushy tail, as was her custom when overwrought, she neared Lemalie's path, murmuring a quiet greeting.

"G-good day, *aiat*," she ventured. "I'm very happy your..." She faltered when the first smile she had mustered in several seasons received no acknowledgment. Without so much as a sideward glance Lemalie drifted by her and left her silently crushed. "…husband…is healed," she finished to herself. Trembling, Raphenie remained with her toes curling and uncurling in the dirt. Another piece of her heart was lost for nothing, never to be returned.

Thetrulengo speaks,

I don't believe I have completely succumbed to the weakness of mind that the mortal suffer, but I am so consumed by many studies that in this most important of my undertakings I may not have delved deep enough into the true driving forces behind the afterlings of the Nhi'Thaun. There may be a need for some explanation on what transpired an age ago; how life came to be at this auspicious stage.

While Ephielipax and Quetzuaul's war raged, there was another strong family that grew in power beyond the reach of either; Miohaelia's nation of Balathide was one of innocence and kindness that dwelt in the sea, until Zeniquorer appeared and took the pure goddess against her will. For immemorial seasons this was the way of life for the poor people of Njaghaadi Nehmahn, the deep abyss, subjugated by a childish barbarian that used their mistress for sickening pleasures while devouring the kindly Balathide and discarding them like refuse when they perished.

Oorghunak was made mindful of this travesty by one of Ephielipax's loyal agents, one who knew of Oorghunak's great love for Miohaelia, and after three hundred thousand four hundred forty-eight days of meditating in isolation the god of poison returned from the depths of the earthplane to visit a wrath on Zeniquorer that poor Miohaelia simply could not on her own. It is said that the pieces of Zeniquorer's body were so small and numerous after a single blow that he could never be restored again. So powerful was Oorghunak, however, that he could not survive his own fury. He too was destroyed.

With this intervention the bondage of the Balathide people was broken, but the heart of their mother was beyond saving. Frightened, alone and carrying the wicked god's child, she was cared for by those few Balathide that remained with her. She lamented Oorghunak's fall, heard his cries of eternal love ring out but, in her weakened state, could whisper nothing in reply. Never before had I wept, never moaned to either outer plane for relief; to know that Oorghunak died without his love returned pains my own ascendant heart in ways I do not understand, cannot appreciate.

In the season that came, Miohaelia begat twins; one daughter who would become the elder goddess Kulibreal, and another who was never given a name. Kulibreal did not allow her to have one. All the clairvoyance that made Miohaelia wise was passed on to Kulibreal, while the other twin received only her purity, gentility and love. Kulibreal immediately felt the burden of her new understanding, assimilated the memories of their mother and knew from the moment she was born what had happened. Just as the horrific knowledge had ached inside Miohaelia's mind, so it was for Kulibreal, and she willed herself to become incapable of feeling emotion ever again. She likewise stripped her Balathide of their own emotions and fused their minds to hers, creating a new nation of countless subjects controlled by her single, dauntless mind.

Kulibreal looked upon her sister and saw with an eye that scrutinized but did not love. She tried to peel away the powerful emotion from the girl, but she could not. After many attempts she became exhausted, thankful she had removed all empathy from herself when the younger sister's sleep became a tumult of nightmares, and she screamed every moment she was awake. Kulibreal, seeing no other reasonable option, removed all of the girl's mind and completely destroyed not just the memories of Zeniquorer but of everything. She emptied the mind, and the body was at peace. Then, amazed by what she had done, Kulibreal realized that she would never be able to repair the damage done and would never truly love her sister. She was an object, a husk. Kulibreal chose to throw the girl into the sea, hopeful that she would either grow into a mortal life or die without ever knowing the betrayal.

~Chronicle of Wonders, the Bitter Mercy of Kulibreal

Lemalie's disconsolate trudge ended at her chamber door, its hinges screeching obnoxiously as she slowly resealed it with herself inside. She stood trembling at its back, bent over and clutched a stray feather fallen from their bed to hold at her breast. Staring blankly at the wall, she could not decide what to think of Keimas' sudden abandonment. Images of their wedding night sprang to her mind. She recalled only being beautiful for him. Turning aside to the mirror across the room she could not help but slouch listlessly, tear-stained, in her plain dress. Her imagination now swirling uninterruptedly, Keimas' fate was imagined: his body torn and burnt by thuell, smiling up at her and winking like his death was worthwhile. Under her breath she cursed him, hoarsely called him unspeakable things while wringing his plumes until they disintegrated. She knelt with loudening lamentations and, in a surge of rage, drove one grasping fist so deeply into the floor that it was no longer visible. There was little pain where she had anticipated none, accustomed to abusing her resilient body without any thought to how an ordinary woman's hand would be mangled by such an outburst. Though justified in her grief she still felt guilty that hatred of her husband dominated her heart. This wasn't the Lemalie she knew, nor the one Keimas had married, nor the one whose word was obeyed by Mantichaena.

Listless, filled with self-loathing, she let her power take hold. Little by little her fingers turned to drips of water, her arms and legs to spouts, and she wholly melted away until a living stream trailed down into the joints and pores of the mortar and baktite, carrying her essence. In this state she was freed from the concerns of her Mantichaena life, unable to perceive anything but the feel of stone all around her and the voices of all the other flowing waters on and beneath the ground. It was like forcing herself to sleep and dream quiet dreams as she drained away into the rock.

The morning assembly of the Council of Archons was called to order as Keimas departed, and though his ascent had only at its peak shown any sign of direction toward Tau it had still caught the attention of a single Patriarch of Ms'egol hurrying towards the great hall. Raru the Thiwa entered the cloister of Nesh where the others were already in session. He dismissed their bleary greetings with nods and leaned in to whisper into Aroch's ear of what he had seen. Aroch's expression soured when the strange sight was relayed and without revealing any cause for alarm he stood and excused himself, pausing only to bow to the presiding Primarch, Nesh Utan Sky.

"Honored father, there is a matter of some importance that requires my hand. I beg your indulgence," Aroch stated, slipping toward the door at Sky's gesture and knowing smirk.

"*Ehueinla, uta.* Go on then and tell the boy I am grateful for his good health," Sky replied graciously.

Aroch exchanged an uneasy glance with Raru as he fled towards the door. Sky meanwhile turned to the remaining council, though his attention was furtively fixed on Raru. Unintimidated, Raru stared back at the Primarch and spoke with purpose.

"*Eihem utam,* what trouble has our city that demands the care of its finest?"

First and foremost was the subject of increasing the number of sentinels pulled from Gazan to patrol Ni'ivitnem. There had been complaints from foraging parties that kuolt packs had been stalking them and the sentinels saw increasing difficulty in keeping them at bay. More and more often they had to kill one or more of the pack to drive the rest away and greater injuries to sentinels was the penalty. Business was business and the patrols would have to be increased, but the root cause would remain. Sanguine was a time of plenty and the Mantichaena were not the only animals gathering as much food as they could store before the passing. Sanguine gave them time to get back on their feet after Mercy, but they had to begin early if stores were to be stocked before the end of Longhand.

Thetrulengo speaks,

The Council of Archons is comprised of the finest leaders

Hanging Gate has to offer; supposedly selfless and benevolent and each a part of the light that guides, the Nesh. Some are well suited to this honor and work hard to earn it. Others took their places by more opportunistic means.

The archons, deemed Patriarch and Matriarch as mortally divisive sex may determine, are chosen by the families they represent. They, Nesh, and indeed all of Hanging Gate, are controlled by a single grand overseer; the Primarch. He alone is the supreme authority in the city, and only by unanimous consent of remaining council members can any of his decisions be overturned.

From the moment of his selection the current one has been known as Primarch Sky, leaving behind his prior name of Nesh Udai Rogan. According to the Mantichaena at large he is a calm and measured Kulo man, known more for his accomplishments through charisma or persuasion than strength. In my personal experience he is...not a pleasant man. While effective as a leader and experienced in the care of people after being a prominent citizen and eventually a very successful governor on Ellel, he remains an unfit husband and father. That, too, is common knowledge among his tribe, though they would only discuss it clandestinely for fear that he would discover their disrespect.

From what I can tell it is considered obligatory by these Mantichaena, being kindly and showing good discipline, to tend to the needs of a lover and any children that may be born. In Rogan's house it was not so. There are rumors within the Hanging Gate that this man took to correcting his daughters' shortcomings with merciless beatings, much as he had done with his wife...whom it seems was never seen again after a particularly vicious bout. I followed these accusations to their unfortunate proof, unseen by the living without disrobing his daughter to reveal the marks he had left. Nepiur is her name, the poor girl. I fear she may never be rid of his foul spirit until his death...or hers.

Under the Primarch, there are many more that serve each house. Seventeen in their entirety if I have not missed one. Nesh has four: Khurk and Aroch the Kubernu, Obure the Thiwa, and Lady Sebashni, a Mearnum. Of course, there's Nepiur, also a Mearnum, who may be present at many of the council assemblies if available, considering her eventual assumption of the Primarch's

85

mantle. She prefers to oversee the tending of the crops while each of the four principles see to one of the four houses branching off of Nesh, composed on their own of thirteen families who are under continual training to act as the voices of authority in any tribulation.

Overall, Nesh is the second largest hall, each Patriarch responsible for the education of several hundred men and women. I would estimate that the city as a whole harbors between three and four thousand. Even with so many, what is the purpose of a thousand leaders? Watching how they behave I have begun to formulate a theory: it is only a choice few who are selected for conditioning toward leadership roles, while the rest are employed in the fields and orchards, catching chlio in the river or simply retrained into other halls. It seems that most of the menial labor comes out of Nesh because the competition for honorable status is fierce. One has to retain an enormous amount of information regarding which broods are best suited to which jobs in the city, how to organize response forces for any dangerous situation and, most importantly, be able to answer questions concerning the daily activities of individual members of the other houses. I suppose it makes some sense. If a member of Ms'egol was developing a new type of anti-venom, then a true leader would be aware of its progress. Similarly, there are some very dangerous practices in mancy, pugilism, construction, excavation and alchemy in this place. Their leadership would be remiss if they did not track potentially hazardous developments and have the distinguished wisdom to put a stop to anything too dangerous.

Ms'egol is where misfits find their home, since it is usually an aptitude for mancy and the sciences that dissociates one from their peers in favor of study. The archons that oversee it only reinforce this standard. Present at all times for the guidance of the alchemical students is a bristle haired Mearnum with the stubbornness of a brak, Mani. He is a pleasant enough sort but, being a master of very dangerous and delicate sciences, he demands absolute perfection from those who train under him, and failure to meet his expectations is often met with reassignment to a new trade. However, his knowledge is well worth the trouble. Naturally, even in my mortal form, I have had no difficulty performing his teachings acceptably, and I can honestly say I have learned a great deal in being taught by mortals. My innate abilities are powerful but uninteresting. I enjoy learning. Alchemy is a special interest of mine, but after all this time I believe I have gained much more from studying under Raru, the Thiwa scholar. None of them have ever asked more than my name. It's curious; education is considered a daily task and a right of all Mantichaena. Even if one is not of a hall, they can simply walk in and begin training at the lowest level, provided they still fulfill their duties in the hall to which they belong.

There is a library in Ms'egol of almost limitless information about how these Mantichaena measure the world, and how they value it. To see through their eyes is a blessing, but to read the life's work of well-travelled folk on their perceptions and feelings is ecstasy. Raru is a wonderful Patriarch as well, never too busy to answer a question or provide his opinions. I have already read eight hundred sixty-two books. I'm not sure why that surprised him. Maybe I'm just a faster reader than most. Anyway, as a Thiwa he's far more amiable than the bitter Boroo codger that rules the Iron Sanctum; Artimecian they call him.

What power I had in my beginnings exceeds the sorcery of Maengir, so I have neither need nor desire to train in something so base. The Iron Sanctum are the weapons of mancy among Mantichaena, the deadliest of gothic witchcrafters. They train entirely in secret, never allowed to leave their dungeon in Ms'Egol, but no wall could prevent me from going to see them. They are adequate for their city's needs, but Artimecian...he is truly remarkable, different from the rest. The only other creatures to wield the kind of devastating power he possesses were gods. I am undone by his supremacy among Mantichaena, for he seems too great to belong here.

The Iron Sanctum is like a small culture of its own, existing only in their cloister and inhabited by a mere eight students. Some pupils of Ms'egol's various sorcerous divisions are taught spells for use in transmogrification. Others learn enchantments from the library if they have the patience, but Artimecian's class leaves Ms'egol only for very important occasions, living their entire lives studying what they call gothic mancy, the channeling of pure, destructive energy from within. Whenever these practices are called into question by the Council of Archons, Artimecian always replies with the conviction of a hardened witchcrafter that the claws and fangs of the soldiers are of no use against thuell, and if they should ever reemerge then only the conjuring of his Iron Sanctum will put them down. I have been inside. I have seen what he does to 'teach' his students. If the cruel practices they endure are considered good and right by Mantichaena then it is a miracle unto itself that they are not all mad. I'm still trying to figure out how they are able to retain the huge amounts of essence that they do, but it makes me uncomfortable. Their method is crude...so much pain.

I haven't spent much time in Voddace Hall. If I did, I'm quite certain I would not enjoy it. It's always so dark and full of moisture, and the faces of statues upon tombs are too grim for me now that I have lived a bit among brighter scenery. Regardless, I did what I could to better understand the ruling authority within and can say little except that there is Klimet the Thiwa, Saketsu the Bakul, and Ritus the Boroo. They three are the overseers that use a strange ritual to lay to rest the souls of the fallen, while apprentices beneath them are employed with maintaining the sculpture of tombs and burial rites for those emplaced. Voddace...it means 'broken hope' to the Mantichaena. Even the name is just...why would they give it such honor, yet such a dismal name? How they balance a vigorous spirit with an almost constant acceptance of the inevitability of their doom is beyond me. The explanation I have been given is that the name is one of many terms that has a literal translation as well as a notional one. 'Broken hope' is another way of saying 'lost opportunity'; the people's opportunity to have further experienced the mind and soul of whomever perished. In that context I suppose it's more inspiring, but I still don't see why they name so many things in an ironic or melancholy fashion.

Tault Hall is a simple affair and easily dismissed in what I have already explained. Metaeu and Mabistu are the figureheads therein, and like their subordinate foremen they are Lugu, thick with strength. Metaeu manages the business of polishing and carving rare stones brought up from the caverns, and his compatriot Mabistu is a vault of knowledge that catalogues all their findings on rock and gem to be stored in Ms'egol, all of which I will study one day. Though they are the voices of Tault, uta

Maurus is its reach. He is not a Patriarch, but he controls the ebb and flow of labor and during most days he is the sole enforcer of the Patriarchs' command. This is not entirely relevant to the models of leadership, but I always thought it was odd that Keimas and his brother were slated to such different lives. I realize he was adopted by Maurus' family, but it still seems like they should have found themselves on similar paths. They are so very alike, apart from the alteration of their Mantichaena blood, though that in and of itself is evidence of buried differences between them.

I can hardly give an impression of the heads of Gazan, 'Great brother'. The nobility of the other halls' principles is earned through years of study and good work, while that of Gazan's principles is earned in a single glorious moment. All of Gazan is an arena, a pit of sweating, roaring crowds and combatants wherein only those of sufficient strength survive. The archons here are not all the great and terrible Bakul, but all are equally dangerous.

Patriarchs Rentish and Simeyer are indeed Bakul, not as large in stature as some others but their spines have grown so long and tough they may fight as many as ten contentions without suffering a single blow to exposed flesh. Their hearts as well set them apart from their fellows, having such a need to prove their right to common respect that stronger Bakul fear to face them. I have seen them nearly beaten by Gazan Udai Dace, a prodigy in the art of war that has studied under them all his young life. Rentish could not be defeated. Though his blood and broken tine did litter the arena, every time he fell to the ground he rose again stronger than ever. A bellow of rage revealed how unaffected he was, and he seemed to heal and become empowered with every step as he charged, hurling Dace from the lofty ring to the ground below in shame. I had never seen such an unlikely victory, but upon closer examination I found the true source of both his and Simeyer's unbreakable resilience: It seems that they had been approached while training under the city guard by none other than master witchcrafter Artimecian – this of course was long before the very beginning of Gazan Hall – and upon seeing what gifted and unfaltering warriors they were he proposed to teach them a style of arabesque mancy that he had developed entirely on his own for the Iron Sanctum's students. Sadly, none of them had mastered it.

The mantic style called 'brave punishment' is a brutal ability that allows the caster to mitigate the blow they take using an absorptive enchantment layered over their skin, draining energy from any impact and storing it to be returned on the enemy. I was shocked to see them fight, holding back and allowing themselves to be beaten half to death so that they could rise and with a single punch send someone their own size soaring into the ceiling!

I'm somewhat ashamed by such base desires but I should like to challenge one of them someday. I would restrain myself to keep it sporting, but they may provide me with a challenge. Beating such a skill would be dangerous. How do you break a wall without any impact?

There are other ways to do battle, and though the Bakul Patriarchs hold the fewest losses in the arena the record for most victories is in a constant state of flux between a short and stocky Kubernu Patriarch named Gazan Utan Novun, and a war battered old Kulo woman, Gazan Aiat Liklita. They both claim in speed what the big Bakul do in strength, and they make their way by almost exclusively fighting opponents larger than themselves. It's obvious they think themselves better than they are, since they rarely have a bout without suffering at least one hit, but they never stop and will spend a whole season playing with an opponent and evoking the opportunity for the killing blow.

I am comfortable in Gazan, fond of these people. If anything, the Council of Archons should have more dedicated warriors, not less. I have seen what effect they have on the citizenry. Even Matriarch Liklita, one of the smallest and oldest Kulo I know of, still commands the unwavering respect of the militia. She is supreme authority in Gazan, seconded by Commandant Schaleikin, who personally oversees training and operational tactics. A Kubernu woman, Gazan Aiat Schaleikin is of a more...decisive temperament. Though not an Archon, she elects to lead by fear and is not the creature any soldier would dare cross.

Unrelated, but today I caught two kut'ifitre. Their silken, rounded wings flutter so quietly as they move from flower to flower to feast. So pretty, they! I watched some children chasing them around and I felt...compelled to do the same. As I took the form of an elderly Boroo, some of the Mantichaena found me humorous. They believed me too old to enjoy child's play, but it's too much fun not to! I no longer care if this life is beneath me. I love being here. Hopefully I will bore myself soon that I may return to some other islands I have glimpsed. Other peoples must be of equal pleasure to...infiltrate.

~Chronicle of Wonders, City of Novel Godlikes

CHAPTER 9: PARTING AND REJOINING

*A*ll life is born of his master. In him the gods house their might. The wind is his voice. It calls the tempest to its service, holding sway over the airborne. The K'hizu kneel before his mighty wing. Across his back he carries the egg, the infant. They utter his praise as he bears them across the sea, across the desert, across the wide breast of earthplane. He carries the children of the world to his house in the clouds. They exalt his inmost light.

In him I am whole. What I am is his from which to shape his affections and in these he finds all that he loves. For him alone I adorn my body with fine linen and the orchids our gardens bear, and his heart and bed do I warm with my desire. His tender skin is beyond beauty, beyond perfection, desire incarnate. On his body my hand prevails to soothe his wounds. When battle tears at him I will ever be there to mend. From his mouth pours the order of salvation for the weak, rejoicing for the forsaken, love for the lost. For his wife he rises in the early dawn and all labors submitted to the city are without selfish gains. They are a boon to the wellness of his wife and future family. He brings her bread and wine and sups with her, spinning words of his devotion to her. She is his great light, so he says, that not even the gods will take it from him. All these things he dwells on in the waning light and the new day, *reveling in what has long been the way of his life.*

Foe of righteous grudge and villain of his stories fall before him. With a sweep of his wings, he smites the murderous, washing away the wicked in the wind of his wing beats. Between his fingers he crushes the throne of the usurper. Upon the flesh of dangerous things he feeds, sates his hunger on the blood of the strong, builds his house from the bones of those who would harm us. He is the truest protector, forged and tempered by truest love until deadly as Mercy's bitter cold.

In my body, my temple, he is held most high. Though his touch destroys the enemy it caresses the heart and becomes the sweet reminder of my life's vast emptiness without. His arms are mighty walls, holding nightmares at bay and dreams closer than flesh can touch. Upon his chest I lay my head and he whispers secrets to me, the elegies of his love for me kept hidden from all other ears. In my body alone he seeks restoration and only in my lips does he find the nectar of passion. His eyes glow when they are on me, and his stone arm trembles to my touch. The almighty warrior is felled by his own adoration, his utmost need. He wants nothing more than to lay down beside her when his struggles end, when his war is done. He can never fall, not before the siege, not before the storm. The gods fear him for he would match their strength and only he can rival their magnificence, for he does not win wars of the heart by showing his strength but by letting it sleep beneath his risen love.

~*Nesh Aia Lemalie*

Lemalie stewed, questioning the authenticity of her own words. From the night of Keimas' departure until the following twilight she had toiled, pouring out her heart, adding new feelings to her first marital poetry. She glanced up, briefly distracted by a small raft passing overhead, shafts of wood gouging the riverbed beside her as they guided it along to carry whatever bales of this or that were demanded as the midst of Sanguine provided the harvest. A small chlio drifted by her in the water, its lidless eyes gawping at her before going back about its business, scooping edible particles from the current with its comically flapping maw. She let her body dissolve into the river a bit, willed herself to be carried along with it and admired the chlio as it meandered. It was innocent, unconcerned, untouched. What bliss it must be, she thought, to have no concept of higher life's tumbling ride which seemed to bruise the soul even in small portions.

The formidable Nesh Aia Lemalie had never been given to allowing pain to overrun her, and unlike Keimas, had always found light in the deepest darkness to guide her way. A respite from her grief had given her clarity with which to see Keimas' ballistic departure for what it was: He was afraid. Only once before had she seen him so detached, so full of wrath that he could not take a moment for peace or even love.

Many, many seasons before, from the bow of a fleeing ship, she had seen the pyroclastic fume that had engulfed Ellel reflected in his eyes on the day their world was destroyed. All the strength of Maurus' father had been tested to restrain the boy as he fought to throw himself overboard and swim back, possessed of the notion that somewhere on that island his absentee father was still alive and searching for him. He was so young, with no solid memory of his infancy, devastated by the deafening roar of flame and the sight of his home burning. Once again that deep fear, coupled with intense and directionless rage, smoldered behind his beautiful eyes. Something had gotten under his skin and again he was a frightened child. The vast difference now was that he had been bred and conditioned to retaliate against a perceived threat with a swift and merciless death. Without her to love or an enemy to hate he was without direction.

Against her instincts Lemalie again prayed for Loi to bring peace over him, petitioned any god who held an ear to earthplane to bless his journey unto a speedy return. Cool water filled her lungs and soothed her muscles, similarly soothing her temper. Floating on her back beneath the surface, her eyes found two pairs of feet dangling overhead, and she was oddly comforted to see them; A disarming reminder that however lost she might feel, life was not all about her feelings. There were greater things to serve.

Two older Kulo ladies sat on the river's edge, enjoying the tepid water between their toes, while the waning Laesis glimmered a faint amber far and away over the Tau. For the wise, which age had made this pair, these few moments of pleasant conversation or introversive reflection on the day's happenings were a treasure.

The ladies' dialogue paused and they chortled together as the partially dematerialized form of Lemalie lazily floated past. The one with a bit more gray in her mane, and a tail that flipped restlessly, nudged her companion and indicated the young beauty. "*Eina*, Cordia, attend you that *aiana*? Little sweetie burbling with the waters?" she asked, conspiratorially. "*Galiltminla*, of love and married now, yet still such an odd one. What do you gather she does down there?"

Her friend was not as amused, being the more sober minded of the two.

"Aroch's babe? Funny thing plays in the water as our smallest do in the grass," she said, dismissively. "Now, wasn't I who saw it, but one that did told me that there was some damage done to her new husband in a race on wings with good Allende."

The elder one concurred "*La*, and no surprise. I had my share of scrapes when I was a bit riper for contest, but those Kutu get their wings in a hurry and gods know what happens if they get in one another's way. Younger were we all when the first battle between those insane critters nearly flattened part of the orchard *thi'svelbis*."

"*Minein*, this was different," the somber woman said thoughtfully. "Something serious befell them out at *Ni'ivitnem*. Little Lemalie is involved now. My sister's boy is apprenticed to Voddace, and he says he saw them have out some sort of wedded head-bashing before Keimas flew so fast he took half the city's wind with him. My *ala* tells me he was for the aviaries, but then my uncle's bride told me she thought she saw him turn Tau."

The grey Kulo snorted and leaned back on her hands, enjoying the last rays of Laesis as they dwindled over the cliffs. "*Laan*. Maybe it's true what they say about the Kutu. Idle gossip or not I have always been in agreement with hearsay that after they get their wings, they start to go ma-a-ad," she warbled, melodramatically. "Besides which, I challenge you to take one look at those bloodthirsty bastards and tell me they're suitable for love. The men are bad enough, I can only imagine what manner of derangement possesses *aia* Miriena. *Ein*, she's a sure killer alright."

"A mighty woman though; a mighty killer, *la*. She loves blood on her teeth a fair distance more than her peers. Her marriage to

95

Allende…"

Her friend's response was cut short as both held out their hands to feel a sudden drizzle. Leaping up, they gathered their scattered belongings and trotted back to Ms'egol for a warming drink before they were caught in another of the Sanguine's pounding rains.

There was little room for error for those who dared to scale the uneven cliffs of Hanging Gate. Though crevices were deep and dark and provided ample room to rest, there remained countless planar walls between that demanded more than just a single bound, even for agile Mantichaena. Sanguine's rains kept the sheer cliffs wet and slick, smoothed by time's pounding of elements. It only grew worse as one reached the highest points, where howling winds polished the stone into deadly difficult grips.

Aroch, fought to climb these walls during the height of the midday torrent. His robe and fur were drenched and weighed heavily, slowing his secretive ascent. Approaching a precipice greatly removed from the ground below, he paused purely out of relief that the ordeal was nearly over. With one hand resituating his robe he used the other to pull himself up by an extrusive root of a blanched thi'tskreol. Its growth and color were stunted by long exposure to the harsh conditions here, giving it the appearance of a withered hand breaking free of the ground. A moment later he was safely standing on a spacious shelf a few hundred feet below the high plateau's edge and the aviary towers beyond.

An unsightly grove of twisted white fungi stretched a great distance to the Hai and up across the rock face. Though he had walked this way countless times and returned alive, the spindly growths scratched at his nerves as he made his way through them. Everything about this very special place was either a danger or a fright, though he had no reason to fear what awaited. It was more a sense of wary respect, acknowledging the many ways to die along this path.

It had been at least ten seasons since he had been here, but he recognized still the zig-zagging cave mouth gaping on his left. Buried amidst the white plants, it might have appeared as just a barren spot unworthy of a closer look. It was both veiled and lined with silken webs that gleamed with moisture on every side, an intricately woven deathtrap that promised little hope of traversal to an unfamiliar eye. Time had cost Aroch part of his mental map of the safe path, but he still knew how to avoid entanglement. Though he held treasured memories of the lair's inhabitant, a part of him always wished never to have to set foot here again. Setting aside that reasonable but morally reprehensible thought, he drew back the elastic curtain of webbing and stepped in, careful to crouch and crawl where necessary to preserve his fur.

He soon lost the light, subsequently found himself free enough of the protective layers to stand and walk slowly into the darkness while, reactive to his arrival, there had arisen a bone-chilling scraping all around him. Hundreds of small deghni scurried beneath the mesh covering the walls and converged on him. He could not help but cringe and shudder as the prickly, segmented little monsters swarmed all around, their pointy feet clacking against blood-encrusted stone. He suppressed his revulsion and, while grateful for the dubious comfort of being unable to see the dreaded swarm just yet, took a deep breath and nearly choked on the stench of dead flesh.

Curbing his reflexes, he hissed into the cold burrow in imitation of its master's voice.

"*Ein, bu'tsssacht na* deghni. *Bethe'beulg* Nagusssta?" The scrabbling ceased, much to Aroch's relief. Barbs had already been picking at his feet, whether curiously or hungrily he didn't care to know. He closed his eyes tight for a moment and tried to shoo them with subtle sweeps of his toes, and they complied respectfully.

A new sound came, this time much larger and louder, and from directly overhead. The grinding voice that followed was both familiar and faintly threatening.

"You sssstmell lik-k-ke ssssstweet meat-t-t-to lit-t-tle onessst...and t-t-to me."

Aroch stared ahead and shook off the feeling of clinging filth, but his tone was kind, even apologetic as he mumbled "I always knew you'd be angry when I finally visited again. If you really must eat me then I suppose I have no words to argue it."

A grotesque tearing and stretching emanated from the black, and six eyes like swirling pits of cinders descended before him until they stopped not a foot from his. He felt a rush of wind beside him as one of his old friend's scythe-like legs swept up and slashed at the dense threadwork overhead to allow the scantest ray of daylight in and allowed Aroch to see his way in the large chamber. The indirect illumination would not damage the Ennedeghe or his spawn, but while his weird laugh vibrated the arabesque hollow a pale light washed over it and a few exposed deghni retreated into the hive walls in a shrieking frenzy.

"Kekekekee! What-t-t can I sssstay my *ut-t-tan*? You dton't vist-t-tit ast oft-t-ten ast you promisssst. Childtrensssst have forget-t-ten your sssctent, andt t-to me you ssstmell like any other meat-t-t."

Aroch shifted his damp clothes and cleared his throat, knowing he hadn't earned his friend's trust and forgiveness, even if it was offered. "Naguza, you fiend," he began playfully, "You know I cannot be up here as often as I promise, less so when my family yearns to tear itself apart. My daughter..."

His excuses were interrupted as Naguza spread his arms and cackled, dropping from his silken cords and rearing upright, his thirty-foot segmented abdomen and its many legs slamming down to shake the hollow. Easily twice Aroch's height, his barely visible chest and head remained somewhat Galaila. Matted black locks surrounded a face dominated by a huge, cracked smile lined with toxic blades that clicked when he spoke. His fingers were melded together into long blades that, like his four, inverse-jointed forelegs were possessed of an edge keen enough to chop the substantial thi of Ni'ivitnem to toothpicks. Giddy to speak with anyone, his dragging posterior thrashed back and forth behind him, its carapaces scraping together and across the netted cobble on many smaller legs.

"Kekekekekee! She gotssst her hussstbandt gone away, yessst?" he moaned mockingly, revealing a knowledge of recent activities. "Tsk, tsk, ssstuch lovely woman ssshouldt not-t-t be t-treated sto." He paused and his clustered eyes strayed a bit before brightening and refocusing on Aroch, his teeth smiling wider. "Issst goodt-t-to ssstee you friendt."

Aroch stood as high as he could and touched Naguza's arm, prompting and accepting a mutual embrace while trying his best to avoid anything sharp.

"*La.* You are well met as always, my *gaz'tskbeulg.* I'm sorry my company had to be under this condition, but sadly it is not for reunion with a much pleasant friend that I have come." Setting aside pleasantries, he regretfully turned to the business at hand. "You are attuned to Keimas' activity it seems. This is good. I only know he has a mind to do as he pleases, a courtesy of the kutliku blood in him, but under its influence and in light of what he's endured of late I now fear for his safety. In his confusion he has seen fit to take wing and it is safely presumed that he makes for the hallowed gate. For his marriage to my daughter, you will understand my worry that he may violate the law and venture beyond it for some unprecedented reason."

Naguza waved him off and hissed viciously at a rambunctious deghni that had begun trying to climb Aroch again. Aroch twitched awkwardly and offered his appreciation.

Naguza wrung his hands together and gestured with a leg to a gash in the underlying net, where sight and sound of deghni commotion was beginning again.

"Mmmy lit-t-tle onessst dto assst they mussst without-t-t my commandt. Wat-t-tch all, Keimassst-t-too. Your Kut-t-tu ssstits at-t the gat-t-te, ssstilent andt ssstill ast the ssstonessst."

"I hoped as much, but did not expect it," Aroch sighed in relief. "I do not wish to send my own after him and reveal to my daughter's husband that I have betrayed his trust…or to others that he has betrayed ours and disobeyed the Primarch's edict. Only please have your eyes watch and your ears listen, and send for me when he moves," he charged.

"Wouldt pleassste me Aroch. My childtrenssst will wat-t-tch assst you asssk."

"Many thanks, brother mine," Aroch replied, and added with a slight bow and a smile, "Additionally, do make sure your sons and daughters do not devour my prized hunter."

Naguza clawed up the walls into his nest, all his brood following.

"Will ssstee it-t dtone," his voice called back, before getting lost in the scrabbling of thousands of tiny feet. When he was almost out of sight, Aroch's suffering conscience got the better of him.

"Naguza."

Naguza stopped, turned and faced him again while Aroch

99

struggled for words. "I haven't forgotten, and I know Artimecian hasn't either. Such seasons we had, things we had to let go of. We both miss you. Artimecian may not admit it but…he loves you as I do."

Naguza said nothing. Whether real or imagined, the sheen of his eyes made Aroch think he was crying, and he felt his heart break.

"What the Primarch did was inexcusable. I know you went willingly, but your acquiescence to his order doesn't make him right. I promise you, when age takes the hypocrite and Nepiur assumes the table's head, you will no longer be an exile. No one will."

Naguza vibrated and hissed, reaching out a great blade to touch the ground at Aroch's feet gratefully, broke his silence at last.

"It-t issst for the bessst-t. I mussst-t remain outcassst-t. I am assst much a night-t-mare assst Ssstalohel wassst. I dton't want-t-t people t-to be afraidt of me…I will alwayssst be happy t-to remember my brother Aroch andt my brother Art-t-timecian, but-t memory is all Nagussssta hast left-t-t."

With that he was gone, retreated to his cocoon to feed his horde and enjoy the life that he had.

Aroch chose his footing carefully as he shuffled out of the cave, hurrying to reach the safety of the webbed tunnel before the spine-tingling sound of its many occupants got the better of him. It was not like him to be frightened by the dark, and he and Naguza had been so close before they had become Mantichaena, but the constant sound of little talons and the permeating stench was more than he could stomach. He thought about Naguza's sustenance; the way the deghni throughout the land mummified their prey and drank them from within. For the briefest moment he imagined his old friend doing the same, shut out the grim imaginings before they could go any further, and gave a quick thankful prayer to Anama that darkness had kept the deeper portions of the hive hidden.

Thetrulengo speaks,

I speak with Naguza often, as time and opportunity allow. I have no restraints on either. He is the kindest soul I have ever known, and always empathetic in his counsel. In no way does he deserve a place outside the people, but their fear of him cannot be helped until a remedy for ignorance is found. I disdain them for it, and I think him as beautiful as any other. He knows me only as the young girl I most often embody, but I have asked him not to inform anyone of my visits, since it could raise undue suspicion about my presence in the city. I think I can trust his word since I am one of the only visitors he receives. And...hiding among the living is painstaking work. It's harder to avoid suspicion when I'm never entirely sure what they will find unusual. To me their whole world is unusual.

The exiles are a bizarre and lethal bunch. As distasteful as it is, it is not unjustified for the common broods to cower from them. Naguza is not the most powerful, but I don't think he realizes that it was not by mere chance that he was taken by the deghni to become Ennedeghe. There is no doubt in my mind that within him is one of the few essences of the elder god whose likeness he perfectly reproduces. In observing the development of some certain individuals...I likewise see no accident in my obsession with this island and this people among the thousands that are. Anama's power has accelerated a process that has previously taken hundreds upon hundreds of seasons; the ascension of the heirs of the elder gods as they drain their power by birthright from the stars. There can be no doubt. One look tells all. Naguza is a rapidly growing heir of the elder gods, the soul-host of the poisonous Oorghunak.

There will be others. There already are. I feel it, even if I cannot see them.

~Chronicle of Wonders, The Poison Progeny

CHAPTER 10: THE GREAT IMPORT OF THE WEAK

Thetrulengo speaks,

*T*he regard I have given Maengir has always been inconsistent and ever-fluctuating, searching its entire breadth from high above the aetherplane, thinking I would make great discoveries. The first era is of no relevance to my work yet, as it was in the second era that the elder gods rose from the embryonic muck of Maengir. From that fetid womb of dark Escharka's creation and the luminous one of Az'Rech's lost essence came the body and soul, married by an unlikely ability to coexist within the same space and strengthen one another if present in small enough quantities. In greater portion they react violently to each other. The conclusion I draw from this is that a creature cannot exceed a certain limitation on its power unless its physical form becomes similarly larger, or denser. In a large body a god is intimidating, but a smaller god of equal power will be extremely durable, its flesh as hard as metal. I learnt this in my study of Ms'egol's alchemy: a particle of matter can only be inhabited by so much energy. To lose control of this balance results in the destruction of the host. I can then reason that Oorghunak's attentions were not simply spent trying to control his power, but to distance himself from the light and slow his consumption of it. He was of such incredible size, but he grew so slowly that he could not expose himself to the full power of the daylight or his body would begin to fragment. Eventually I will need to perform a study of how Mantichaena and other diurnal species are able to live in it constantly. My expected result is relatively simple: there is very little essence left in this era. Most has already been consumed or started homeward to Az'Rech.

While alive, Nhi'Thaun were of minimal concern before I realized that, while they may destroy one another without plan or purpose, one of them invented a new way of living.

Miohaelia was the very creator of love and of purity. By virtue of her being, she invented the first thought of love. The result was both the learned affection of Oorghunak and the distasteful perversion of Zeniquorer, two opposing uses of the same sensation, and their collision was her tragic end. This story I have dwelt on for so long, anguished as if mortal for the unceasing pain of sweet Miohaelia and her true love Oorghunak, but now it seems the greatest undoing of wicked plans is upon them at last; Maengir has engineered a second chance at lost love.

Kulibreal's sister, the one she discarded...I think I have found her at last. By peering into her I have seen evidence that contradicts what I had always believed her condition of mind to be. Kulibreal, in her self-appointed wisdom, I do recall trying to scrape all grimy emotions from her younger sister, but the tiny goddess' soul was more the shared child of her two parents than of her mother alone. Kulibreal's conviction ever drove her to action, but within her meek and delicate twin the souls of Miohaelia and Zeniquorer twisted into one. In trying to cleanse Zeniquorer's touch from her sister's mind and erase all memory of his existence, Kulibreal could enter only the pathways left by the blood they shared in calling Miohaelia mother. The parts of her born of Zeniquorer's greed were too raw and erratic to be controlled or even discovered by Kulibreal. They remain, intact, lurking and hungering.

Tormented by the feeling of Zeniquorer inside her, the little sister subconsciously gave control of herself to the will of the father. Kulibreal battled to restrain her, eventually tried to destroy her mind and displaced her to the seaplane, but the indwelling of

Zeniquorer desired a certain destiny for her. Only now have I deduced that cycle after cycle of lonely seasons and being adrift in the deep and winding currents of the sea had robbed the forsaken girl of the last bits of her identity and memory, completed Kulibreal's work in scouring all memory from her shattered mind, even of Zeniquorer. Her soul remains, but it could have no master until her inner war yields a victor. The last memories of either her mother or father have to destroy the other in order for her to assume the birthright she's destined for...whichever it may be.

Her celestial essence spent, the orphan's powerless body fell out of the veil's flume and was washed ashore on the island of Skin. The Mantichaena took her in, thought she was one of them, for when her soul found them it believed they were her kind, and created for her a flesh in their image. No one gave any thought to what family she belonged to. No one but me. She caught my attention, I saw in her what she truly was, and I bring her to the font of my voice upon pages of mist. Herein Maengir will know her fate as I will ascribe it to the kindness of strangers. In looking into her broken mind, I have seen nothing but the pieces of her past, no sign of either elder god to tease her one way or the other. Her woefully heavy heart belies her affinity to Miohaelia, but the disquieting cravings I can hear in each of its anxious beats can only be the fingerprints of Zeniquorer. Even in death he reaches out to take her.

She is like me, confused and eager to understand, unable to discern what is good and evil. This is my advantage, but not so for a goddess lost among the mortal. Out of rash curiosity I have mistakenly knocked continents from the higher earthplane before I understood how my actions affected the world and its creatures. What havoc could this one wreak if she realized her power and lent it to the service of Zeniquorer? The Mantichaena may rue the day they discovered the orphaned girl with no memory and no name. They gave her the name of 'innocent's unburdened dream', an omen, calling her fate to fruition. In birth she was called Jimnalbpia. The Mantichaena call her Raphenie.

~Chronicle of Wonders, Sleeping Child

Patriarch Khurk swayed and finally stooped, his bony chest heaving with exertion, and drew dusty breaths that burned inside him. A footrace up from the freshly dug warrens of Nesh, for which Khurk had not been prepared, caught his salty bones off guard and reminded him that age was inescapable. He glanced to the hall he had passed and quailed, huffed that he was not able to push through the pain as a young man would.

Impatient to continue and swollen with smugness, Matriarch Sebashni tapped her stubby Mearnum claws along the wall a few strides ahead, slowed in expectation of his likely surrender, and strutted lazily backward from him.

"*Ein*, stiffen your belly Khurk! The malleable beaches of Ellel tired a leg far worse than this hardy stone and still you shamed me on them day after day. You wouldn't give dominance of your own Hall to a child, would you?"

Khurk smirked and responded to the challenge. Thrusting out his gut and filling his lungs with the stinging air, he whipped his tail up and darted after Sebashni. Recharged for the moment, he overtook her before she could turn back down the avenue, but her ego baiting was no idle sass. Sebashni regained and held her lead, provoking him onward until Khurk's regard for his screaming muscles was forgotten. He basked in the memories she spoke of, so awash in how it had felt to race in warm seasons along the beach that he nearly forgot where he was. They fought onward until they neared the doorway into the atrium. Only one at a time was going to get through that door and neither would yield, but a sideward glance from Sebashni to Khurk stole her verve away; he had the look of a young man again. His mind was full of the glory of their old lives and the eternal pursuit of speed and victory. Sebashni took his pain unto herself and felt suddenly that, in comparison to his young heart, hers was the old one. It was a matter of character. She had given herself completely to the duties and responsibilities of an elder while he had taken the Patriarch's seat with the heart of a child that still had so much wonderment for the world. She resigned and slowed with a bark of disappointment but laughed happily as he launched himself with a flying leap from the top landing and plummeted down to the center stage. His heels struck and he slid agilely along the dusted rock, settling on shaky legs to face and bow to a defeated Sebashni. Hobbling down the slopes beneath their entry, her tail and toes dragged across the ground though she clapped for him and congratulated him with dignity.

"Someday, elder mine, I would hope to be as fresh without as you are within." For a moment Khurk turned about and held his fists high, but immediately felt the consequence of poor breathing habits, collapsed in fierce coughing.

"Bahaha! And now you have grown old again," Sebashni again teased, panted and set her hands on her hips. "Perhaps next time I will not remind you that you always win."

Khurk tried to laugh through agonizing breaths and eased himself down from the stage.

"*Minla*...when I am...gone and buried...you will still...never beat me. My spirit will...always race alongside you and...death will only make me faster." They exchanged hugs and turned to face the fire burning comfortably in the hearth. Khurk walked carefully, leaning heavily on his company's attentive shoulder.

"Where go you from here, *aiat*?" he asked at length.

Sebashni bobbed her head and turned to the ramps opposite them, the route to Keimas' room, wherein she hoped to find his wife.

"Here ahead, toward Nesh Zet'Tau, in hopes that our watery beauty has come home. I see her pain in how her father worries for her," she fretted. "Since she went missing in like style with Keimas good Aroch wrings his hands more than usual, and fails to find peace. I would wait there in hopes of catching and interrogating her for his easement. What of you, *Utan*?" She turned back to her old teacher. "Haven't you more pressing engagements than footraces with younger, faster and more attractive beasts?"

"Hah! *Minein minseba sil'thav*! Evidently not, as there are none here!" he burst out cheerily. He paused and thought to answer more honestly, and his glee wavered. "Though, in a happy manner, yes. My business is to prepare Nepiur for her long fight to be laid on a husband's breast as Lindu breaks."

Sebashni stiffened and searched Khurk's face to find he was serious.

"*La, wektein*? Nepiur offers herself tonight?" She could not keep the concern from her voice. "I suspect it will be to a certain man who tends to the fire, the blind caretaker she's so often with, *la*?"

"*Uta* Capheif," Khurk confirmed. "He has been of love to her for some time, and she to him for even longer. Have you not seen her watching him when he goes out to sing by the river, waiting on him as he lights our conflagration here in the wall?"

"It seems I notice nothing of great importance, if I have lost my eye for the someday-Primarch's passions. Maybe I have allowed myself to think this deep empathy unwieldy when held for more than one Archon's daughter...*minein*, how long have they been seeking to keep and rest one another?"

"Nearly since the start of our latest Mercy, following many other seasons full of secret affections and stolen kisses," Khurk muttered coyly.

Sebashni grinned. "Limitless joy! I am so pleased to hear Capheif of love with such a woman. But these secret affections you relay, are they known by more than a few? I don't expect the Primarch knows, or I expect his bitter thumb would squash any desires in her, save what she can muster for her birthright to his position."

Khurk closed his eyes and huffed, dropping his head to his chest and scowling. He too had noticed the Primarch's harsh treatment of his daughter.

"He knows. He knows all too well and in no way favors it. He has far more clout now than back when the affairs with his wife arose, but not the opulence of pocket to drown out the excessive outburst that would surely follow the violent climax of his loathing." He trailed off and closed his eyes, the stench of that memory creating haze in him. "*Ein*, by Anama's grace the arrogant man has not struck her direly over it, though not for lack of desire," he said in disgust. "He refuses to see her. She, the only daughter he hasn't yet driven away to exile. He swears his soul to Vaeba if he ever smiles on her again and curses the name Nepiur at its very mention. I, for one, am proud of our little heir to the Primacy. She does not flaunt her love before his disapproving eyes, but neither does she show fear of his retribution. She has found the courage to stand as a woman of love, not a girl of silent obedience."

Sebashni growled and lifted her eyes to the partially hidden door beside the fire pit. Beyond it was the caretaker's quarters where their friend, Capheif, ate humble meals and sang humble songs of romance.

"I cannot abide Sky's violence, even if justified as he would have us all believe. To claim he would disown his own daughter simply because her promised man lacks sight?" Khurk paced a little as his ire mounted. "*Minein*, a position he would not call honorable to his family? He behaves like a beast that has begot a runt and yet his daughter is the fairest and most deserving of any *aiat*. It is beneath his station to harbor such prejudice towards one of his own people. More so his own daughter! Capheif faced Nepiur as any man, fought with her bravely to earn a place by her side, and his victory came despite his handicap." He ceased his rant and turned back to Sebashni. "*Malpael*, I am in the wrong. Sky neither knows nor learns, that much was clear when he threw his eldest to the wild. It is foolish to think he wouldn't do it again."

"*Aia*, it is not my place to say," Sebashni replied.

"I have known Sky since before he was governor back home. A pure hearted Galaila then...at least in youth. He wasn't this skulking tyrant. It's as if an evil has set itself on him and changed him. I remember well a time when he would have recoiled from striking anyone, even in duty and the recipient a scoundrel with stolen goods in hand."

"Until this place."

"*Minla*, until his wife. She was his first. Ferraro's wrath was perhaps a fortune for him, sparing him the vengeance of his wife after he cast her out of Tieg Raev." Khurk shook his head in disgust. "But ah, what bitter taste this puts on my tongue to speak of! I tire of it. Instead, I will bless your attendance to Lemalie, and may you both be in good spirits to meet." He embraced her briefly and departed in silence for the hallway situated beneath the ramp that led to Nepiur's chamber. Sebashni watched him go for a moment before turning to seek out young Lemalie.

After the archons left the hall, the great fire continued to burn, lighting the room and chasing away shadow. Only the antechamber closest to the escalating walks were veiled by dense shadows resultant of the height and shape of the stage. Unseen and

108

unnoticed by the archons, a gentle soul sat, mournful tears trailing through soft white fur, to drip silently onto the stone floor. A single alabaster-furred foot eased out of the cloak of shadows, a timid precursor of the rest of the young Mearnum, Ms'egol Aia Raphenie. She slunk into the light with her soft and bushy tail twisted in her little hands, while the rounded ears beside her drooping head twitched. Skirting the hall, she sat again, conflicted, and held her knees beneath her chin. Her misty blue eyes ached with envy to follow Sebashni and comfort Lemalie. Deterred by the surety that she could provide no help to the great lady she instead looked on the path taken by Khurk, tried to control her despair upon hearing that the only man who had ever shown her kindness had the Primarch's evil eye upon him. Not all was lost; Capheif was yet alone, in seclusion until he was summoned to marry. The realization brightened her face though still she gnawed her lip. She scooted toward an open hallway beside the door through which Khurk had gone. She thought to herself *Loi, Anama, be good to me. Let me be a comfort to the pained, balm to these wounds. Help me stop their hurt.* If Nepiur's imminent marriage was such dangerous territory under the harsh gaze of the Primarch then perhaps Capheif, too, was in need of some company. She hoped he was, most desperately.

She found herself outside his door, surprised by her own audacity. It was big, old but sturdy, and loomed over her; Capheif himself if he were a door. Her small fingers made the slightest tapping sound against its dense wood, and she knew before his reply that his marvelously sensitive ears would hear it.

"Come, please," he rumbled from beyond.

She pushed the door open slowly, not wanting to make any unpleasant noise from a corroded bolt, but neither certain she had the courage to see it opened all the way. She tried to match his tone; salty, concise, but was poorly equipped to imitate strength.

"*Udaian*...thanks be that you welcome me. I do not mean to invade you."

Without a word Capheif chewed the remainder of a seasoned chlio he had been devouring, leaned back from his hearty meal and sat a tall wood cup before the opposite seat. The great muscles in his finely constructed figure flexed and flowed with each movement. He was bare apart from a skirt of simple green that fell from halfway up his abdomen to his knees and a headdress of the same color draped around his neck and shoulders over thick braids of black hair. Vibrant white horns curled around his ears like perfectly leavened bread dough. As he sniffed the air, took in the girl's scent, his pointed beard bobbed with his mouth and scrunched nose.

"Hmm. A Mearnum, a young one. Too young to be my betrothed, *la? Minein*, but instead it is the hidden flower that grows in the academy, enjoyed by all, seen by none. Raphenie?" He paused as he perceived a new scent. "Oh no, my child, are those tears?"

Compassion replaced curiosity as he turned to face her and rose from his seat. She shuddered happily to know he had not forgotten her, and he searched about with sudden fervor for a basket of neatly folded cloth he kept next to the table for indeterminate purposes.

"*Ein*, certainly it must be you, little Raphenie. *Eina*, come closer now. You may not weep," he said gently.

Raphenie could not help but smile at the blind Kubernu, accepting the rag he offered with trembling fingers. He ushered her to his table and drew a seat for her.

"Poor thing, sit you here and share in my feast." He was always this paragon of civility, startling to see in a fortified tower of a man.

"*Minla* sir," Raphenie said, bowing sharply and backing a step away. "I would not survive the guilt of so rudely sitting for a meal with a man of another's love, not alone." She blushed furiously, hoping secretly that he would insist and certain that he would.

"*Malwekt*! Nonsense girl. I always keep a little extra something at the ready in case of company, and I'm sure Ms'egol's strict dietary regulations have left you with a craving for chlio prepared with the savory secrets of Nesh Udai Capheif's pot." He stepped precisely over his seat and moved by memory to where a heavy cauldron boiled with broth over the dying fire.

"Likewise, I would be far more honored than distraught if you should have something to ask of me, or perhaps something to tell me? My mind slumbers all day without stimulating conversation, but with the wedding on approach it is best I stay here and reflect on who I am to become soon."

Raphenie's romantic mind convinced her he had already gleaned everything she felt. It was not uncommon for him to do just that with whomever he met, being an intuitive beast with a knack for sniffing out the feelings of his guests.

"My *Utan*...did I give something away?" she asked shyly. "Do the walls speak to you of what troubles me?"

Capheif spooned some steaming potage into a bowl and returned to the table, broke a loaf of dense bread in half, placed the broth before her, moved the cup beside it and lifted another dripping chlio from a nearby plate for her. All of this without a stumble or misplacement.

"A bit, but I assure you it is only by your presence. I train my mind in common sense the way you and the apprentices of Ms'egol do in mancy. I can smell flesh and wine as I always have, but through time, I have unfortunately never learned the scent of thoughts or feelings. I only know that when a girl so solitary as you comes knocking at my door she comes with purpose, which suggests conflict."

Raphenie took the gutted chlio from him and placed it in the broth, shredded it daintily with her tiny claws. She relaxed, more at home now, though she blushed increasingly as he revealed his knowledge of her intent.

"*Malpael*, I apologize for my resistance," she nervously said. "I was compelled to come to you after hearing of your marriageable love."

"The word and hand of Primarch Sky no doubt an adjoined subject," was his rough response. Raphenie nodded silently and Capheif pursed his lips, taking her silence for agreement and reason to dismiss her weightiest of thoughts. "Do not allow the unfortunate disposition of one man to pollute your goodly spirit. The flight of his hand has never been the fruit of hate, only confusion and fear. Despite being *Utanan* Primarch, he understands so little of how to be a man, and beyond the things he does not know there are countless more he never will. He vaunts his intellect because it is well suited to governing in times of trouble, which have been many for us, but not to fathering nor to being husband. He does not understand love, nor does he kindness, only control, and a singular conviction regarding what is good and worthy. Hence, his distaste for me may in fact be justified...from a certain point of view."

Raphenie chewed a bit of flesh solemnly, shook her head in silent wonder.

"A gift," she ventured, "that anyone could be so understanding of such an awful man."

Capheif leaned on the table, staring hollowly in Raphenie's direction.

"It is not such a bad thing that he is so, for he is wholly devoted to the laws that kept our people safe and certain for a time. It is only to us that dwell on love and do not understand the burdens of such demanding leadership that his way of life seems flawed. A great many are loath to understanding what they are not, and without understanding they will often fall prey to fear and distrust." Capheif stood and moved to the fireplace, his voice losing its congenial shine and becoming a grumble. "My blindness he sees as a weakness, and who can blame him? I can barely see the light of day when I stare headlong into Laesis, and colors and shapes come to my blackened sight only when my mind plays tricks on me. If he were to know me, he would know my power in its entirety. It would be a nice respite from the glowering contempt he shows me otherwise. Though I wish he could be different, I do so selfishly. He has the right to decide who he is, as do we all."

Raphenie sat in silence, her meal barely eaten but torn to pieces as she counted the possibilities of what could transpire next between the two families.

"Raphenie," Capheif prompted again.

"*La, Utan?*" Her heart leapt at the unexpected invitation to talk further and the intimate tone he used.

"I have heard you walk; I have heard you speak and I have heard you eat and breathe and sit by the water. In everything you do, I can hear worry upon you. It is not the desire of your heart, this I know, but anxiety surrounds you with a weight unlike most."

Raphenie took another drink of broth to keep herself busy while she thought of how to respond.

He continued "Believe me, dear girl. I know fear. It came upon me not when I was a warrior, but for a handful of seasons when I was first stripped of my sight. I could not find my way, nor could I feed myself. I couldn't perform the simplest task without knocking something over or tripping on whatever insignificant stone presented itself as a mountain to my uncertain feet." Firelight glowed in his eyes, and Raphenie basked in the warmth of his words. "But all the while, when I was most helpless...it was then that I became stronger than I had ever been when my eyes had done their work. Colorful pictures dimmed to shadows, and soon the sky blurred into clouds, then everlasting night; my nose grew keener, my *sepituum* more eager, and my ears sensed things that vision could not have provided me. Regrettably, even with all of this I still longed to confirm my own existence by sight and to know the look and form of the world. I dreaded the darkness in my eyes even after I had overcome it." He sat again at the table, returning to his meal. "You came here to offer me comfort I think, but first you must have comfort of your own to give. You are as blind as I am to the true shape of the world because you can only see darkness. Just because you cannot see the light beyond doesn't mean it's no longer there. If you become convinced that life is synonymous with darkness, and that you alone are the light, then the darkness within you grows, unchecked. You depend solely on what you see outside of you, not what is within you, and that is when you become truly helpless."

Raphenie's shoulders slumped and she pushed her bread back and forth between her hands.

"Light cannot have darkness in it," she argued.

Capheif smiled gently and adopted a quizzical look.

"And if light truly believes that then will it ever look inward? How is one to understand the darkness without until it has understood the darkness within?"

Raphenie's ears wiggled as she tried to focus on his voice. There was wisdom here, but as so often happened in his presence, other thoughts and feelings intruded, interfering. As he spoke, she felt an upwelling connection to him, a bond of desire that gradually suppressed her reason and gave way to new and oddly intense, yet unfamiliar thoughts. Though her eyes were fixed on his creased face, her vision blurred and she felt disoriented, carnal fantasies thronging at the doors of her consciousness. A heartbeat drummed in her ears, whether his or hers she could not tell, but of her only friend she suddenly felt a demanding lust. She felt as well, for the first time, that she could be pleasing to a man. Had she been aware of it, it would have surprised her that he was to her, in romantic and sexual desirability, everything that Lemalie was in imitable womanhood. The two were opposite yet the same in their effect on Raphenie.

She was jerked out of her reverie by his hand grasping hers, igniting in her a fresh and dizzying swirl of cravings.

"Our world will never be a perfect place for either of us my girl," he rumbled. "This dreadful existence was made by gods who feared just as we do, then faded into the veil and left us here alone. We battle and bicker and show no kindness to each other because we are all equally lost. This existence is not our true home, but we smile and make amends because it's the only home we have. The purpose of life is not to be without fear or danger or evil, but to survive it together and build the new upon the old, strengthened each day as one until we can overthrow it. All good things and indeed all the good or evil in this world begins as a spark in a single heart."

Raphenie barely heard him as she sat gritting her teeth, hungry in a way the food before her could not satisfy. Chastened, and recovering herself only by the fear he spoke against, she recoiled from his grip and rose from her seat. Capheif was stunned into silence by the sharp movement, reaching out with his senses as he rose with her. The fire had fallen to the toasty glow of a bed of coals, and without strong flames there came a gloom around them that honed Raphenie's arousal, forced her to hide her face instinctively with handfuls of her hair as she stared at the chamber floor. She tried to speak, but her lips and tongue refused. Capheif was unsure of what to make of the situation and grew increasingly concerned that his rough and direct speech had distressed her. Raphenie, only partially eased by separating herself from physical touch, backed towards the door hoping to further dull her strange lust. Capheif slowly reached out, and not finding her where she had been, he circled the table and searched.

"*Ein*, are you alright *sumearaiana*? Where are you?" He was not rewarded, and his hopes sank as he heard the overly harsh squeak of the door hinges betray Raphenie's furtive departure.

Ignoring the forlorn baritone of his belated farewells, Raphenie sobbed into her folded hands, wrenched from her by the unbearable crisis within. Her lungs and gut ached from the effort of preventing her grief being audible to Capheif. She slouched against the wall for a moment then bit her tongue and stumbled away toward the antechamber, aghast at her treacherous thoughts. She could not control her emotions, had never been able to. Now they crashed over her, a wave so unlike her normally gentle heart, as if she craved him more out of anger than love.

It seemed now as if she had always felt it, a rampant craving. She wanted his power, his sex, if only to be Nepiur and be taken by this beast on their wedding night. She dug her claws into her shoulders while cradling herself. Groaning, she moved faster and faster down the hall, and heard her own voice repeating one terrible thought in her head until it twisted to suit her: *Their wedding night. Their wedding...our wedding night...MY wedding night...*

CHAPTER 11: NESH UTAN ROGAN

In the Council of Archons' sanctuary, Aroch stood at the far head of the long stone table that was its centerpiece, opposite a dourly brooding Primarch Sky. All the halls' elevated figures, mothers and fathers distinguished by superior insight, stood around the periphery of the room in isolated pairs. Aroch had preempted normal business with the abrupt announcement of Keimas' 'apparently directionless' flight, that he had dispatched Naguza's brood to locate him. Collective concern rippled through the room until Sky became impatient of the obvious lie, and at his insistence Aroch finally confessed that Keimas had flown Tau. Assurance that he lingered before the great wall had placated many, but old fears were awoken, particularly when words like 'thuell' arose. Time was limited in which Keimas could return before the council would be obligated to punish him. The Primarch cleared his throat sharply and, with a wave of fingers, ordered the archons to reseat themselves and the session to resume. Conversations broke off as they swiftly reassembled. A calming tone was set when Sebashni's lyrical voice took the floor.

"My familiars, all equally esteemed, let's take a moment before judging too hastily what we do not know, that we might be open to every possibility." She glanced meaningfully in Mani's direction, who touched his chest lightly and bowed his head to Sky in apology for his earlier loss of composure. Ill will appeased, Sebashni quickly stated, "Regardless of what time we have, we must act as though it were little. *Utan* Govan will be the first to notice his absence, and others will follow. We will have to silence all rumors if we are to avoid an unfortunate reaction, even panic."

Aroch smoldered as she spoke, but before he could interject Obure's willfully optimistic smile and reassuring words rang through the hall.

"*Minla*! Let Govan rave that his prize hunter has not nested! Keimas has been through a great ordeal. We have seen as much in his unsettled sleep and terrible sweat. In Voddace he seemed near death, and not surprisingly, after falling into a place that must surely be cursed from our betrayal of Loi. We have only kept Keimas until his body healed. Who can say when his mind will be right?"

Mani stood boldly, his tail lashing back and forth in agitation. "And do nothing to quell rumor? Raru SAW him part from us, and that beat of wings was of a ferocity incited by purpose. He did not simply find himself flying but flew with intent! Others must have seen it as well. We cannot risk gossip that he has gone anywhere but back to the aviary."

"You're making too much of nothing, friend," Obure retaliated. "He's just being prudent with his reputation. Perhaps he seeks the purifying power of the gate, *la*? If he turned to Ms'egol for aid they might publicize his needs. A Kutu cannot afford to be seen as unfit by the people that rely on him. It's best that we simply assure the city that he is perfectly well, back in the aviary with his hunt."

"Is he!?" Mani demanded forcefully. "You heard his mutterings, his feverish dreams. Something happened in that accursed place that he will not speak of; something we cannot ignore."

Aroch's tremendous fist smashed down on the tabletop and silenced the quarrelsome pair. Ignoring Sky's disapproving glare he commanded attention, spoke slowly and impatiently.

"You two...you fight like children," he growled. "In fairness, we've been in session for much of the morning and I know skins are thinning, but you will NOT speak of my son in this manner, nor of our first and greatest godly benefactor's hallowed house of worship." He waited a moment for his words to sink in, then tried to redirect the course of the argument. "*La*, it is expected that he still feels some illness in him, whether mind or body, and seeks remedy. Our enchanters divined the words that adorn our gate for the specific purpose of destroying anything unclean such that no thuell, nor any other toxic thing, could ever pass through or nearby. There may be some truth to Obure's speculation."

Obure rapidly nodded his approval, while Mani shook his head in annoyance. There was more support than dissent for this determination, until Artimecian, hands firmly locked and eyes intense, leaned forward from his seat to challenge forbiddingly.

"And what if you're wrong?" he asked. "You'll forgive me, *Utan* Aroch, but what if he is deliberately secretive? Our burden here is to prevent panic among our halls, not merely to protect the honor of your daughter's husband. We're all fully aware, as you yourself are, that Keimas is in the habit of taking upon himself beyond what is expected or even allowed of him. He hunts alone, scouts alone, no matter what chastisement Govan doles out. His mind is awash with self-aggrandizing thoughts that often turn to scheming, then to actions unmitigated by his betters. It's no stretch to consider that perhaps such scheming is occurring now."

Aroch's capacity for hearing accusations was stretched thin, and it showed in his face and voice.

"*Ueinla*? And what scheme is he hatching, Artimecian? Does he plan to incite panic himself so as to overthrow the council? Will he break down the gate and expose us? Tell me what you would have us believe my son will do to destroy us!"

"EXACTLY THAT!" Artimecian thundered.

Aroch was enflamed by the outrageous notion and the entirety of the council shocked to attention as Artimecian dominated the table.

"Why else are we keeping word of his flight secret? People may be scared that he has seen something evil in Ni'ivitnem. Let them be scared over such a trifle! A much more pressing concern is what they will do if they learn that a hunter-killer has left the city to the most forbidden of outlands without the consent of the council. Do we want every warrior to believe they are free from the law and permitted to come and go as they please? Keimas' entire life is an insult to the rule of law! We must bring Keimas back before his recklessness incites rebellion."

"How DARE you!?" Aroch retorted, lurching from his chair and rounding the edge of the table with bared teeth. "Keimas has never, EVER betrayed a direct order of the council or the duties of his position! His urgency is a sign of real danger, and you would tarry on wild assumptions that the entire city will be flung into anarchy if a single law is bent by a trusted man!?" Artimecian did not budge, only folded his arms as Aroch advanced on him until Sky's voice shook the cloister and stayed Aroch's approach.

"*Minwekt, sauv!*" The Primarch bellowed, ordering them to sit. The tension among the council was tangible, but Sky seemed to feed off it, calmer than ever. "Aroch. Sit. Down." His finger dictated movement, his face not revealing one glimmer of sympathy for the worried man's point of view.

Aroch backed away, plopped down and gripped the underside of the table resentfully. Artimecian shared a furtive glance with the Primarch, then sneered at Aroch like a child who, when locking horns with a brother, was certain the parents would take his side. His juvenile surety was proven when the Primarch spoke again and Aroch could not believe his ears.

"Father Artimecian is precisely right." Sky began in a greatly softened tone. "Keimas' disappearance could either be damaging or empowering to this council, depending on how we use it. As *Utan* Artimecian has wisely said, it is the fear of the thuell that has kept us focused on Ni'ivitnem for sustenance, instead of turning back to the Tau. With the fear of the Thuell that still infects the simple minded, any madness such as Keimas' the people will interpret as Thuell taint. Who would be willing to hunt and forage then, if Ni'ivitnem has fruiting Thuell bodies stalking its depths? Our foremost concern is to convince them that Keimas' injury was nothing more than a simple accident, and whatever he may or may not have said while under the fever's influence was just that: fever." He shrugged nonchalantly, dismissing Aroch's words with open disdain. "Furthermore, it is in our best interest to ensure it is well known that Keimas parted by order of the council…that we posted him to the gate to ensure it and the surrounding plateau are safe before we send Ms'egol enchanters to assess how well the enchantments have held up to time."

Mani and Raru exchanged perplexed looks, then presented their confusion to Sky.

"Primarch, we've not been told of this plan until now," said Mani. Sky smirked and held out his hands to placate them.

"It's just become the plan." With a snap of his fingers he accentuated his command presence and directed one hand to his witchcrafter. "Artimecian, take two students from your Iron Sanctum for this task."

Aroch's snort of contempt pulled the Primarch's attention to him, and his gaze met Sky's unwaveringly.

"Of course," he spat. "Artimecian and his mad zealots who know nothing of classical enchantments will be sent to inspect them?"

"Aroch," Sky rapped his claws on the arm of his chair in annoyance. "You will not forget your rightful obedience in this chamber, lest I have you removed from it."

Aroch's gaze searched the room for any support, but only Sebashni would make eye contact, displaying her own distaste with a sad sigh. He had no choice but to bow his head and submit, clenching his fists as he stood slowly and moved to the corner table of assorted refreshments where he poured himself an excessive amount of wine. Sky, meanwhile, emerged from his elevated seat and waved his hands dismissively. "This has drug on too long. We will retire until this evening."

The palpable tension in the room ostensibly abated and the archons departed to their respective halls and bedchambers amid casual conversation. Aroch's gullet rumbled as he downed a second and then third cup of wine. His melancholy brooding was broken with the sound of the door slamming shut behind him, followed by the gentle touch of a hand on his neck. He leaned against the wall, turned and saw Sebashni's kind eyes, so close to tears that he felt compelled to set aside his own troubles to comfort her. Her pleasant arms surrounded his waist and her head rested on his chest. She was despondently confused.

"Aroch...what have we just witnessed?" she asked wearily.

Aroch stroked her hair and leaned back with a finger beneath her cheek. "The inevitable end of all politicking, when those long-accustomed to power and a peaceful life forget how to let go of it. *Eina,* my son enters my family only to disgrace it. If I had said nothing then it would have come to light one way or another. I hoped securing Naguza's help would placate them, yet now realize this was the highest order of foolishness. Sky twists the truth to serve his schemes. He already has everything he needs to end me."

Sebashni squinted one eye skeptically. "What is that? You sound as though Sky, and even your own son are conspiring against you."

"Not Keimas, but Sky I know to be," Aroch said. At Sebashni's surprised look he rubbed her shoulders and closed his eyes. It would not do to allow his own distress to take hold. "I have known for some time now, ever since Sky learned of Nepiur's engagement to Caphief. He intends to pass the Primacy not to his daughter but to Artimecian, very soon I suspect. I imagine the mockery of justice we are about to witness will be heralded as a great act of civil service that will ensure the arch-witchcrafter's future place as Primarch."

"That's impossible! His own daughter...it was he who made the very law that secures her as Primarch."

"A law that no longer suits him," Aroch reminded her with a disgruntled slap of his hand on the wine table. "He would rather see her out of Nesh, out of the city itself, than have a Primarch so wedded to a *gal'tskhain*."

Sebashni struck him in the ribs, then held his face to hers in both hands. "*Mintaudai*! You should not speak that word."

He pulled himself free of her and slouched into a nearby chair. "I am fearful not of speaking the word but of the man who invented it. Whether or not Capheif is a worthy man, the absence of but one sense is enough for Sky to look down on him." Sebashni was not wounded by his behavior, even laughed a little, causing Aroch's anger to burgeon.

"What!? Why do you mock me!?" he demanded.

She sighed and grabbed hold of his robe tightly, refusing to be moved away from him. "*Utan* Aroch, the power of the veil shapes the world as much as the living things tied to it, and always toward balance. I do not hate Sky for his ignorance of Capheif's virtue, I pity the loss it brings him. Nepiur was friend to Capheif for so many seasons, but it wasn't until he lost his sight and Sky decreed him an...undesirable, that Nepiur revealed she was of love to him, as if to spite the old man. I love that you are so concerned for all this, but the girl is not. Nepiur doesn't value the Primacy, leastwise over her devotion to Capheif. Sky can preen and strut and flaunt his authority all he wants, but Nepiur is no more a slave to him than any of us are."

Aroch's lips puffed and he grumbled back at her sarcastically. "Of course, we don't belong to him, which is why a roomful of our tribe's leaders sat here and gawked at the ground while he and Artimecian blatantly disdained my family, practically announced that they would sacrifice my son as an example to maintain their authority."

Sebashni pursed her lips and patted his chest. "*Quo wektein,* it's not good. He's been Primarch too long, but until the people see reason not to trust him there's little to be done to take the Primacy from him."

Aroch scratched his beard and considered her words. "A little may be all that is needed." Before Sebashni could respond, he put his arm around her and whispered to her. "Take a message to Raru, I beg you. If Sky sees me moving about the other archons he may try to corner me and keep me under watch."

"Certainly, whatever do you need?" she agreed readily.

He smiled his appreciation and ushered her toward the door.

"If the Primarch intends to lie for his own ends, then I will spread truth for mine. Tell Raru that I have reason to believe Artimecian's iron pets have no intention of examining the gate but go only to bring Keimas back by extreme force."

"I'm certain he knows, same as all of us. It's obvious..." she began.

"And Keimas, given what he is and the power of what drew him Tau, will go willingly?" Aroch inquired quietly. "I do not think this and neither does Sky, or he would not have sent the savages of the Iron Sanctum. I believe he will make an attempt on Keimas' life."

"What!?" his paramour cried incredulously.

"Please, tell him," Aroch repeated. "A man who rules by fear, disdains his own people if he thinks they might weaken his regime, will not use Keimas' safe return to bolster the city's spirit. I would be lying if I didn't confess that I agree with Sky in part. Keimas is keeping secrets. There's nothing a despot fears more than that. He will either kill my son or bring him home to a life of chains and cut the truth out of him, by Artimecian's hands no doubt."

Sebashni silently contemplated his words before sharply

nodding and taking Aroch's hand. "We'll take no chances," she said decisively, "if Sky could really do something like that."

"*Ein*, would you expect better of him?" Aroch asked.

She hated that she shared Aroch's suspicion, but the more he spoke the more she recalled the Primarch's occasional use of violence to stem disobedience. One who would abuse his own family would not hesitate to strike against the family he loathed most when the opportunity arose.

"I will urge Raru to intervene, with his best men to match Artimecian's. With luck there will be no need for confrontation at all, assuming the Sanctum is deterred by witnesses alone."

Aroch kissed her forehead and watched as she passed through the door, fled down the hall past a few children and workers coming in from the fields. It was hard for Aroch to watch her go, knowing that his worst fears were becoming reality. He knew he wasn't paranoid. The feud between him and Artimecian had been going on since they were young men on Ellel, and it seemed his rival had gained the support of the Primarch.

Sebashni had traversed half the fields between Nesh and Ms'egol when Sky appeared between the rows of fruiting thi to block her path. Hardly distinguishable amid the multicolored shadows of the petals and fronds, she recognized him only by his superior tone and postured silhouette.

"Primarch," she greeted him suddenly, her mind working fast. "Your daughter weds tonight. Shouldn't you be preparing for your exaltation?"

Sky approached with hands nonchalantly clasped behind his back.

"Silence and absence are the only honesty I could offer." He was obviously aggravated by the reminder, but undeterred. "I will be indisposed, when it occurs. Eina, have you misplaced something in Ms'egol, *aiat*?"

"Forgotten it," Sebashni fumbled. "Mani has therein a tincture I'd hoped to give Lemalie, to steady her."

"*La*, of course. The young lady must have trouble sleeping," he stated disarmingly. "How did she fare when you saw her today?"

"Still vacant, the room."

"I see. And with this tincture you will wait idly for her?"

"I will, father, before and after the wedding if she'll not be there."

"Mhm..." He grumbled, stopping by her side and staring beyond. "Matriarch, I would have a favor of you. As you do your good work, I ask that you also give the woman a kindly reminder that her first duty as a daughter of Nesh is as your own; the confidence and welfare of all people. If she were to become aware of anything spoken of privately in council, that would benefit no one, herself least of all. *Eina*, it would be unfortunate if her father's place on the council proved unsatisfactory protection from the fitting punishment due those who would undermine the Council. That's assuming he retains such a place."

Sebashni was unshaken by the veiled threat.

"If I were to give your ultimatum as stated, perhaps she would not grasp your full meaning, my *Utan*," she retorted boldly. Her challenge was quickly rewarded as ego overwhelmed sensibility. Sky seized her wrist and compressed it until she winced and faced his accusing grimace. He spoke very quietly.

"Let her grasp this: Aroch's limited influence is the sole reason someone of her excessive power, an inherent danger to MY city, has avoided exile. Unless she yearns to be *gal'tskhain*..." He sneered and released her, his last words singeing her ears as she pulled away from him, "...She will keep her tongue curled."

Given Aroch's recent warning, Sebashni now realized that the task he had given her was more than a precaution, it was the start of a long defensive against a ruthless adversary. Sky had showed his intent, entirely certain he could not be stopped. Ensuring he kept that confidence would help blind him to potential danger, which was critical if she and Aroch hoped to survive him. To feed this, she easily feigned submission, recoiling and bowing meekly.

Sky eyed her distrustfully as she silently moved past him and disappeared into the growths. Weighing the veracity of her story, he stared back at the doors of Nesh. Therein, the atrium fire had been refueled and it would not be long before citizens started to gather for the marvelous marriage. Sky's disgust for Nepiur's betrothed had driven him to pass off the honor of presiding over it. He had given it to Khurk who, among the Patriarchs, was Nepiur's closest friend, other than Sebashni herself. Bitter thoughts of his daughter enfeebled Sky's ability to take control of the situation.

His will was in Artimecian's hands now. Unbeknownst to him, it would soon be in Raru's as well.

CHAPTER 12: MOST LOVED BY THE STORMS

The wedding came and went with suitable revelry. The celebration momentarily stemmed the spread of rumors, giving Aroch time to further contemplate Keimas' protection, and Artimecian time to plot his demise. For one more night the people of Hanging Gate would enjoy peace. As dusk built and Lindu rose, Capheif and Nepiur took their leave of the revels to spend their first night as one. The party continued until the hundreds of drunken celebrants took to their beds, and Sebashni made one final attempt to locate Aroch's daughter.

A sopping wet and windblown Lemalie gazed out from her window at the gathering silvery light over the mountains Thaun. Lindu wrapped like a halo around the north sky that looked close enough to touch, yet so far away there was no telling what was beneath it at the other side of Manti. Sanguine Star, now beginning its way back into deep sky, cast a pastel blue streak as Longhand Started to descend. She always felt bereaved at Sanguine's end, loved it more than any other season for the frequent and torrential rainstorms. They made her feel stronger, intensifying her power with every drop that touched her. Longhand might bring water as often, though without as much force and far colder. Regardless, to touch her element and be touched by it was where she found her joy. It was ecstasy akin to her love, and it too was soon to abandon her. She languished at her window and allowed the last drops of a once great and now perished downpour to caress her bare skin. No shiver of chill coursed over her skin, even after a full evening of this. Her body responded to only the most extreme cold.

A knock at the door shook her from her musings just in time to throw a dress over herself before Sebashni's kindly face appeared, her gaze briefly flitting about the room before smiling brilliantly at her.

"*Aiat*, my sweet! I'm glad you've returned."

The Matriarch's face showed no sign of pretense nor of concern, just happiness that her wait was no longer fruitless. Lemalie responded with an obviously disheartened attempt at the same optimism.

"A pleasure, mother, and my first in a day."

Sebashni entered quickly and closed the door, hurrying to Lemalie's side and taking her hands.

"*Minien*! Your father was nearly in his grave over you." Lemalie jolted at the small vial stealthily planted in her hand, raising it to be examined, and Sebashni wasted no time explaining its purpose.

"A potion from Father Mani. Something to sleep easier, rest of the mind and such. Take it quickly so I may not injure you with grim news, for before this, all else pales; Keimas' leave." Her last words were stressed, and Lemalie's ears were tweaked by her gravity.

"*La*? Tell all."

Sebashni grunted in frustration and led her young friend by the hands away from the wide window.

"News is not of him but about him, urgent and deadly. Your father receives word on his state by the servants of black Naguza. He is safe, but only thus for the sloth of Sky's dregs."

"What? Did he really do it? Did he go Tau?"

"*Minla*, he keeps to our side of the gate, or so your father says, but it is ideal fortune that you've come back. Sky sends the students of the Iron Sanctum to retrieve him."

"Then he thinks Keimas will resist? Why would he send

Artimecian's thugs?"

"Not resist, but fall, perhaps die," Sebashni said. "Your father and I fear Sky grows suspicious that whatever privileged information Keimas has could damage the people's complacent trust in the council's promises, more precisely his own."

Roused from the lethargy that had permeated her soul since Keimas' departure, Lemalie cried angrily, "*Jioumin khainilt!* What wretched scum he…he has nothing to gain, no secrets to learn. My husband is as baffled as the council," she revealed.

"He confided in you?"

"Unwillingly, and not with any clarity. He is not himself, uncertain of what he knows but driven beyond consolation to find answers. There is an old madness in him now, and as it was not soothed by me it will not be subdued by Artimecian's conjurers."

"You knew he was for Tau?" Sebashni asked, perturbed. "What is he doing there?"

"If I tried to explain, I would fail. He rambled about a spirit, a voice…said that there were or would be many dead, and there is one or many responsible." Lemalie had been so focused on Keimas' disregard for her that she had not fully understood what he was saying. Repeating it aloud made more sense.

"Sky is right to fear," Sebashni sighed. "Most have sacrificed a faith they've known all their lives to place a new one in *golaiat* Anama. I cannot imagine if Keimas speaks of such devastation at her hand."

"I think he is after proof," Lemalie admitted. "He spoke of sight but not word, a yearning by the spirit for his presence."

"At the gate or in Thonsfa? Did he have a face or name for this messenger?" Sebashni queried.

Lemalie's patience for conversing was fading fast.

"Not a face, only many eyes, and at the gate or beyond I cannot say. *Minein*, he's gone to do what he thinks must be done. What that is I don't know. I never know," she finished petulantly. Sebashni was surprised but gleaned from that baleful voice that Lemalie didn't want to discuss the man's mind, though she was clearly concerned for his safety. She had to get through to her about the direness of the situation. Leaning forward, she grasped Lemalie's hands, her intense gaze drawing Lemalie's.

"*Eina*, my girl, I trust in you and Keimas to be noble and *Jioum* as surely as Laesis will rise. But *golvulilt, aiat,* did you not hear me? Sky will stop at nothing to fetch Keimas, and if he does not return willingly, they will kill him!"

"Let them try," Lemalie dared, head tilted back and spine straightening. "Sky is a madman and Artimecian is no better, but they cannot catch a Kutu. He may not return but neither will he be caught."

Sebashni was aghast at her stubbornness, "Even in his weakened state?"

There was no reply, and so she grabbed Lemalie by her shoulders and shook her like an impudent child. "Lemalie, stop this! Your dismissal of his life is unbefitting a wife, or any decent soul!" Lemalie stared at the ceiling, unmoved, and Sebashni concluded "You...really don't care?"

Lemalie brushed the constrictive hands away and flounced back on the windowsill.

"*Minein*, I don't have to. Keimas kept himself fine for many seasons without me fretting over everything he did. Why would a husband be different from the man he once was? He's never been injured in a hunt. The only harm he's ever taken was resultant of his own pride."

"Will pride in this shrouded purpose be different, or is that not worth your concern either?" Sebashni accused.

Lemalie's stubborn silence resumed and Sebashni turned away in annoyance, retreating towards the door, stopping only to stare back pityingly. Friends and admirers sympathized with the girl's plight, and there she sat with one foot up on the bench beside her, one swinging down as she fondled the vial disconsolately. Sebashni's heart took some solace in seeing Lemalie toss the sleeping mixture listlessly on the ground with a clink, forced a little smile and opened the door to leave. Clearly, despite her contest with Keimas, Lemalie didn't want a quiet mind. She wanted to worry, as love would do. Some wished for sleep, this one wished only to think deeply.

"*Ein aia...*He's still your husband," Sebashni whispered. "In my advanced age I have finally started learning a few things, foremost being that a man or woman who thinks life better without companionship is destined to live in regret. We are flawed creatures all, made to need one another to find the best in ourselves. Some have a need greater than others, and that is why we seek the person who loves us at our worst, but sometimes…oftentimes we let each other down."

There was no response for a moment, then Lemalie reached down to retrieve the receptacle and imbibe its contents. She hesitated after already taking in the liquid, grasping the vial to her breast before muttering "Could you stay a moment?"

Sebashni's smile widened, but she tried her best to suppress her eagerness in returning to the window.

"I'll stay as long as you like, little river." There was only a moment of comfortable quiet before Lemalie gripped her Matriarch's hand and confessed, "When you arrived…I was thinking about last Mercy."

"This most recent one? *Quo*, why?" Sebashni was surprised by the sudden change of subject, and what seemed like a positive change in Lemalie.

"That was when Keimas offered himself to me," Lemalie said. "But there's more to it than that. Would you…can I tell you a secret?" Sebashni nodded and squeezed her hand encouragingly. "Keimas…we broke the law in our own way."

"How is that? His challenge?"

"*La*, issued as required and for the fourth time," Lemalie stammered. "I always fought hard because I didn't want things to change. I loved him, but I also wanted to delay taking a child so that I could still protect my city." She looked down at their entwined hands before confessing, "He never did defeat me."

"But there must be proof. How were you allowed to marry without proof that he could keep you safe during childing?"

Lemalie looked up and said, "My father. He was the only one who was required to have any evidence, according to Sky's modern edicts. He thought he had watched Keimas beat me with his own two eyes, but it was all a trick."

Sebashni settled herself at the window and listened intently, as Lemalie explained.

Thetrulengo speaks,

Love: a chain of energetic impulses within the body that join with that of another to create the sensation of wholeness for two broken things. By spiritual design it is exactly as it seems. The mortal obsess over its many effects and perceived importance but squabble about where it comes from. I'm not sure why its origin is so important to them, but at least they can agree on its value for the most part. I still have not found any emotion or personal value that is collectively loathed or adored, but love comes the closest. There will always be many that resent the notion either because of its absence or their own failure in it. A mortal despising love further explains creatures such as Zeniquorer.

Excited by all the changes to their lives, I was anxious to wait and hear what Lemalie had to say of her husband during this insightful meeting with her elder mother. I was expecting more curses than fond reminiscing, but Lemalie seemed intent on recounting how her life had become mended to Keimas'. In this way she regaled her Matriarch with florid prose brought on by what I maintain is love, but even she had forgotten a few details. I was there, after all. Yes, distracted by the study of thi'tskreol atop Ms'egol's garden spire, but I alertly remember how it all unfolded.

It was Mercy season, as she admitted. Keimas took his favored woman in his arms and flew up to the top of Hanging Gate. They stood before the aviary where, as I recall, his inscription extolling her virtues is now engraved. He wanted the setting to be perfect, wanted to show her from the top of the cliffs what it looked like when the Mercy star finally broke back into the high ether and the Sanguine Star took its place. They waited and talked flirtatiously about...inconsequential things. I was more observing than listening. Though for some reason couldn't take my mind off Keimas' wings. They were always at rest when he was grounded, but at the time he ceaselessly waved them behind him. I grew attentive when Lemalie became sad, expressed her worry that they would never be married. She did not describe then the laws which she referenced, but I had already learned how such engagements were to be made.

They try to kill each other! Minla, I bless the mindless creatures in their derangement, for they actually try to hurt one another to prove their love. I'd never seen it done before and apparently it is uniquely determined by the Mantichaena, after they were turned thusly by the island. They believe that, as a woman, if you are strong enough to protect the city then that is your first duty, but as a parent your first duty is to protect your offspring. By that right, a woman becomes a gal'tskhain, an undesirable, if they ever conceive while serving as a warrior. Some, like Lemalie, worked their entire lives in the fields and the river or gathered in the forest, but if ever any Mantichaena joins the fight against any threat they are decreed a warrior and elevated above the rest. A warrior woman cannot marry unless a suiter proves their strength. This ensures that the mother is in no danger while she is full of new life. When that life is matured, they are a warrior once more.

K'hizu are vicious and often attack the city. Lemalie, being as powerful and courageous as she is, was compelled to protect her kind. This is how she came to be such a prominent lady in the community and respected by the soldiers. However, it was a curse to her. Aroch wept for her the first time she killed because he knew how powerful she truly was, far more so than even his favorite among her suiters; Jiou Keimas.

I have just learnt that word, Jiou, or Jiaia if it be a woman. It is a figure much like nobility but more specific. It refers to anyone who is given special honor, a hero or idol. The only meaning is one implied: 'Worthy of prayer as well as praise'. Is that not something? They believe that if someone is as good and honorable as they are powerful, they begin to ascend in spirit, becoming capable of answering prayers and granting blessings. My response to such a belief is another word I have often heard from them: 'Zet'itka.' Half-head.

I should retake the subject at hand. Lemalie became increasingly dejected even as her relationship with Keimas grew. Once, twice, then three times Keimas tried to conquer her, but having already revealed her power, and with an entire city watching, she could not simply submit. They remained prisoners to a code of honor. She being the prize of beauty and power that she was and he being a paragon among the most dangerous Mantichaena, those close to them expected not only their union but a ferocious engagement preceding. The world was watching. His struggle to earn the right to protect her must be memorable. She had to suffer through vain attempts by her beloved and each time threw him down in defeat despite his great power as a hunter killer. Lemalie had been forced to keep hidden the majority of her strength, first so as not to be seen as a danger and be safe from exile, but also because even as a child she knew that she desired a husband more than glory. Among her many gifts is one that few immortals have ever achieved: glorious invincibility. So fluid and unbound is her flesh that even Keimas could not draw blood when he tried. Water can neither be cut nor beaten, and she is water.

That brings us to the day so fondly remembered, when lands bloodied by Mercy shattered as the star reaffixed to deep sky and Sanguine began in a brilliant bloom of cerulean light that enveloped half of Maengir, sparkling in the young couple's eyes.

It was beautiful, and they were happy. What days they were; calm, until Keimas took the greatest risk of his life. I think he believed that, despite all evidence to the contrary, maybe his lady wasn't indestructible. He was wrong, but so was she in believing they could not convince father Aroch of his worthiness. It was she who could make it possible, given the chance when Keimas devised a plan to...ein, it was no plan, really. He threw the two of them off the cliff.

Ah, love. The two of them tangled together as they plunged toward death. I was expecting a bloody mess to result, but Keimas kept screaming his ultimatum over and over while his wings dangled behind him uselessly: either she yielded and he would fly them safely down, or deny him and he would die for her. Half the city was below watching as they fought nearly to the ground, watching still when she realized his ploy. No one else but Keimas and her father knew her strength, that she would be unscathed by such a fall. The display was not for her, it was to make sure their love was never questioned. She happily cried out in surrender so everyone could hear, and they alighted together by the river, intact and betrothed. There was little to raise protest of their union, which was much desired by their friends. With reasonable proof of Keimas' ability to protect her, Aroch accepted him as his son, and there was no doubt that his daughter had made her choice.

No one's ever dared to ask, even since Lemalie discovered wilder abilities than what could be done with her own body: Is Keimas truly stronger than her? No. No he is not. However, it is an *unparalleled example of a fundamental truth of being mortal, perhaps the one I have been searching for: in a battle between love and law, love always wins, thus denying the importance which law places upon itself. If love cannot win in flesh it will win in spirit, and the veil will be colored by its purity. I suppose something to that effect is how the stars became what they are. Love is as powerful a force as vengeance, if not more so. Does that perhaps mean the reason Maengir is not destroyed by the lightning and heat of Zeniquorer's Nhi'Thaun is because Oorghunak still hinders him from beyond death? Does Quetzuaul's Mercy not choke the life from everything because Ephielipax's Sanguine restrains it? If only to know the minds of dead gods. But la, to me they are nothing but lights burning in deep sky. I cannot know their intentions until they manifest.*

~Chronicle of Wonders, The Secret

Sebashni could not believe what she was hearing. It had already been postulated that Lemalie could disperse her body, and it was common knowledge that she was tough, but completely unbreakable? It strained credulity that such a person could exist.

"What...what would Sky think?" Sebashni pondered.

"*Minghen!* You cannot ever speak of it, mother!"

Sebashni patted Lemalie back to calm and lowered her voice, kissed the girl's hands as promise of her loyalty.

"I would never, but the idea worries me. Is this really true? Can you not be hurt?" she asked.

Lemalie was flustered.

"I don't know! I didn't know until much later that if we had struck the land Keimas would have broken like baktite and I could have simply stood and dusted myself off. If anyone ever found out what I can do..."

Sebashni held her head to her breast and shushed her.

"No, no, don't say such things, precious. Your marriage is now done, and no one can take it away from you."

"Keimas can," Lemalie grumbled bitterly.

"That's why you're angry?" Sebashni suddenly understood.

"You want to help him?"

Lemalie's eyes gushed and she wept into Sebashni's chest.

"And I cannot! Mother, I'm only married for a few short days and already I am forbidden to fight! I cannot go after him, or the law will turn against me as it has him!" She cried in anguish.

Sebashni held her tight, stroked her hair and knelt to see her, face to face.

"Sssssh no, my lovely. I'm sure he doesn't think in such a way," she cooed consolingly. "You are a warrior just as he. It is part of his love for you. If you fought with him, he would feel only pride and gratitude."

Lemalie groaned back "You do not know."

"*Minein*, I do! Look at me..." Sebashni grabbed Lemalie's neck and kissed her forehead. "Dear, he is used to people expecting him to defend them, not to fight beside him. Keimas is Keimas, and would not have married *aiat* Lemalie if he did not respect Lemalie the warrior. A pox on conspirators and autocracy, myself and all archons with me if it is we whose word cuts you apart. If you want to go after him, you still have your right. You're still just a married warrior." Lemalie's face contorted but she could not look away, her desperate eyes becoming more pained as Sebashni spoke. "*Hemnla*, you have no child, no reason to stay here..." Her words ceased and her face stilled as she noticed Lemalie's distress. Lemalie fell on her Matriarch's lap in a mist of tears and wretched weeping, and Sebashni's heart fluttered when she sensed the ill-timed truth. "...Oh...oh my precious woman." Sebashni was no sanctifier, but she still knew a bit about using her light. She slipped her hand deftly along Lemalie's lower back, using the girl's weakened emotional state and their emotional connection to sense what was within her. As sure as Lemalie felt it herself, Sebashni too sensed the little raindrop growing inside her.

CHAPTER 13: A GAME OF THREE MASTERIES

Thetrulengo speaks,

I *have seen war. I have witnessed travesties that mortal man has purposefully been made unable to comprehend. There was a time, one known very well to the servants of Az'Rech and Escharka, in which man was unable to reason. Az'Rech freed them from this state when he rose on a wave of glory from the Far Edge. However, when the battle ended and his armies were victorious he unwittingly set a fire to light the dark minds of men as his remnant power soaked into their flesh. This energy, the very essence of Az'Rech, became light, heat, the forces that move each and every particle and thereby form the basest foundation of all mancy. Whilst the elder gods shaped their mancy as they saw fit, it ultimately fell into three distinct disciplines, all of which are taught in the Hall of Ms'egol in some form or another.*

Taking hold of the mechanical forces of nature and creation, an act of maintaining balance by transferring knowledge into manifestation and manifestation into knowledge, is what is called classical mancy. This is a calculated and rigorous field of study for men called enchanters, in which they learn how to bend the veil and convert material to energy, replace it with something new, relocate it or simply give it a little nudge. The students of this style are patient, even-tempered and very focused, as they require more study than others and much less emotional fuel. Classical mancy requires having all the aspects of the veil completely under your body's control and knowing how the tiniest shift in temperature or motion can drastically change the flow of a spell.

Sometimes it's a bit boring, but I have done my best to observe and review practitioners of the discipline of romantic mancy. They are known as sanctifiers. They gain their power by stimulating their affection and altruism, using acts of kindness to consume positive emotion from the veil space occupied by others. Advantageously, since witchcrafters must use pain and negative emotions to retain their energy, they can have such high expectations of others that they are constantly heartbroken by the state of their fellow man. Like their classicist counterparts, romantic sanctifiers will live a very long time from how often they refresh their essence. Students of the veil's romance will learn to mend broken bodies, fractures both within the veil and in mortality, as well as the difficult task of entering the minds of the living. Romantic mancy is truly an art, requiring tact and a delicate touch as opposed to sheer will. It is also one of the fields where a great deal of its techniques are triggered verbally instead of physically. It's fitting that auditory acceptance of a trigger word is what makes a recipient more vulnerable to the spell. For example, a very common bodily healing spell in Ms'egol has a long duration and takes a long time to speak, but begins with the words 'Do not dignify pain, do not give in. Surrender your broken heart and take mine which is whole'. What a haunting phrase. Although, for someone who does not understand what is being done to them I can see the intent. You can feel mancy taking hold of you, so it's important for healers to craft trigger words that give a sense of security and establish trust. As with so many things, there is a darker side to romance. Abuse of the power to garner such trust can be a problem. Sanctifiers who fall prey to this temptation become exactly what Zeniquorer was; lustful spirits who can no longer feel love, only cravings and entitlement. They are called adulterers.

Gothic mancy is the beating heart of the veil, the vein that connects with its very core. If the veil was of the same laws as Maengir, then its Laesis and Nhi'Thaun would be the little spark of energy that lives inside each person. Az'Rech's essence within living things is so concentrated that, when enough has accumulated, it will create a force that repels excessive energy and causes the body to overflow and wick away power. Circumventing this natural inversion and closing the floodgates is the ultimate goal of students of gothic mancy, and it is the phenomenon that spawned the six original elder gods. This is not to say that all gods or powerful beings use gothic mancy, but they are masters of the principle that gives rise to it: a heap of sand will spill and tumble from one's hand, but in carefully stacking each grain there is no limit to how much you can hold. Even Miohaelia, if she had the desire, could have been very destructive. It is more poignant to say that godhood is often the insatiable dream of gothic apprentices. This practice has nothing to do with balance or control, only releasing stored energy to inflict pain. A student of gothic mancy first searches for the spiritual center of his power, something that makes them feel frightened and alone, then focuses all his training into forcing as much fuel as possible into that furnace. This is done by evoking strong emotions like love and hate that digest energies from the veil, tapping into it as would any other maker of mancy, but understanding how to use the volatility of dark thoughts to harden one's spirit again and keep its contents from spilling back out. Energy building emotions soak more of Az'Rech's essence into them, while spiritually depressing emotions, such as those that come from sorrow and helplessness, break down the soul's ability to release it. I understand that this is not a perfect topic for my personal light to luminesce upon, but I despise the gothic witchcrafters. They injure themselves to enkindle their inner fire, then their comrades chain and torture them to break their spirit and stifle the draining of their power. They stay awake for days on end, scarred and bloody, losing all aspirations beyond their next infusion of energy, and when they can next use it to rip a piece of the world away. It's a barbaric way of training that was much more common in the old world, but the archon Artimecian has kept it alive within his Iron Sanctum. Its volunteers are almost all orphans, and antisocial, but some of them are just ordinary children possessed with a passion for becoming the most powerful of all. At first, I thought they must be mad to enjoy bondage and torment, but I realized at length: perhaps their power gives them a *sense of security? With so much essence sealed within themselves they are able to heal quickly, and the sheer knowledge of what they have become capable of seems to make it all worthwhile. I have never seen one fight, but if Sky's wish to have them loosed on Keimas is fulfilled, then I will certainly be there to witness it. I know better than he what hunts him, and he will die.*

~Chronicle of Wonders, Scions of the Essence

Artimecian rose with Laesis' first ignition on the Hai, as had been his custom for as long as he could remember. On the day following the assembly that decided his path, the day that Longhand had first begun to fall and signal the transference out of Sanguine, he awoke with a mind to accomplish great things with the resources life had given him. Like the schiis that slithered on its belly, he barely stood above a hunched position as he slunk out of bed, avoided the intrusive light of day invading through his window and snatched up a small sack from the nearby dining table.

His chamber was nearly at ground level, the sole chamber furthest east of the dormitories of the alchemical students, and far beneath them. The hall that connected the academy to his residence continued past and into a dimly lit pit around which spiraled a dusty stairwell. All of these were places he alone was permitted to enter, and only by his order were any allowed to leave.

After washing his face, but with little regard for dressing or grooming himself, he made his way down the hallway and onto the stairway without so much as a candle to light his way. It was a long journey down, rough, uninspired in its crafting and completely dark. He traced the wall with his knobby old fingers to ensure he did not near the inner edge, and after escaping what small light intruded from above detected a single torch below, marking his destination. Beside that torch the pride of his discipline and its students was hidden behind a simple wood door, darkly painted with potash and the pulverized bark of black vines. He inserted a hand into a hole at its center and gripped a handle, twisted it hard until a hollow click allowed the door to open. Entering, he paused at the top of a series of circular landings above a morbid grotto. Despite his promises that all goings on here were entirely necessary, if anyone but the gothics were to see it the witchcrafters would surely be disbanded and the Iron Sanctum deemed an unclean place by such riotous demand that not even Sky could stop it. Indeed, exile would be inevitable with or without the Primarch's support. This was why he made its seclusion certain. What the people would surely view as pure evil he and his students saw as the only answer to a world of monsters that tooth and claw could now hold off no better than spear and shield had in the past; monsters like the dreaded thuell. Artimecian often thought himself the savior and true ruler of the Mantichaena for just such reasons. Without his preparations, they would not survive another infestation.

A crust of blood was embedded in every grain and seam of the floor, walls and ceiling. All stone surfaces were covered with sheets of brassic, and on each level there were diabolical instruments that intense and devoted study had finely tuned to inflicting maximum pain.

There were eight souls in the wretched place, four men and four women, each without a stitch of clothing on and kneeling with eyes closed and hands folded neatly in their laps. Apart from the six days per season they were allowed to sleep, this was their nightly rest while awaiting the grand master's arrival. The noisome groan of the door did not disturb their meditation, their unwavering focus on controlling every cell and drop in their bodies. At night they remained awake but hardened to withhold essence. Artimecian smiled, so proud of his devoted soldiers who had consigned themselves this way. No matter what anyone on the outside said, they were good men and good women, true believers for whom no sacrifice was too great when it was needed.

To reward their devotion, he threw the bag he carried to the floor which, upon striking, fell open and released rolls of bread and salted-crust cuts of sumear. After a watchful moment, he turned his back, hummed to himself and waited. A short pause was followed by the voracious sounds of tearing flesh and breaking loaf. It made him happy when his students were happy. After a few short breaths he faced them again, stepped down slowly from one platform to the next and shook his head admiringly at the witchcrafters' violence of action. All the food was gone, not a crumb left behind on the floor or on their lips. He turned the bag over and undid a tie beneath it, releasing a heap of ragged clothes onto the ground. Stomping his foot once and tossing the satchel aside he briefed them on the day's unusual work while they burst to life, and each fought viciously to be first at the best pieces of clothing.

"I couldn't be a prouder father, my Iron. You have done so well with your studies and practices. At last, two of you will have the chance to test yourselves. There has been an incident in the city which unfortunately involves a grievous failing by one of our beloved hunter-killers, Keimas." The students, now all decently clad, drew close to him to kneel at his feet. The Kubernu man Gogol, oldest and arguably the leader among them, spoke aggressively but with deference to Artimecian.

"Father, the Iron Wind will serve, whatever the need!"

Artimecian noted with pleasure how Gogol took his brother's hand as he spoke. Haerulf the Kulo, significantly younger, lit up like the morning behind his bedraggled hair. Artimecian continued to search the faces of his students, and all seemed hopeful that they had be chosen to go, though each would acquiesce not to Gogol's word but to time-honored proof that he and his partner were the strongest.

"*La*...Good, you two were of course to be my first choice," Artimecian said. At this affirmation the group of eight all raised their hands, exalted Gogol and Haerulf as they stood:

"IRON WIND!"

Artimecian's face hardened, and he seized Gogol roughly.

"You have until I reach the top of those stairs to say goodbye to your fellows. Catch up quickly and make way to the high gate Tau. Rise!"

They obeyed, their skin crackling with streaks of uncontrollable essence as they embraced their brothers and sisters one by one. Artimecian gave them their time while ensuring they understood the gravity of the situation.

"Share your love now, my boys, for you may not return alive. Nesh Udai Keimas has flown Tau against the edicts of the Primarch. The man is insane, driven by an evil presence within him to break our gate end expose to us the danger of the Thonsfa Tau. You do not face a citizen or even a man, but a creature in the dark. Treat him as such and protect yourselves and our people."

Unanimously, the collective student body bemoaned the

unwelcome order of execution and beat the brassic floor beneath them. Scant tears flowed for they mourned that their victim must be Mantichaena, but joyfully their skin brightened and flecks of light danced around them. Here was a chance to prove their skill to the master. Any and all emotions they allowed to fill them, being possessed of the habit which fed their essence.

"You will be the greatest examples to our people," Artimecian concluded as he climbed to exit. "If you fail there is no telling how many will perish at this lunatic's hand! Use all you have, all your long-suffering in the service of your Primarch! Kill Keimas!"

The smaller mouth of the canyon, where Keimas sat in contemplative silence, was almost completely absent the chilly winds of the night, making it ideal for his prolonged internal search for guidance. Sumear raced on tiny feet between the rocks and made themselves known, readily available sustenance. Apart from them the only K'hizu presence were the many hidden deghni gathered in crevices, staring all night long with beady eyes. He could smell them, thought of them only as pests. It never occurred to him that they were there with a purpose.

A face floated in and out of his mind, one he had never seen before except in his dreams, one that only that night he realized had been beside him at the fallen temple. It was the face of the beast that had taken him by the leg, the one that begged him to venture out into dark places. It was a blur that raced through his head, reminded him of things he had never known, then snatched the thoughts away before he could understand them. When he envisioned the spirit, he smelled smoke and blood, tasted fetid water, felt sand between his toes. He was certain that the face that eluded him, taunted him, was surrounded by a brilliant mane of flowing scarlet braids. It was such a small detail, but the most striking he had ever seen upon a head. He had never seen red hair before, never heard of it nor heard of anyone who had heard of it. It was like a memory from a story he had never read. If it was at all indicative of his tormentor's true form, then either it was another unique Mantichaena who called to him, or something stranger; No mere Galaila, and certainly not a creature born of the gods. He wanted to fly, wanted to tear down the great wall and streak across the desert to confront the presence that beckoned him but was stymied by the overarching truth that he didn't know why he was here. His confrontation with this sacred wall had stalled his resolve long enough for him to wonder if there was time to turn back.

Through the moist and heavy silence of the canyon, his patient ears heard the faintest shifting of dirt. His eyes flew open and he bared his claws, whipped around with a beat of his wings to heave himself onto his feet, eyes searching the warren as morning light blazed through the mist in moving beams. Two shadows emerged from the road behind him, two tattered figures approached with heads hung low as if shamed.

"*Ueinwekti*, present yourselves! What are you doing here!?" the mighty Kutu demanded.

They stopped without answering, the taller of the two raising one hand and waving Keimas over. Annoyed at the summons and wary of others hiding nearby, Keimas cautiously approached, wings still half raised.

"What do you want?" He insisted. "I am here with a purpose, and you are disrupting it!"

They stood stoically silent, and revelation came as Keimas drew nearer, catching the tiny flashes of sparks skipping across their filthy bodies and the horrid state of their hair and faces.

"Gods, is that...Gogol, is that you?" Keimas asked incredulously, then excitedly "It is. *Aurb'dae* Gogol, how long ago have I laid eyes? Ten seasons or more?

Some small amount of filth had been washed off Gogol and Haerulf's faces with the tears that even now cut paths down their cheeks, and both of them twisted their clawed feet against the ground anxiously. Gogol shakily took his brother's hand, and together they each held one out to Keimas.

"Nesh Udai Keimas, or whatever evil thing I speak to now, under the authority of the Primarch by way of the grand master Artimecian," Haerulf stated factually, "I consign you to death."

Stunned and shamed, Keimas only now realized he was a criminal caught in the act.

"What!? Friends, you must be...surely you wouldn't..." he said laughingly, holding his palms open to them as he relaxed his massive wings.

Haerulf's cracked shout silenced him, harsh proof of how serious he was.

"Do not play the fool, Kutu! Our father has told all. A devil inside you stirs your mind. I will..." He hesitated a moment, scrutinizing Keimas and seeing no difference in him. He seemed the same man he had known many seasons ago. "...I will give you one chance to stay judgement. Stand down from this gate and return to the city without trickery, or I swear on my mother's head you will burn here and now!" Both his and Gogol's bodies shuddered as a gale of energy built up inside them, so much so that they crouched lower and lower to keep their footing as they vibrated erratically. The brothers' hands clenched tighter and Keimas took a step backward. It became apparent he had no intention of obeying. Haerulf's eyes teared up again and angrily he accused Keimas.

"It's true...you really meant to break it!?"

To which Keimas stuttered "W-what? Countryman I..."

"YOU WILL NOT HAVE THE CHANCE!"

Too impassioned to hear reason, Haerulf carried out his orders. With the effervescent energy building in his chest, it hissed and split with an eruption of white light that condensed into a spiral of flame billowing onto Keimas.

Keimas' reflexes were fast, but his reaction was delayed by the confusion of being attacked without provocation. His folded wings now hindered him, too cumbersome to move adroitly as he tried to leap aside.

The blazing jet advanced to swallow him, but the ground at his feet mounded upward to deflect the blow at the last moment, a high wall of stone growing from the ground right before his eyes. He tumbled to his back, confounded by the miracle, blinded by the fire fountaining around the slab as his savior skidded along the ground to stop in front of him. In the eye of the storm stood old man Raru, palms thrust against the stone and leaning into it with all his might.

"*Ein'tskaria*, hunter!" the old Thiwa laughed nervously, with a cocky challenge. "Do you hunt your imberuc from grounded back as well!?" The assault abruptly subsided and, with a multicolored flash from his fingers, Raru whirled against the stone and it leapt forward at crashing speed. From the far side it was exploded with another attack of flame, and The Iron Wind fumed at the foiled attack while the rubble scattered around them, gnashing their teeth at Raru's deft impediment of their power.

Keimas launched himself up and into a ready stance, unfurled his wings, whipped the dust from them and came alongside Raru, primed for a fight and praising the enchanter's name, gratitude for the welcome intervention calming his nerves.

"*Gal'zetlaan*! I never thought I'd be so happy to see you, father!"

"*La*, and I never thought I'd barter my life for yours," Raru retorted as the flicker of fire and a shockwave of heat heralded another volley from their assailants. Keimas watched as Raru, ever firmly rooted, used no earth but rather deflected Haerulf's bolt with a single finger, arcing it away into the north cliff.

"Raru, what in god's name is the meaning of this!?" Keimas demanded.

As the Iron Rain's screams and a hail of attacks were lobbed, Raru was forced to raise another blockade and Keimas took to holding it with him. Blast after blast the stone held, but each time Raru strained harder to rebuild it between winded sentences.

"It's the Primarch, boy! He's afraid that your desertion...of the city...will incite either panic...or disobedience...I'm not wholly sure on the...details, but he and Artimecian devised some-*MNEM*!" He thrust Keimas aside, both of them barely escaping a bolt that broke through between them and the shrapnel it created. Then, as if nothing had happened, continued "Some sort of plan to kill you, use your actions to destroy your family and oust Aroch from the council!"

"Insanity!" cried Keimas. "No one would stand for that! Are you certain?"

"*Malpael*, son, but people are already scared of you after the way you came back to *Hauan Etain*. Rumors abound about the temple, and what happened to you. If I were a gambler, I'd bet it was the Primarch himself who whispers them." Raru turned his head skyward, bellowing up to his unseen reinforcements hiding amongst the cliffs, "*Quo khainilt*! Do you plan to help some day soon!?"

The assault of flames stopped dead as four of Raru's pupils appeared on the low outcroppings either side of them, each pair holding corners of a long banner they unfurled to the ground. Shouting annoyance and urgency, the Iron Wind tried to get one last shot off, but as the flags opened the glyphs embroidered thereupon began to squirm and glow, almost instantly forming a barrier of shifting crystalline strands that screeched and trembled as the fire skipped along their surface. As each attack landed, they were transmuted into dust and water, falling sloppily to the ground. Now, taking a deep breath to settle himself, Raru took Keimas' shoulder and turned him toward the gate.

"Son, it's time for you to go," he ordered.

"To the Tau..." Keimas hastily considered. How could they know? Was he not doing what he should, such as his actions had pitted witchcrafter against enchanter? Without any answers to justify his actions he felt overwhelmingly guilty, panicked in the moment.

"*Utan*, I don't know what I'm doing anymore!"

Raru huffed, tightly pursed his lips, said "Neither do I, child, but all the nights my sanctifiers and I watched over you I learned a bit about you. I don't know what you expect to find out there, but I know how ravenously you dreamed of it. I knew your course would be something unexpected, but if you are convinced that this is the one you must take, then you carry my desires with you."

"You seek the Tau?" Keimas asked incredulously.

"Survivors!" Raru thundered. "What if there are still survivors out there? If there's anyone left alive in Thonsfa they need us. It may be against the Primarch's decree but you are the one chance we'll have to find them!"

"But the Primarch..."

"*Sula* Keimas!" Raru's old, leafy fingers squished Keimas' cheeks together as they jerked him closer, jostled him forcibly to end the arguing. "Boy, use your reason! This city is about to have more than a few troubles thanks to that old bastard, and futures where you get to keep all the blood you currently have are dwindling! I don't know what you saw, I don't know what you could POSSIBLY need to do out there and I don't particularly like you either. You're arrogant, you're selfish and you're rash...but I know you're not crazy. *Minein*, you're certainly crazy, but not dangerous. Not to us." This he said with a touch of intensity, shook Keimas' head again and reiterated "Whatever you're doing, I know there's no malice in it. Mother Sebashni's word in your defense is all I need to know that you have a good heart. Now follow it."

Keimas relented and without a word further took off with a powerful stroke of his wings. He soared up and out, beyond the heads of the surrounding statues and became a shadow along the cliffs until he arched and dove over the height of Raru's own magnificent gate, gone from the battle in mere moments.

The enchanters quickly pulled up their barricade as the Iron Wind charged forward at the sight of Keimas' escape. Like children they stammered and jerked back and forth, glaring after the rogue Kutu and unsure if they could pursue. Even if they could, there was no reaching the wall. Raru's presence demanded attention and his smug demeanor foretold his commitment to keeping them right where they were.

He shrugged patronizingly, reasoned aloud "Now, my amateur friends, do you not see what little harm is done? He flies alone, breaks nothing, exposes us to nothing. Let him go."

"Th-the Tau is absolutely forbidden!" Haerulf sputtered.

Gogol's whole body began to ignite, swirling fire all around him that scorched his clothes.

"He persists...Father Artimecian was right. Only one possessed would enter that condemned sand!"

"Then let him die as an undesirable should, *la*?" Raru countered. "To pursue him would accomplish nothing but to make yourselves undesirables as well. Tell Artimecian that he has gone to his death, and I am certain Anama will bless you for your wisdom."

Haerulf envisioned that; telling the grand master they had lost their prey, that one who had broken the law would not be caught and punished. Tell him they failed? Return with nothing to show for all their training?

"I would sooner die out there myself!" the impetuous boy screamed. "For the master...if you will not stand aside, then you go with Keimas to Vaeba's bloody shore."

Haerulf swung his finger down and released a blinding explosion that upturned a huge wave of rock and dirt, chased and enveloped by Gogol's fire until it became molten. Raru raised one hand with a disdainful sigh, and right at his fingertips it stopped midair, cooled to stone once more and the waves fixing like statues at his sides. The Iron Wind disciples looked up at the enchanters, furious at how they chuckled amongst themselves. They hardly had to intervene anymore, so confident they were in their teacher's sublime abilities.

"Be gone, mongrels!" Raru commanded the pair. "If a traitor you seek then retreat to your hole and accuse its master! It is his lies alone that serve to twist this city into anarchy!"

"You are with him," Haerulf seethed, blinded by singular loyalty. "You are an obstacle to justice. YOU are the traitor."

Gogol was harder pressed to speak. His little brother never knew Keimas as he did, had been raised entirely in the Sanctum with no childhood outside its walls. He knew in his heart that the Kutu would never pose a threat to the city, but Artimecian's word was the only law he had known himself for most of his life. Far removed from the Sanctum, their master had told them exactly why they were needed, and limited memories of a good boy meant nothing compared to the arch-witchcrafter's order.

"He has a demon inside him," Gogol snarled, wincing at the inner conflict even as he resolved himself to fight on. "That's not Keimas. It is evil…you're all evil."

Leering up at the classical students where they skulked, Haerulf's skin boiled. Raru may be untouchable but his students were not. If they could not destroy his body then they would break his heart until he yielded. Whirling fire in his palms, Haerulf set his sights on the apprentices, menacingly cried "You are conspirators! Rebellion! Y-you will all be ashes!"

CHAPTER 14: THE SURVIVOR

The Council's morning assembly would adjourn early when news of the Iron Wind's order to retrieve Keimas was cleverly explained by Artimecian: "Decisive, with as little bloodshed as possible. The extent of any violence would be entirely Keimas' choice." The reassurance was satisfaction enough for the Primarch in whose pocket the arch-witchcrafter resided, but there was a heavy wave of discomfort across the rest of the silent council. They feared Keimas' injury or death as much as they feared his intent in nearing the far gate, but after their prior deliberation and the decision to send Iron Wind there was little hope of changing course against Artimecian or Sky's decree. They were both so heavily armored in aplomb that they disdained any questions between them and purposefully avoided the eyes of Aroch and Sebashni.

In reality, both Aroch and his shrewd partner were poised to entertain all the arrogance Sky and Artimecian wanted to give them. They only exchanged a few sly looks between themselves as the meeting continued without Raru. Remarkably, Sky had not yet made the connection between their relaxed attitudes and Raru's absence, but it was only a matter of time before he discovered their dealings. The Primarch was, after all, entirely business when business was afoot. However, it was no secret that he had ears to all the ground of Hanging Gate, and his agents were numerous.

Toward the end of their talks, adjudicative action was requested of Sky by the archons of Tault regarding a recent discovery below ground: a void that seemed connected to others, and each lined with strange and unfamiliar gemstones. While Sky posited unanswerable questions about the nature of the voids, Artimecian had the opportunity to slip away without even Aroch's notice. Pursuant to questions of his own, he had a long walk before him, a most annoying one, for he felt doubt tingling in his skin that Sky's plot would have the desired effect. Formidable as his students were, he suspected he would have to ensure it himself.

"What else was required but my instruction?" Artimecian demanded, vexed beyond reason from the first sight of the catastrophic and utterly pointless bloodbath at the far reaches of the canyon. "What have I not provided you to elicit some semblance of success!?"

The Iron Wind silently paced around a fair distance from Raru, who stood resolutely in a cracked crater that had been beaten into the ground by fiery attacks against the orbicular aegis of stone plates spinning around him at incredible speed. Their palms dripping with molten rock, the witchcrafters bombarded his shield again and again, driving it down into the ground but never disturbing its immutable strength or Raru's cool concentration. He sat back in a restful stance, eyes narrow and hands waving back and forth as he twisted the stone around him and made it flow as easily as water, filling the breadth of the pass with swinging columns that threatened to smash anything coming near. Haerulf, who was winded and sweat-drenched, flailed in frustration before turning to face the master's condemnation.

"He will not budge, Father! The vinous *gal'tskhain* continually blockades us with this unassailable charm. We leap over and he knocks us down; circle around and he beats us back!"

Gogol withdrew from the circle as well and spat at the charred remains of Raru's students dangling from the cliffs. Very little was left of the corpses; bones and cinders blowing away in the occasional breeze.

"It has taken all we have to put down his cubs, father," he explained. "We thought it would do to draw him out but..."

"He still wouldn't move," Haerulf finished nastily.

Artimecian only stared, mouth slightly agape at the two of them until they were finished making excuses. He was wholly bewildered.

"*La*...truly, you are the pride of my stock," he said sarcastically as he stepped over the corpse of the one enchanter who had dared come down to attack at ground level. "You will always be of value to your people..." his voice peaked as he turned on Gogol and kicked him to the ground, continued to stomp on him as he shrieked "...THE NEXT TIME TAULT NEEDS DIGGERS!"

Breaking off his beating, Artimecian clapped his hands together, parted them slowly and infused a blue light from one into a spark from the other to create a streak of lightning that forked into the ground all around Raru's defenses. Rocks shook loose from the cliffs, the air tightened with electric power and Raru felt his constructs breaking apart as the ground trembled. He refused to be uprooted and tried to maintain his concentration. The swinging plates began to hang and slow as the unceasing lightning ricocheted between and tore into them, blinding Raru and forcing him to recoil as they finally shattered into pieces. He tried to gather the rest of his arsenal to him, but Artimecian's overwhelming power was too much and his attacks too numerous, dozens of bolts dancing all around Raru and leaping from the flying pillars onto his woody flesh until he could suffer no more. At last, his charm broke and he fell, clutching his burning skin and gasping for air as his pillars broke from the cliffs and thundered to the ground. Without breaking stride Artimecian stormed back to Gogol and hauled him to his feet by one filthy ear.

"And as if that weren't enough of an embarrassment to you..." he glanced around in mock surprise at the dead, turned Gogol's face to see as he did while Haerulf knelt in shame. "...It seems that, among the numerous brothers you've massacred, not one is Kutu!" He hurled Gogol down harshly and turned to glare at Raru.

"And YOU! God's blood, disappointments throng my doors! Imagine my revulsion in finding that an archon of Ms'egol, a lowly Thiwa, has the audacity to defy our Primarch's...of all the insufferable..." So enraged was Artimecian that he was momentarily at a loss for words, stammering over mixed syllables of hatred. Suddenly he stopped, held his breath, and then released it with an uproarious laugh as he snatched the barely conscious Raru by the back of his neck and shook him like a leaf.

"You have made a grievous mistake in thinking yourself above the law, above me!"

He looked down at the unfortunate classicists who had come between the Iron Wind and their prey, then leaned back into Raru's ear with an almost apologetic whisper. "I wish it didn't have to be this way. In my young life I admired you, even looked up to you…but you've let yourself get soft. You don't have the stomach to lead this city anymore. Look at the price your people have to pay for us to keep order. They are full of fear, unable to see the great truth of how they must be if we are to hold the remains of our world together. Sentiment will not save us. Sky sees it…why cannot you?"

Raru groaned and managed to take hold of his peer's shoulder, trying to lift his head, his own eyes defeated as they flicked around hopelessly at the students he had lost.

"Sky…is a murderer," he grunted breathlessly. "Your children are murderers. You are a murderer."

"Sky is a visionary," Artimecian corrected him derisively. "And I…well, I haven't forgotten who it was that led us safely out from Ellel. It was Sky who stood above us when savages failed time and time again to overrun Tieg Raev. It was Sky who opened trade with the Memgnari and Agualti. It was Sky who gathered Galaila nations to the flotilla and saved not one but three cities when the heavens fell! It was Sky who started us toward the Hai when the thuell rose! Every moment of your miserable life you owe to his decisions and his rule!"

"He has…forgotten what it means…to rule," Raru said painfully.

"And you have forgotten what it means to OBEY!" Artimecian roared and threw Raru down in a heap. Calming himself, he stepped over the inert Thiwa and approached the grand gate. "Patriarch – and know that it truly saddens me that you will not understand this – you and your impressive creation are about to serve this city more than ever before." He stood for a moment and contemplated the gate, imagining the future he and Sky were creating. The sacrifice would be great, but the unflinching loyalty it would inspire in the tribe would be greater still.

Raru struggled to breathe while the vines that grew from his Thiwa flesh gently prodded the soil around him in search of water to refresh his strength as he fought back to his feet.

Softly, Artimecian insisted "But perhaps you will. I hope you will." He stirred himself once more, ignoring Raru as he stared up at the gate with crinkled lips and a twitching eye. "Keimas is just a tool, to be used as the Primarch and the council see fit. Even as a lawbreaker he is of use. He has strayed from his divine role in the city's order, become an agent of disarray. Word of his possession and dark spirits could have damaged the city if not kept in check, but this? This goes so far beyond betrayal of the city. It is regrettable that your pupils, like yourself, must die to keep the peace but... peace will be kept. All tongues that could fuel distrust of the Primarch must be silenced. They MUST believe that Sky has absolute control, or they will no longer allow themselves to be controlled! Your little show here...all you've done is to make Keimas an even greater enemy of the people." Artimecian's tone changed as he worked things out in his mind, recited to himself proudly how he might phrase the situation later: "*Einwekt*, your offer to aid my Iron Wind in the capture of Keimas was noble, but he was just too dangerous...possessed not of the thuell but an insidious *vaetn* that gave him unholy powers." His words gathered speed as he grew excited about his own lies. "*Einta*, I barely arrived in time to witness the final moments of a horrific battle, which my own students had sufficient training in their art to survive, but poor Raru and his ramshackle order fell before the mad Kutu's..."

"FATHER LOOK OUT!"

Artimecian heard Gogol's voice, but his certainty of Raru's defeat had made him careless. He was unable to turn quickly enough before a serrated bramble tore through the ground and along his side. Reacting poorly, he tumbled away from the viscous tendril as it coiled after him. Screeching and ripping a fistful of thorns from his hip, he bitterly savored the echo of Raru's dying screams as the Iron Wind enveloped him in a punitive wave of magma and burned him to nothing but a black scorch mark in the sand. In a rage he staggered back up, tossing the bloody spines away and shuffling around aimlessly, his mind blurred by humiliation and hate as he shouted orders.

"Get them out of here! Make certain the Primarch knows exactly what I have told you." Gogol and Haerulf bowed and backed away to comply, only to be stopped by their master's bark and brooding countenance. "No...no, wait. This Is not finished yet. I'll handle the regaling. You finish the task assigned to you." With one hand on his wound, he extended the other so that his palm was almost touching the face of the high gate, and the Iron Wind watched in horror as he took the plan in a new and unimaginable direction.

A tiny particle of violet light vibrated beneath his wrist, joined by myriad ribbons that flashed out of sight and into the locus from along his arm until it was burgeoning with energy. The purple glow washed all around him, consolidated into a pinpoint beam at the base of the gate, and like a whip he arced it back and slammed it down to cause a jarring eruption at the target point. Gale force winds ran up the inscribed wall while the light opened phantasmal fissures all through it and in the blink of an eye burst outward from Artimecian, blowing a massive hole in its face and nearly cleaving it in half. Dust hung in the air, refusing to settle as arid wind from outside the canyon swirled through the menacing opening. Through the haze, Gogol and Haerulf could barely distinguish the Patriarch's visage, but his voice was clear and commanding.

"Get after him! Neither he nor you have anywhere to run but back to the needle and fleshraker! No ultimatum, no peace talk and no mercy! I want his bones to bleach in the sand!"

The two could say nothing as they scrambled, against all good sense, out into the dire wasteland. Their skin was parched by the hot dust, their hearts pounding from the dread of what the cost of a second failing would be, with all the tools of torture Artimecian had at his disposal. There was no future for them without Keimas' blood on their hands.

CHAPTER 15: BRANCHES OF BURNING THI

O blivious of the morning's destruction, the toiling masses in the fields and orchards worked from the crisp dawn onward with routine vigor. They stalled, growing sluggish in the sweltering heat that followed, uncharacteristic of the germinal days of Longhand. Laborers with little time for deduction regarded it merely as an annoyance of fate. No one suspected that it may, in fact, be the consequence of one man's actions in destroying the wall that had sheltered them from the parched Thonsfa. So far down the twisting canyon was the shattered wall from them that the wind from beyond barely crawled as it reached them.

Among these poor creatures slaving over the luscious fruits and billowing thi'tskreol leaf pods was the maiden Raphenie. She was stooped humbly in the shade of a taller bough and, with the hearty twist of a wooden needle, coaxed a steady stream of succulent nectar from the bulbs, engorging a leather sack fastened around the end. Lovely enough by night though they were, by day the bulbs were transcendent in their pink and white splendor that fairly sparkled with sticky secretions. Just to see and touch and taste these beautiful things was Raphenie's reason for choosing to work in this manner. She was not too vain or proud to consider herself above the long and tedious chore. It gave her a quiet joy, and so became her life's work.

As she was not officially a member of the academy, Ms'egol never seemed to value her during the passing as she worked the alembics and cauldrons with the other alchemical students. However, it was during the bearing, as she lent the harvesters her hand, that production in the academy took a noticeable downturn. It would forever be believed that it was due to more than one student taking a leave of absence as she did, only because no one knew what great efficiency and perfect touch she had with all her work. Her wit and dexterity gave advantage in nobler pursuits than gardening, but to her this simpler task was nobility incarnate. Food was what kept them alive, not science. Any way of feeding those soldiers whose much more challenging and dangerous profession kept them safe from the harsh wild was to her the penultimate honor. The only role she held in higher esteem was that of a wife and mother, which as yet eluded her despite a heart full of passion. She dreamed of it; tending a lover and child as she tended the orchard, watching love grow into the most beautiful of flowers. Dreaming in this way was commonly thought childish for Mantichaena. Sufficient occupation for most was the adventure of self-discovery that came as their blood intermingled with the K'hizu Manti'ilt. It seemed that, like animals, Galaila taken by a creature's blood gained a new innate sense of self-worth, something that gave them a new level of identity. It was stronger in some than others; Keimas, Capheif, all the soldiers for certain and many others who had risen high in the city's social hierarchy. Compared to them Raphenie felt as though she was broken. Her sense of purpose was comparatively diminished on all but her most ambitious days, and only love pried such ambition from her, for she did not desire fame in life or death, only love.

This day, two days before the end of Sanguine, had nearly become one such day of ambition. She boiled from within from thoughts of Capheif and resented his wedding for interfering with her hope of a future with him. Though she could not suffer the pain of being present at the marriage of her utaiam – her social superiors – Capheif and Nepiur, she concurrently obsessed over him and writhed in shame at her own jealousy, maddened by the prospect of the two lying together. A thought crystalized in a corner of her afflicted mind. With a smile and dreamy giggle, she assured herself that her disconcertion was unfounded, manifested by excessive worry. Moreover, she was convinced that in the true world, her world, Capheif pined for her. He certainly was just shy, settling for a lesser woman, and Nepiur...*Nepiur will not be the end of our love. We know what to do.*

Today, Raphenie's attention was less upon her chores as it suffered repeated and frequent distraction. Not a stone's throw away, Capheif and the other orderlies that kept Nesh so clean and bright were spending their morning helping with the last harvest as a kindness, not unlike herself. *Such a good beast*, she thought as she stared at him. She admired his diligence, and though it had not made him a noble member of the family he was appreciated by all, save his marital father.

Her chest tightened at the sight of him working, her skin as flush as the fronds overhead and her hands trembling so awfully that, barely slipping their grasp, the needle's connection to her burgeoning sack was severed enough to douse her in sticky nectar. Her wayward thoughts were shocked back into their due place and she frantically wiped away the liquid that hadn't soaked in. She quickly made for the shallows of the river, so flustered that she dropped her tools and spilled most of her product.

To her relief, attention to her blunder was minimal. People cared more about finishing the work before the oddly hot day cooked them alive. No one pitied her or chided her, rather silently felt for her, each remembering having made that same error a hundred times. And yet, as always, they did not care to know who the girl was that went to clean herself. To them she was just a clumsy girl and must have always been. It was certainly untrue. For Raphenie, it was humiliating because it was the first time she had done something so ungainly in all the many seasons worked. She had been preoccupied with her racing mind all her life and, having grown accustomed to it, never allowed it to hinder her in a task. It took no extra thought to realize what was new about her situation. The object of her obsession was slipping away to the arms of another.

The chill of the water immediately soothed her and all the aches and frustrations drained away. She was almost back to reality, but no sooner had she begun scrubbing nectar from her dress than she began losing herself to fantasies of Capheif again. The stains disappeared acceptably, and she took a moment to refresh herself with a drink before a fearsome noise downstream caught her interest.

Children whose natural inexhaustibility was enhanced by rich juice – stark contrast to the languor of their elder caregivers who were equally enhanced by liquor – bathed at the water's edge. It was a pleasure to watch, always calming knowing that things in this special city were not so terrible. She wanted to believe she missed being a child and longed for younger years, but the sad truth was that if she had ever had a childhood, she could remember nothing of it. Perhaps that was why she still was called a child by some, having been discovered at her present age and size but never growing up as the others did. Mantichaena at large developed quickly but aged slowly, yet she still had the girlish look and underwhelming size she had washed ashore with. Almost sixty seasons had come and gone and she remained a runt running abreast her herd of K'hizu, a pup among grown beasts. It surely did not help that the K'hizu caste of her body's remaking was the meekest of all their kind.

Maurus' family had taken Keimas in after the fall, and Sebashni had been like a mother to Lemalie when Aroch's wife was put to ground. Every orphan was scooped up in times of loss and given a warm bed and warm plate, but never Raphenie. No one recognized her when she was plucked from the beach, nor did she have any memory of any person or place, even Ellel. Instead she was an oddity without friends to claim her, a waif wandering underfoot who was welcome in the tribe but not in a home. This was her earliest recollection; being a Galaila among others of her kind, but not really one of them, and yet believing as she changed and became a Mearnum that she must be where she belonged. The only outstanding trait she possessed was her unique white fur, but that was not enough to draw the attention she wanted. Capheif could not see her. She often wondered why they had bothered to save her at all. How long had she been laying there like driftwood cast ashore and abandoned by the sea? She never asked such questions. To her, she had simply come as the others had, but absent their fear of home and the East. A blank slate.

A distant cry broke her musing. Shadows darted along the cliffs and the boom of Kutu wings shook the air. Govan's otherwise deep voice was warped into a feral shriek as he descended from the aviaries, then reached sufficient proximity to be heard shouting repeatedly, "From the Hai! From the Hai! Gazan at the ready!" An attack was imminent. Hungry K'hizu must have found their way up the west cliff again.

This was a common emergency during seasons such as Bone and Mercy, when hunger made the K'hizu of Sekhaadi Ni'ivitnem desperate and daring. It was much less so during the bearing, though still a concern, so no great panic was incited from the alarm. Nonetheless, swift obedience was given to the guidance of authoritative figures participating in harvest as they echoed Govan's signal and directed groups of non-combatants back to their halls.

Raphenie instinctively searched for Capheif, her heart pounding while seeking a glimpse of white horns through the crowd, unable to find his. Her presence would be demanded in Ms'egol for the sake of accountability...or would it? She thought perhaps she could slip into Nesh, seeking another incidental meeting with the man. Sadly, she could not see him and so by nature she retreated to Ms'egol. Certainly, she would see him again when the danger was dealt with. Departing thereto she leapt upon the knee of one of two statues either side the academy's yawning doors – two humbly knelt scholars holding an open book between them under which entrants would pass – and craned her neck to see for herself what the danger was. There was no hope for any rogue predators as those young and eager to become warriors charged out toward the West, a squad of screaming militia ushered out of Gazan and the Kutu streaked overhead. One would think Anama herself had sent an army against them by the volume of the retaliation, but as Raphenie climbed higher on the sculpture she saw nothing of danger at all. She was only able to discern a pair of robed vagrants, stumbling and constantly looking over their shoulders as if hunted as they approached, one in blue and one in black. She ogled only momentarily before she was ordered to fall in line and enter the safety of the academy if she was not going out to fight. Stealing another glance westward before obeying, her last sight was a chilling one, something she had heard stories about but never personally seen; the character in black was notorious in the city. The darkly silent visitor held the one in blue from beneath the shoulder as they limped as fast as they could, the flicking drafts of dust at the mouth of the canyon parting like grain before a drooling echelon of wild-eyed kuolt seeking to swallow them whole. These animals were different, not natural. Their fur was matted and crusted with blood that scattered into the air as they ran. Had they bathed in their kills? Worse still, what could drive so many of these creatures to pursue their prey so recklessly into certain death.

It was nothing the Mantichaena were not prepared for, and proper to the season or not the city had no shortage of claws for defense. Govan led the hunts and other Kutu with a piercing cry and picked off the easy targets, disrupted the pack and kept them from reaching their prey until Gazan's coordinated response crushed the kuolt like a battering ram. Throughout the brief skirmish the belly-laugh of the soldiers resounded as every animal was crushed or clawed to death, amidst the jeers of "More meat! More meat for supper tonight!" It was over so fast that many field workers hadn't enough time to get inside. Turning from their flight to shelter, they cheered for their favorites among Gazan's forces and watched on as the assault came to its gruesome end. Raphenie wanted nothing to do with such things, had little love for any soldier. Her tender heart hated the sight of a dying creature, even one so foul. She would never understand what about death gave such sick pleasure to breeds like the Kulo and Kutu.

At the behest of Sebashni Sky was informed of the travelers' arrival and that one of them was terribly wounded. He commanded their admittance into the academy for whatever treatment they required and the convergence of the council posthaste. The orders were relayed swiftly to all corners of the city and all archons appeared readily, all but Raru and Artimecian.

The small entryway within Ms'egol's doors, and the steep but short stair after it were not fire-lit and so carried a musty, abandoned feel despite their frequent use. The glow of gelatinous thi sprouting from the cracks shined dimly on the way, but the final step into the premiere room, the academy, presented an array of colorful lights and intriguing scents from all forms of alchemical experimentation.

The room was spherical and immense, but not spacious to walk. As much workspace as possible was crammed onto platforms suspended by chains. These were connected not just by stairs but also by vertical tubes in the rock containing counterweighted lifts that descended into or rose up and about the rounded walls, like veins transporting blood. The side of the concave roof opposite the entry was less crowded, a giant half-circle hole leading all the way up to the plateau above and pouring daylight down into a tangled web of wooden walkways and baths therein that housed herbs, rare vegetation and various fungi.

The black robed visitor, who had kept her hood close about her face and refused any treatment or inspection, immediately surrendered her injured cargo to the capable hands of the apothecaries and sanctifiers. Wordlessly, she turned to wander up onto the bridges and among the resplendent thi'tskreol, stopped to smell and touch each one as though they were her only reason for coming.

Sky and the council gathered in the basin below, where several students moved back and forth taking turns applying various remedies to their guest's wounds. The subject was not clothed for travel, wearing a flowing blue robe interlaced with white leather tarnished by time. His old face reflected his apparent frailty as he struggled for breath, his body lacking muscle to the point of unusual emaciation. A young Thiwa girl who had helped him up the table remained with him as the rest of the students finished their work and moved away.

Sky commanded Patriarch Rentish to spread word that the alarm be rescinded before turning back to the young Thiwa, taking charge of the situation.

"You, *aia*, what is his name?" he demanded.

"*Ein, minghenwekt*, Primarch. He does not say," she responded in a small, deferential voice.

"Of course not." Sky glanced up at the darker figure and huffed, eyed her distrustfully. "What of that one? She's said nothing to anyone?"

"A woman, I think," the girl provided. "Her brood I cannot tell. She shared that the man approached her encampment from the Dhai, along the southern cliffs near Nikhaadi Ansax, injured and panicked, and begged her for guidance to us." A small flurry erupted at the door as Patriarch Novun and Matriarch Liklita arrived belatedly and approached to listen at Sky's back.

Sky scowled, suddenly annoyed at the battered traveler's presence. He looked him up and down, noted the short fur, round ears, whiplike tail and blunt claws. He was a Boroo, well-suited to the wilderness, and garbed unmistakably as an enchanter from a faraway settlement. Sky was familiar with the color and style of his robes. They were the raiment worn by the acolytes of Aes'bethil, the village of visions.

"Long, since god last defecated on me," he cursed, thinking aloud "He's a *Bet'hvaebeulg*, a priest of the seeress. Give him rest and rations and send him on his way before day's end. I'll not have his kind here."

"One of Bethaali's folk?" Liklita burst excitedly.

"Primarch, what if they are in danger?" Novun protested, eager to learn about the distant colony.

After a quick glance at him, Liklita ventured,"Primarch, you mustn't simply cast him back! We've heard nothing of Bethaali for so long. This is not a good sign."

"*Utan*, attend your advisors," interjected Gazan Utan Simeyer in support of their point. "If there is a hazard in the Dhai then we must assess it. It may be the same form that attacked *Utan* Keimas."

"More devils?" Sky jeered. "Do not be ridiculous. It's no doubt more like the kuolt pups we've just slain."

"Ask him, father. At the very least ask the man his story."

With so many insistent stares fixed on him, Sky pondered his options and eventually acquiesced.

"*La*, fine. When he is later revived, I will inquire."

The weak figure rose laboriously to a seated position, brushing off the students' efforts to keep him bedridden. Leaning heavily on the workbench beside him he wheezed with effort to give a proper introduction.

"Esteemed Primarch of Mantichaena...city Hauan Etain...I am here at the behest of the godlike Manti *Golaia* Bethaali, dreamer of dreams and seer of the outworld."

Sky bristled at the unwelcome heralding and was on the verge of another outburst, but held his composure.

"I'll thank you not to use such audacious titles in the presence of true believers, or you will be expelled," he said disdainfully. "This city worships our true lord, not a mortal pretender. What message does Bethaali the EXILE send?" he demanded.

"A plea for compassion, great Primarch," the acolyte begged. "There are...things out there...things dripping with the black spoil of the ancient thuell!"

The council moved fluidly to distance and silence hovering students, creating a space to keep the general populace out of earshot. Sky never took his wary eyes off the man, bending double to peer coldly at him.

"You must tell me now if you exaggerate, messenger," he warned. "And be assured, if you utter a word of such an impossible thing without due consideration, I will have you skinned and burned."

The envoy was undaunted, almost emotionless as he relayed his message.

"Primarch...I witnessed a dozen of my brothers and sisters perish in its jaws. It came up from below, right in the goddess' sacred ground, as black as night, skin squirming like it yearned to tear away from the body inside. I have never seen any creature such as this. With hands like sickles it cleaved its way through our village, indiscriminately smashed buildings to rubble and flesh into meal! *Aiatan* Bethaali herself languishes from a terrible wound! We call for aid!" he cried, casting his eyes about, hands reaching to grasp the Primarch's arms in his earnestness. "Witchcrafters! Soldiers! Anything!"

Sky slapped the man's hands away as they groped for him, rolling his jaw back and forth pensively. He directed the Thiwa attendant away with a flip of his fingers and stood alone to brood.

Seeing a chance to be heard, Liklita incautiously petitioned him.

"Primarch, we have more than enough hunters and sentinels here. We cannot sit idly while one of our own is overrun by such a thing! With this man to guide us we can finally find where Bethaali has made her colony, and it would take only a small contingent of the Iron Sanctum to bring a lone thuell down!"

Rentish returned and attended them, adding his own voice to the argument.

"*Einla*! She's entirely correct. We have spent more than fifty seasons preparing for this day, and we are ready for it!"

Sky silently approved of his courage, in that it gave their people confidence, but he would not allow such rashness sway in his council.

"*Udai*, and what if there are more? What if there are scores? Thousands? Have you forgotten how suddenly the poison spreads? What good would it do to spend precious resources to protect a city of exiles when we are blind to the extent of the threat?"

Aroch asserted himself on Rentish's behalf, hoping an appeal to Sky's political shrewdness would rationalize the proposition where an appeal to his humanity failed.

"Primarch, you yourself often speak against postulation beyond what there is evidence of. This creature does not sound like any thuell, but what threat it poses to Bethaali may soon fall upon us. Exiles or not, deserters or not, they are children of Ellel, and now Mantichaena like us. Perhaps their return home remains unwise, but they may serve as allies. If we strengthen them in their need and bolster their defenses, then perhaps the danger may be stemmed at their borders instead of our own."

Sky swallowed the bait whole, eager to boast of such a wise move to the public. He was loathe to do Aes'Bethil any favor, but having the village strong could indeed serve as a line of defense to the South. As much as he hated Aroch, he loved the idea.

"That is...an exquisite observation, father Aroch," he said as a plan unfolded in his mind. "We, a benevolent city, should offer some small assistance to the *gal'tskhain*. In this, we provide aid while simultaneously maintaining a safe territory between our borders and theirs. Of course, we cannot just send warriors to do the work of a diplomat. We must send a head of Nesh to represent us, along with a pair of gothic witchcrafters for her protection. Such assets will need to retain their essence until absolutely necessary, so a small troupe of Gazan will be assembled to escort them."

"*Her* protection?" Sebashni inquired. "You already have a choice in mind for the mission?"

Sky was so hard pressed to hide a wicked smirk that his lips quivered excitedly.

"*Einla*. I should think this is the perfect opportunity for my youngest to have some real experience in negotiation and prove she is ready to serve as one of my archons."

There was a thoughtful silence, then all from the council except Aroch and Sebashni quickly approved the proposal. On the surface it did make sense, but to those attuned to the Primarch's motives this was an obvious ploy to put as much distance as possible between Nepiur and the throne of the Primacy, and the same between her and Capheif before a child could be conceived. With this one decree, justified and supported by the council, he could banish one of the dissenters to his rule. Aroch was especially terrified, knowing how little Sky valued the lives of his family, or anyone, when they crossed him. There was no knowing the true intentions of such a power mad creature. For all Aroch knew, Sky was trying to put his second daughter in a situation she could not handle and allow her to die.

"I defer to you, mother Liklita," Sky continued with heightened enthusiasm. "Since you are so adamant that this be done, let it be one of your own champions who leads the caravan. And since Artimecian is not here," he added resentfully, "I surrender the remaining selections to my trusted advisors. With any luck we can identify this new monster as the source of the attack on young Keimas and allay all remaining concerns. I pray it is a single entity and one that will not turn its sights towards us. Inform me when you have made your choices."

The ensuing discussion swelled as Sky retreated to the entry stair with only Sebashni's inquisitive alto following him.

"Primarch, what demands your time?"

His preoccupied voice was forbidding, "I must correct an inadequacy."

Sebashni cared only as far as his voice reached her, and as he fled so did her regard. The duty of assigning suitable members to the rescue caravan weighed on her but was overshadowed by a sense of foreboding brought on by the woman in black, who had yet to speak since her arrival. Allowing her to roam free in Ms'egol was inexcusable, and Sebashni had no intention of permitting it to continue. She listened for a moment as the gathered archons debated who best to assign to the expedition. Nepiur was educated and fiercely intelligent, but no warrior, unprepared for the wilderness. Tests of archonship aside, this might as well be an execution unless she was provided with the right escort. Knowing the discussion would continue for some time she turned towards

165

the other matter.

Properly excusing herself, she made her way up the stairs surrounding the academy to the gardens above. There was no obvious sign of the visitor but Sebashni was certain the black shroud would be easily spotted against the upper flue's greenery. She was quite right. Where the walls came alive with carefully trained and trellised growing things she saw the skulking stranger by a basket of amphiraeds, caressing one of the newly flowering beauties with a hand hidden by her sleeve. Sebashni scrutinized the solitary figure while rising on one of the lifts, landed to approach her with some trepidation as she crossed the creaking walkways.

With frightening alertness the eerie hood swiveled to acknowledge Sebashni, and her poor heart nearly stopped beating.

"*Aia*, good day," Sebashni began respectfully. "I'm told that the man you delivered stumbled onto you in your home?"

A nodded reply.

"And will you be staying for some time? I imagine you'll want to make sure your friend is in good health before returning."

No reply, verbal or otherwise.

"*Malpael*, forgive my candor," Sebashni continued, "But I must demand that you show propriety regarding your identity while you are a guest among my people. If you will not reveal yourself, then speak, but if you will remain dumb then allow me to see who stands before me."

There was an uncomfortable silence, followed by a sigh from within the hood. A slurred voice, hissing as if it rose up from boiling oil, spoke.

"By she who ruled here long before you I was called 'storyteller'. If you share her good sense in leaving me to my own affairs, then you may give me whatever name you please."

Sebashni was taken aback by the strange voice and outrageous words but she recognized the name, had heard it spoken as though it belonged to a mythological being.

"Storyteller...I have heard of the woman you claim to be. Some of our hunters have professed stumbling onto you in the heart of Ni'ivitnem. They describe you as some eldritch ghost, roaming the deep woods without a care, but never again found in the same place. They call you storyteller and mythspeaker as well, befuddled by riddles of truth you weave for travelers wherever you meet them. I must admit…I half-expected you existed only in the imagination of the superstitious and lost.

"As I would have it remain," the visitor explained. "Some of yours have sought me in the only home I know, wishing to see for themselves that I am flesh."

Sebashni was intrigued.

"You sound offended, yet all who return with a tale of your company paint you beautifully, saying that you gave them food and shelter, spoke of the ancient world and interpreted their dreams. They also claim to have returned with an aroused hunger for knowledge only to find that your territory, previously marked with banners of fur and bone, was absent as if lifted from the ground and carried away without so much as a blade of grass out of place."

"…*La, aia*. Their simple ignorance is a blessing I cherish."

"I insist, do you have a given name, then? Or only the taken one." Sebashni asked, increasingly interested in the woman.

"I am only a storyteller."

"Perhaps I would better know you by a false name if you would but show your face," she invited once more, perhaps pushing more than she ought.

"Then call me nothing. I have obeyed you in speaking, and my gift to you is to say that I will be only a few days among you before returning to my den."

Sebashni's ears tingled from the raspy voice, and very cautiously she extended her open palm facing the woman in agreement.

"*La enta*, I will give you the benefit of our council's trust, but we will be watching you. If you require rest then you are welcome here in Ms'Egol. There are unused rooms higher up, but please do not touch anything without the supervision of the researchers."

The woman stared at the oddly positioned hand, trying to understand what it signified. Sebashni waited uncomfortably until the gesture was returned. The cloak's ragged sleeve never slid away from the hand it hid even as it touched Sebashni's, and her mouth went dry when she felt very soft but deathly clammy flesh. With that, the storyteller turned and drifted away up the walkway, leaving Sebashni alone and confused. Though the Matriarch was congenial, she remained wary. Quickly she retreated and acquired one of the alchemical scholars a short distance away, ordered him to observe the woman at the expense of all other work, at least as long as she roamed in the open, and report to the council if she acted in any way suspicious or unsavory. No doubt they would hear from him, if only because of the haunting way the shrouded creature moved and silently inspected her surroundings. She looked uninterested in most things, as if she was merely stalling for time.

Meanwhile, the storyteller found her way to the upper levels, but did not seek a room to occupy. She crept out into the light on the terraces of Ms'egol overlooking the city, made her way to Gazan and entered almost unseen. Once in, stepping around prostrate combatants who had already finished their training for the day, her ears were assailed by the sounds of smashing bodies and roaring crowds below. She had no way of disguising her presence, but having never been seen disrobed she moved unhindered, confident of her anonymity, though she still stood out amongst the nearly or completely naked warriors. This was not her first time here. Upon each visit she would spend time in one or more of the halls, had always done well in deflecting questions about her presence. If anyone recognized her, intent on speaking to her once more, she would vanish with impossible suddenness into crowds or corridors and elude them. Though she showed kindness to people in the hostile Ni'ivitnem, she brought none with her here. She was searching, waiting, wondering if today was the day she found what she sought, but never hopeful for it.

Gazan was gruesome and noisy to many, but for the storyteller it was soothing. She had often enjoyed the show within, familiar with the flying blood of combat and excited by it. Smelling it in the air, she moved to the edge of the promenade surrounding the arena and instantly perceived the palpable energies of pride and violence that permeated the mist of perspiration therein. Not wanting to be noticed, much less touched, she found some personal space and sat herself on the ledge, humming contentedly to herself as she watched two young women below beat each other senseless.

No one of special importance was engaged in the arena, but it didn't matter. It was the lifeblood of Gazan to relish each match, and no matter how fresh or undertrained the participants were the fights were always met with equal enthusiasm. Each victory was a celebration of this hall's power which even the loser shared. There was no shame of failure in Gazan. To win was to be strong, but to lose was to learn.

The storyteller peered all around at the cheering faces and below at the blood-soaked platform, smiling dryly beneath her hood at fond memories of when she herself had been feared, when bones filled her gut and sinew hung from her teeth. What wonderous days long-passed, when the world was young and she had no need to hide from it.

She was roused from her thoughts by the tepid monotone of a small girl who appeared suddenly beside her, uncomfortably close.

"Good bearing, storyteller."

How unexpected, she thought, that a child should even know she existed, let alone be familiar with that moniker. Just how prevalent were these fireside rumors of her? No one seemed to care that she and the little miss were talking, so there seemed to her no harm in responding.

"Good bearing," was the reply as the storyteller snuck a sideways peek at the waif. She was younger than her voice indicated, no more than four or five seasons, soiled rags clothing her soiled skin. They eyed each other blankly before the girl yielded, tilted her head and giggled.

"I want to know why you're here. Tell me," she demanded sweetly.

"I'm...looking for someone."

"Your brother?"

The storyteller's breath caught in her throat. It was a suspiciously specific guess, but she did not want to give anything away to such a stranger.

"You're called a storyteller because you tell stories," the girl continued upon seeing the visitor's hesitation. "I like stories. I have never seen you before."

"You're a bit young. It's been some time since I visited your city." As she spoke, the storyteller noticed something remarkable about the child: She was Galaila, no indication of K'hizu alteration. It was exceedingly rare that any child reached three seasons without showing at least some sign of change. "*Aia*, how aged are you? Have you not been taken by a brood?"

"Tell me a story," the girl requested flatly.

"I...I'm sorry, I do not have the mind for it today," she avoided. "I am preoccupied with he for whom I wait."

"I'll tell you one then," The girl replied immediately, forcefully.

Rising to leave, the storyteller found herself hindered by a small hand grabbing onto her cloak and holding on relentlessly. The unexpected jostling caused her to gasp and grapple to keep herself covered, briefly exposing a boney hand, armed with sleek black claws which her stalker examined closely. She smiled at them, look up at the Storyteller and said:

"...A story about three children; three children who murdered their mother. One son whose eyes saw all, one daughter whose hearts felt all, one son whose teeth devoured all. The eyes would watch as this Maengir grew old, the hearts would feel the numbers of its people, and when the many lands and seas became full of life, the teeth would tear open the darkness and unleash their mother, and she would eat us. She would eat everything."

The Storyteller was chilled, staring into a child's crystalline green eyes and seeing the face of something else behind them. That face stared at her with agonizing certainty. Its blood flowed from the beat of something that was not a heart. It smiled with something other than teeth. Not knowing what she faced, the storyteller lost control of her voice, its sickly dribbling tone fully revealed.

"*Ssskhain aien enta*...how did you here such a story..."

"I know who you are. I also know who he is. He is here. You will find him soon" the girl whispered hurriedly, before skipping away.

Her robe released, the storyteller recoiled and the girl smiled back at her. No one else seemed to notice she was there, though she sang in a loud soprano all the way to the stairs: "I know whooo you aaa-aaare!"

Thetrulengo speaks,

Incredible! I do not believe my eyes! I thought no discovery would come of deviating from Raphenie to inspect this seemingly simple recluse, but she is the treasure to which the hell of the

Manyflesh itself is drawn! What enormous idiocy has made me blind to her? All unknown parts of myself, harken to your whole and see what eyes have seen: a child of the dark edge as I live and br...well, as I...mortal colloquialisms are inapplicable, but I am happy! What luck! What strange, stupid fortune has made this horror a friend of the Mantichaena? All this time, a simple shroud and simple living has made her invisible even to me? La! As I gaze secretly beneath that dreary hood and now look up into eyes like broken metal, I see that these Vulgoli are tricky things indeed. Perhaps I have not credited them appropriately for the cunning in their...hearts? Inner workings? I dare not say soul, lest they themselves mock me and call me fool. Nonetheless they have occupied the surface of Maengir most expertly, without my notice...and also without the death and carnage synonymous with their name and heritage. I expected their return from their hiding places to herald oceans of blood and the splitting of earthplane, but I can see now that it is not just the son of teeth or his brother, the eyebeast, that has become...diminished. I did know who she was, but I didn't know anything about her. Such a wondrous woman of uncharacteristic curiosity now, far afield from the slithering reptile she was in the old day, wearing the entrails of mortality like jewelry and nesting on their bones.

Between the moment when the Mantichaena's Primarch looked upon her and what followed immediately afterward – as this was the moment in which I examined her for the first time and saw her for what she was – I decided to revisit the libraries once again and peruse what books I could find in their archives for any recording of her lessons and recitations received by hunters or those who had become lost in the wood. What I found was startling.

I suppose I can finish this in the time it will take for my little Raphenie to take one or two more steps...so what reason have I not to?

This devious demon has somehow kept herself hidden from Az'Rech's luminous Deina in the most obvious of places and has been recounting to these mortals stories that they have no business knowing. I am undone, as this tribe alone is privy to knowledge of the Age of Unravelling. To think what could happen if they learnt their true history, the unlimited power that can be taken by one soul murdering thousands...there would be yet another generation

171

of genocidal gods, making the clouds rain blood as they tried to steal each other's essence.

Worse still, might she be inclined to share the location of the Dying Wish? The Commanding Voice...even Hollow Among Graves. How could she know such things herself? If she has spoken of any, then Mantichaena might discover how this blighted canyon is the very place where Escharka's limb was cut from her, and that upon their beloved island is the unnatural mouth of her prison and the final resting place of Rogkt'sokai, Brother Blood, the Son of Teeth. Has she announced in florid verses that the thuell they fear so terribly are in fact the fallen pieces of her mother, cut out of her when she was driven back into the dark edge by Az'Rech? Certainly not, or they would live in the same waking nightmare as this woman; eternal, inescapable fear of their creator's return.

They are likely too ignorant to decipher what little she has told them, but...it's all here in their archives; almost the entire history of life from the moment Az'Rech came upon Maengir. It is written in a manner that conveys fiction, fantasy, even satire. They think she is a storyteller alone but...she is a historian. Among these fantastical misinterpretations is hidden the most ancient of truths: the real reason for their existence, which I am certain would rob them of their very will to live. The records mismatch in some places, and some tell of things it would be impossible for this Vulgoli to know...is there someone else yet living here who was witness to the first day?

Why is she doing this? It seems she is taking precautions to ensure that only very few hear her words but what terrible risks she takes in speaking them, all for the sake of...what? There must be something else at work here, something she expects from them perhaps? According to the text, she has never asked price or favor for entertaining weary journeymen. It's as bedeviling as the words written here...but no more. I cannot suffer these scribblings to be. Perhaps they will not even notice they're missing? I'll take what ink and coal I must from the books and leave them blank. There's no sense in taking a chance. If any of them knew what awful things were buried beneath their feet, dread disgrace! Lamentation! If a mortal selfishly seeking glory would take up a weapon such as the Dying Wish then ruin equal only to Escharka's advent would befall this mortal coil.

Mijamaon...Sister Sleep...it's her, I have no doubt. She looks so different now. I wonder what has become of her brother? Could that be who she's waiting for? Is Brother Bone still up there? No. He was freed almost a hundred seasons past so...perhaps he is evading her?

For now, I will continue with my studies of Zeniquorer's child, but I will keep one wary eye on this woman of the dark edge while the other seeks her brothers.

~Chronicle of Wonders, A Beginning of Vulgoli

CHAPTER 16: CONSUMPTION

Raphenie's mind raced and her head burned with fever, trying to keep pace with her rambling lips. She confided in the indifferent walls of a deserted library cloister, tracing the cracks in the wall with her fingers and periodically striking the smooth face as she tried to talk herself down from frenzy.

She hated Capheif. She loved him. Hated to love him and loved the way he made her hate him. He could not see; they were meant to be. Even his marvelous heart was unable to feel what love she held for him or what perfect romance she could offer.

No one loves you, the voice in her bones rumbled.

"No one," she hoarsely agreed.

She hated Nepiur the most; Mearnum like her, young and beautiful like her. Was she really so much more deserving? No, that was a trick played on Capheif by that manipulative whore. It had to be a trick. Nepiur was repulsive, a foolish bore, insufficient for a man such as Capheif. What justice was there that she should be consigned to isolation while a woman of pitifully inferior caliber reaped golden grain from the field Raphenie loved? She felt always stifled, cheated by an ignorant world, denied what it owed her.

The tiniest of voices inside her muddled brain chided her for her selfishness, but she refused to heed it or feel the guilt it should have inspired. Empathy wasn't empowering, and her newfound greed snuffed it out, leaving a bitter shame as she ground her knuckles across the baktite walls until they were raw and bloody.

"Raphenie?" came a very special voice.

Suddenly the storm of emotion was driven away, and her soul lifted as if to the stars. Quickly she hid her injured paw beneath the folds of her dress, turned a bright smile toward the wondrous vision of Capheif as he trudged around the bookcases to her, sensing she was there as expected and inquiring casually:

"*Eina aia*, Cisiveo had to point me in your direction. What are you doing still in here? Reading a bit?"

Raphenie was taken aback by the realization that she was among books. She had been completely unaware of where she was as her temper led her all through the academy. What luck that he found her here, a far more reasonable place than somewhere public.

"*La*...reading," she affirmed unconvincingly, snatching a book at random from the shelf she stood beside, forgetting in her discomfiture that he could not see what she did.

"*Kaiba quo*. The scuffle outside was nothing," he said with relief. "The council has everything under control, and it sounds like they will have their hands full this season. *Aia*, we have our work too, but I did not smell you in the orchards after our release. Are you fit? I have been concerned after the way you left my table so abruptly."

She was elated by his consideration, and his unexpected awareness of her whereabouts.

"Thank you, for your concern" she replied, a little breathlessly. "*La*, I live well."

"*He wants you. He just doesn't know it.*"

She barely heard the conniving voice. Capheif's presence made her heart strong.

"*Uta*, are you not of Nesh?" she continued clumsily. "You were holed up here during the attack. *Quoenta?*"

"Hmm-yes, *laan*. I was to go to Nesh but, as I removed myself from the fields, I heard a pained sound. After searching with my ears, I realized that a goodly old man who had been working near me had been pushed down in all the excitement. No one else seemed to notice he had been left behind, so I carried him here quickly and made sure he had adequate care."

Raphenie's heart melted.

"How…how good of you. *Minla*, I wish I was that strong."

"*Minein*! You are strong, my girl. Come now, set yourself to work and become stronger!"

His smile charmed her into compliance, but in this unique situation the voice within saw opportunity. Stimulated by his praise, she felt the strength he spoke of. It urged her to delay their departure from comfortable isolation.

"Capheif, come in."

"Capheif, come in," she invited, practically demanded.

He did, with a curious look. She was pleased. She had never so forcefully requested anything of anyone, and so no one had ever obeyed her. What a feeling it was to have even that measure of control over someone.

"*Aia*, are you sure you're well?" he asked.

"Always, *Utan*…always." She let him come closer, nervously biting her lip as his scent filled her twitching nostrils. "I don't want this anymore," she groaned. Then said, with some aggression, "I want something…better."

This was unusual for her, Capheif felt. He could not help but wonder what agitated this bashful creature.

"*Quo*, why has your tongue always been so puzzling and your conversation so evasive?"

Raphenie placed her hands on his wrists and felt her heart race, pulling him so that he stooped as she craned her neck upward.

"Take him," goaded her inner fire.

"My tongue can be many things," she teased. "Tell me if you taste something puzzling."

He did not respond, barely moved. Her lips hovered off his without meeting, while their eyes did. In his she saw something that frightened her. Their milky depths reflected her own face, womanly and in command, taking something that did not belong to her. It was unsettling, but what truly upset her was how heavy and lifeless his complexion became.

In this moment she knew what was real. He should be resisting, if his love for Nepiur was true, or succumbing to Raphenie if the world was as it should be. Instead, it felt as though his mind and soul were wholly vacant. She felt no heartbeat on her fingers, no breath on her cheek, and the dark impression slowly overtook her that this was not Capheif. He just stared, lingered, hung like a marionette.

With a twinge of dread, she released him, and no sooner had her skin left his throat it blew a roar of pain. He cradled his head, lashed his tail and stumbled away from her, knocking over shelves of books and collapsing against the wall. In a shrill voice he screamed accusations at her and painfully clawed his way out of the room. As he fled down the corridor his lamentations echoed back: "*Sehilthsi!* Darkmade! Creature of Salohel!"

Raphenie stared in bewilderment, listening closely as her body explained to her what she had just done, and how to do it again. It had frightened her a moment ago, yet when she felt the very real power coursing through her she became galvanized. She had felt her way inside Capheif and become him, taken control of him. It mattered not how it was possible. She wanted to feel it again.

Moments later, Mani came flying in the door, hands grasping the frame for stability as he searched, wide-eyed, for the source of gentle Capheif's uncharacteristic lunacy. His eyes landed on Raphenie, giving him pause as he let out a sigh of relief, followed by a wary stare.

"Ah! *Aiana*? Is it just you? What has happened here? I could have died when I heard *Utan* Capheif…"

His words were cut off as Raphenie lunged forward with silent, voracious speed. In the blink of an eye she moved through the air and now stood nearly in Mani's arms, her fingers resting on his chest. His stuttering lips became cold and silent. She felt it again, a unity, like his body was an extension of hers. It was a rush to be so attuned to him, feeling his body as though it was her own. She stretched her mind and reached out to his, felt no resistance as she instinctively detached a small grain of her consciousness inside him. She released his skin without fear and, as though nothing had changed, he continued to stare slack-jawed back at her. She tilted her head and he tilted his. She glanced at the door, and he went to it without a word. She could not suppress a mirthful smile. This was a gift, a miracle endowed to her, one that meant that she could finally have…everything! Everything imaginable. She walked up behind Mani and giggled, touching his shoulder and listening inside him again. She felt the faintest struggle deep therein. His mind rebelled, crying out in pain. She had never been so happy. She could have anyone. The world could be hers, but there was no need for such drastic measures. Fate had granted her chains to bind Capheif, to finally have the love she deserved.

Thetrulengo speaks,

I have lost my euphoria over this reappearance of an elder goddess' soul. Mostly I wonder how such a young girl will assess her own condition. She doesn't show any sign of questioning it, hasn't stopped to solve the mystery of how now, and very abruptly, she is capable of so much so quickly. I myself am slow to understand.

This is danger. Have I not been present for something that happened to her? Have I not asked the right questions? This woman needs someone to understand her even if she herself does not. Miohaelia never had anyone to protect her from the power of Zeniquorer until it was too late. Her daughter deserves better. Manyflesh, I entreat you, devour Kulibreal in her egotism. Woman of oceans, kneel before the ancients and pray as the mortals do for forgiveness. Abandoned and frightened, your sister wallows without you, and you have excised what little in your heart would suffer for her. If you will not watch over her...I will. Gods always take this path of abuse when their powers emerge. If anyone has earned the right to explore it, it is this girl. Still, I hope she chooses a greater path. I have seen this look before, that which sparkles in her eyes now; hungry, depraved, innocence swallowed completely by greed. It was the dark fire that burned in her father, but he never had this power of indwelling. La, that beast of a man never saw the need. He was loathe to fill his victims' minds with obedience, preferred that they resist him, that they thrash and struggle and scream. It was that which gave him pleasure, not the act itself. It was...sport. As the father, so the daughter; the desire for ownership.

~Chronicle of Wonders, A Change of Heart

CHAPTER 17: RETALIATION

The sound of a plethora of heated conversations met Artimecian on his return from the Gate; a din from the windows of Ms'egol more suited to a drunken rabble than to the respectable company of archons. They were rabid, arguing over something to do with a great venture beyond the city. Strange that among the chaos of voices he could not distinguish that of his only superior. His attention was diverted by the patter of tiny feet on the interior steps as he drew close, and young Raphenie burst from the door in a rush that nearly sent the Patriarch flying backward. To himself he mumbled *"Minamaia,* silliest of girls" and moved to enter Ms'egol and assess the disturbance. Eyes instinctively following the hasty adolescent for a few steps, he noted the graying head and bent shoulders of his Primarch near where the little Mearnum forded the river. He didn't react to her passing, seemed intent in studying the water's surface.

Artimecian swallowed hard and hesitated. Reluctantly he changed course and approached. Sky had been perched there for a long while, judging by his slumping posture, on a boulder dipping from shore into the shallows. He was no doubt anticipating Artimecian's arrival with well-rehearsed wrath, evidenced by the imperative wag of a few raised fingers, signaling his pawn should come closer. Surprisingly, his voice had not the slightest hint of dissatisfaction, but was deeply contemplative as Artimecian arrived.

"Stand here. See as I do," the Primarch commanded.

Artimecian obeyed quickly, eager to do right and soothe his master's mood.

"*Seweih*, Primarch, the Iron Wind subdues him n…"

A gently erected finger stifled him.

"I said stand, not lie."

Artimecian buttoned his lips and stared, following Sky's fingers to where, before the submerged portion of the stone, a school of chlio swerved in unison against the lazy current.

"The life you live is very sequestered," Sky droned. "Removed from many of the realities of our life here. Do you know, who is the greatest teacher in all the world?" Artimecian was silent, sure that Sky was being rhetorical as he never broke concentration on the quietly moving creatures. "It is the world around us, the spirit of Maengir and the Veil. From Vaeba's pit in all its infernal and bloody splendor to the endless void of Aurba. There is irrefutable law in Maengir, decided and enforced by natural forces so that all things populating it fulfill their roles. Without obedience to that natural order, all life would crumble."

Without warning, Sky grasped his subordinate's shoulder and directed him to the water as the chlio were joined by a much larger one that passed them. Though they were different species, the newcomer, a predator and a faster swimmer, settled at their head and they fell in alongside it and clung to it tightly.

"*Beth'ka!* Do you see? These creatures do not comprehend my words, nor the law I speak of, yet they obey it. They are made to obey it. We think ourselves so far above the beasts, so powerful and wise, but look now about you and see how each creature flocks to its better." Sky lifted his somber face and gestured across the river to the orchards. With a soothing voice he praised the quiet diligence of those who labored in the soil and thi. "They move with purpose, even if only directed by one more capable. The *chlio iltcha* could surely swim upstream on their own but that is not their nature. They wait for the dominant *chlio du'amn* who, by its size and design, hides them from others who may prey on them, and yet it will devour some of them as they go. Some must perish so that more can survive. It is in their nature to value comfort over freedom. They want to follow. They yearn to be led, to be protected even when that protection does not apply to all. They worship a predator because they believe there is a worse fate awaiting them. Do you see? Some of us are born to rule the world, while others are born merely to inhabit it." With a burdened sigh, almost an apologetic one, Sky released Artimecian and turned his eyes up to the windows through which the raised voices of the council continued to spill over each other.

"You and I, we are of a kind. The souls residing in us have made us the keepers of the lesser, though fate and chance have placed me above you. We each have a purpose to serve, and without serving those purposes we become obsolete or even detrimental in the great game of survival and the continuation of our species. As your superior, I would be remiss if I did not make it clear to you that your friendship to me is the natural result of your utility and loyalty to that cause." Artimecian's throat went dry as Sky continued, "I have never had reason to question your loyalty, but with this most dire threat to the council's control flying against my decree and your apparent inability to contain it, I begin to question your utility."

"Primarch, I beg you, do not disdain me!" Artimecian pleaded, clutching the folds of Sky's robe. "Victory is imminent with the return of the Iron Wind."

Sky took hold of the cowering witchcrafter's forearm and squeezed the blood from it. The pain stimulated Artimecian to sweat and ache so profusely that his skin illuminated as it released energy. Though the discharge singed Sky's fingertips they held fast, and his condemning gaze did not waver.

"Do not take me for a fool, you obsequious scavenger! If you had captured Keimas I would feel HIS skin crumpling beneath my fingers. If you had killed him, I would not be troubled at all. Instead, you return empty-handed, hoping I'm too dense to realize what you've done out there! If Keimas is gone beyond the Gate, then I pray you tell me how it's possible that the Iron Wind pursues while the Gate is intact!? Tell me why my skin dries while Sanguine is barely at its end."

"*Utan, prostas!*" Artimecian whined, "My disciples were thwarted by one of our own archons! Raru arrived before us, I know not how, with enchanters to quell my sanctum's flame! It was only after I joined them that he was defeated! But he was too powerful for..."

Sky tortured Artimecian's arm with a vicious twist, dropping him to his knees and effectively silencing him. Dragging him on all fours out of the public's eye and into a shallow alcove among the cliffs he berated him without the consequence of witnesses.

"Say that again! SAY THAT AGAIN!" he roared. "You promised me perfec...I cannot..." Artimecian writhed in the Primarch's remarkable grasp, gaping as his master paused and shifted his grip thoughtfully. Instead of further punishing his archon, Sky hauled him to his feet and thrust him against the wall, his fingers lightly pressing and prodding to ensure Artimecian was still while he schemed, face aglow with inspiration. "...We can salvage this. We can still use this."

"P-Primarch?" Artimecian stammered, hopeful for redemption.

"Control your tongue. Let me wander within myself."

"But Primarch, Raru's life, his academy! Some of his students were with him! I had to make sure they would not become more troublesome. Their absence will not go unnoti..."

"Sssssssh! Ssh! Not another word," Sky hissed and jerked. "Raru was not acting out of benevolence. His interference was a deliberate act of rebellion for which he paid the due price, by Keimas' sin, no less. Heed this and put it to others' ears as opportunity presents: your men were not alone in their examination of the Gate, for I reconsidered my proposal to you after the assembly." Sky released Artimecian as his brilliant lies congealed into a satisfactory plan. "As was proper, we entreated Raru to aid you, for fear that the enchantments had weakened or been damaged. By your wisdom, Iron Wind was dispatched as a precautionary measure, in the event that Keimas was lying in wait. However, they were...insufficient."

"Insufficient to what task, Father? I must confess I hoped to convince the commonfolk of the same story, but the enchanters are burnt to ash! No one will believe it was Keimas' doing."

"They will believe what we TELL them to believe!" Sky snarled, quickly searching the mouth of their hideaway. He continued in a more subdued voice, thinking out loud. "Before we could silence Allende, he confided in his wife. Now, with this repulsive *bet'hvaebeulg* appearing out of thin air and raving about a thuell resurgence…even ensuring that young Lemalie stays mute, there is little hope of containing this conflagration of unrest. My mistake was in trying to prevent it. Rather, I should have respected its power and recognized that it is inevitable. I should have been providing it with a victim."

"Keimas," Artimecian caught on.

"The bastard himself. He is already fated to be made a symbol of my authority if now we drape your blunders over him. Few have seen him since his encounter, even fewer heard his voice. An accusation of some evil possession is not completely groundless; we make him the source of all danger, not by way of the law but by way of morality. It will take some…creative explanations on our part, but if we can put my seal on any gossips then it will not prove difficult to convince the people that the creature in the West is searching for its master, slave as it is to the devil that consumes poor Keimas."

Artimecian wholly supported focusing fear on Keimas but was unsure of what they stood to gain except to cover their own grandiose lies.

"Then we rescind all action undertaken? The stories we kindle and breathe upon, *la*. I understand this, but what of the council? His wife?"

"Leave your counterparts to me," Sky gloated. "I have enough experience in shaping their perceptions that they will pose no problem."

"*Einla,* and Aroch, the same?"

"Hardly. He will require a special degree of pressure, though only as a final defense. First and foremost is to take advantage of his vulnerability as a locus of blame while we have the chance."

Artimecian bit his lip and sneered at the wall of Nesh, growled, "Finally. I have been waiting for the chance to see him shamed, if only to gag that smug, self-important mouth."

"Not yet," Sky admonished. "Stay far from him for now, and Sebashni as well."

"What? There's no limit to the damage they could cause if left alone!" Artimecian objected.

"As I said, they are my responsibility, and I will handle them. The damage you speak of concerns you, it would seem. If Raru alone alleged that you were meant to end Keimas, then all is well.

But I encountered Sebashni seeking him the very night we set our plan in motion. I was daft not to interfere with greater force. I should have known that guileful bitch was in service to Aroch and his rebellious brood."

"*Utan*, then what am I to do?" Artimecian asked.

"Only stoke the fire," Sky replied. "Spin whatever tales you must, but all that was needed was Allende vomiting suppositions about a voice surrounding Keimas in the dark. Such a story has the stink of a demon and will be easy to peddle. We can no longer keep the city free of fear, so we must harness and give it prey before it turns on us."

"Well decided then. I am engaged." Artimecian scuttled away, hunched and ugly in spirit though his body was upright and composed. Despite his revulsion at the witchcrafter's failure Sky always appreciated his fervency and the ready adaptability he exhibited.

The furtive Primarch mentally formulated the exact words he would use to notify the city of the situation. A proper sell was critical, demanding that he address them in a manner that demonstrated unique importance. In preparation, he emerged from his hiding place and beckoned a woman busy bathing her child downriver to attend him. In simple and easily recalled words, he gave her a message to deliver verbatim to the citizenry as soon as night began to fall and the ground to cool; a message that every man, woman and child should gather by the river and set torches enough to hide the stars, and there hear words of the utmost importance to their survival. Fear was best used when the danger was unknown, and here it played upon the worried mother with superb effect. Nothing made a subject more malleable than the need to protect their poor, innocent child. *How foolish that is*, he thought as he watched her go. *Children are born to usurp us. It is always in their hearts. There is nothing innocent about them.*

Although word of Keimas' disturbing ordeal had been effectively spread, worriedly by Allende and strategically by Artimecian, there was little accuracy in the stories passed along from listener to listener. Outrageous speculations were perpetuated as Artimecian's inchoate lies added to the sordid details of Keimas' spiritual fall.

Sebashni was yet unaware of many of the goings-on she had planned to monitor for Aroch's sake, as she waited both stubbornly and hopefully by Lemalie's bed. Once again, the young lady had gone missing, overwhelmed as much as Sebashni after letting slip she was with child and now clearly obviating her social and agricultural obligations.

Sebashni's patience was finally rewarded. Her ears perked up at the captivating sound of Lemalie in liquid form coursing up from minute fissures in the corner stones behind her mirror. Waiting no longer than it took for Lemalie to fully reassemble, the elder Mearnum threw her arms around her and nearly took them both to the ground without even waiting for the stunned girl to put her dress back on. "Gods and stars and all good things ban your power, *aia*! With each disappearance I am apprehensive that you will never return."

Feeling revived herself, waking from what felt like a long sleep, Lemalie reacted with a shining smile, greeted her father's lover with an embrace and kiss to the cheek, then with an awkward haste moved to her bed and clothed herself.

"Apologies, Mother. I am not despondent as before. If I'd clarity enough to know I was so missed I would not have languished alone for so long."

"Pay an old woman's worry no mind my sweet, only tell me, is your spirit righted?"

"Muchly, and my body with it. The water restores what deep aspects of me food and drink cannot," Lemalie explained contentedly.

"I wish I had such a release, dear heart. Well...other than your sweet father, that is." Sebashni took Lemalie's face in her hands and pursed her lips, eager to gain Lemalie's involvement in important matters but hesitant to ruin her good spirits. Sensing the mother's jumbled thoughts, Lemalie patted her head by its side and in a hushed tone relieved her of the need.

"Matriarch, do not contest whether or not to share the grim news of the bloody battle that has been fought over my husband's fate. I already know."

"*Quola*!? How is this? You were able to follow?"

185

"No, but then a sudden yes." Lemalie's tone was serious, though not strained. She relaxed further even as she revealed unsavory news. "I did not follow Keimas, but in a stroke of luck was adrift below water, near the insidious tongues of men I once lovingly called fathers and leaders. I could not see them but undoubtedly recognized the voice of the Primarch, listened in disbelief as the man he was with confessed to failure in an attempt to slay my Keimas. Though my anger mounted, I kept my head so as to attend to what they now plot; deceit and misinformation meant to dissuade the people from exalting Keimas as a hunter killer, instead to vilify him as the host of a demon and the root of all the sudden dangers we face."

"He wouldn't dare! The repugnant *bpotuis vaeilt*, I'll cut his heart out!"

Peaceably, Lemalie took hold of her friend and held her close.

"Don't let his untruths emblaze you. Allende's mistake they may capitalize on, but I have a mind to vex the city as Sky does."

"*Minla*, you think the people will hold your word over that of Sky?" Sebashni doubted.

"He will have his numbers and we will have ours. Whomever, by virtue of friendship and respect, would choose to hear us will ensure that he does not possess the whole body of the people."

With a sigh Sebashni accepted that it was the best defense they could hope for.

"*Aia*, it's no victory, but at least it will bolster skepticism and protect you and your husband from annihilation."

"It's all that can be done right now. No doubt my father's place on the council is already in question among his peers as Artimecian's tongue slithers among them. I cannot sway them as much as you, but together with the help of our families we can ensure that my father's removal from the council would be met with immediate rebellion."

"Is that our plan? To incite a revolt?"

"Unlikely, but Sky is convinced that he can manipulate the city however he sees fit. We wage war against deception with the revelation that he is the true enemy of the people, if only to rouse them from their complacency in believing Sky is as much our guardian deity as Loi or Anama."

"You speak no lie...*la*. I will go among the council and unearth allies to embolden, likewise in the families of every hall, and you go to those who trust in you to be a testament to Keimas' efforts on our behalf. That remains true, *la*?

"I'm..." Lemalie faltered when faced with the unanswerable. "...I'm not wholly certain."

"But certain the man is not possessed by any *vaena, la*?" Sebashni's heart sank with Lemalie's scowl, and she became silently pensive. Together they envisaged internally the maneuvers they would undertake to succeed in their preparations. At length, the memory of what state had driven Lemalie into hiding made Sebashni place a gentle hand on the girl's still flat belly, a new sparkle in her eye. As if to force happiness upon Lemalie, she asked quite soothingly "Can you sense your child's presence?"

Lemalie smiled and laid her hands on Sebashni's.

"Only just, so distantly that it feels as though she flies up from the furthest place in the veil to find me."

"She?" Sebashni's voice was exhilarant. "Already you can sense the soul?"

"No, *minein*, I am only hopeful. Keimas always wished to have a daughter...or rather hoped not to have a son."

"*Eina,* I will not condemn such a strong feeling. A son without a father will always question who his blood flows from, and thence comes a fear of failing one's child. But Lemalie, it is joyful! My heart overflows for you. And you?"

Lemalie tried to appear pleased, though the muscles in her face conveyed the turbulence of her emotions. "I merely repair the holes in mine. I am happy to be of a family all my own but dismayed that I know not when I could share its awakening with the sire."

"My beauty, I wish that once in life I could have felt as you feel in any form. Do not let yourself fall prey to despair. The presence within grows stronger and I'm sure your husband will feel it with you no matter how far the wind carries him. The far-reaching knowledge of young life in his heart will draw him home."

"I hope it reaches him. While I could suffer his absence our child absolutely must not."

"She will not," Sebashni stoically assured her. "As you feel your child, so do I feel this: Keimas is no more than a man, and on one day or many may fail you, but when your child joins us in the morning light her father's face upon her shall shine even brighter, and her love will remake him just as yours did."

CHAPTER 18: PATHLESS WITH BODIES BELOW

The word 'Thonsfa' was more of a colloquialism to the Mantichaena than a noble word inherited from generations past. Originally it had meant dust, or barren stone. After the devastation wrought by the thuell, it had taken on a mythical quality synonymous with 'Nikhaadi', dangerous lands devoid of living things – whereupon merely setting foot could kill. The old Galaila had passed on many words for corruption and decay. 'Thonsfa' now conveyed the image of a grave and reminded the living of the dead still buried in the dunes.

The oddly flat and long plateau dividing the wooded Ni'ivitnem from the East Nikhaadi had long checked the putrid wind that rose from Thonsfa's brown sands and black thi'zech, the legacy of the thuell. In the bearing season it would have been felt as wet and stale, but in the passing it was so scalding that it ached in the lungs and could hardly be survived.

The onslaught of the thuell had burned away what few living things had once populated the land, leaving little but sand, rock and ash in their wake. Even now, after so much time had passed, only very occasional patches of tall and intertwined thi'zech brambles crawled over the dreary dunes, roots digging deep in search of what clean water remained in the clay deeper down. These skeletal remains had grown staunchly thick with bark and thorns that did little to stop the winds, but for the occasional schiis and some particularly hardy sumear who had evaded the wretched pestilence they provided infrequent shelter from Laesis.

For such pitiful shade, Keimas was exceedingly grateful as he staggered gracelessly through a particularly nasty stretch of the treacherous groves. He had flown as long as he could bear, but after half a day the unexpectedly fierce heat had nearly boiled his brain and forced him to proceed on foot. Shade notwithstanding, he trudged on, cursing the vicious briars while his prized wings dragged behind him. Had he not been exhausted and dehydrated he still would have been unable to fly for fear of betraying his location to his hunters. For a time after his abrupt departure from the gate, he had continued to debate moving forward, but the crash of stone following the gate's destruction sent a dread message that the Iron Wind was not to be dissuaded from their pursuit. Still, he swore aloud that his greatest enemy was the wretched thi'zech he grappled with now.

"Damnable things!" He groused as he fought free of yet another sticky vine. "Anama is no friend of fleshy things for how her spawn aggress. A pox on it all!" His heat induced torpor was abruptly broken as he realized that the vicious little barbs were visibly moving to catch him as he passed, most likely a survival instinct to reach for moisture even in other living things. Individual bramble tips bent as though to wrap themselves around him like sinister fingers if he tarried in one place too long, dripping odious sap that clung to his feathers. The little buggers moved slowly enough that he could avoid them fairly well if he kept moving. Pausing would most certainly be an inconvenience, but then pausing was not really part of the plan. He winced as he dislodged a thorn with his teeth and spat it angrily into the sand.

Travelling entirely on foot was not something Keimas had suffered since before the people's escape from this place, certainly not a day of fighting his way through thickets. Such filthy and degrading transport was for the landed castes.

Exhaustion taxed his senses, enough that the intermittent sounds of cracking bark and limb from far behind at first did not register. As the noises slowly drew closer Keimas dismissed them as auditory hallucinations until a particularly loud snap – this one close enough that he could hear an aggrieved shout concurrently –

shocked him awake. Shaking the lethargy from his wings and head, his blood began to pump faster, and he turned to face the mysterious source. Crouching low, he sniffed the air. He was upwind and could not trace them, but the hair of his neck bristled with each unnatural sound.

They were gaining a distance, he realized. His mind raced and he moved covertly, eyes casting around for a diverting route. There was little question as to who followed, no surprise that they had caught up to him; Kulo were adept at footed travel, terrifyingly fleet even while navigating these monstrous plants. Worse, their noses were surely sharper than his. Every thorn that caught him took a little blood with it, and every drop was a beacon that called to his pursuers. With his wings constrained he stood little chance of outdistancing them and it seemed his options for avoiding detection were few. Still, he formed a desperate plan. Roughly slashing the thicket to his right, he forged a path, before backtracking a short distance. Coming upon a slightly thinner infestation, for it could be considered nothing less, he combined stealth and patience to slowly but painfully force his way through, beyond, and finally behind and under yet another thick cluster to lay beneath it. Flattening his wings against the ground he wriggled as deep as he dared before making small sweeping motions to upturn the fine sand and dust beneath him into a fine cloud. As he had hoped, it settled across his feathers, dulled the vibrancy of his wings, melding the shape of his body into the ripples that surrounded him. He had seen all kinds of schiis employ this trickery before to evade larger predators and could only hope it was effective against Mantichaena. He forced himself to lay limp and deathly still, like a blanched corpse, barely daring to breath though his heart pounded in his ears.

He clearly heard the immediate arrival of Gogol and Haerulf, darting swiftly through the brambles. They bobbed past on all fours at an astonishing pace, fixation on the signs ahead making them less attentive to that which they passed. He suppressed a derisive chuckle as the Iron Wind's chase took them out his false exit and along the periphery of the thicket, overheard them bay and bicker once out. They sounded convinced that the Kutu had taken flight once more, scuffled about to find further sign then took off over the dunes in a more southerly direction. Enjoying the minor victory, he silently repented for cursing Anama's diabolical inventions and praised her for the single brittle thorn that had given away their approach not a moment too soon. He continued to lay silently beneath the brambles and over time felt that his body had begun to cool in the deeper, moister sand. With the scant shade from the thorns providing some protection, he settled in, remaining partially buried and rested until the desert's hot breath began to mellow with Laesis' gradual descent. His eyelids drooped the moment he felt safe, and so focused was he on listening for the return of the Iron Wind that they eventually closed. Little by little he fell victim to sleep.

Only when the radiance of day was captured by Lindu in the Thaun, and dusk encroached on the wastes did Keimas wake again. Brief and inconsequential dreams turned to a cutting pain, eventually rousing him to the realization of danger. His parched throat wheezed, and his limbs jerked against the pull of hundreds of curling brambles that had ensnared him as he slept. Ignoring the pain as they tore into him, he clawed and bit at the skeletal vegetation with reckless ferocity until he could free his arms and unwrap his neck and torso. He slashed the nasty things from his legs and stumbled out of the grove, altogether bloodier and once again in agony. Kicking free of the last tendril he turned and stepped backward into the air, ignorant of the steep slope beneath him and soon on a tumbling, yelping journey to its foot. Irritated, thirsty, aching in every imaginable way, he lay in defeat and stared sideways at the horizon. Had he brought a single water skin this journey might not have been such a nightmare. A lot of things could have made a difference, but once again he had no one to blame but himself. Was this the mighty hero of the Kutu? What had happened to his sense? Only two days since this venture was undertaken and from start to finish his mistakes were compounding.

His miserable thoughts were interrupted by a sudden splash of cool water from above. Sputtering and grunting from shock he dismissed the sensation of drowning, reactively savored the few drops that splashed his lips then wiped the rest around his face. Clearing his eyes, he tried and failed to stand, knocking grit from his wings with each movement. He collapsed again in an ungainly heap, lying still and staring blankly at the emergent stars above.

His befuddled mind replayed the events of the day, confusion circling around the possible origin of the lifesaving water.

He smacked his mouth, already resenting the absence of water, tried to lift his head to search the vicinity. His weary neck crackled with the effort and still didn't see anyone around, nor any springs or any sound of rain. Then, just as startling as the cold splash, the hillside next to him appeared to move in the darkness. His eyes traced it warily, as a curious face separated itself from the surrounding twilight and eased into his field of vision from overhead. The eyes and nose were recognizable as that of a Mearnum, though with features made more indistinct by the addition of caked-on layers of dust. Loosely fitted clothing of rough brown fibers with a hood and face-wrap hid the rest of the body from sight and, not surprisingly, gave the strange creature the perfect camouflage.

"*Anhalat!* Well met, dirty *kutlikudai!*"

Keimas could do naught but stare back in utter confusion and mimic the absurd greeting.

"Kutu, actually. Good night, dirty Mearnum."

"*Quoth?* What is that'm? A Mearnum, mmm…what say you?"

"You. It's you. You're a Mearnum."

There was a long pause as the stranger pulled down his mask and his bearded face shifted in thought. At length he smiled and replied happily, "*Alaaan,* I'm a Mearnum! Good'm, good'm, so on your feet now!" This he said snatching Keimas by the throat and lifting him upright with a single hand and little effort, perturbing him. "And you'm Kutu? Galaila you were once, just as we, *la?* Came from Ellel, or born hereabouts?"

"Ellel. Our ships I'm sure are long decayed on the seas far Tau."

"Oooh *la'm gnoth.* Good'm your fortune friend, and good'm mine! You came ahead of us'm ship! Came from Ellel too, found'm your flotilla but not yourselves. Thought you done'm follow the coast and were off Thaun. Looked, no Thaun, just upside-down mountains."

Keimas scanned the garrulous creature curiously. Its speech was strange but bore no accent alien to his own Maen'hgan.

He answered slowly "In the north mountains? No, we were forced into the Hai, beyond the great plateau."

The boisterous fellow's mouth gaped and his brittle hands patted Keimas all over as he became increasingly animated.

"That wall in'm cliff? You'm built it!? *Minueeeein,* marvelous! Us'm mancyfolk and physics could find no answer to how it came to be, but priestess did...predicted," he nodded sagely at the name. "Wouldn't say, said'm couldn't say, but Gaijala know'm everything. Talk'm to stone god."

"Stone god?" Keimas said skeptically.

"*Alaaa,* it is the earthplane! He'm earthplane and see everything; prophet."

"A prophet," Keimas repeated. It was a hint of direction anyway, he thought, derisively, assuming the being really existed and was perhaps capable of guiding him. Summoning what remaining optimism he could gather, he probed, "*Eiha uta,* can I meet this prophet of yours?"

"I-mmm don't see how," the dirty creature responded thoughtfully. "He'm welcome grand physic only to speak with. *Mineina enta,* only speaks with the priestess." He then brightened with "But I'm sure a 'Kutu' he'm think special to talk at!"

The odd little Mearnum shuffled off immediately, North over the crest of the dune, and Keimas gathered himself to follow. Despite his exhaustion, or maybe because of it, he felt comfortable in the man's presence, or perhaps merely disarmed by him. After the day's misfortunes he dismissed any lingering concerns in light of the creature's unexpectedly helpful attitude. He still had not given any thought to the meaning of this meeting, barely recognizing that he was speaking to a Mantichaena who had never made it to the West.

"*Eina graan* for the help," Keimas muttered with a tired smile. "Lead on, very dusty one."

Together they ventured into the dead hills, never noticing how the nearby sands shifted in many tiny streaks of movement. Beneath the surface, pointed feet and segmented bodies swam, unaccompanied by their usual high-pitched chatter. A small army of the sneaking deghni turned about, burrowed back Hai through the sandbanks to their father to deliver the news that Keimas lived. More importantly, that he was no longer alone.

CHAPTER 19: THE EXCEPTION

Nepiur and Lemalie had never really been friends, though to an observer they would seem quite similar. Both were educated, respected, generous, desirable, destined to great marriages. It might be said that Nepiur was of a higher class due to her father's position as Primarch, but individual quality was better appreciated than social standing. Neither of the women disliked the other, though while they had tried to engage one another in conversation they had not found much common ground. Lemalie had committed to Nesh only so that she could be nearer to Keimas, forsaking her old life as militia initiate of Gazan, while Nepiur had lived there since the city's making, obligated by a destiny to one day be Primarch and lead the Mantichaena.

Destiny notwithstanding, the primacy was not what Nepiur would describe as her ultimate goal. It was more of a means to an end; the only practical way she could finally make a difference. Many archons had voiced their support of her, citing her social grace and political acumen as justification. Thankful for their endorsement, she remained humbled by what her aptitudes could produce: not fame or power but a finely bound connection of her own wellbeing to that of the tribe she loved.

Like most hearts, there was one hers loved more than all others. Capheif was the most thoughtful man she had ever met, and that was the trait she yearned for most in her mate. Selflessly, she had postponed marriage until she was sure that her future was here in the city. Having finally believed her position secure enough to engage the relationship, it now seemed her precaution had been for naught. Father Khurk had delivered the news that Sky had chosen her to be the voice of Nesh and lead a troupe of warriors on a mission to reestablish communication with Bethaali and assist with an unknown threat presumed to be thuell in nature.

Concern weighed on her face as she contemplated her task. She was excited at the honor and opportunity she had been given, though she had to balance it against not only leaving her new husband but the inevitable consequences it would have on their reputations. Lemalie's circumstance was evidence enough of that. Talk of Keimas' abandonment was rampant; suspicions followed of Lemalie's culpability to her possessed and traitorous husband. Nepiur knew Sky's ways and his dislike of her husband. While it was only against the law for her to depart if pregnant, she was certain that this was Sky's effort to prevent her from becoming so. There was little doubt that her father had plans to further alienate her from her husband and her people once she was removed from the city. Every day that she led in her own way instead of his drove her further from the Primacy, and the only secret she could still keep from him was that this was her intent. Her concern was not for herself, but for the consequences to Capheif.

Sebashni had just that evening relayed to her the morning's events and the terrible implication of Sky's unremitting schema. Nepiur was no more shocked than if she had been told the river was wet. She knew her father better than anyone and felt rather victorious that others were starting to see his true colors. To the honorable Matriarch she wholeheartedly pledged to stand by Aroch's family if the worst should happen but warned that Sky would anticipate where her loyalties lay. It was certainly another reason she had been chosen for the long and distant mission. In a single order, Sky could disrupt her marriage and distance himself from a powerful ally of the one who challenged his authority. She had no desire to sidestep her duties in this, nor any reasonable possibility to do so, but was loath to make a final decision without consulting the man she would be leaving behind. That, she told herself with surety, would set her apart from the disgraced Keimas.

Nepiur had already put in a long day, working alongside overseer Maurus in documenting newly discovered gemstone deposits beneath Tault. Then, the relaxing evening she had planned with Capheif had been spoiled by the news of her selection and the ensuing briefing. Khurk had waylaid her for longer than necessary, mostly because she was too tired and distracted to give him her full attention. At long last, she gained her freedom and made her way back to the long hallway behind the fire pit. Outside the door of the bedchamber, she now shared with Capheif she rested against the wall, took a few calming breaths and entered peaceably.

It was entirely dark within but a sudden rustling from the fur-strewn bed told her she was not alone. Reaching to put flame to the single sconce by the door, she groped about for the striker that should rightly have been hanging from the wall. Excusing its absence, Capheif's voice rumbled lazily in the darkness.

"Forgive me. I forgot to replace it after starting the fireplace this morning."

"It's not needed," she replied as she closed the door behind her and felt her way along the wall to join him. "Your work was tiring today it seems?"

"Tiring," he repeated heavily.

"Grueling more like, for us both as it sounds," she continued as she moved nearer. "Though, we need to discuss something, and I would prefer I could see you." It was true, but as soon as she said it, she realized how thoughtless it sounded when entreating a blind man. "*Minein*, I suppose that's not important either. I am embarrassed by how I rely on my eyes to feel closer to you. *Eihs rysha,* slave to them as I am, they are not my only tool for loving you." She quickly disrobed and slipped under the thick pelt covering her husband and nestled into the crook of his arm, noting how strangely absent was his usual vigor in holding her as he grumbled his reply.

"You need not be ashamed for your flaws. I assure you; you have none. What did you want to speak of?" He was surely drained. His voice carried little inflection, as if each sentence was factual, but devoid of interest.

"I must...*eina*, a message arrived today from Bethaali." She paused for a moment, but when he had no reply she continued, "It may be there is some justification for our worry about another infestation by the thuell, for there they have seen it. The council intends to dispatch warriors and witchcrafters to excise it, though I cannot fathom any reason for my father to care what happens to the seeress. Since her exile so long ago I am disinclined to think his hatred of my sister has subsided, yet *Utan* Khurk insists that we will be reaching out to her."

"You must go," came the immediate reply.

She was startled by his assertion, especially considering what she had already shared with him about her father's plot to separate them.

"But we've so little time together. *Malpael,* I haven't seen Bethaali for all seasons, but you are my family now. I cannot just leave. My place out there has nothing to do with my ability and everything to do with moving me far from you and our home."

Capheif's voice warmed a little, but still sounded as if asleep.

"Perhaps, but he's snared himself with his own plot. Either he can suffer us here together or he can reunite you with the daughter he spurned and cast out; the sister he stole from you. You will be with great love either way. *Eina,* I already have this love to fill my heart. Has Bethaali any?"

Nepiur squeezed him tight and tried not to cry. He always seemed to know exactly what she needed, even when it wasn't what she wanted. A niggling feeling worried at the edge of her consciousness, but she could not seem to keep hold of it as her eyes drifted closed and she fell sleep.

"*Eihs rysha, utasa.* Thank you. All you say is true. I want to see her again as well. She deserves that."

Into beautiful dreams Nepiur drifted while, not an arm's reach away, another little Mearnum stood behind a wall hanging and leered down at her with a sickly smile and turgid eyes. Internally howling with laughter, Raphenie manipulated Capheif's words and more. One little trick was all it had taken. Without the fire striker Nepiur would never see the cracked mirror, the overturned table, scattered food and debris that evidenced Capheif's terrified struggle as she had come upon him. As she rose and he slept on she would leave none the wiser, hopefully gone for good if she met her end in the wild.

The little maiden had never known peace, but now she no longer obsessed over hearts she could save or the pleasures of love. Her power's sudden emergence had overwhelmed and engulfed her. She stood stooped in the darkness, grinning down at her victim, brushing his hair gently while his wife slept, blissfully ignorant, at his side.

"You will be mine," she whispered.

"You will be mine," hissed another voice beneath her own.

Thetrulengo speaks,

Perhaps Kulibreal's work on her sister's mind was not entirely ineffective. There is a force surrounding the youngest daughter of Miohaelia, something I do not fully understand, but it does not seem to be what ails her. It would seem the fractures Kulibreal created in her may have been a boon, allowing one part of Raphenie's mind to piece together her own stream of thoughts that eventually became a complete personality, apart from her true self. Young Raphenie was created from a fragment of her old mind but, as those cracks began to heal, something appears to have invaded that could not reach her before.

Once I hoped she would gain her man's affection. I am no longer certain I approve. I was so thrilled to have found this long-lost elder goddess but now – and I anticipate this is due to my predisposition that an elder god is no more than a mortal with a mouth larger than its heart – I want only to see her fail. Without question, there are many more repugnant creatures within and far below mortality, though not many as destructive as the soul I now see has risen in this dark virgin.

If my most unfortunate fears are correct, the descendants of the six stars may retain the traits of both of the gods from whom they descend. If the parent entities are not in harmony, then it is possible that their influences will fight for control. Oh, my heart, I draw courage from a new thought: Miohaelia was so gentle in her lifetime, unable or unwilling to protect herself from Zeniquorer's puerile hungers. Perhaps her child, having built her own mind from nothing, will be better able to fight back. There may yet be something of Raphenie to save, though to wake it she must resist.

~Chronicle of Wonders, an Unwanted Love

CHAPTER 20: THE EXPECTATION

The industry of the Mantichaena was tenfold what it had been in the early days when tools were made of stone and malleable metals, easily broken and difficult to repair. Their creativity had always been great and had led to enormous leaps in scientific and artistic knowledge. Conversely, with bodies now redesigned to smash, dig and cut like never before, they had entered a new era of constructive efficiency. Even with their tribe's diminished size they put the ingenuity of their brightest minds to the task of guiding the strength and size of individuals who equated whole divisions of laborers and were capable of completing an entire day's work before breakfast if properly employed. Tools had become a thing of the past for all but the most precise of tasks.

Under the direction of Tault Udai Maurus, the abilities of the Lugu were engaged to collect a heap of fallen thi from Ni'ivitnem at daybreak following the bet'hvaebeulg's arrival. Their stalks were lashed together by the fibers of their intertwining canopies to form a structure that would add a sense of grandeur the incipient public presents, as well as many more to come. At its completion, the buoyant construct was situated upon the river, wherein most of its weight was held aloft by the water while supports embedded in the banks served to hold it in place.

Always one to dramatize his speeches, this entire project was to provide a place for Sky to host assemblies where he would be far loftier and better heard by all, not just the few score that could fit into Nesh. It seemed to him fitting that he be above his fellows. A reminder to them of the right order of things.

The labors of Tault were complete, and so as Laesis passed over the city and began to roll off into the Tau they wiped sweat from their faces and sat to rest and marvel at their good work. The time of big words was drawing near, and others settled alongside them, anticipating something wonderful. Maurus and his crews refreshed themselves in the silken waters, were brought fresh delights from the orchards by doting lovers and altruistic citizens to help them regain their spirit after such heavy work. One by one they rose, invigorated, and melted into a growing crowd straddling both banks all around what had come to be called 'The Pyre'. The manner in which Maurus had coined it was comedic and spiteful, made to be an allusion to the joke he had made several times during the project: 'Another day wasted building that which, to an archon's discerning eye, is a testament to their own greatness. Meanwhile we that slaved at its invention see only a temporary tool of vanity that will be discarded in flame once its purpose is served. A proper reflection of every one of us in the eyes of a god! May every archon of Hauan Etain think so little of us, that we should go to dust at the end of our usefulness!'

Though he always followed this commentary with uproarious laughter and slaps across aching backs, the bitter tone in speaking it awakened resentment among Tault's earthmovers who recognized the truth of the futility of their work. Everything that often went unappreciated was built on their backs, almost always at Sky's command such that his grand works would be remembered forever. Regardless, they worked voraciously for the pride and exaltation not of the council but of Maurus, the leader to whom they truly owed allegiance and respect and who understood best the importance of one's duty regardless of personal feelings. Like others who directly influenced the activities of the halls, Maurus was considered an icon of Tault, more so than either of its political Patriarchs. They had the power, but he had strength of heart. Not unlike its partner hall of Gazan, this was what the Taultudaiam revered.

Such heat had already soaked into the ground that, at the first emergence of the archons from their domains, the dirt burned even hotter than the air. People crowded in what shade could be had, and those left in the light shifted awkwardly to spare their feet. many more stood close by the pyre in the river, and in several shallow places they were gathered in such numbers that some were forced shoulder deep into the water, floating freely at its center or tiptoeing on hidden boulders. It was clear that even the Primarch suffered from the extraordinary heat they had been cursed with, sweating profusely, though he had only just walked from Nesh to where the pyre was anchored between Voddace and Ms'egol.

The climate presented new challenges for the Primarch as he would give his address to them. Those in comfort and plenty were malleable. When times were hard, people could still see reason as long as they understood their situation. This was an anomaly, a freak heat wave uncharacteristic of the season that baked everyone's brain and made them impatient and demanding. He would have to redouble his charms if he was to be persuasive.

Sky drew Artimecian close as they approached the base of the platform, delaying the short climb to confer secretively before leading the council upward. Gripping his servant's clothing he hastily demanded information.

"Was Mani not informed of this? I should think the master of the academy would be inclined to attend so public an address."

Artimecian sensed his ire and knew his answer would not satisfy.

"I could not attain him, father. One of his girls came to me and, with a frightful air of concern, revealed him to be gravely ill. I went myself and found him sitting on the floor, limp."

"Sitting? At the floor, and without any words of his own?"

"Only utterances, and those were senseless. I fear he has a fever, or some other malady that addles the mind. He wasn't himself. He looked as though he had risen from the grave, cold and squalid."

"God's blood. If true, then what a fever indeed," Sky replied, considering. "If it is so, I can forgive a single absence."

"You are a benevolent man, Primarch," Artimecian muttered halfheartedly.

"I very much am."

As they parted, Sky made the fairly easy journey up the steep but even alignment of logs that acted as a crude stair. His archons followed, falling into rank behind him. He was momentarily caught off guard at the sight of the dark-hooded woman who had brought them the messenger of Aes'bethil. Though he could not see her eyes he could surely feel them. She was watching him with an uncomfortable intensity. With some effort he turned away to address the people. Her intrusive stare was of little consequence right now, though the reason for her presence both in his city and these proceedings preyed on his mind.

Sky sought in all things to resolve conflicts – at least those that would not benefit him – by exposing them in a public setting, thereby limiting variance in their interpretation by the commonfolk. With this in mind, he opened his address by raising both hands for attention and gathering all his pomp.

"Friends! Countrymen! Beautiful families which, together as one, have made our city the vision of the new life we always dreamed of; I welcome you to a brand-new day for our land and its colonies!" He paused for a moment as a few quiet cheers came from those who were perhaps too fond of his leadership. "For those of you who've not heard, we have with us a man of Aes'bethil town. Crippled by the dangers of Ni'ivitnem we of the high Gate have learned to master, this man of the exiled houses has come to us, asking that we would extend to them a branch of kindness. My eldest daughter has, in her departure from our furthest borders, unknowingly led her followers to harm. This man returned from her brings word that their community is under attack by a vile creature of old, and perhaps of a form we've not yet encountered. Disregard all you have heard and know only the truth, for it may be that which we have long feared: the thuell have emerged once more." He silently congratulated himself, for what followed was not panic but a rapt silence that hung on his every word. How masterfully he could adjure others to calm while speaking words that should bring fear. "I will not deny it, because I do not fear it! Will you? Will anyone ever again? I say you NO! To you and this man, beset by the dark thuell that dares to threaten us again, I instead make challenge! Let the monster rise! Commanding the fires of in the inworld we are ready for it, and we are not afraid!"

The crowd fed off his energy, swept up into a blind sense of superiority. Aroch closed his eyes and marveled. He may not have liked it, but he had to admit Sky was a natural with words. Even if he spoke wrongly, anyone who heard him seemed to fall in line, full of faith.

"For the thuell," Sky dropped his voice dramatically, building in intensity as he continued, "We, your *utam kaiba*, have prepared a special welcome: A force of flesh from every hall – wanderers, warriors and witchcrafter – not to drive away this feculent thing but to send it screaming into Vaeba! Your Primarch has assembled a force by whose presence the colony of Aes'bethil will be made safe and the denizens of disease reminded that it is Mantichaena who rule this land!"

At last, he had the crowd and stirred their ardour, though a few skeptics remained as he raved on. One of these was Lemalie, who sat arm in arm with her companion, the Kutuaiat Miriena, under the shade of an amphiraed thi and hissed disdainfully to her.

"*Enta Aia*, 'made safe' until they realize that this is only to prove that his daughter and her people remain under his control and survive only by his clemency, even in exile."

Miriena huffed in concurrence, jostling Lemalie to soften the mood while verbally hardening it.

"Such is the path of a man who thinks himself a godlike, walking with such heavy footsteps that the flowers either side are choked by the dust he raises."

"*La*, but flowers are watered from the ground beneath, not the dust above. Despots never truly change their people. Our strength comes from one another, not him."

Allende was close at hand, leaning against the rock by Miriena's other side and added his own input to the analogy.

"But a phototroph needs the light, *la*? Enough dust billows and the water will not make a difference."

Miriena shushed him, still sensitive to Lemalie's displeasure at his prior advertisement of Keimas' experience in the forsaken temple. But Lemalie was fully capable of defending herself and could not resist chiding Allende for his part in starting rumors of Keimas.

"*Minein*, he's right. Our struggle is already begun regardless of whatever *mintazet* may have aided our opposition by wagging his tongue to any who would listen. He raises an excellent point; who is our light? If Sky were to fall from power, which of the council would take his place? Is Nepiur ready for it?"

Allende's pride moldered in silence as Miriena responded.

"Surely he's taken precaution against the opportunity. I have it on good authority that she is part of this scheme. He sends her away when doubt of his rule is mounting. This venture into the wilds coincides conveniently with your little rebellion, don't you think? But then, what of your father?"

"Not while Artimecian remains. The architect of the Iron Sanctum will never cast his lot so," Lemalie reminded them. "He has far too much power at his and only his disposal."

"Would he cast for any but himself?"

"None but Sky, more like. People adore Sky, but they fear Artimecian. Even my father is wary of crossing him. He knows he could never be elected fairly, but whoever has his support is not likely to be defied."

"Perhaps only by the most courageous among us," Miriena reassured her. "Pitiful," she then spat, "When rightness dangles at the end of a string by a self-impressed puppeteer and his pet witchcrafter."

On the pyre, Aroch's eyes flitted back and forth, pretending to attend Sky's audacious speech while secretly watching his daughter. She seemed lighter, perhaps happier. At least now she opted to venture out and be with her friends. It was more than she had done for him since Keimas' departure, but he knew that a father's love was oft taken for granted. For her, it was unnecessary to offer it until she had been long enough without it that need compelled her to draw near him again. He could wait. She would seek him again, he would smile, she would laugh, they would reassure one another that Keimas would return safely, and life would be bright again. For the moment she needed the support of her close friends.

Sky's climax caught Aroch off guard as his wandering mind was pulled back.

"...Under the supervision of Nesh's defensive strategist, Nesh *Utan* Aroch." the Primarch finished.

With an artificial smile and very real confidence, Aroch took Sky's place at the forefront of the pyre and began his heavily rehearsed account of the council's selections for the venture, continually turning about so that all could hear, except when indicating particular persons chosen. Of these distinguished men and women only Nepiur was aware that she would be part of the delegation. The rest had been told only to attend and had been given no warning of their impending charge. As Aroch claimed the crowd's focus he was grateful Lemalie's came with it, relished the momentary meeting of eyes as though it was a private and meaningful conversation with her, then pressed onward.

"As the Primarch explained, our detachment will include a multifaceted group of individuals, all of whom will be essential to the mission. First among these is a woman whose qualification requires no introduction, though we take this opportunity to finally grant her the mantle of Matriarch. As a wise and respected ambassador for the Council of Archons, proven to be of sound judgement and great understanding, she shall be our voice across Ni'ivitnem. The newly appointed mother of the council and fifth archon of Nesh: I give you Nesh Aiatan Nepiur, Matriarch!"

Nepiur stepped up onto a rock, whose occupants quickly vacated so she could present herself to the council and public.

"Primarch, to serve the Gate I do go as your voice." She responded assertively.

Aroch continued, competing with rising and falling waves of praise after each name was listed.

"Secondly, due to the likelihood of a thuell threat, we have elected to send out two of our witchcrafters who have demonstrated that they are more than a match for this disease! As the agents of the Iron Sanctum's extreme power, we acknowledge Ms'egol Udai Rashala and Ms'egol Aia Ronsha, the Iron Rain!"

The husband and wife, both Kulo, climbed up from the crowd to land atop a low ledge beside Voddace's door and loosed an ear-splitting shout.

"Primarch, to serve the gate, we do go as your fire! IRON RAIN!"

The pair's friends and family, long apart during their seasons of training, went wild over the unexpected appearance. Ronsha and her man Rashala showed their gratitude and excitement by whooping to the sky and throwing bolts of lightning up from their fingers into the cliffs. Aroch waited for the display to subside before continuing, starting to enjoy himself as he played to the thrill of the crowd.

"Adding his unsurpassed strength to these mighty gothics that he might preserve and protect their company; I give you the son of stone and keeper of Tault's underworld: Tault Udai Maurus!"

Maurus vaulted up alongside Nepiur, much to her surprise, and threw his long shoulder claws up in salute to Aroch, though his voice saluted Sky.

"Primarch, to serve the Gate, I do go as your strength!"

"To defend against any foe," Aroch continued, now enthused by the drama, "We announce one who is whispered of in terror at the tables of Gazan. An awesome force even to the archons who handcrafted him in the arena. Born into battle, his given name became the one he earned: 'Smash'! The bonebreaker! Gazan Udai Dace!"

The ground nearby vibrated as the enormous Bakul shifted from all-fours onto his hind legs and stood to his full height, dwarfing the Kubernu around him. Long spikes thrust out all across his back, limbs and the sides of his thick, smiling face.

"Haaah! Primarch, I do go to kill many things!" He cheered comically.

"Indeed," Aroch muttered at the informal response. "Lastly, to guide our envoy through the treacherous wilderness, we require the one who has led the discovery of nearly all the western lands we know, rendered nearly every map we possess of the borderlands and beyond; adventurer of old who inhabited Manti and wandered its endless hills even before our arrival. Master scribe of the academy, Ms'egol Udai Haxelinopsis!"

There was a somewhat less exuberant reaction to this news, more a tangle of confusion and some laughter. Dace, known to be one of the few friends the scribe possessed, became the center of attention as he lifted Haxelinopsis' limp Boroo body from the ground by his tail. Tattered clothing fell across the rumpled fuzz on his face and a half-empty jug of wine slipped out of his unconscious grip to clink on the ground as Dace replied on his behalf.

"*Laan*, Primarch," he shouted, "As *uta* Hax does carry your will, so do I carry him! Bahahaha!" Dace turned a full circle, his great guffaws silencing the crowd's jeering but not their incredulity.

The council as a whole gestured its annoyance and took a brief aside to murmur among itself, insulted by the disregard that Hax's semi-permanent inebriation represented. Dace shrugged and grinned unapologetically amid raucous scorning at the expense of his Boroo, and Sky hastened to move on from the undignified lapse, taking Aroch's place over the masses to conclude.

"Your Primarch has ordained that these messengers of peace will depart on the coming dawn, providing security to the colony of Aes'bethil and a renewed bond between our two peoples. Give your utmost praise to these chosen ones, for they endure the trials of a journey never before undertaken! In great Loi's name, let Mantichaena prove their divine right to rule this land! Blessings of Nhi'Thaun be ours! All glory to Hanging Gate!"

The crowd cheered proudly, riotous as they thronged to congratulate the caravan's membership.

The council conferred amongst themselves briefly, until a tremendous shout rang out over the crowd, abruptly interrupting the revelry and replacing it with uncomfortable silence.

"WHAT ABOUT KEIMAS!?"

As Sky had anticipated, there was some worry among the citizenry that rumor would coax to a blaze. A situation he was prepared to use. However, this was a bit more extreme than what he had anticipated and made less manageable by a wave of grumpy agreeance resounding along the river. He kept his poise and raised his hands to silence them, scanning angrily for the source of the outcry.

"*Prostas*, steady yourselves! Be certain that Patriarch Artimecian's Iron Wind is engaged…"

"Has BEEN engaged for two days!" rose a swift retort.

This was a new voice, and more were rising in quick succession from those less acquiescent to Sky's charisma.

"*La*! What is happening out there?" came another cry.

"Father Artimecian told me himself, *Utan* Keimas is a *vaena* apostate!" came another.

"Just as I heard it, that! Thuell don't possess, they burn! Why are we sending out warriors beyond the very place where a hunter-killer was taken by a demon!"

"Why send anyone!? Who knows if the Iron Rain can even kill

such a thing!"

"*La aia*! We should be protecting our OWN city!"

One after another, voices raised their fears and suspicions until it devolved into a cacophony of demands and accusations, both for and against the departure of the caravan.

Lemalie's blood boiled at the implications of the protest, especially knowing who was behind it all. The target of her antipathy, Artimecian, mounted the platform at Sky's side and demanded attendance, shouting above the din.

"Do not let your fears be misplaced! It is not some legion of ghosts and demons that trouble us, but one man whose corrupt and undisciplined mind has been opened to the influence of dark denizens! Soon he will cease to be a danger to you!"

As he strutted and built his case, Lemalie was quite literally breathing steam, infuriated by the defamation of her husband. Miriena held her fast, adjuring her to remain calm as nearby citizens in turn either sneered condemningly at her or gazed in heartfelt pity. More than having him beside her to defend himself she longed to utter just one word on his behalf. He was a lord among them whom none had the right to demean. What surprised her most was the lack of support from Miriena and Allende. Even Govan, Keimas' teacher who knew and loved the man almost as much as Lemalie herself. All three stood in frustrated silence.

The mood of the crowd was abruptly changed when a young girl's startled voice pealed, "*Bethe*! Look at the stars!"

Voices quieted gradually as everyone looked up into the deep sky, where the Nhi'Thaun shone brightly. They were disorderly; one of their great and prophetic stars had fallen closer to earthplane several seasons before it's time.

"It's...impossible," Nepiur murmured in disbelief. "The Bone Star...how has it come so soon?"

"It's an omen!" an enchanter decreed. "The Bone comes now, in the advent of Longhand! It brings the heat that burns us!"

"Udai, this is a sign! What if you are wrong?" someone loudly postulated to Artimecian. "Could it have been a godly spirit that possessed Keimas?"

Voices erupted again in speculation and a plentitude of absurdities. Some suggested the unprecedented sign meant redemption for their people, that one of them had been chosen by a god, while others believed it was a sign of futility and the displeasure of the stars.

Lemalie stood, unable to suffer any more of this idiocy. Striking her heel down she dominated the unruly mob.

"Stop this, NOW! Am I surrounded by a herd of beasts without the sense to trust their own eyes and hearts over their imaginations?" Silence resumed as all eyes turned to face her. "You have more faith in children's tales of gods in the stars than a friend you've lived your whole lives with!" she accused. "One who has served as your protector, fed you and watched over you since we first set foot on these stones! Neither god nor ghost nor demon resides within Keimas but the soul of a man who cares for nothing but a safe tomorrow and long life for each and every one of you. Any allegations to the contrary are idle gossip."

Allende's conscience took a much deserved and well-struck blow when she met his eyes with an admonishing finger. She turned and directed it then between Sky's scheming eyes, venting her ire with carefully chosen words.

"Gossip proliferated in salacious lies concocted by a Primarch who would rather see my entire family, indeed ALL families who would dare question him, torn apart by the very people who once called us countrymen and honorable Mantichaena!"

Sky was taken aback. Though he anticipated revolt from Aroch's brood it was madness for them to show their hand so brazenly. He whirled towards Aroch, whose face-splitting grin and loving eyes deviated from his daughter just long enough to savor Sky's expression, his calm more devastating to his own than anything else. With trembling jowls and clenched fists squeezing their own flesh white, Sky's skin then crawled when he realized there was no mass protest against Lemalie's accusation. No one had ever spoken so disrespectfully to him, and yet there was no voice in his defense as there should have been. The crowd stood silently before him as if anticipating his response, or perhaps eager to see him talk his way around it. By sheer force of will Sky suppressed his outrage and gave her an acknowledging nod before reassuming composure.

"Perhaps we have all been taken by hysteria in this debilitating heat." He tried for a lightly mocking tone. "It's clear that at least one poor and especially anxious girl has nearly lost her mind, *la*?"

He feigned indifference, like an aloof parent at a child's meaningless tantrum, "Let us be tranquil and not war among ourselves over things that we mortals cannot foresee. What is important now is what is most at risk; our children, our brothers and sisters in Aes'bethil. They are in danger without the aid of our tribe's strongest, and we are not so cruel as to deny them protection so that we may remain comfortable, cowering behind our walls as some would suggest!"

Lemalie looked on with disgust as he continued to manipulate the crowd with his smooth machinations but was moved not to escalate the conflict after what she saw around her; his trite words of a greater good had a greatly reduced impact, the majority of listeners no longer allowing themselves to be mollified. Whether they believed him or not, many were beginning to lose interest in watching fights break out. They mostly began to disperse, some to pout, others to congratulate Nepiur and her party members. Too many of them were not paying attention to Sky any longer. It was clear his command presence no longer interested them, and he could not abide it. Still, he droned on, louder and more erratic, desperately trying to keep attention on him until, finally, he stopped mid-sentence and stood in silence. Face frozen to hide his rage, Sky turned and demanded in hoarse mutterings that the entire council convene for an emergency session. Aroch knew punishment was coming but his fool's smile persisted. His heart swelled with pride in his daughter. Whatever else had happened, he felt security in that Lemalie's show of force met no resistance. At last, they were heard, and once in the minds of the people their voice would remain. Sky was no longer all-powerful. The faith of all had been shaken by hardship, which served Aroch's family for now, but they must take care and treat the multitudes delicately. The cycle of the stars being in upheaval was a frightening notion even to him. While there was nothing to be done about it, it was another aspect of fear that needed to be kept in control.

After a verbal thrashing which persisted so long that Sky's throat had gone dry, his tireless stomping around the council chamber ended with his face thrust up against Aroch's with a decisive threat.

"I swear on Loi's name," he fumed, face vermillion, "If I EVER again hear such treasonous words out of any member of your family you will all be exiles! I will make the lot of you *gal'tskhain* of such revulsion that even Naguza will not harbor you!"

Aroch absorbed Sky's words as readily as iron absorbed rain, blankly staring at the Primarch's forehead until the foul and caustic breath on his face abated. He grumbled some submissive phrase to pacify Sky but there would be no convincing him that he would fall in line. He was not surprised by Sky's final words, though they shook the other council members to their cores.

"Nesh *Utan* Aroch, as of this day you are stripped of your title of Patriarch and your authority as an archon of my table. Leave these proceedings and return to your simple life."

Instantly and passively, Aroch walked without argument from the room. In passing through the door, he left the council with a quiet reminder to those trapped under Sky's heel of how their order was supposed to function:

"If that is the will of this council, then let it be."

It felt surreal to be walking down that corridor for the last time after so many seasons of fighting for justice and equity for the city, but in truth he was amenable to the decision. The obvious corruption of the city's governance had been growing for longer than he could bear, and now he was positioned to create the greatest change of all, especially now that he had no obligation to that table or its occupants. However, he did feel a great vindication at hearing his fellow archons protest his dismissal in such volume that even behind closed door and many steps down the hall he could still clearly identify the voices: Novun, Liklita, Saketsu, Mabistu, Sebashni and Mani. They would certainly be silenced, but not before they had their say. All told, it was a victory to know that Lemalie's rebellion had given the archons, and perhaps other voices throughout the city, the courage to speak up.

Stepping out onto the top of the north stair of the atrium, he peered down and saw his girl coming through the outermost doors, surrounded by many old friends and some new ones. She felt his eyes on her and in meeting them began to weep uncontrollably as she raced toward him. He descended to meet her, calming her as their supporters gathered to them. She begged him to forgive her thoughtlessness, apologized for exposing them to attack but he quieted her with a finger and pleasant smile.

"*Quo kalib pertai*, my wonderful, courageous daughter. You did what you were entirely in the right to do. It seems the time for pretenses has come to an end, as has my need to feign loyalty to our oppressor."

The entourage were taken aback by his comment, particularly when coupled with their own observation that he was alone in exiting the council chambers. Lemalie, of course, noticed as well.

"Father...he could not have..." She complained.

"Indeed, he has. My time with the council was certain to end, though not without a boon to us. Opposition of the decision was not absent at the table and now we know whom we can trust among the archons."

"In no way a proper payment by fate or law! Both are coldly insufficient for what you are owed!" Lemalie argued. Still, her father seemed completely at peace.

"I am owed by law only what I have been given, owed by fate only what I take from it forcibly. The latter you and I will do together."

"This is an outrage!" cried one Kubernu, and soon all of those who followed Lemalie joined the furor.

"Unacceptable!"

"Let any other archon be called poor of character before you!"

Aroch felt many hands on his shoulders, and silently acknowledged the faithfulness of these few brave souls. His eye caught one among them whose face he loved as dearly as Keimas', like a son never born. While the rest of the caravan prepared for their task, Maurus remained in defiance, fiercely devoted to his brother and the family who stood by him.

"Good Aroch, consider me your left hand to the end," he said. "I'll not listen to such lies about my own brother, whose good spirit is as the blood in my own veins."

Lemalie put her arms around Maurus and kissed his cheek gratefully, as Aroch queried, "Maurus! Not abandoning the new Matriarch's party are you?"

"In part, *Utan*. My body will go where it must, but my heart and its prayers are bound to you here. Mother Nepiur knows I am here. She sends reassurances that you are not alone, and gratitude to Lemalie for her bravery."

Aroch took his hand appreciatively.

"Thank you, friend. I promise you, when Keimas returns it will not be to the Primarch's retribution. Do your work for our Aes'bethil and we will do ours for your brother."

Maurus nodded with a resolute grimace and departed.

The calm had finally broken. The storm was imminent, and the stage set for any number of underlying struggles within the council to break out. Whether in acquiescence to Sky's will or retaliation against it, each archon had no choice but to choose where they stood now, and each battle had to be carefully waged for the war to be won. Aroch pondered the situation as others around him discussed it. His principal concern was to anticipate the time when all conflicts would be made public. The Primarch's regime had suffered a blow, but it would not be easily overthrown. With Artimecian and the Iron Sanctum at his command, Sky could do irrevocable harm if pushed too far too suddenly. His need for control would become a terrible vengeance. The only way to defeat him was to take away his power, take away his followers, leave him with nothing to rule. Someone like Sky could always claw their way to the top as long as they had one powerful servant. Artimecian was his greatest asset, and only by stripping him of that asset could they strike the final blow.

Aroch's eye caught movement on the wall, a deghni that darted around vying for his attention. With a quick smile, as though he had glimpsed an old friend, Aroch excused himself and hurried out of Nesh. He swerved to avoid running into the towering presence of Capheif, nearly trampled young Raphenie on his way out the door. He apologized, though neither paid him any regard. Had he not been in such a rush he would have considered it strange how Raphenie walked so closely beside Capheif, holding his arm and guiding him to his chambers. Perhaps he was ill, for he certainly looked it.

Breaking into a jog, Aroch covered ground quickly and circled around to the foot of the Dhai cliffs. With a flying leap he sank his claws into the rock and scrambled upward with strength borne of renewed hope. At last, Naguza had news for him.

CHAPTER 21: NOT A DEMON

Thetrulengo speaks,

T he Galaila had worshipped the starry sky because of their god, the 'omnipotent' Ephielipax, whom they had known only in visages of wood and stone, carved by their ancestors and enduring beyond the generation that witnessed his birth and rise. He disappeared almost as suddenly as the war ended, and as time led the Galaila away from memories of their true father and unto the worship of his wicked son, they eventually forgot the great collapse when all elder gods had fallen to their shining graves. The mortals' holy scriptures taught that, in his life, Ephielipax was enthroned in the highest place above the clouds and among the Nhi'Thaun. Their religion optimistically dictates that every soul becomes a star when it dies, and by blind happenstance their faith intersects with truth. The dead indeed become the stars, each one of them a soul that lights the darkness as it ascends homeward.

Loi was considered chief among those stars as he occupied his father's throne, and as a figurehead in their faith they were convinced he was responsible for that from which they sprang; the spirit world they call the Veil. They were ignorant that their true creators were already dead. In fact, Ellel was only of interest to

Loi because it was the place of his birth, and he believed it was his by right. Galaila of this new era were so long without the direct influence of their godking or any other that they became lethargic and domesticated, forgetting their barbaric past. None but an immortal would remember that they were first given form by Ephielipax for the sole purpose of conquest. They were bred as an army to smite the unbeliever and subjugate the weak. Now they are blind animals who have forgotten what they once were or even what gods they had served and opposed. Their only faith in the elder gods now comes from fanciful stories, pabulum that benevolent Loi will forever judge them from on high. But Loi is unpredictable, devious and dangerous, acting so violently and erratically that even I cannot guess at any motive other than unending dominance. He has a plan for this world. One that begins here, now, with a Vulgoli whose favor he owns.

~Chronicle of Wonders, Enemy of Achievement

Above the mountains and the higher earthplane, very near where the surface of the ether undulated and entirely obscured by the dust and daylight that blind mortal eyes there hung an otherworldly construct of the most glorious beginnings. White as the clouds its every surface, it was strong as marble, for the luminous energies that composed it were so dense and pure that they did not permit any physical matter or vision to pass. The result was a sparkling structure of no practical shape. It was silken yet jagged, like a snowflake, with hundreds of splintering branches of solid light projecting outward around it. The only surface that was not obscured by these extremities was perfectly smooth, featureless. There was no door, window or any other opening or marking, though an immaculate stairway protruded beneath it and descended a few hundred feet into the open sky before fading into nothing. It was of a broad and shallow grade as if it were meant to host ceremony, but rarely had anything walked upon it.

To an observer it would appear little more than another stay, so high as it was. Even some gods had failed to take notice of it. In the first era, when a shining messenger visited Ephielipax and urged him to peace, it had warned of this place. While trying to teach the blue god the virtues of peace and unity it alluded to the star as the source of divine providence and called it only 'Home'. Ephielipax was so taken by the being's beauty and sublimity that he succumbed to its words, and therefore swore to uphold this pursuit of peace. The messenger departed and Ephielipax called out for its name, but when it did not answer he called it 'Angel'.

The marvelous fortress was not meant for any creature born of Maengir and so word was passed that the living gods must never go near it. This great mandate died with Ephielipax. Like so much of the early ages, though priests had recorded the words of their gods, mandate became legend, and legend became idle story. Now, deeply buried under an eon of dirt and decay and the ruins of Ellel only forgotten stone tablets remain containing this scripture. For many lifetimes these were the only surviving objects in all of Maengir where the star's name was enscribed in any language: 'Ax'lahantskinam Yerhemanit'dahnik - House of the Living Sky'.

For uncountable days the steps before the open face of the fortress had been barren, ghostly and still as the air surrounding them, silently waiting. However, something had changed when Ferraro fell and Ellel met its end. For the last sixty seasons the hallowed stair had an occupant, something unclean, a mortal enemy of the House's designers; a creature that had touched the real treasures within and pined to have them again. This lone entity, a man of sorts, knelt before the immaculate and shimmering walls of the House, constant, needing neither sleep nor food nor drink. Peering deep into the world, he meditated, with knees folded beneath him and arms tucked tightly to his sides. His fingers were extended, coal-black claws twitching as he dreamed waking dreams. His long and perforated ears were buried in a mass of bloody crimson hair that hung in long, unkempt knots. Unlike most of the Mantichaena on the island far beneath it did not cover his body, instead confined to his backbone, down his arms to the elbow, the backs of his legs and across hunched shoulders. His tail lay limply on the floor behind him, twice longer than his height and splitting every few feet like a forked whip into five independent tips, each hiding a retractable spine. His skin was hard and decorated with self-applied scars sliced deep and rubbed with ash, creating indecipherable images of pain all across his sinewy and emaciated body.

It was time. His arms twitched and extended as he slowly

emerged from his trance. His mouth dropped open to reveal a curved row of fangs that dripped a reeking black scum. His eyelids opened painfully to reveal gruesome, colorless pupils reminiscent of fabric that began to tear when stretched too far. Such eyes opened across his whole body, each as loathsome as the last, covering his arms and chest. Including the two blinking beneath his troubled brow they were twenty-three in all. On beastly feet as lethally armed as his hands he stood and turned in a single motion, trudging with somber purpose to the iridescent wall. He cleared his throat to speak, shaking off the long period of immobilizing numbness. His speech was slurred, tongue raking the dangerous fangs and occasionally drooling on himself amid poorly articulated words.

"Success. He is coming now," he said directly. "Will all unfold as you wish?"

The walls vibrated and a winding shower of light coursed from inside the stone to form symbols of the creature's own language. They would appear, swim briefly aside, then disappear one after the other.

Make ready.
Erase worry from mind.
If Golgamet fails.
Tzychala must kill man.

"Yes…I understand," the monster replied.

How long.

"He has almost reached the shrine. I have visited your prophet's servant and commanded her to send a guide to bring the man before Golgamet." He hesitated a moment. Then with a perplexed voice, asked *"Bsstore*, I am curious; was it necessary to deceive him so? I could have dragged him through the Veil myself. Time is short."

Man must decide.
Man must choose.
Man must believe.

"Are you certain he is the one you want? His soul is not clean. He has the eyes of a man weighed by sin."

This makes Loi.
Want him more.
Exile doubt.

Tzychala has no soul.

To judge man.

"Rethink speaking down to me, fallen *Jiou*," the eyebeast retorted. "What service I offer you is payment, not gift."

The subtle threat hung in silence for a moment and the air around him thrummed. He had sufficient time to consider his own wisdom in provoking a god before words again glowed on the face of the monolith.

Loi is grateful.

Fulfill promise.

Loi will fulfill his.

"I will, to its completion."

Despite his brief bluster, the monster knew that intemperate words here could prove fatal and were of no aid to his goal.

"What leads you to think this man will give up his soul to you?"

Love.

"Does...does it really incite such obedience?" he could not help but ask.

Do not underestimate.

What harm one brings.

When afflicted by it.

Coupled with ignorance.

In the case of.

Loi's father and.

This man.

"We will see." The creature retreated down the steps. "For now, you wait."

Despite all his many eyes, the creature did not look to see if words followed. He instead peered down from his perch to the island of Manti in all its dreadful tedium. With a hissing sigh he leaned forward, tipped from the edge and fell to freefall from the ethereal temple toward earthplane. For the first time since before the stars were born, he would touch the warm flesh of this delicious world.

Thetrulengo speaks,

Shackled gal, bonds their own, let them weep and bleed.
Their punishment is meant to last, and death would set them free.
Watch them suffer, watch them writhe, too shameful for the stocks.
Still, they dance and smile, singing praise for chains and locks.

Shackled gods, cursed are they, trapped inside their seed.
Their punishment is meant to last, impossible to free.
Suffering, their tears are bread wrought from bitter grain.
Feasted on by afterlings empowered by their pain.

I have never tried my hand at poetry before. I don't enjoy it as much as I thought I would. At the very least I'm becoming more capable as a wordsmith. It's taken me a long time to try it, but I'm glad I did. The measure seems a little...I don't remember how they describe it. No matter.

I'm listening to the stories of the old folk here and comparing them. In leafing through all their books and repeating their words I begin to understand how they view their past. They are like me, unable to perfectly recall every detail of their experiences, and so over time the truth changes. What I have found to be uniform throughout is that they are blissfully unaware of the laws set by the elder gods at the end of their great conflict, particularly so of the involvement of the one the Mantichaena fear and despise the most: Ferraro, the gol'itkaia of unknown heritage. Half mortal and half goddess, she was holder of all things subterranean, the fire and cave and darkness which men of the open air and field have largely dreaded.

On Ellel, the existence of the gods had never been questioned or considered anything but common knowledge, even after they all disappeared, and no proof remained of them. The idea that their deity would one day reemerge was a frequent topic for a very long time, but he never did. Generations grew and withered as Ellel became a garden of man's great accomplishments, and over time it seemed that the almighty Loi was no longer needed. Some abandoned his worship altogether. Many began to dismiss him as archaic nonsense and some turned their worship to their own sciences. That is, until the day of the fall, when all faiths were renewed by the loss of the culture where Galaila worshipped their own invention. Not surprisingly, the remnants of Ellel now seem to be returning to that way.

It can be understood, knowing how easily mortality is frightened, that when Ferraro appeared on Ellel they believed she was the great destroyer come to slash and burn. Without warning, wave after wave of undulating flames billowed across the inland regions as Ferraro fell from the sky and throughout the island the ground cracked and vomited molten stone from her wrath. The Galaila looked on her and knew their time there was ended. Some fled to the coast and boarded as many ships as could hold them, others seized their fate in their own hands and, instead of waiting for their god, took up arms and challenged the goddess' power with their own. There were many thousands of deaths, hundreds of thousands, but it was not the day of reckoning the Galaila's legends foretold.

Since time immemorial they had been taught that Loi was to be adored and Ferraro to be feared. The appearance of flame and quake incited great fear of Ferraro, unaware as they were that the inferno in which their world perished was not born of Ferraro's anger but from her dying body. A demigoddess fell dead on their home and her explosive demise wreaked havoc on the land.

What those that would one day become Mantichaena do not know, likely will never understand, is that Loi had been there as well. High above, he had looked down on the Jioukhaadi he had inherited and done nothing to save it, for it was he who cast Ferraro down. She had chased him there, to the steps of the House of The Living Sky, fought him in hopes of protecting the Galaila where he sought to enslave them. The destruction unleashed on Ellel had not been her intent. She loved the Galaila just as their creator did, as much as she loved her own offspring.

The heart of Ellel is now a crater that reaches nearly to the bottom of the island. There is nothing left of poor Ferraro, for the earthplane was so distraught at her death that it crumbled in despondency.

All this was because of the House. When Ephielipax told of its presence and the message delivered by the angel he only stirred up more contention among the gods. They yearned to know what power abided inside this marvelous star. Ephielipax knew how *dangerous it was and when Quetzuaul slew him she gained not only his power but also his memories, and thence when Loi devoured her in turn those memories were passed on to him. The young god who murdered his mother was beset by Kulibreal and Ferraro, a united force that threatened to destroy him if he did not agree to abandon the world-consuming conquests of his parentage, though they did not know that he was privy to the secrets of the angel's home. Loi refused. He vowed to bring the Galaila back under the heel of his father's legacy and thereafter to take control of his mother's Hischates, a united nation that would make all Maengir his own. First, there was something else he desired. Through his mother's flesh he knew the way into the forbidden House. As he made his bid for it, Ferraro saw his flight only as the beginning of his war, departed from her own homeland of Apos to put an end to him once and for all. I suspect she knew she would fail, not because her power was lacking but because Kulibreal did not come to her aid as she had promised. Kulibreal of the sea had watched and waited for the outcome, believing that if Ferraro failed there would be no danger to herself or her mother's Balathide kinfolk in their deep Njaghaadi Nemahn. Cowardly, yes, but also shrewd.*

Poor Ferraro's sacrifice was needless. Just as no god or mortal knew for what purpose the House of the Living Sky was first created, they likewise did not know the law which governed that purpose, as set forth by Az'Rech himself:

Only one may abide within to divide what must be apart.

For the one set inside there will be no freedom.

Should a second seek the light, they may only enter through the dark.

If the second does find the light, the first shall not remain.

And there, into the annals of legend, goes the great secret. The House of the Living Sky is a trap the likes of which no creature imaginable, be it of light or flesh, could ever escape. Loi could not understand what his greed for power would set in motion or how doomed to failure he was. Now, the soul that suffered inside from the very beginning kneels before it and weeps, for it never wanted to be free. Loi weeps as well, for he has taken its place. The first is

Tzychala, the Vulgoli called 'Brother Bone', son of eyes, and middling child of Escharka the Manyflesh. Now he walks free, hidden from all sight but my own, even from his own siblings it would seem.

~Chronicle of Wonders, The Missing Piece

CHAPTER 22: HALLOWED GROUND

Keimas' wings trembled from the cold, ached from the dust collecting between his feathers. After a night trudging through the vast wasteland of Thonsfa, his talons and plumage drug through the sand behind him. His energy continued to wane no matter how often he demanded water from the skin strapped across his guide's back. Though he knew deep within that he must press on, the voice of reason chastised him constantly for being out here. There were too many unanswered questions. This man before him was a Mearnum, something that could only have been created on Manti, yet he arrived after the thuell had burned this place. He must have been taken by sumear to become Mearnum and if sumear lived then there was still edible foliage. How many others had come with him? How were they sustaining themselves?

That question was answered, and Keimas' assertions proven wrong when the man stooped to take sand from the ground, putting it to his mouth and swallowing. A Mearnum that ate the ground? Keimas' mind and stomach turned at the thought, but he was intrigued. Lugu could consume certain minerals from the ground and Bakul ate whole rocks to grow their armor. Perhaps these Mantichaena were not limited to one breed. Perhaps the influence of Anama did not facilitate only a single bond but many, however a Mantichaena's environment demanded.

Conversation was minimal as the Mearnum trundled onward with alacrity through the rocky dunes, without ever turning his head to see if the Kutu followed. Keimas was winded from trying to keep up, taking brief but painful flights every so often to give his ill-suited legs a rest. His guide had revealed little of who he was, except that his name was Hopi, that somewhere out here there was a nameless settlement and somewhere within was cloistered a seer.

"Overall unimpressive disclosure," Keimas grumbled to himself, "After a night's travel." Yet, here he found himself, gliding across a forbidden wasteland in the tow of the most abstract person he had ever encountered and bound for a city he began to suspect did not exist.

It was the last breath of night before dawn and the pace had been increasing steadily, stretching Keimas' endurance to the limit.

"*Ein, udai*, why so hurried?" he complained.

After a night of few short, brusque answers, his companion suddenly became more garrulous as together they crested a rock formation overlooking a great depression almost as broad as Voddace and Ms'egol combined. It was empty, nothing but a pool of sand.

"Mmm...worry'm no more, wing'm friend. We'm arrive!" Hopi slid down the steep fringe of the valley as Keimas landed on the stone he had abandoned, exasperated. He should have known he was led on by a zet'itka, a halfwit. If there was a home here it was likely a pitiful barrow with a scrap of cloth for a door and piles of sticks littering the floor that this man's isolation had convinced him were friends and family. For a moment Keimas suspected Hopi had not landed late, but had survived the carnage of the thuell, his mind broken from the trauma. It was deeply saddening to see Hopi racing down the hill toward nothing but sand and a fever dream of a prophet. He must have somehow survived and done what was needed to cope with being the lone survivor on this side of the Gate. With a heavy heart, Keimas let the wind carry him down after Hopi and hovered over him, speaking softly.

"*Udai*...Hopi, you must stop. There's nothing here," he said.

"What'm? Haha, mmm oh you are soon'm witness something beyond your wildest thought! My city is'm magnificent place, fit

225

for'm godlike such as you."

"Hopi…" Keimas dropped beside him and walked with a hand on his back. "…Hopi, there's nothing left here. Everything we had out here was burned by the thuell. There are no survivors."

"No surv…wait now, what'm thuell?" Hopi asked.

Keimas was stricken briefly, lingering behind then dashing to catch up.

"You don't know? Have you never seen…?"

As they reached the very bottom of the basin, Hopi turned to the side and waved his hands downward like he was braiding a rope. Tiny markings of classical enchantment aligned with the design, which fell to recreate it on the ground. The air and sand rippled and shifted before Keimas' eyes, and the illusion of bare terrain wafted away to reveal an archway; the mouth of a tunnel leading down into the hillside. It was not brassic or basalt, appeared to be obsidian or perhaps something he did not recognize. Whatever it was it didn't sparkle like cerrubite, but its surface was polished with the utmost care. Torchlight from deep within danced along cracks within it, bringing it to life and replacing Keimas' wariness with curiosity.

The floor was rougher, with many narrow channels impressed. A putrid stench permeated the tunnel mouth, emanating from a viscous mixture of sand and red ooze that bubbled up from the floor and trailed down the hall along the grooves.

Keimas swallowed hard, unsure of what to make of the sludge as he followed Hopi down.

"Friend, I realize this is not a reasonable thing to ask…but should I be afraid?"

"You can if'm you like, but I don't busy myself with'm fear and neither should you. This is safety; a gift so'm Galaila would have'm home."

Keimas considered the possible meanings of the explanation until they neared the end of the tunnel and entered an expansive grotto filled with crackling fires and smiling faces. A wave of excitement flowed across the room when Hopi crossed the threshold, and a cheer of pleasure arose as a number of similar Mearnum raced to embrace him. Keimas received many strange looks amidst the flurry of hushed questions directed to Hopi. The man waved off his interrogators and, extending a hand towards

Keimas, proclaimed to the thirty-some Mearnum:

"Peace, good'm folk! The prophet spoke'm truth again for again! I was out where'm said would find a man with'm wings. See'm word!" He stepped back as he spoke, and the crowd surrounded Keimas.

With wide-eyed amazement, they reached out to touch Keimas, entranced by the color of his feathers and strange clothing, chattering among themselves, though without actually directing any questions at him. He tried to shrug them off, but they were quite intent on touching every part of him, as if feel and gesture were part of their language. He called to Hopi uncertainly, dancing aside to avoid the ooze as it crept between his feet.

"Hopi, damn it all man, you knew I would be there? What game are you playing?"

Hopi shrugged. "Apologies. Priestess said'm prophet said sent'm out. Said'm find you but never said'm why. Said'm very important I shouldn't say about knowing."

Lost to translate that, Keimas gave up being subtle and pushed his way past the weird savages in their weird tomb, surveying it as he followed Hopi.

Each of these folk had some sort of workspace very like what he had seen in Ms'egol, and right beside each one was a ramshackle bed of rock and fur. There were simple cauldrons carved from the ground, luminescent weeds wrapped in coils and all manner of crude contraptions. There was little metal to be seen but they seemed to have made do with thizech and brassic. For a band of desert scrapers their system was almost as impressive as the academy. There were many side rooms where the walls were not the crude brown stone as the central chamber was, but more smooth black surfaces. They were similarly equipped and firelight within revealed all kinds of geometric carvings covering the preexisting faces. They were not pictures of anything he knew and did not seem to be lettering, just ornate pathways in the stone. By appearances they were not the work of this group, more likely the subject of their study, though Keimas could not conceive of how alchemical work coincided with carving.

He felt a cold breeze from an unlit passage on the furthest side of the chamber and felt subtly drawn to it, peering into its winding depths.

"Is that the way to the prophet?" he asked as he rejoined Hopi, his impatience showing.

"Yes'm. I say you, be'm polite and respectful," Hopi warned. "He'm only let you come led by acolyte."

"Whatever he wants, I don't care," Keimas acquiesced grudgingly. "Who'm acolyte?" His mockery of Hopi's speech was effectless, answered only by the appearance of a slender, straw-haired woman in the dark tunnel. She was clothed far better than the others around him; some ceremonial raiment preserved from Ellel, though by its design he could not tell which village. Decorated with numerous hanging strands of beads, some bone and some a sort of clear crystal, it had well-fitted folds of red and black that tightly covered her from neck to ankle. Without expression she bowed to one side slightly, raised one bound arm and beckoned him in silence. He crossed to her, noting as he did that the others made a conscious effort not to look at her directly. He ignored their reverence and did not avert his own gaze, wasted no time in venting his frustration.

"At last. I pray YOU will deliver me to my summoner. I'm growing tired of madmen who seem to know all about me yet refuse to enlighten me."

She shook her head and smiled wryly, turned away without any of the flailing or chatter that seemed to be customary with this people. Keimas thought this to be a good sign and followed with anxious speed. As they moved down the grim tunnel, she finally broke her silence and spoke easily but with great care.

"Forgive our Hopi's manner. He's not as mad as you think. He's actually quite a brilliant physic. Tell me though, are you not of the desert, kutliku-man?"

"Keimas, born Tieg Raev, now *Hauan Etain*," he said plainly for introduction. "It is beyond the cliffs Hai. What of you? Clearly you are apart from these odd folk. Are you from the same village as them or are you merely a more practiced speaker?"

"Well-spotted. My home was Pnaefahan in the South. Some of the others are outlanders, but the rest were mostly of Tieg Aalitskne. I have no notion of where Hopi came from. He is more...relaxed," she said, then added conversationally, "He's the outsider among us. We met him on Ellel, and still are not certain where he hails from. When we saw the carnage to the north, and

228

your ships setting sail, we considered following you, though we could not determine where you meant to go. He came running over the hills, screaming that the gods had brought war to Ellel. We packed what little we could and boarded our little fishing boats, not knowing the full extent of what was happening until we were already out at sea...nothing but smoldering wreckage at our backs. We had hoped to join your flotilla, but in your wake were caught up in a great storm which carried us quite a way off course. Your people must have just escaped it, for when it passed you were nowhere to be found."

"*Laan*, I remember that storm. It must have been worse than we knew if it caught your people as well. It's a miracle you found this place at all. We thought Ferraro had bullied what souls infest the sea to conjure it against us."

"She may well have. Half our ships were sunk, and thirst killed many of us on our way here. But the physics plied their trade and caught us what food they could from the water. I tell you, water drunk from a chlio will make you pray for death."

"Hah!" Keimas was amused but stifled shamefully for taking her words lightly. "*Mineina enta,* I have no doubt you are right. We were here for a full season without seeing your coming. To be astray so long must have hurt you all deeply." The woman's expression was increasingly dour and distracted. Keimas thought about the rest of what she had said and was struck by one familiar but unfamiliar term. "Hopi used that word as well; 'Physic'. You use it strangely."

"Physic? It is just a common one's word for what we once called a 'Magician of the material'. We are not unlike your metalsmiths and fluid-makers of Tieg Raev. My village strove to understand the connection between the kingdoms of the material world. We do study some classical mancy to that end, but our focus is on shaping the world by the manipulation of its own laws rather than recruiting the aid of the Veils."

Keimas was silent, fascinated by this one who spoke so openly of what, among Mantichaena, was oft considered taboo: home.

"*Prostas*, acolyte, but I'd prefer you not speak the name of my city," he said.

"I...*malpael*," she responded. "I am dismayed to speak of my own city after seeing it lost. I should have expected the same of you."

"*Minla*, I have no bitterness. Among our people it is considered…not against the law, but detrimental. I suppose our masters want our focus to be on surviving here, not lost in the past. But please, continue."

"That is all," she shrugged. "We believe in the natural order above all else, survival being our ability to fit into that order by discovering its innermost workings. I must say, even in this desolation we have made amazing discoveries and even invented our own."

"Including this sanctuary," Keimas marveled, recalling the black stone. "The masonry is immaculate." I've rarely seen anything so finely carved.

"*Minein*, not this," she said. "We found this place abandoned. Every tunnel is a dead end except this one. All are sealed by heavy slabs we dare not breach."

"And where does this one go?" Keimas asked. "To your prophet of science?"

"I'll thank you to not be snide" she replied smartly before returning to her more genial demeanor. "As the appointed leader of this company I was offered a private place to my work. Once settled, I tried to go deeper. That was where I found the prophet."

"That's how you came to follow him? You stumbled onto him by chance?"

"Not by chance. He was expecting me just as he expects you."

The hall emptied into another cave, this one lined only by the familiar sandstone of the island, and once again firelight danced across walls and furnishings. Keimas was captivated by the numerous apparatuses and bubbling concoctions neatly organized on rows of stone tables across the uneven floor. The acolyte moved confidently between them, pausing to carefully measure a smoky liquid, then pointed lazily to a bed in the corner made of thi'zech fibers woven together.

"You can rest for now," his host sighed. "The prophet will call when it is time for your audience."

"I'm grateful of course, but I'll stand."

"As you will."

Keimas glowered at the uncomfortable looking bed, then at the further depths of the chamber. It curved up and away, eventually disappeared around the bend of an unlit passage. There was nothing beautiful or even decorative about the recess to indicate the presence of a spiritual guide therein. Keimas' presence here, along with the unreserved acceptance by this alien people were the only indications that he might be in the place he was meant to be, not just a victim of unfortunate coincidence.

Turning round and round to examine the mysterious vessels and technologies surrounding him, he was stricken by the sight of an amorphous mass of black tissue almost as tall as he was, suspended in midair within a sheet of transparent crystal. His first instinct was to scream himself hoarse, but the substance's inert state calmed him.

"*Eina*, acolyte..."

She rose from behind a jar composed of the same crystal and filled with yet another unknown brew.

"*Eihs* Gaialja," she chimed.

"As you would, Gaialja. What is this thing before me?"

"Ooh! Your kind have not discovered this? It is a liquid sand, melted under tremendous heat and rendered transparent. Like water, it can take the shape of any vessel it fills."

"Fascinating, I'm sure, though I refer to this monstrosity contained within."

"*Uein*? Oh, that's Uru. I found him while I was digging for metal grains. He seems a lot like his more fluid relatives out there in the sand, but he was strangely inactive so very easy to capture. We poured our clear sand into the hole, and he barely reacted."

"His more...Gaialja, how exactly did you find these things?"

"They can be found many places out there. Most of the time we find them living in the heartwood of the thiz'ech or hiding underground. Any exposure to Laesis or our own fire tends to make them...combust."

"YOU'RE KEEPING THUELL AS PETS!?" Keimas roared.

"If you're going to yell, you're welcome to wait in the hall," Gaialja scolded, ignoring the urgency of Keimas' voice.

Keimas controlled his outrage but was not satisfied.

"*Zet'tskhain*, you do understand that these are the very creatures which destroyed our people here and caused us to flee to our home beyond the Gate?" He described in some detail the Mantichaena's brief and tragic history with the thuell. To this, the acolyte listened

231

respectfully before replying, apologetically at first.

"*Ryshatsk'vae,* I had no idea. We have had no such trouble with them, ever. Physical contact has not been possible because they wither and catch fire when exposed to any degree of light. We have to search for them at night, but even torch and star are enough to hurt them. What you see here is only the tiny amount we were able to preserve. Why the coating protects it is something I still study. Presently I suspect it has something to do with it not being exposed to air and light simultaneously. At any rate, he is no danger. I can appreciate your concerns, but Uru is more a victim of our curiosity than we are of his nature."

"So this...all of this, you made it yourself right here in this cave?" Keimas queried, somewhat conciliated, though equally confused.

"Mostly, yes," Gaialja affirmed. "It's a very quick process. The time wasted is that spent testing the sap from the few living samples I find. I'm not the only one working. Everyone has their *ini'na* areas of study. *Minein,* my own research is a bit obsessive."

"I can see that, and I do understand," Keimas replied. "My wife has the same sense of focus and wonder."

"You've wedded? What's she like?"

"As I have described, though also a fair bit wiser than myself," Keimas replied with a grimace.

"*La?* And not just for being a woman?" The acolyte asked, trying to add humor.

It worked well enough and Keimas chuckled at the discriminatory jest. Gaialja was a pleasant soul, one who expertly conveyed real empathy as her smile warmed. She looked remarkably young considering the destitute situation of her people and by her more relaxed attitude he was reminded again of his love. Certainly, the strongest thing he felt was shame in how they had parted.

"No, certainly not. Her true nature is sweet and tender but the misfortune of being of love to me has made her accustomed to suppressing her own emotions so that she may, with a superior mind, keep my own steady. I believe in my absence she feels free to express her true self more, and if given the choice between wisdom and kindness she is a slave to kindness. Only when afflicted by my monumental stupidity does she reveal her divine strength of mind."

"You regard her wisdom more than her kindness?"

"I do. Though her good heart is truly precious, her mind serves me best in protecting me from my own shortcomings," Keimas admitted.

Gaialja considered his words briefly before swiftly approaching him, dusting powdered minerals from her hands and inspecting his wings as she chided him.

"Your self-deprecation is nonsense, *udai*. Love, by its very definition will make you all of these things you admire in her, and her all things you are comprised of. Her wisdom and goodness, if it does make your own seem pallid, is not a failure of one but a triumph of both. You are one soul and should celebrate your differences, not as differences between two but as the versatility of one. *Einla,* marriage is as a single hand that wields two weapons."

Keimas nodded absently, distracted by the thought of his wife's face, the heartbreak that had shown in her eyes as he pushed her away. He was haunted by those eyes, cringing at his own insolence as he remembered his vow to let her rest in him, a vow he had broken and revealed to be of less value than the seductive whispers of a darkness he knew nothing about. Though the memories pursued him, he had never turned back. They were valuable to him, but nothing had pierced him more deeply than Gaialja's reverent words, which stung all the more as he felt he should have already known them. His heart fluttered as the woman fondled his wings and he realized suddenly that she was cleaning them for him.

"Do you mind? Your physiology is fascinating," she murmured.

He shook his head 'No', swallowed to wet his parched throat. His exhaustion had melted away under curiosity and they were both relaxed for a moment as Gaialja began to speak again.

"You are fortunate to be requested by the stones. It was I who stumbled upon our prophet and none but me has ever been allowed to set foot before him. Why do you think that is?"

Keimas looked at her for a moment and got no sense that she was being rhetorical. She was eccentric, honestly wanting to know his thoughts regardless of how uneducated they were. She seemingly didn't know any more than he did, which led him to consider that this prophet may very well be genuine.

He somberly confessed, "Because you have beautiful insights."

She hid a smile, but her gaze remained focused on her task.

"And what of you? Why are you brought before him?"

"An accursed insight; visions. I received some sort of memory gifted by a spirit. Only bits and pieces there were, and they did not fit together."

"*Prostas,* explain," she requested.

Keimas hesitated, then relented to describe, in simplest terms, the exalted creature and their nation dead beneath it. He begged her, if she could, to explain its meaning.

"I was chosen to relay the prophet's words to others, those who are now his disciples in the service of our father Loi. It has never been my place to interpret dreams," she replied, contritely.

Keimas accepted her humble answer. Within the rejuvenation of rest inside the cave and the eventuality that his journey was nearing its end he turned to consider only his current place.

"I am intrigued by the balance your people hold between mancy and science. I am a hypocrite to inquire so, but does your tribe's doctrine not instruct you to sacrifice the world and have faith in Loi alone?"

"Haha! Of course not, *udai.* This world was created for us, if not by Loi himself then by his ancestors. To study it as diligently as we pray is to become immortal alongside them, glorifying their creation and so glorifying them. Science does not countermand belief in our god, it brings us closer to him."

"This is a good thing," Keimas marveled. "Many of my people are of the same mind, but our beliefs are not as united as yours. As many have made the sciences their first love, others still look to god and spirit for knowledge and assurance."

"It may not be right to assume that science is their enemy simply because they have faith," Gaialja reasoned. "Many people cannot imagine more than a single road to their destination. It is a weakness of the mind, not a flaw of character."

Keimas smiled broadly, enchanted by the easy debate and the manner with which Gaialja spoke. He agreed with her, as did an increasing population in Hanging Gate, but the religious still held sway over social order there. He grew excited and left her to meander through the many benches, considering their individual burdens with a quizzical eye before reaching the table at which she had been working. There, a weighted wheel indolently churned a font of pink goop.

"I am surely one who cannot see the many roads," he confessed. "I was blessed with strength, not brain."

"And how does the blessing of your birth decide the blessings you are capable of giving?" Gaialja offered.

His wings glowed and he was again charmed by her cleverness.

"Could you...teach me?" he asked. Wouldn't it be marvelous, he thought, to understand so much? To understand the world as he had always believed no warrior could?

"Teach you?" Gaialja asked in surprise. "To be a physic?"

"To see more than one road."

Disarmed by the twinkle in his eye and the genuine thirst for knowledge which she identified with, she said "I...suppose there is time."

"*Laan!*" Keimas exclaimed, "On my return I should love to be able to converse about such things with the greatest among my people...my wife for one."

Gaialja bit her lip thoughtfully, this being the first time she had taken a pupil of her own volition and having no idea where to begin.

"*Eina,* there's something very interesting I can show you. I have studied it for most of my life here and still its true meaning is unknown to me. Even the cr...prophet will not answer my questions."

"Is that so? What is this secret thing?" Keimas asked conspiratorially.

"Keimas, there is no knowing. Of that you can be sure," she laughed.

"But you have learned from it?" He pressed.

"*La,* things I never dreamed of. Come, and see the road even I cannot understand."

She rushed to his side to grasp his hand and together they ran back the way they had come, avoiding the main chamber where her kind dwelt and squeezing into a second passage. So narrow was its mouth that he had not noticed it before, distracted by conversation. Into its darkness they went. She had lied, Keimas realized. There was indeed an open door in this place, and what lay beyond it must have been kept secret even from her own people.

CHAPTER 23: A DARK PLOT EMERGING

The Division Age – A Historic Record
Article 61
Unknown season, Windsong Star falls, Longhand Star remains,
Bone Star falls

I *was wrong to have such high hopes for this bleak time of the cycle. Our loreknowers and studiers of the stars have no notion of what insanity is occurring in the heavens. Longhand approaches its end, and yet the star does not ascend? What's more, Windsong comes gradually while the Bone Star descends so suddenly ahead of its time. It's as though the stars themselves have forgotten their place. The weather burns. Hot winds from the East and the light of the Nhi'Thaun scorch the ground. Some of the crops are starting to fail, thus the Kutu have been needed more and more recently, and now we are down one hunter-killer. There is still no official record of why Nesh Udai Keimas departed the city when the passing was coming. Madness can take one from time to time. It wouldn't be the first time someone has become so like the K'hizu that they could no longer handle life in the city. We have enough hunting parties that we should not go hungry, but we must fill stores quickly. Time has betrayed us, and we are not prepared.*

On the twenty-eighth of Longhand there was a smoke signal in the Hai, down in the green of Ni'ivitnem. At first, we thought it was just the initial camp of the caravan dispatched to establish contact with Bethaali's settlement but upon scouting it was reported that the temple where Keimas was found injured had been set ablaze. Nesh Utanam Govan and Allende led a group of Gazan's best rackers to investigate the surrounding area. Everything was gone, only rubble and ash remaining.

The elders have been in assembly all day trying to decide what to make of these ill-timed omens. The misalignment of the stars has made the earthplane burn, but actual fire? In Ni'ivitnem no less? I hear rumors that the thuell annihilated the temple to hide from others what Keimas had uncovered. Rumors only. The thuell cannot think, they cannot plan, they just react to our presence. I feel this is just more paranoia born of what Sky himself perpetuates. In fact, I think it was not the thuell but one of our own who burned it down. I opted to do a bit of snooping myself. I was out of order to do so, but...gods, Mani cannot keep me locked away here forever with these ridiculous scribblings.

I was in rare form, and a short distance from the ruin I discovered in the thi a patch of very distinctive scarlet hair torn away by a thorn. Perhaps left by the culprit? I have never heard of such a thing as red hair. No Mantichaena, no Galaila, no K'hizu has ever been known for it. Whatever it belongs to should be easy to find...but then we would have found it already if it was around. I am wary of bringing this to the attention of the council or the academy. With the state our city is in I don't think they will listen to any more theories without making the worst of them. People just want to pretend everything is fine. Anything out of the ordinary is always troubling to...lesser minds.

We've been busy defending the city. Since that fire we've had more and more wild K'hizu attacks, not just on our scouts but at the near borders and even upon the cliffside. The kutliku are restless too, even the cocks among them...something is drawing them to us, something that frightens them and makes them aggressive. Even Jiou Boa has been sighted out over Ni'ivitnem. Whatever this is, it is not a fluke of nature. A wound has opened somewhere, and the island is in pain. Whatever is going on, it cannot be a simple change in the weather. Every living thing is reacting to it. Utan, can I please get back to work that means something?

~Ms'egol Aia Cisiveo

Lemalie was the only Mantichaena that craved the passing, for no work would be done once the harvest was in. She was not lazy, only preoccupied with more important personal matters. She was a thinker and a dreamer, prepossessed to thoughts of the world's nuances thronging at the doors of her ceaselessly working mind. This was not new for her, though it might seem so to some, knowing as they may how focused she was among familiar faces. The excitement of being with people and interacting with others had always eclipsed her deeper musings, making her a perky and pleasant conversationalist, one that always brought energy into a room. That girl was gone now, though she was not entirely different, simply more evolved. Her vitality had been replaced by anxiety over the fate she and her father would suffer if things continued along their current path. Even worry for Keimas was pushed to the back of her mind.

Longhand was meant to be a bearing, yet each day struck harder with a cruel heat that grew increasingly worse. The crops were already dying, the river narrowing, the coffers barely meeting the required levels for survival of a single passing. Every available body in the Gate had been drafted for field work to rush all that could be saved into storage, but it was not adequate. If Longhand did not return to its normal plenty the insipient Windsong would starve out the city. No one knew what to do but ration what was had and pray the hunters were able to flush out more prey than usual.

To answer the unavoidable question of where the heat wave had come from, Sky and Artimecian were without options and forced to adhere to the story of Keimas' possession even when it made no sense. Now, placing the blame for all their worries on him was less believable as word of Loi's temple being destroyed reached their table. There was even suspicion among some that Sky had ordered it destroyed to try and add credibility to his story. The loyalties of the people were becoming starkly divided and the fear he fed on was growing out of his control.

The council was as afraid for the future as any other citizen, especially after hearing how Keimas had destroyed the high gate. Indecision overtook them, then outrage as Sky continued to forbid either enchanter or foreman from traveling Tau to mend the broken wall. He had inexplicably raised the punishment to execution for anyone who defied that command, which was strongly enforced by his supporters but also increased the numbers that swayed to Aroch's camp. Rumors started to ring with truth as more surfaced that even the fall of the gate was Sky's intent. It was more believable that Artimecian would do such a thing than Keimas, at least to those who knew both of them.

Little of the law was known to an organization as secluded as the Iron Sanctum, and so the loyal specialists Artimecian had sent out were completely unaware that their mission in the Tau would condemn them to death upon their return. The law gave no concession for what was ordered, only what was done. These faithful agents would kill the traitor Keimas and return home triumphant, only to suffer the same punishment. Sky's authority would be absolute, and no one would dare disobey him ever again, or so he assured himself. Only then would he reseal the gate to regain the trust of many, reward the servile, punish the dissenters and bring lasting order to the Mantichaena.

His plan might work if Thonsfa had anything to do with the rise in temperature. Day was day out there, just as it was in Hanging Gate. As the Bone Star shone brightly Sky knew that nothing would push it back into deep sky before it chose to go on its own. Many knew, yet still they clung to the stories he peddled: Keimas had brought this ill wind on them by tearing down their wall. He just had to maintain his authority until the time was right, claim responsibility for Keimas' death just as the Bone Star retreated and secure himself as the divine benefactor he was when he rescued his helpless citizens from Ellel's incineration.

Meanwhile, citizens and archons continued to secretly seek Aroch with their desperate complaints that Sky must be mad to sacrifice safety in order to make an example of Keimas. He consoled them as a former Patriarch but, when one revealed themself to be earnestly against Sky's rule, he began to include them in his plans to challenge the tyrant's hold. He had no desire for battle or bloodshed, so at his assurance of change the rebellious kept silent and waited patiently for the time when a revolt would become their only course. He prayed often that success would come another way, worried about the suffering that would come with a violent coup.

It was still a hopeful time, an exciting time. There would be a new order, a new council and a new Primarch. Perhaps his friends and family were right; him, a suitable Primarch? He was. He promised himself he would be the greatest Primarch the Mantichaena had ever known. As more people came and pledged themselves to his leadership, he became more convinced that Loi had blessed his family's success. He would be the next Primarch. The stars had ordained it.

There was still much work to be done with the city. While a few archons had fallen prey to Sky's timely explanations, the better half of the council and the families that followed them withheld their praise as he appeared among the halls to fan the flame of discontent aimed at Keimas. A demon within the Kutu's flesh was such an easy target for the superstitious that many even blamed the alleged mass reappearance of the thuell on him. To a zealot it made sense that Loi was allowing these terrible things to happen to them as punishment for abandoning his patronage for Anama's. But could they accept judgment upon themselves for such failings? Never. It simply must be the fault of Keimas the violent; Keimas the reckless; Keimas the unfaithful. He and all his family were a danger to the good folk of Hauan Etain.

A horrible piece of Keimas' past resurfaced as these tongues wagged. Long ago, his youth had been full of so much anger. He had met Lemalie at the height of his transformation, and the beautiful and supportive girl had brought out the best in him and quieted the turmoil in his heart, tumult caused by seeing his mother perish in the fire that had taken Ellel. Lemalie saved him and brought him into a world of love, yet still there remained a pain inside that drove him to commit his most unspeakable act. In his youthful lust, he had lain with another woman, betraying Lemalie's trust most shamefully. She had somehow found it in her heart to forgive him, trusted his suffering before her as true repentance. He had vowed to be hers, to be ruled by her will, to forsake his own desires and live entirely for her. It was not a promise easily kept and one he could not sustain long. Time and again he acted impulsively in running off to seek adventure, but never again did he repeat the crime that had broken her heart. She understood him well and continued to forgive, even after this most recent abandonment, but her love was not enough to make the world see him as she did. His flaws were many. The more they were shared, the more it was said that he was no different today than he was then, vulnerable to evil and always succumbing to it. As Sky's agents painted him in increasingly dark colors it was all too easy to bring transgressions to mind and revive scandals long passed, to conspire and extrapolate and convince themselves that the demon within may have been there all along. Without a father he had always been called the son of a whore, despite his adoption into a wellborn family. Born in fire, reborn in the Kutu's blood, his every action was redefined as those of a creature destined for the dark.

Equally spread about was Sky's influence among the religious community. His divine claim as rightful Primarch was solid, in part because they believed he was chosen by Loi himself to protect the people of Tieg Raev and all the great western ports of Ellel. He had given them prosperity and, when disaster had overtaken them, he had led them to safety. When the thuell rose, he once again found them a home. To those of a mind for Loi's will, no upstart Kutu or his malcontent of a marriage father would mislead them from the path Sky had them on; Loi's path.

A schism was born between halls Nesh and Ms'egol. The witchcrafters and apothecaries of the academy were deeply vulnerable to Artimecian's tongue, while news of Raru's death had shaken the loyalty of his enchanters. Both demanded to be told everything but believed nothing they were told. As Nesh grew distrustful of Ms'Egol, so Ms'Egol grew distrustful of its own, and the feud was beginning to overheat.

Nesh's people, to Sky's humiliation and Aroch's bitter delight, had become openly hostile toward the Primacy. From the moment of Nepiur's departure it was spoken like common knowledge that her assignment to the caravan had indeed been exile, even execution. Long forgotten rumors that Sky's eldest daughter had not left of her own free will were revisited. A flood of detailed stories circulated of how he abused his family, bullying Bethaali into leaving, even threatening her life, just as he had banished his wife from Tieg Raev, never to be seen again. It was not for infidelity, not for treachery, but for disobedience. Things once dismissed by a people with unfailing loyalty to him were now seen for what they were; the actions of a cruel and selfish man.

Soon Sky felt unsafe roaming his city as he once had, reduced to sneaking from one hall to the next and keeping the constant company of his faithful for fear of facing those who opposed him. However, he might justify his behavior in his own mind, he could not risk answering to others, nor even maintain his composure if confronted.

The very situation Aroch had strived to avoid was now reality. Sky had started a war when he sentenced Keimas to death. There was nothing to be done to protect the man and it was only a matter of time until tensions at home turned to open conflict. Aroch would realize this soon enough.

Lemalie reclined against the wilting fronds of a great albalithaed, bereft now of its cyclical crop of heavy, succulent seeds. The sun warmed her, though she scarcely noticed as she lay deep in thought. No longer did she grieve the loss of her husband. Her personal grief must be set aside in the face of the changes facing her home. Specifically, how to end them peaceably.

A rustling sound startled her, and she looked sharply over to see her father suddenly laid against an adjacent frond. He was smiling, faintly at first but soon his head rolled over to face her.

"From our guileful friend atop the cliffs I have received word of Keimas' good health."

Lemalie's heart leapt, but she did not sound so pleased.

"If he lives, then not all is lost. You went to Naguza for help?"

Aroch sighed and shifted to a more comfortable position.

"Long ago. It was all I could do. Sky dismisses the strange as quickly as he does the innocent and so would never consider that I had enlisted the help of an exile."

Lemalie eyed him worriedly, said "You'll die with Keimas if he finds out what you did."

"I have given him a hundred reasons to have me killed or cast out. For all his blustering he cannot destroy me yet, not while I have the favor of the people and certainly not after this most recent development."

"*La*? What development?" She asked eagerly.

"The Iron Wind took up a path divergent of Keimas' and he eludes them still. If that were not miracle enough for you, heed this: he is not alone. Someone else is out there. The deghni spied a stranger reviving and caring for Keimas when he was weakened and fallen."

"*Lauein*! Whom?" Lemalie cried. "From whence does he come?"

"Friend Naguza could not say. *Aiana*, imagine what it could mean for us if the Tau has been cleansed of thuell, at least to the point of habitability. Whoever is out there, they are surviving in the waste we have always feared."

"*Eina*, then the law is nothing! We must make this known! With the thuell gone Sky must lift his taboo!"

"And lose ground to accuse Keimas of a misdeed, if it has led to this," Aroch beamed. "Naguza's word will mean nothing against his, but Keimas' testament could spare his life if it has the chance be heard. If the gods will it, perhaps survivors will return with him as proof."

Lemalie threw her arms around her father and rolled across him into the dirt, then sprang to her feet.

"We have to go, spread this with every breath," she whispered excitedly.

"Not quite yet," Aroch cautioned. "We need a balanced attack. We cannot wade in swinging wildly. This news could be the spark that sets the whole city ablaze. If it does then people will die. Artimecian will protect Sky to the last and that means more lives lost than saved if the arch-witchcrafter fights for the Primacy."

"Then we take him first!" Lemalie argued.

"Cool your spirits. This is good news, but the plan must remain, a lethal conflict our last resort. We have an advantage now that will allow us to disprove all that Sky has fabricated, but we need Keimas to come home. Together, with truth in plain sight, we will face sky before all the people."

"*Ein*, I am with you Father. I suppose in my husband's absence I feel a certain lack of reckless bravado which I must now fill" she said comedically. She knelt again at her father's side with shifting eyes, suddenly distressed. "And that might have been my death. Sky is clothed in lies but also an armor of convention, history and confidence. Whether we see it or not, he remains the heart of the city's strength. If we are to remove him then there must be a new heart to replace him. You have said the same."

"A decision that need not be made today. Tempers are high but ours must be measured. Keimas is alive. We have no reason for haste." Aroch concurred. "Let Sky stew in the people's distaste. Let him cower while they palm stones with an eye for the back of his head. Very soon there will be a confrontation, with or without our interference. It is in how that conflict is handled that the city will see its new Primarch."

"And Artimecian?" Lemalie asked.

Aroch shifted thoughtfully. Artimecian was a zealot, unpredictable. Still, he felt confident that he understood his opponent well enough.

"*La'ekt*, I surmise that the man is no more than a leashed beast, begging for the hand that feeds it. I know Artimecian better than any. Many may think him insane but no, he fights for what he believes is right. As with all his other creatures, Sky knows no discipline but the whip, so like any beast I suspect Artimecian has already thought about biting back. Until we can understand where his heart lies, we can only assume he will defend Sky's rule to the death, because he truly believes in him. We must continue our work and unite as much of the city as we can; defend Keimas' honor as one family, defend the lives and dignity of our kin. They will cry out for new leadership and our family will be waiting with open arms."

Lemalie sighed and took his hand, knitting their fingers as she reclined on the shrub again.

"Primarch Aroch." She muttered

He hummed happily, savoring the thought.

"To be Aroch Sky…I am warming to the idea the more it becomes a possibility. I want to be the servant this city deserves."

"Honor again to you, Father."

"Honor again to you and your husband."

Looking skyward with hopeful eyes, Lemalie sighed, "Honor again to mother."

Twenty-three unblinking eyes fixed on Lemalie, wide and full of bewilderment. Twisted hair like trickles of blood flowed around them, while black claws and sickly legs held them aloof. The scarlet-haired creature who, like a child not understanding its own fascination, gawked at the loveliest of mortal women with a hanging mouth and clammy hands. Like a leaf he had ridden the scalding wind across the sky, landing just an arm's reach from the one thing in all the world that piqued his interest: any woman whose husband would sacrifice everything to keep her safe. The horrid Vulgoli man believed it after hearing her words, seeing for himself how exquisite she was, though his feelings were painful and indescribable.

Enshrouded in the Veil so as not to be seen, he reached out to touch Lemalie's hand upon Aroch's, felt a twinge of emptiness when his fingertips passed through as though she were a dream. He could not feel her warmth or substance, though he felt her spirit and her inner light singed his cold flesh, frightening and captivating him. There was something extraordinary about her that spoke to the world and commanded it to revere her. It was not mere beauty, rather divinity that her own father could not see. She was an immortal, the chosen heir of a Nhi'Thaun.

"*Gazeihs,* you desire her too?" hissed an eerie voice akin to his own.

The eyebeast levitated off the ground and, swimming in the Veil by force of will, whirled about at the audible echo of his thoughts to see the black-hooded storyteller watching him from within an aura like his own. He returned to the ground, a nervous smile revealing his ashen teeth. Though her face was obscured by cloth he knew the mystic felt no joy in seeing him, her displeasure glaringly apparent when she spoke.

"I've not met a man who does not," she said, leaning over to peer again at Lemalie and Aroch, "But never considered her so beautiful that she could lure you back to earthplane."

Shuffling forward a step, Tzychala felt shamed as she retreated the same step. His head drooped, and he willed himself to show sadness he could not feel.

"Mnavaelle, I am sorry."

"No, you're not." she grumbled coldly.

"I wish to be, truly. I know remaining here must have been testing for you."

"Testing!? For what punishment? Perhaps this accursed light? Starvation? The only hardship I have faced since these wretched things rose from the sick that spawned them was looking to the stars and knowing that I would never see you again! When I felt your presence again..." She shivered and her hood drooped sullenly. "...I thought you would come back to me, that you would seek me out, not this ignorant creature."

"Forgive me, sister."

"More than two thousand days!" The storyteller screeched, throwing back her head and swiping at him as the Veil reverberated with her voice. He did not defend, cringing as she clawed through his chest and threw him back, his intangible form falling through the two mortals at his back.

Her cloak tossed over her back, she appeared as simple a creature as a Vulgoli could, though every aspect of her wept for its own hideousness; eyes like clenched teeth, hair like blood, tightly matted and trimmed with beads and pieces of bone, claws unliving and a tail wrapped around her waist to remain hidden under her garment. It unfurled slowly and from its sharp ends there dripped a caustic venom as she raged. She did not have his many eyes, yet what she possessed was no less precious and matchless: two of his own kind that misted with her tragic rage. Her blood rushed under the pounding of four hearts in her chest, each bursting with the emotions her brother imitated so poorly. One by one they steadied as she looked upon her only kin after so long apart, broken by his absence.

"I only wanted...Tzychala, I thought you had forgotten me," she moaned.

He recognized what he was seeing, had seen it in mortals often enough. This was hurt, not anger. At the sight of a tear coursing down her face he raced forward and wrapped her in a fierce embrace.

"No! *Aias mith'naine* unending pain be my fate if the first true feeling I had was one to take my memory of you! I wanted to see you more than the shores of *Ireapos*. Your hearts should have told you that much."

"My hearts could no longer hear yours when you were confined in that awful place. You were inaudible, removed from me," she lamented.

"As it should be," the brother replied. "What you might have felt within me would bring you no pleasure."

Memories chased each other across his face as he continued to hold her. Eventually she stepped back from him, pulled her cloak around her shoulders and smiled at him.

"Then it is well ended. My pleasure is in seeing you free; free at last." With a spontaneous kiss on the cheek, Mnavaelle pried his thoughts, almost excited.

"Why are you suddenly returned? On your emergence I felt things from you I have never felt before. Did it...are you remade?"

Tzychala's smile flickered, a mixture of hope and despair.

"It did what could be done with one such as me. It was a fool's errand, childish even to believe I could create a soul of my own in this way, though it was not without a few small triumphs. From each soul that passed through me and into the Veil I gleaned a wealth of memories. Many of war, but just as many of...other things, better things. As each penetrated me, I felt as they did...but as soon as I was released it all went away. In the end I have only memories of living."

"Do you feel different?"

"Tell me yourself," he invited, his arms spread.

Mnavaelle paused to scrutinize him, seeking that inner connection they once had. Her hearts touched him, their fingers crawling through his body and looking for signs of a different man. What she felt was not a soul, but neither was it the raw darkness of his making, like he was neither Vulgoli nor Maengir.

"You feel...unique, strangely fearful. Why?"

"I do not know," Tzychala considered. "I must be feeling something but cannot give it a name."

"Then you did succeed," she replied. Then, warily she asked, "Do the Deina know of your escape?"

"I suspect not. I lost my will to resist them but never my caution. I make every effort to conceal myself."

"As do I, though it may not be necessary. I have not felt their presence for a very long time."

"Long or not, time will see them soon aware that another has taken my place," Tzychala spat.

Mnavaelle caught his arm as he turned aside, "Perhaps, but for now you are free."

As his sister tried to soothe his troubled mind Tzychala laid a mournful gaze on Lemalie's marbled skin, her azure hair and eyes. He had never left the steps of his prison since he had escaped it, trapped by an itching need to serve its new owner in the hopes of finishing what he had set out to accomplish. After being trapped so long he had never seen what the breeding stock of Maengir became when they absorbed the light of Az'Rech, could not have imagined that the puerile, slithering masses his mother had planted here could become something so different. Now, seeing throughout the world with his far-reaching eyes he was disturbed by how different life was than what he had known of it.

"Yes," he finally agreed. "But I realize too late what purpose I served by succumbing to the will of the enemy. We did not save these things any more than we saved ourselves."

"We did save them," Mnavaelle rebuked. "We saved them FROM ourselves! We changed the world, changed fate, ended their suffering."

"Suffering is all they do!"

Mnavaelle shuddered at her brother's tone, her hearts jumping as she sensed his turbulent changes in temperament. "Mnavaelle, you have been here with them, watching when I could not. Have you ever known them to be better than the food they were created to be? The soul has turned simplicity to insanity! These past ages the only thing I was able to experience was the dying breath of every mortal soul that was thrown screaming through my flesh. Do you know what I felt from them? Anger. Anger and sadness, panic and contempt. Can you imagine the regret they felt in knowing their short, empty lives had come to an end? Have you felt the anguish of a mother watching her own child die in her arms? Do you understand what a terrible curse we placed on them by sparing their lives? We turned on our brother, our mother, so they could live. We died so they could live? No, we stole their innocence! We lifted one curse and gave them another, made them to suffer the unquenchable fire of a soul that torments them every day!"

He panted furiously but Mnavaelle's face was drained and

heavy.

"And yet you whine like an orphaned mongrel that you cannot be cursed with them," she accused. "You knew how much pain they felt when they came to life, so you chose to be their savior; the one thing that would allow them to be more than fodder. You have no passion for what they are, only for what they remind you of, the thing you truly are and from which they were made."

"Am I not as you are? Are we not one?" Tzychala asked spitefully.

After a momentary pause and a deep breath, Mnavaelle corrected his arrogance.

"Perhaps, if I were blind and deaf. You want, but only because you can't understand. What you want to feel is so much more powerful than you know. Your curse is to want, mine is to resent."

Tzychala had forgotten to whom he was speaking, though he had not meant to be judgmental or condescending of her. Rather, he was jealous of her burden. She knew this and could not hold it against him. Despite both being presumably incapable of possessing souls of their own, Mnavaelle had, for all time, been able to feel the emotions pursuant to her hearts that bound her with all mortal ones. Tzychala wanted that passion, that immense link with other creatures, yet while he bemoaned its absence his sister could not escape it. She felt everything at once, all of Maengir within her like a whirlpool of indiscernible needs screaming inside her. Just so, he could not prevent the visions his many eyes glimpsed of the many veils.

Mnavaelle raised a hand to halt Tzychala's approach as he tried to apologize for his ignorance, wiped away another tear, stiffened her jaw resolutely and made herself clear "You've never been wrong about them. I have to drown in the ocean they create with the essence they were given. They spend the lives of their own children to purchase the deaths of another's in equal measure. I understand entirely the hatred you feel for the burden of life."

Tzychala was frozen, hopeful that his response would not injure her deeper.

"Brothers and sisters all, we are. To suffer alongside them I thought would be a gift, to have new brothers and replace what we have lost."

"Do not speak of him!" Mnavaelle reprimanded. She was

unstable already, feeling more at odds with Tzychala when the topic of their youngest sibling came up. She could not speak without sobbing and tried no more, leaving Tzychala to prattle on.

"Mnavaelle, I confessed to disdaining them, but you understand why all I want is to be like them. All that draw breath are made vile simply by doing so, yet it was they who earned the blessings of death. We are wretched purely for what we were born as, while they make themselves so by misusing the sublime gift of being able to choose their own purpose. I have no loyalty to the god of my saving, nor to these swarms, I only…"

"You hope to purchase mortality by your subjugation to yet another lightful master," Mnavaelle scoffed.

"I exchange what I have to attain what I need. It is as the living do," Tzychala defended.

"Committed to emulate what you despise?"

"As much as I despise what I envy," he sadly explained.

Mnavaelle laughed at his obtuseness.

"I neither envy a soul nor need one of my own. Neither should you. Az'Rech's essence was not meant for us. Just the fractional presence that gives radiance to Laesis and warmth to the earthplane is enough to sap our strength. If it were any greater it would cripple us. If it resided within us, we would be destroyed. If what you say is what you truly feel, then you are envious of a painful death."

"To live and die in pain is to me more desirable than to exist eternally numb," Tzychala professed. "After witnessing it such countless times it is the only satisfaction I can imagine: to be unmade."

Mnavaelle touched his chest, the scars she had left on him, feeling four sad heartbeats within her and none within him.

"You are a fool of the highest order, brother. Mother's affliction that I should feel their pain has not been for me the gain it was to her. I have tried to silence them, taking no pleasure as she did in hunger and thirst beyond satisfaction. Yet it is crueler still that the only heart in which I find solace is this empty one. Do you not, with your mind alone, feel for my hearts as much as you covet theirs?"

"I love you, my sister, in whatever pitiful way I am able. Before this world ends, I need to understand as you do what it means to love, not so that I might walk among the living and dying but so I can walk beside you."

"You do, even if you don't understand it," she promised, imploring him to hear. "What need have you for a soul to attain what you already feel?" Tzychala pondered the idea in silence for far too long. Feeling the indecision that plagued him, Mnavaelle grew impatient. "Brother, do what you will. I have been away too long." Swimming shadows gathered around her silhouette as she retreated, Tzychala's conflicted expressions not slowing her. "No matter the outcome, I know I will see you when the time is right. Still, I hope all that you seek is found."

The Veil crackled around her as she faded away, appearing as a mirrored reflection turning about until it could not be observed. Tzychala was left in a dismal muddle. He had a purpose to fulfill at the behest of his unintended savior but, here among mortals, his curiosity about one in particular prevailed. He had taken something from her, the thing he himself wanted, yet she was still happy. She spoke of war and still smiled, was destined to rot in the ground and still held her head high. That had to be the power of a soul.

An odd thought occurred: he could not have helped preserve this world simply for his own survival, as he had sometimes argued. Had he unconsciously made the sacrifice he had for their benefit? Vulgoli didn't have souls, never had and never would, if he was to believe his sister. To feel anything for these lower forms of life was asinine but he, if only for one woman, had to feel it. Mnavaelle would never understand his longing, he could not explain it to her. Her hearts overflowed to bursting, so how could they understand emptiness? He feigned affection for her, lying to both of them that he felt what he did not. His captivity and the constant transfusion of souls had gained him nothing, only taught him to mirror what he saw. He would never have said it aloud, but his bitterness stemmed from his utter perplexity at seeing in himself the insatiable longing that almost every dying soul carried with it. He heard it, saw it, understood it existed, still its nature remained alien to him. All he could do was savor brief glimpses and hope that, if he sacrificed sufficiently, he would find the key to filling the hole inside himself. If one more mortal had to die a few seasons too soon for him to attain that dream, then so be it.

Right now, there was something far more important at work here than his search for a soul. He could not put a name to it but something inside him moved while observing the woman Lemalie. Since regaining his freedom he had watched the world from afar as an observer, telling himself it was all to learn how it moved against itself, how to survive living. He was wrong, terrified that its inhabitants were not as he conceived. He spoke of them from the tips of his teeth but only as a habit. It was not what he believed. Whatever lens he was beginning to see through it was not one of loathing. Mortality excited him, drawing him in like the scent of a thorned flower.

Thetrulengo speaks,

I am not unhindered by the passage of time. Without a form capable of ruination, I do not age or weaken. Yet the days become seasons and seasons end in turn. Much to my annoyance I am trapped in one single moment that multiplies upon itself. Conversely, the median veil in which I reside is unaffected by my being unless I act upon it.

Just as I am formless, so am I limitless. Wherever I choose to be, I am, yet sadly I cannot escape time and am unable to return to ages past and see that which has already happened. Like all other beings I have encountered I rely on memories to justify my future choices, as well as determine what I write upon this book of the mind. That alone has told me a great deal about why I am and what obscure purpose, if any, I could be serving. Yes, a great deal, though nothing approaching complete understanding. My purpose, like my being, I must define for myself. It is difficult, as I am unable to establish whether my quintessence exists principally in the material or ethereal domains. I feel I am nothing, yet with a thought I can become anything. Had I been born a deity with the power of an element – Ferraro of ground, Ephielipax of sky, other such titles – I believe I would be the goddess of nothing and nowhere.

This is only a brief explanation of what I believe makes me a cousin of sorts to these bloody-red Vulgoli. I dare not say I despise them, for in fact they have much in common with their nemeses, the shining Deina of Az'Rech, whom I have equal regard for.

Only Bolgaia or Garcharen may tell a story befitting the true nature of the war between the opposing edges of all that is, but in my adequate understanding of what draws these worlds against each other I can say with the utmost surety that the Vulgoli are just as vital to the preservation of Maengir as the Deina are. Any examination of either's motives or ends is thick with irony, principally in how they hate each other with such explosive zeal while unknowingly serving the same purpose: balance, an equilibrium of forces that suspends Maengir where it lay. The loss of one edge would cause all veils to cascade upon one another, each into its empty hole.

All I have seen to do with the ancient era began with the events following Escharka's release from the dark edge, though preceding her clash with Az'Rech, thereafter the coming of the champions of both edges rising to seize victory for their respective creators.

The Vulgoli were three and the Deina two – the latter were Moghredaios, the arch-Deina who breaths the light, and Naotogallion, arch-Deina who swallows it – and their battle was one mortality should be grateful they did not witness. Even in such meager numbers they devastated half the world. Neither side could defeat even one of their opponents, for their weapons were only the essence of their being and therefore inadequate to destroy one another in equal measure. So, the Deina began to effuse fragments of their own massive souls, employing something the Vulgoli did not possess: the power to control other beings. Though the remnants of Az'Rech gave light and life to the feral mortals, the raw Deinaim fragments remade those they touched into Deina'itka, light-likes. They sired an army in a single day and the Vulgoli were conclusively overwhelmed.

The battle had torn the earthplane asunder but the final blow from the god of souls that drove Escharka back was right here, where I now record these words and where Maengir's most enlightened species makes its home. Manti, which even these unknowing creatures call 'Skin', was the battleground where Escharka was driven back. Moghredaios cleaved the mountains in half and Escharka's limb with it. As she fell, so did the Son of Teeth strike down the Jiaia of Deina before he himself was betrayed and cast back into Ireapos by his siblings. Buried now beneath the feet of Mantichaena are the shattered remains of the children of the lonely soul and the Manyflesh, the only fingers which allowed them to grip Maengir.

This day was one of many occurrences, not all of which I was witness to. I will likely never understand the deeper meaning of that first dawn until I further eavesdrop on the illustrious storyteller...assuming she lets slip necessary fact and not just fictional verse. As the Hischates say: to know the story of a battle, one must hear it from those who fought and died, not the Hoening who order them forward and lived.

I digress; the first dawn was the time when the arch-Deina Moghredaios fell to his knees and, in mourning of Az'Rech's defiled essence, sang bitterly. Just as the Vulgoli watched their mother shredded by the light, he saw his father and sister infected by the darkness. By his mere presence, Az'Rech had inadvertently given his light to the fleshy things Escharka's brood had affixed to Maengir, and with it they grew strong without knowledge or understanding of whose power had infected them. As the Deina grieved by the thousands, the Vulgoli emerged from hiding. They surrendered. Moghredaios withheld his wrath upon seeing how they severed their mother's connection to Maengir and cast down her third child, heard them profess their disdain for darkness and become traitors to their realm. Moghredaios agreed to suffer them to live, but only if one of them would offer him a sacrifice to prove their earnestness.

Brother Blood, the youngest and most terrible of Vulgoli, had slain Naotogallion. With her gone there was no way to reclaim the light, so a bargain had to be made. Moghredaios raised his left hand, whispered the true name of Az'Rech into it and a blade forged of pure light arose from his fingers and became the Commanding Voice. With it he bid the radiance of the newborn Laesis to obey him and from the scattered oceans of light erected a monument to set above the sky. Cut as though from the heart of Az'Rech, this prismatic temple would shine just as bright, residing forevermore at the very pinnacle of the aetherplane.

The arch-Deina's ultimatum to the dead ones was simple: one of the two remaining Vulgoli would be charged with entering this hallow of Az'Rech and become a purging fire to the souls of mortals. As Naotogallion could consume light and protect it *within, so could a Vulgoli peel the flesh away from a soul. Moghredaios' construct would be a two-edged sword, absorbing the souls of the dead for two purposes.*

First and foremost, the House of the Living Sky would strip the affliction of Escharka's essence from souls, leaving only a light which would slowly fall back to Az'Rech's grove. All of Escharka's influence would be incinerated within the House or cast back upon Maengir, returning it to its condition before the clash. Secondly, by facilitating this removal of their power, it would act as the single physical opening between mortality and the veil, enabling the Manyflesh's creations to age, deteriorate and die, thus preventing them from accumulating too much essence and becoming a danger to the Deina'itka who remained to watch over the new world and ensure its decline. Fate, however, makes fools of even the Deina. Awakened by the light, some were destined to drink more of it than others, prolonging their lives and one day finding themselves the gods of the ancient world. Fate reveals itself again, for those ascended animals guaranteed Moghredaios' success when they began to kill one another.

It was the Vulgoli called Gaz'toeg, 'Brother Bone', who accepted this duty so that his sister could perform a more crucial task. Moghredaios accepted Gaz'toeg's offering, placed him in the bonds of Az'Rech's beacon and made a pact with him that so long as he remained in bondage and performed his function the Deina would never again return to Maengir. They had need to. Over time the House would return every last drop of Az'Rech's fallen essence to its origin and decay from the middle veil.

The Deina'itka were commanded to honor Gaz'toeg's martyrdom and ensure that his place was not threatened. Clearly their watch was not vigilant, though they did revere the eyebeast as they did the House itself. They bestowed upon him a symbolic title befitting the awesome power he had fought them with, as well as in remembrance of how he, a darkborn, gave himself to Az'Rech's will and purpose: Tzychala, slave fire.

Mortality was allowed to persist and Moghredaios' plan for their souls was proven a triumph in all except a few cases. Most souls were easily cleansed and are now so far away that they appear as mere specks of light as they make their way home to the Far Edge. Know now in looking upon the ages which six of these would become Nhi'Thaun so awesome that they could resist the power of the House and the purge that came with it. Their bodies lost, they retained all the memories of their immortal lives, consumed by unfulfilled purpose and a need to realize it. The six seasonal stars are the only failed experiments of Az'Rech's glorious machine which, through the ephemeral lives of the gods' mortal disciples, has been whispered of as the greatest power in existence. No one, not even Ephielipax, was ever told of how the great weapon of the Far Edge could be turned from soul savior to deadly harbinger if a being with the power of an arch-Deina took control of it. But legends have a way of teaching truth. From memories gained through murder the impossible might of the House eventually rested in Loi's mind, and it was that power which he desired most of all. Too late he realized he was not destined to be its master. But then, what is his plan now? He is the son of Quetzuaul the Deceiver, after all. Her line cannot live without hidden schemes, nor apparently can Ephielipax's live without conquest.

~Chronicle of Wonders, the Bounty and Trade of Stars

CHAPTER 24: A DARK CITY SLUMBERING

The delving of Keimas and Gaialja into the eerily quiet bowels of the underground was an uncomfortable journey for the Kutu. No sound could be heard throughout but their hasty breaths and gritty footfalls as she pulled him along at a run. His mind raced with a torrent of possibilities: all the things he had never learned, the gift of his wings having determined his hall without any choice. It was not as though he had ever wanted to apprentice in Ms'egol, but what if he had? This mancy of the material was everyday work for the academy. How might his strength and speed compare to the power of reshaping the world? He embraced the multitude of ideas until they reached the remains of a great slice of the same black stone, shattered at the center and laying in two halves against the walls. They flew through the opening before halting abruptly, presented to the room beyond and the enormous monument within.

'*Golvulilt*!' Keimas exclaimed.

His expansive wings dropped, his face draining at the sight of an awesome yet sinister arch. Gaialja released him and circled it, admired its hundred-foot stature and smooth curves. It was the only finely crafted surface within, as featureless as any they had passed, though it had the same linear grooves. Between the two sides there was a plate embedded in the ground into which were engraved innumerable glyphs of a pastel red hue from discolored sand crammed into the finely carved lines. At first glance it was extraordinary by its sheer size but, after his initial shock, Keimas stood mutely analyzing it. It was not as bombastic as his Gate, yet the balance and ornamentation of the arch were of a unique glory.

Gaialja saw in his face exactly what she had hoped for and entered his view at the object's base with eyes that gleamed.

"Now begins your lessons," she said proudly. "Tell me what you see."

His brow furrowed.

"*Minein*, I wanted to learn what I don't know, not embarrass myself by showing it."

"Please," Gaialja cajoled, taking his hand. "Only try."

"It's out of place," he said plainly.

"*Uein quo?*"

Keimas hesitated, then stumbled through what he thought was a pathetic observation:

"It doesn't belong here. I have seen obsidian before, but this stone is not known to me. There are no joints between it and the foundation, as though they are mended together, not merely placed one atop the other. It must be the work of mancy but…it's very old; older than you or any of us that came as refugees. As I see it, this was surely the work of Ferraro, or some other god of the ground."

Gaialja bobbed up and down excitedly, squeaked with happiness and jerked him closer to the writing in the floor, professing "*Laan*! I thought the very same, postulating that if this stone has stood for as long as I think then it must have preceded any Galaila presence here. Bless my brush, you were born into this! Tell me more. Tell me everything you can. I promise I'll only be impressed."

Keimas became immersed in the moment as he applied his hunter's senses to this new realm of exploration. He sniffed the ground around the markings and felt their texture, tracing their progression along the base plate. He thought of how he might stalk prey from the air and what might keep it hidden from him, saw this object through that lens.

"Whoever made it, if I were to pretend knowledge of them, was likely ashamed of it. *Mineina*, not ashamed but wanted to keep it

258

hidden. It is solid as a mountain and would not fall to wind or rain, so why not build it above ground? Its creator wanted to make sure it went unseen.

"Correct again," Gaialja said, delighted by his insight. "Upon exploring the entrance to this labyrinth I've concluded that whoever left this behind had a use for it but might also have lived here and guarded it."

Keimas was at a loss, mumbled to himself about what it could possibly be. Gaialja trotted over and knelt tight to Keimas' side to run her fingers across the writing in its base and hurriedly explain.

"It is…I cannot make guarantees, though I have an idea. You can read this, *la*?"

Keimas followed her hand but felt woefully unable to do as she asked. True, the symbols were familiar but even those he recognized were misshapen or appeared to be out of order.

"It's not proper *Maen'ghan* words."

"Or perhaps a much older dialect," Gaialja corrected him.

Keimas looked at her, shared her amazement, then threw himself on the script to unlock its mysteries. Reading excitedly, he became increasingly confused and dismayed.

"*Eina*… 'Talk this river fields of…parent. Talk this river…down twenty-three wood?' It's like it was written by an idiot child," he said.

"Quite the opposite, my friend. It is we who are the children. This was the original language, the very first language, before our oldest ancestors began changing the meanings to common words because they could not pronounce them!"

"That's absurd. Who would have created a language their own children could not speak?"

"A parent we did not know," Gaialja looked ready to burst. "Something that came before us but was not of us, something completely unlike mortality but is the earliest form from which we take our own."

"Like a god."

"No, something unlike even a god. At least, not like Loi," she contradicted.

"What thing would have a need for something like this?"

"Does its form not reveal a purpose to you? Forget the notion that these ancient creatures are different from us. What would this be to you if you had built it?" Gaialja inquired with tense expectancy.

Keimas knew his answer, wondered if it would make any sense if spoken aloud.

"It's...a door?"

"*Einalaan!*" she cheered.

As understanding dawned, Keimas was infected by her exuberance.

"But to where? For whom?"

His teacher took his fingertips to place beneath her own upon the words, whispering to him her own translation of what he had read.

"Open this way to the fallen of the field, open this road to twenty-three heads."

That was enough for Keimas to think on, but to his surprise it was not all Gaialja had deciphered.

She went on, "Give us to the dark below. Mother masters child, child masters the blood. Open this way and wake the nest. In the name of a dead woman, open the twenty-three veins of the outworld and fill the drowning pool."

"Twenty-three heads," Keimas grumbled.

"*Quo?*"

"Nothing. Nothing at all."

Gaialja dismissed his reflection, but Keimas felt anxiety nip at him. Could it be that Gaialja had misinterpreted? Twenty-three seemed certain but was 'hands' a mistake? Could it be eyes? He was shaken to his core to think the ghastly visage who had appeared to him was the very being who had set this stone in place. Was he meant to find this? It simply could not be. All their observations told him this was not a strength for the many-eyed ghost, rather a weakness; something that could reveal its nature and secrets.

"It's a lock," Gaialja interrupted his thoughts, tracing the glyphs again. "A verbal lock to make sure no other was capable of accessing it. You see the symbol here for 'open'? It has these flares on its outer edge and this tail beneath the character." Keimas tried to clear his head as she spoke, tried to piece together what she was saying as she critiqued the shape. "Our tongue is founded on that which was lost to us, the old tongue. This is the character we

Galaila adopted and used for 'open', but that's not what it means. It's a secret word, one that probably means the same thing but that no one has seen written this way. I have repeated the incantation over and over to no avail. All I can surmise is that the words themselves are not the key, but the exact sounds as they are written. The original pronunciation was one we can never uncover, leaving us with a word we can never know."

"A secret protected by a dead language," Keimas groused.

"*La, udai.* Just imagine; a hidden race that has been using these monoliths as transport, possibly throughout the Veil to realms we cannot even conceive of. I believe they are still among us, watching us."

This conclusion came with a strange pitch of optimism. Keimas recognized the tone, at once hopeful against all opposition and brimming with joy. Gaialja's face was full of life, a reminder of that of his wife. For the first time he noticed that she too had sparkling blue eyes. By rationale he was forced to believe it was a coincidence but the look she gave him was a meaningful one. To be here, learning about things that made his own existence seem trivial and intrusive on a world far bigger than he thought possible, he recalled the first time he had felt such a sense of insignificance. It was the first time he had seen Lemalie's smile, the moment he had caught her eye and his became enthralled to her. It was when he had fallen hopelessly victim to love and felt so small and meek in its clutches; the greatest feeling he had ever experienced.

Gaialja squeezed his fingers and instinctively Keimas reacted by applying equal pressure, barely aware that it was hers and not Lemalie's as he reflected. Gaialja blushed and withdrew, feeling the passion that Keimas exuded. She felt vulnerable to him and so was especially put off when he mentally shook himself free of his musings, his voice becoming rough and demanding.

"I need to see your prophet. Now," he ordered.

"I told you, he must not be approached. He will summon you."

"He HAS summoned me! It was all for his summons, which even now I have not been told the purpose of, that I abandoned my bride and my city. I nearly died crossing that infernal desert!" Fuming as his Kutu blood started retaking his mind, he marched off toward the passage from which they had come. "I never should have let myself be distracted. Your business is not mine and I do not care for the employ of either physic or spellmaker. Mine is the warrior's, and to be a fool on a fool's errand and traitorous to my bride was a mistake I should have recognized!"

Gaialja was hot on his heels, tugging at his wings until she was forced to cut him off.

"Stop! Keimas, arrest your impetuousness. You cannot go there!"

"I can and I intend to," he growled.

"You came here to us, asked us to present you to him and accepted his will. Why are you suddenly so hostile toward it!?"

"He took me from my wife!" Keimas' rampage down the hall halted and his face went dolorously limp, tonguing the words he knew he had to say but sorely hated to. "*Mineina*...he showed me...and then I left her."

"Just so! YOU left her." Gaialja's congeniality had completely dissolved in Keimas' caustic affront to her beloved prophet and she loosed her ire on him. "Have you forgotten!? Have I stuttered!? You left your wife! YOU! Do not dare accuse our lord Loi or his disciples of tricking you away from your wife when you chose to come here and seek them! This is your last chance, kutliku-man. Either have faith in your god or run home like a sniveling child!"

Keimas was humbled at the sudden onslaught. Guilt and shame at his irreverent words followed, thereafter thronged by pain at the thought that he may still be very far from the end of his journey. He knew she was right, that he had given himself to this purpose at the expense of another. It was the duality of his mind that made every choice he made such a burden, not some futile struggle against the preordained.

"*Eihs malpael. Malpael* Gaialja. Gods forgive me and I beg the same of you. You are right, I did choose this, surely in the worst possible fashion with no regard to how it would affect anyone but myself. I was selfish and it was my own vanity that made me blame you and yours. Absolve me my offenses."

Gaialja still pouted, injured by his apparent lack of belief but impressed by his modesty.

"The forgiveness of gods I cannot promise. Mine is freely given and I apologize as well for my cruelty. I too left a lover to serve my god. To my great embarrassment I will admit to fleeting times of regret about the decision."

"You were of love?" Keimas inquired.

"And made one. Quite newly at the time, like yourself. He was a hard man and a hunter. He was with us when we arrived but there was some…conflict of desires between us."

"He was no follower to Loi?"

"A better one than I, actually. You believe in Loi, *la*? Do you believe the stories of his throne in the clouds?"

"*Minla.* I did when I was very young. Some called it that, others the 'Aurba Door' or the 'Seat of Laesis'. It's hard to believe a story that changes with every telling."

"Those indeed were the same names jestingly spoken of in my village. Travelers brought these stories to us all my life, stories of the god and goddess who had begotten Loi residing in a stronghold of unimaginable size and splendor, raising our newborn lord in a home built of wind and teaching him who we were and how best to care for us. We all enjoyed, but my mate was completely obsessed with the thought of its existence. The idea that Loi ruled from a physical place that mortals could enter led him to repeat the tales without end, enkindled by the same manic fervor that had led others to their deaths in distant lands."

"What happened to him?" Keimas said, intent on her story.

Gaialja's eyes fluttered closed from time to time as she recalled her misfortune.

"It stopped for a time when we were forced to leave Ellel. He stayed by my side thence but when we arrived here…gods give me patience, that woman was practically waiting for him. She was Galaila but strange, not like us but very similar. Encamped in this very cave, she welcomed us at first, spoke about her unending search for that holy place. Takinoxote, she called herself. Fanatical, like my husband and swearing on all she held dear that it would be she who found the Jioukhaadi of the god and bade all who desired true salvation to follow after her."

"He believed it," Keimas said, closing his eyes. "And he left you."

"Like a wide-eyed waif. He barely even said goodbye. So great was his love for Loi that he journeyed with this woman into the wilderness on a quest to find his presence."

Keimas was not unaware of the similarities between her story and his own.

"*Eina malpaelan*, Gaialja. I am broken to think that my wife feels as you do now, betrayed for an end that may be nothing more than morning shadows."

Gaialja wiped her eyes and smiled weakly at him.

"Don't ever think that. There is no shadow of the will of Loi. Shaken by days of loneliness I likely would have chased after my beloved Bandta purely out of love, if the prophet had not appeared to us immediately after. We each made our choices, both believing we were doing what would bring us closer to Loi. He was not alone either. One of our others went with them; Kjan another hunter."

"I suppose it wouldn't be the first time that differing interpretations of the same belief drove people apart," Keimas said thoughtfully.

Gaialja turned away, hiding her grieving eyes.

"Yes…that's why you can never forget that somewhere inside your wife there is a piece of her that knows what you are doing is right. There are limited alternatives for her. Either that you truly have been led away for a purpose, that you are delusional, or that you are a liar. If she really loves you there is only one she will willingly believe."

Her compassionate words found their mark, soothing Keimas' aching heart. He opened his mouth to reply but the ground beneath his feet began to vibrate and a cold wind blew out from the place of their ingress. With it came a low and rumbling sound, like a groan from the throat of the rocks. Keimas fluttered his wings to stay standing, fighting the wind until it died and he could settle again. Gaialja endured the disturbance without moving, bowed to Keimas and said with some finality, "This is the end for us, Keimas. I hope I will see you well…someday. For now, your path lies ahead. Go up from my study and you will find him. I cannot go with you."

He said nothing, mirrored her solemnity, suddenly unnerved in wondering what waited for him.

It had been a short journey to reach the stone arch, yet the return felt like a lifetime. Each step echoed around him and the wind that had called to him seemed to rise and fall in time, each gust shaping the sound within it more and more into the faintest words. He could not distinguish them but felt they implored him to come closer.

On entering Gaialja's workshop he felt completely lost without her. All bright light was doused and his path through the tables was lit only by a glow emanating from around the distant bend, refracted in the transparent stone surfaces nearby him to create the feeling of wading through the stars to reach Laesis before it disappeared in the Tau.

He reached the far side and turned the corner, saw that this light must have been burning all along, dim and unnoticed next to the lights kept by Gaialja until they were suddenly snuffed out. Oily substances fueled a blaze leaping from a trough along the right wall which ended at a dark recess, more hole than door. He stepped through, leapt away from the flame as the ground beside him seemed to crack and spread apart to make way for it. It was following alongside him, lighting his way as he ventured deeper, now very anxiously. The cavernous route wound upward, then down, then up again. All the while the oil slithered through the rocks and pulled along the guiding flame. Keimas felt a new respect for the power of the prophet, as well as increasing certainty that its relation to Loi must be a complicated one. This was Ferraro's mancy, not Loi's. His doubts would persist until he heard the revelation he had come for, but this was no amateur trick of illusion. There may only be a few enchanters in Hanging Gate with the skill to move liquids with such precision. Visions and predication could be considered impressive but this thing awaiting him was more than a clairvoyant. Perhaps it was more than a prophet. He would not challenge its power but neither would he lower his guard.

CHAPTER 25: A DARK DREAM STIRRING

The enemy of Raphenie's unrequited love was gone at last. To her immense satisfaction she did not have to suffer through manipulating Capheif to dote on Nepiur further before her departure with the caravan. It was not expected to be a long journey and with the shortest and sweetest of partings Nepiur had gone out at daybreak to join her company. They had gone away like ghosts, with only the earliest of risers to see them off.

Quietly, now with complete freedom to cherish her property, Raphenie lay in Capheif's arms with her hand firmly latched to his throat and her face as limp and expressionless as his. She had induced in herself the same state she had in him, their minds entwined.

Her triumph was short lived as she came to feel the limits of her power pushing back. Mani remained in her possession, safely stored in his room, mute and lethargic and unable to ruin her game. Maintaining the bond with him required only some of her concentration but controlling both he and Capheif had become taxing and unsatisfying.

The emptiness she was now feeling only worsened her bitterness. Having Capheif now was disappointing. He only did what she told him to, said what she said, never with genuine ardor or even a glimpse of emotion. She felt his mind, like Mani's, fighting back while trapped under her hand. She was desperate, hungry and afraid of losing her hold on him, then had an epiphany. She thought perhaps they could be closer if she could see him within, leaving behind her own body and making them of one mind. Stepping out of herself she had entered him and conjoined their thoughts in their purest forms. However, her power was still immature and she could not control all that was within her, for there was more than mere emotions. Unwittingly, she had made herself vulnerable. Shaking the roots of her mind had disturbed the ground beneath, waking the worms and maggots that bred in putrefied memories.

Thetrulengo speaks,

Memory is such a fickle river, so easily diverted for use by more advanced intellects or simply blocked until it overflows destructively. Kulibreal knew this, perhaps even invented the very idea of turning a single memory to stone so that other, more dangerous ones could not be reached or flow past it. Upon herself and the sister she wanted to protect she performed such a ritual, preserved their sanity before the rancorous memories that haunted them could tear them apart from within, for they carried the very soul of the one who had put them there. With time I have come to respect Kulibreal's intentions, though more and more I see that her failure makes them irrelevant now.

I should have paid closer attention during the second great war, when Maengir and its peoples were new and the elder gods full of mordant passion. Ephielipax may have been foolish but never weak-willed. Perhaps he was not taken by Quetzuaul, rather truly fallen in love with her. She and her brother share the power to take possession of minds. Could she have touched Ephielipax and overwhelmed him when he welcomed her to his lands to make peace? Otherwise, perhaps her treachery slept until she found herself mated to him, waking only when she was certain his full confidence was hers. Their son has a fraction of this power too. The elder god Loi made her ability his own, binding any soul more fragile than his own. It was this terrible power to enthrall whole nations that made Ferraro and Kulibreal believe the war would end very poorly if they gave him time to amass armies gathered from the willing and unwilling alike. They moved quickly to force upon him a truce, a mutual retreat into the Veil, while they still held the advantage.

How deep do the roots of the elder godhood go? They died out as suddenly as they appeared, only living for a few thousand cycles. I wholly overlooked what bonds entangled many of them. Even of Quetzuaul's protection of Zeniquorer I was only marginally aware. With his nomadic nature and her unmoving empire, they never directly opposed one another. Yet, each time another god assaulted Zeniquorer, Quetzuaul would appear to fight them back. She was so full of malice and pride and still she seemed bent on protecting him. Surely, this is why Oorghunak never tried to save Miohaelia for so long. He feared Quetzuaul, as every living thing did. It was only when her son was born and subsequently consumed her that Oorghunak was free to finally annihilate Zeniquorer and protect his love.

Quetzuaul and Zeniquorer...they were siblings? Yes, that must be it. He was the younger brother and she defended him, perhaps even cared for him. He possessed her same powers, tried to use them against she whom he lusted after, the virginal goddess Miohaelia. However, her purity of heart and mind was too great for his cruel tricks to capture, so he took her by brute force.

Now, a hundred generations hence, the lost product of their union seems to have inherited more than just her mother's essence. I dare say she has gained more from their father than Kulibreal was able to protect her from, more than she could withstand. Raphenie is more powerful than any of the other heirs I have seen risen from mortality, though she cannot use her full power. Its two opposing halves conflict with each other. Like light and flesh, they cannot coexist in their truest forms. If these two natures cannot shed their power and therefore bind, then one must be destroyed...only one of this woman's minds can survive.

~Chronicle of Wonders, the Two Faces

On a floor that did not exist, illuminated by an inner light that did not shine, Capheif's soul lay prostrate beneath a silent tempest of white smoke that crept indelicately over him like fingers and hands. Gripping and binding him, they pricked his skin, held his mouth tightly shut and tightened all the more as he screamed and struggled. The pain of being pushed down deep inside himself was almost unbearable but was eased somewhat when Raphenie's consciousness joined him, willing comfort upon him. His agony less, he did not feel gratitude as he saw the image of her emerge, thrashing no matter how desperately she tried to heal him with her love.

She felt for him, wanted him to see what she saw. It was no doubt difficult to comprehend that these terrible means could be for a beautiful cause. She had to find a way to make him understand. He had to. He had to see that she was doing no wrong. Her love justified all.

She strove relentlessly to fight him down and convince him of her affections with desperate words of affection until both of them were spent. While he still moaned before her, she loomed with baleful eyes and chewed her lip until it bled imaginary drops of blood. Every time his lips crept free of the bonds he screamed in denial of her. The more she tried to wheedle him with sweet nothings the more hateful he became. It was his own fault she had to trap him like this. It was his own damnable fault that he would not accept her.

As he writhed, Capheif saw a sudden change in his captor. The Raphenie he had known reemerged, succumbing for the briefest moment to the sinking realization that she had made a mistake, that he did not love her. She imagined moving on without him, and her heart broke at the thought. However, it shattered entirely as she saw the pain she caused him. This was wrong. It had to end now. He had done nothing to deserve this. She trembled, and the surrounding void trembled with her, like a sudden clap of thunder coursing through their demi-world.

"My turn," came a haunting voice that seemed to both cover and fill her. More focused behind her, it was accompanied by a burning hand that crept over her shoulder and around her throat. She panicked, shrieked in alarm, crooked her head slightly and saw a forked tongue of ash and twilight flicking near her cheek as sickly sounds slipped from between smacking lips, *"You had your time, whore. Would you like father to show you how to take?"*

Her skin crawled, lips quivered and heart pounded as boney fingers slid over her skin and grappled her. She could not possibly understand what was happening, could not fight it, closed her eyes in prayer that this was a horrid nightmare. The specter gripped her tight and threw her to the dark ground beside Capheif, whose face was contorted in disgusted terror at seeing what spirit now haunted them. Together they witnessed for the first time that which lurked within Raphenie, her secret soul, the monster that scratched inside her.

Its body was lavender-hued with skin that moved like candlelight, crudely imitating the form of an ordinary man. Its twisted head was dominated by round, unblinking white eyes that twitched with madness. Though it stood tall, its arms drug along the ground. Its bowed and shriveled legs staggered freakishly, as though it had never stood upright. Neither alive nor dead, its energy was so sinister and giddy that it defied comprehension as it howled and flailed down to trap Raphenie once more.

She wailed on and tried to crawl away, helpless to escape the vicelike grips on her wrist and ankle that drew her back and held her down. It snatched her jaw and turned her head to Capheif, whose pained whimpers now reflected fear for both of their safety. His anger toward Raphenie washed away as the intruder jeered:

"Look what you did! Look and see what you did for me! You think you are a woman? A virgin woman? You are your mother's child. You were BORN a whore! You are disgusting! You are nothing! You let me in! This was what you wanted!" He turned her face back to his, grinding his lopsided jaw. *"Because you're weak, like your dirty mother. She didn't even fight back."*

"W-who are y-you?" Raphenie's shrinking voice whispered. The phantom purred and bristled in turn, visibly aroused by the sound of her fear unto shudders of pleasure.

"I have been waiting inside you, drinking your tears every time you cried yourself to sleep. I'm your soulmate, the soul you should have had..." His mouth gaped and gnarled, blocky teeth seemed to grow from its shadow. He bit her cheek and savored the taste of her light as it flowed like blood, releasing her only to lick it away. *"And I had to watch you live like a coward for so long, fighting you for freedom while you wallowed in shame. Finally, FINALLY, you let me out...mm, you taste like your mother."*

Unseen and unimpactful, another stood among these three; a being beyond life and time. It looked on and wept. Though for incalculable days she had spoken with the purpose of immortalizing her passing thoughts, this time her whole body crackled with hate, real and pure.

Thetrulengo speaks,

This is not right. I don't know what could truly be good or right but this is NOT it.

Why do I feel this? There is nothing to love about the living, and their suffering is only a part of everyday life. Am I becoming something less than what I was made to be, or have I woken to the very same? I'm standing in a woman's soul and feeling its screams upon my skin. It's like...like watching that little Hischates girl burn to nothing. I let her die, did nothing to save her and...

Thetrulengo the eternal, Thetrulengo the unbound, remembered the day she felt she was truly born. In her own revelation, she felt as though born again.

I felt so helpless, so afraid of how I might accidentally alter or injure this world if I intervened that I watched her die, even stole her name in some misguided attempt to keep her memory. Thetrulengo...she died because Ephielipax's war found her home in the lands of Quetzuaul. She was not unique, not destined to change the world but...she was innocent. Raphenie is innocent. All these creatures...are innocent, victims only of the torturous duality of their forms; the hungers of soul and flesh as they collide within.

He is here. He is really here, a revival of old malice! Of all horrible acts that I have seen, this is the most truly evil thing I have witnessed.

I want to kill him. How can that be? I hate him. I want him to go! I want him to DIE!"

Like a bolt of lightning Thetrulengo struck through the veils, through flesh and through Raphenie's mind, excited at the thought of Zeniquorer's soul snapping between her fingers. It did not come, even as she saw them close around his throat. She stared, disbelieving how her touch passed straight through him. She struck again, then again, affecting death upon this feculent god no more than she could upon herself. Once more she felt changed, different than ever before as she looked at her manifest appendage and saw how it evaporated at the touch of this soul. In a flurry she tried to seize Raphenie and pull her free, yet neither of their lights would allow her to take hold. She could move mountains, reshape creation, yet could not control the lighted soul. All this time, all her experiments and curiosities had not shown her this truth and her one limitation was at last revealed. She felt fear, confusion, then only hate. There was no time left. She had to act in any way she could. There were other weapons living in this city and she would make sure they found their way to this creature's throat. There was one in particular whom she must reveal herself to in order to bring it upon its ancient foe.

An other-worldly cry of pain echoed throughout the great walled city, making the hair of all that lived in Hanging Gate stand on end and quiver. Fieldsmen and fruiters threw down their work and sprang to their feet, tense and fearful. They heard its direction and knew it had come from Ms'egol but as they raced to intervene they were perplexed by the same din emanating from within Nesh; a scream not of Maengir. Something terrible was happening.

Nesh heard the cry within its deep reaches and its archons responded quickly, searching for the source. As they made their way to the atrium the main doors flew open and father Mani barged in. Voices stilled as he staggered back and forth among them, shouting feebly:

"Find her! FIND HER!"

Sky, still groggy from sleep and only half dressed, took a flying leap from the precipice of the rightward stair and landed nearly on top of Mani to take hold of him angrily.

"God's blood, *udai! Wektinapael*, what's wrong with you!?"

Mani's eyes were afire.

"Find the girl; the Mearnum alchemist with the silver hair! We have to kill her! She's a creature, a plague, a demon herself, *bsache*!"

The hallway beside the stage filled with firelight and frantic cries for help as an unfamiliar young girl appeared, flapping her hands and shouting for aid. Without further explanation, Mani pushed past Sky to the girl, half the council in pursuit and some just now entering the hall, following the pointing fingers and nervous direction of concerned citizens.

As quickly as she had appeared, the girl was gone. Whisked away into the veil, hopeful that she had rallied enough attention to keep Raphenie safe for now.

The doors of Capheif's chambers sailed off the wall when Mani's palms struck them with the mountain-shaking power of classical mancy. As the mob intruded, a wretched spectacle was spread before them: Capheif lay fetal in the far corner, rolling back and forth and clawing at his temples with blood-soaked hands. By his side was Raphenie's battered body, face down on the stone with blood pooling between her legs and scratches covering her throat and back.

Sky cringed and nearly vomited. Sebashni and Obure fought back the crowd and demanded they retreat from the scene. Mani was struck dumb. He had suffered Raphenie's power and believed her to be the danger but this travesty, ostensibly at Capheif's hands, was a more brutal act than any he had ever seen. Sky called for Khurk and Artimecian to get Raphenie to safety, and together they lifted her gingerly. Artimecian ripped a fur from the bed and swaddled the girl's hips in it to help protect her and hide her injury. The moment he had finished, she woke, first with whimpers they tried to comfort to silence. Then, as she escaped her delirium, her eyes flared at the sight of the archons bearing down on Capheif.

"Don't! It's still inside!" She screamed in protest while reaching out to him.

They fought to drag her out, but the room fell quiet as the clamor of Capheif's howling faded, replaced by a distorted, jerking laugh. Raphenie fought her way down from the fathers' arms and tried to crawl away through the crowd's legs, constantly ensnared by hands reaching to protect her while only preventing her escape. Crying desperately for them to let her go, the cackling caught her with a chill and, rolling over onto her back, she faced Capheif. He stood and steadily grew in an aura of swirling violet embers, becoming so large that his shoulders pressed against the ceiling. He held a finger out at Raphenie and opened his eyes for the first time, revealing eerie, pearlescent firelights.

"That...belongs...to me..."

"NOOO!" Raphenie screeched, barely escaping Capheif's grasping hands as they smashed through others to reach her. Khurk's taut old muscles grabbed her, hauling her past the other archons and stampeding down the only egress. He sprinted her away even as she squirmed and wailed in his arms, finally setting her at the tunnel's mouth and bellowing for soldiers.

The thunder of Capheif's paws shook the hall, his pursuit slowed only by his own girth as he swelled and pressed against the walls, which now could barely contain him. Terrified archons and citizens piled over one another in flight, shouting for every family to abandon Nesh.

Raphenie looked back from the outer steps as she fled, stood petrified as others thronged the vestibule and passed her. Tears inconsolably streamed as she saw the back wall of Nesh cracking and buckling under the assault of the man she loved. The thought that this living hatred cursing him had been part of her turned her stomach. It didn't matter who it was in. She was all it wanted; possession in any way it could find. As the doors closed, she could not imagine any light that could part that darkness, no love that could shine through a hatred so extreme.

CHAPTER 26: JOURNEY MAHAURBA

For a long time Keimas stood in the final, tomblike room of the ill-lit burrow, nerves taut. This was a very different world from Gaialja's furnished laboratory. An unnatural silence pervaded the mist and stones. Even his own breath and movement were noiseless. The fire that had accompanied him had ceased at the threshold, leaving him straining in search of any sign of life in the profound blackness. The air moved about him again and he felt purpose in it, like the vibrations were the prophet's call. As it came rushing against him, a renewed firelight moved with it, darting into a web of troughs all across the floor, increasingly expansive as the fire revealed it.

Many crisscrossing stone columns leaned into the slanted roof of a cramped chamber that appeared to have been displaced by an earthquake sometime in the past and was now tilted and twisted in several different directions. The slinking flame coursed up along the face of the furthest pillar and into a ring of similar carvings on the ceiling ahead. Keimas' understanding of the room was already warped by its shape and path but his attempts to discern its construction were abandoned when he noticed that the circle that now burned furthest from him did not spread about as though seeking the sky, instead licking downward toward the ground. Adjusting his eyes as the conflagration came to rest, he saw a shape sculpted into the wall beyond the upside-down fire. Warily moving closer, he saw it was a simple face. The journey across the odd room was disorienting to the point of nausea, as if each step changed the way the surrounding earthplane pulled on him. However, he neared the warm glow crackling overhead and, much to his surprise, did not go careening up into it. Wary of further surprises and with eyes narrowed quizzically, he craned his neck to closer examine the relief. It was merely a carving, flat-lipped, with rounded depressions for eyes. It had peripheral edges but lacked even ears, a completely unimaginative image of a living thing.

A guttural chuckle nearby perked up Keimas' ears and, retreating from the effigy, his gaze fell rightward on a similar face he had not noticed before. Like a thespian's mask in the wall, it was frozen in revelry. A gentle breeze again came, carrying a deeper laugh with it. The greater face did not move no matter how Keimas waited for it and finally he turned away to the entry, nearly leapt from his skin as he was confronted by the sight of hundreds of faces no bigger than his own staring back at him. They were contorted into every expression he could imagine, yet none moved, covering the arches, the walls, even emerging from the floor. He had not simply missed them. They were emerging one by one. It seemed any flat surface was claimed in time and reformed as part of the weird gallery of eyes and mouths.

"They've never seen someone like you before," a voice at his back explained.

The voice had a calming effect and Keimas settled, serious but unalarmed. It was deep, incredibly so, but not aggressive or pompous. It sounded rather like a Bakul, large and pleasant. He turned back to the prominent face. It smiled, finally moved, speaking quietly as a friend.

"A Kutu; that is what you are? They do not know of your kind as I do. They are not of Manti and do not watch the above world."

Keimas' long withheld anger reflected in his voice as he demanded, "How closely do you watch, Golgamet the earthen prophet?"

"Closely enough to know that it is impatience with only yourself which compels you to speak to me with such an impudent tongue."

"*Minuein*, you have done all in your power to push me to it."

"And who can say with what ease I did so? Your regret at being parted from your woman has made me your enemy even before I speak," the sculpture retorted.

"Yes, it has," Keimas rejoined, with no indication of repentance. Finally confronting the locus of his problems, he would tolerate no more nonsense and entertain no more ado. Throwing his arms apart as though one whose time was more important than a god's, Keimas mockingly exclaimed, *"Eina taultutana,* speak! Reveal what you have kept for me! Your acolyte has provided no useful insight, so my life is wagered on the value of whatever you have to say."

Golgamet replied with perfect equanimity.

"I commend your passion, both for the love of your wife and for the will of god. It was these that brought you here, not me."

"Minta, my head aches. I'll take little pleasure from idle conversation," Keimas warned.

"Very well. Since you will not play into the secrets of my word, hear me now. Your god demands your devotion, Blue Sky Raptor. You have presented yourself because you fear for the safety of your wife. Is this your heart?"

The prophet spoke slowly, deliberately, carefully choosing each word. While it worsened Keimas' headache, it nonetheless revealed how much the prophet knew about him. Likewise, it was said in a manner that paid respect to Keimas' priorities, contrary to Gaialja's disapproval, for holding his wife above his god.

"I grant you," Keimas admitted, "You are adept at...whatever gift has allowed you to know these things. *Eina,* this day has seen my capacity for explanations into all the workings of the world filled, except those that concern me."

"Dues are nearly paid," the prophet assured him, "For all that you seek and more, oh man of god. Do you praise the lord Loi?"

"By virtue of my tribe I am submissive to Loi as much as the next man," Keimas said, wearily and without reverence.

"And yet your tribe does genuflect before his daughter," Golgamet replied.

"La, the *golaia* Anama, his daughter she is? She is most contemptuous of him."

"She is his only child, but a traitor to the elder gods and an obstacle for the *Jioukhaadim* Aurba. Loi's voice, through the eyes of the creature that first came before you, has reached far in search of a powerful mortal who could serve as a weapon to cut away the rotting flesh of the world. He has found you."

"Explain! What does Loi expect of me?"

"Kill for him. Kill Anama," came the slow response.

Keimas' throat closed and his wings dropped to the ground. It was a preposterous command, his thoughts a jumble at the impossibility of carrying it out. At his silence, Golgamet pressed further.

"Do not shy away from the task your god has given you," he insisted. "I was once mortal like yourself, yet in the glory of Loi I was remade as a hammer to smite the foes of the almighty, as you also will be."

"How? How can a mortal raise a hand to a goddess? What you ask cannot be done."

"It can, and your hand will," Golgamet insisted.

The pain behind Keimas' eyes grew even worse. He massaged his forehead as he paced in confusion. He had been so proud in the past, so vainly convinced of his own excellence among his kind, even to the point of resenting Govan for being his only better. Throughout his time with Lemalie she had chastised him for it, made him mindful of his pride and helped him control it. She had made him a stronger, more disciplined man. Now the voice of Loi expected him to be capable of so much. It was senseless, even by the standards of a man who had recklessly chased that voice unto his death if not for Hopi's intervention. He could not believe, no matter how hard he tried. There was no chance.

"Prophet, *quola*...why me?"

"Among mortals on this island and all across the world, with their many blessings, you are yet more rare. You are touched and taken, encompassed by the soul of your ancestor. You are your father's son and every marvelous power that was his is destined to be yours. Through me, Loi can awaken your inheritance."

"Prophet," Keimas droned, "I come from a family of masons. Poor ones. My mother bore me without a father to know and so young was I when she died that I cannot even remember her face."

"Man, your father was not for you to know. He is of the highest order and not given to appearing before us. It is his very blood within you that makes you fit for the blessings of your god Loi."

"My father was a philanderer," Keimas hissed.

"You father," Golgamet soothed, "Was Loi's father."

Keimas' heartbeat pounded in his ears. He waited for laughter, praying the faces would jeer at him as though it were all a game. They waited as he did and the face before him glowered while he took in the news. In the end, his mind was not so easily turned about.

"Perhaps he should have been a better one…to all of us." He shuddered as he said it and the images of what he was shown returned to him. He had no faith in Loi, neither had he any left in Anama. There was some truth in what he witnessed. There had to be.

"But," he finally conceded, "I will bear whatever blood you ask if you will but tell me the meaning of what I have seen."

Golgamet grinned deeply, and the spooky faces all around him tittered obnoxiously.

"Good! Good, man! I knew you would see your way to god!" he said, triumphantly.

"No. I do not." The revelry abruptly ceased at Keimas' grave rejoinder. "I enjoy stories as much as any other, but I have no intention of giving Loi the satisfaction of using me like some pointed tool with which to pierce she who gave us safe haven when we who trespassed against her." His temper built again, reflected again in the volume of his voice. "Each time you or one of your ilk promises me answers I find myself captured by pointless diatribes presuming my loyalty to the gods, demeaning me for questioning them. Not once has anyone bothered to take notice of my lack of concern for their prayers, for they have never heard mine! You expect gains on my yearning to protect what matters to me, *la*? Why then, without a single word as to the gains of my own people have you presumed that I will kneel? *Wektminta*, Ferraro purged our land with smoke and cinders and Loi did nothing! Nothing! Families burned to dust in the inferno, and where was Loi? We arrive here and are met with the thuell. Where was Loi!? Now he calls to me and demands my service!? *Eina*, WHERE IS HE NOW!?"

Golgamet's face wrinkled and cracked, lips grinding in distaste.

"You are untrue," he growled. "You are not loyal."

"Do not speak to me like a beast of burden!" Keimas retorted.

"You've given me nothing but the charge of an executioner and hollow reasoning without explanation! If Loi would have words with me then let him speak now!"

Golgamet's eyes drooped, as did the many faces beside him.

"I am sorry, mortal. I truly am. Loi cannot speak to you. He is a prisoner."

Silence stretched on for a few moments as Keimas thought.

"*Utan*, how can that be?"

"By the treachery of his daughter, I'm afraid. You know the evils of Ferraro. It was Anama who shared with her the secrets of how to defeat Loi."

"Why then does Anama shelter us?" Keimas shouted, gripping his head and irate from the inexplicable headache. "Are we not her father's people?"

"Anama does not shelter you, oblivious creature. This island is a trap. She is no longer the beloved child of Loi but a collaborator with the enemy. You believe she shields you from the dangers of this world? Who, my young Kutu, do you think unleashed the thuell upon you?"

Keimas' face roiled with heat and tears, his mind blurring.

"No...no, she...NO!" His great fists crashed down upon the already cracked ground and he beat it until his knuckles spewed blood, lashing his wings and raising a whirlwind of dust while his anguished screams echoed. When his fists could take no more punishment, he shifted to assaulting the floor with open palms, the fore of his head, his chest and elbows. Spittle formed between his fangs, and he collapsed in a destitute heap. "It cannot be. We worsh...we worshipped her."

"She is the greatest trickster of all, sired by your god who loves you and traitor to he who cherished you."

"She killed so many," Keimas mused aloud. "The thuell killed everything."

"And when she failed to exterminate the children of her father," Golgamet continued relentlessly, "She enslaved you with sweet promises, taking from Loi the last thing he possessed, pacifying you and making you her own."

"On the one condition that we never seek her out...*einla*, that we never confront her..." Keimas concluded, lifting his filthy face to match Golgamet's. "...And in return she would not allow her

'Favorite children' to consume us."

"The thuell," Golgamet sneered. "The threat she wielded against you and the token for brokering your worship are one and the same."

"How could we?" Keimas marveled. "How could I?" He ground his teeth angrily as the full depth of their patron's deception assembled itself in his mind. At last, he weakly knelt in abject fervor, "I believe! Prophet, I am loyal! Please...let me kill her."

After a moment of silence, Golgamet's dire air turned once again to triumphant levity.

"Yes. Good. You will do as you have always dreamed, Kutu. You will armor your love and all your people in the benevolence of the lord god by rising from the ashes of his test. The promises of Loi are not as empty as Anama's. Your god rewards his champions.".

"*La! La*, let me be this! Tell me what I must do." Keimas' energy was renewed as he became filled with new faith.

"Anama is an adequate temptress and skillfully disguises her true form. She is beguiling, though strong indeed for a young goddess. Her essence is vast, permeating even the rock and thi and all living things, and by that essence are you taken and made like her mindless beasts of field and foliage. You must possess Loi's extreme power if you are to defeat her," Golgamet declared.

"*Eina*, tell me how!" Keimas demanded.

"Curb your impatience. Your loyalty will be tested again to know the cost."

"Let it be even my soul!" Keimas dared recklessly. Just as Keimas insisted, Golgamet confirmed.

"It is exactly that."

Keimas' impassioned words halted. Risking his inmost essence? He was, however, a Kutu, and one of love to his wife. There were more important things than survival, even of his immortal light.

"I will pay with it...for those who have died," he finally said.

"Is it so simple?" Golgamet asked.

"It is." Keimas stood slowly, setting aside the grisly thoughts of having his spirit ripped out of him. "To ensure my god's betrayer can never harm the woman I am part of, nor any of my countrymen ever again. She whom I love and call wife has, for seasons uncountable, tested my patience with lessons about giving myself in service to others. Now I will do this to the full; sacrifice myself in all ways unto absolute death. If that is the price, then let it be levied."

Golgamet listened as Keimas thought on the peril he faced.

"Man, this is true. You need not fear death. As Loi joins your body you will become the very embodiment of the godking!"

"Loi will be within me?" Keimas asked.

"Only in part. It is the legacy of those in the ancient bloodpool of Loi's mother that they are able to take control of lesser souls than their own, placing a part of themselves therein. The unfortunate consequence is that the host soul is suppressed. In such a robust presence it is sometimes destroyed."

"But...no, I cannot. My woman..." Keimas recoiled, thinking of Lemalie's reaction if he went willingly to the grave. Golgamet saw his fear and was ready for it.

"Do not be afraid, son," he said. "I will ensure Loi does not damage your little light. In compensation for your compliance, he will permit me to remove it from you and safely retain it within myself."

"Then will you not suffer the death you spare me?" Keimas asked.

Golgamet's expression soured, a halfhearted smile then arising on his craggy lips.

"It is you who is vital to the great plan, not I. This is the one god's will."

Keimas was deeply moved by this. That Loi would sacrifice the life of a powerful servant in order to spare his was enough to gain his service.

"Then make it so. *Malpael*, know I am saddened that you must pay my passage," he said with heartfelt humility.

"It is a minor cost," Golgamet declared, "To restore the lord most high to his rightful place."

"*Laan*, it is. For all that we will attain with the death to come."

As the somberness of the moment thickened, Keimas was overcome by the hesitation that accompanied all great and momentous decisions.

"Prophet, you called me something I have never been called before. In my heart of hearts, I believe you meant something in saying it. *Einta*, why have you called me 'Blue Sky Raptor'?"

"It is your true name; the name of the great spirit within you. It was the name of your father."

"Loi's father," Keimas repeated.

"It is that star that shines upon you."

"Explain," he demanded, feeling urged to know all that he could before being locked away, possibly forever. Golgamet favored it, apparently enjoying their conversation equally.

"Your father died long, long before you were born. Like all elder gods his body decayed, not in this world but in the veil that surrounds it. In that spiritual plane their essence was swept away, and they found new bodies, hosts of sufficient physical power to sustain them."

Without needing to hear further details, Keimas was prepossessed by an assumption brought on by his knowledge of the mythic Nhi'Thaun and their progeny. Legends he dismissed in youth suddenly made sense.

"My mother was home to a piece of a god?"

"No, my boy," Golgamet said with wonderment. "The Blue Sky Raptor did not simply find your mother. He fell in love with her. You are the result."

"And the Kutu, *uein*? Are we all descendants of the same elder god?"

"Just so. As all your kind grow in the presence of Anama, so did her connection to your elder awaken his bloodline in you. The fragments of his body chose you to live on in, beneath your notice but influencing who you would become. You, however, are not like the others; you are perfect, a firstborn. Your father visited your mother in her dreams and when a piece of him was finally able to touch her she became with child, immaculately conceiving you. Your others are born of his death, yet you were born of his love."

Keimas was dumbfounded. He had known hardly anything of his own family, believed what Maurus' had always told him after they had taken him in; his father was a vagrant and deserter, took his mother and abandoned her, not to be seen then or ever again by anyone of Tieg Raev. That man must have lived, though surely was not his sire. He felt warmed to know that the broken family he thought he had come from was more of an unexpected one, an unknowable gift.

"*Udai*, who is this god? Who is my true father?" Keimas asked.

"The entirety of his being you would not understand. It would take seasons to educate you on the rise of the elder gods and their great war that lifted him up from among his peers."

"*Eina prostas*, only tell me his name," Keimas pressed.

Golgamet hesitated. He thought hard but knew that a name in itself would mean nothing in the end.

"He was called Ephielipax," he confessed. "Elder god of the kutliku and all that soar on wings."

"I share the blood of a star," Keimas mused to himself.

"And with it the blood of all Ephielipax's descendants, communing with it like no other mortal can."

"And what of the other Kutu? What of Govan? Miriena? They are similarly descended?" Keimas demanded.

"They are, as I have described," Golgamet affirmed.

Keimas took this in, measuring the veracity of his words. "Then why me?" he asked at last. "Though I admit it reluctantly, Govan is twice the man I am," he confessed.

"That is truth only in that you believe it," Golgamet admonished. "By the love that created you, Ephielipax's presence is far greater in you. Though this place is far from Loi's dominion it is the unwitting cradle of Ephielipax's most potent seed. You bear wings, which was not intended by him who created you. Anama's power, combined with the pieces of his soul, have created in your kind more than just hosts, but reincarnations of his living form. What has made you the jewel of Loi's desire is the circumstances of your birth. The rest of your brothers and sisters were pierced by Ephielipax's soul after they had already grown, merely colored by it, but not you. You were born as if from Ephielipax himself, wholly formed from his soul and knowing its power since you were laid a droplet in your mother's womb. All men have sons, gods even more. It is said that by their children mortals achieve immortality. For the elder gods that is a limitless truth. Have you never wondered how your Kutu spirit so quickly grew to challenge your superiors? So great in you is the presence of Ephielipax that you slowly reap it from others of his line. You drink from all springs, depleting other Kutu and becoming even stronger."

"Do I hurt them?" Keimas asked.

"They are lessened around you, yet the soul always heals

itself..." This he said with a very knowing tone. "...Even growing a body anew as long as the soul persists. They will live and you will grow a hundredfold beyond them," Golgamet said.

Keimas pondered this, remained at odds with himself. There were a thousand things he wanted to know but had already been forced to absorb so much that he rose and dwelt on it silently. He was so internalized that he seemed to Golgamet as if asleep.

One by one the shattered pieces of Keimas' past, present and intended future fell into place and became clearer. Hands seeking the faces upon wall and pillar, he moved about to keep focus, eventually speaking again at a quick but articulate pace and with an exhilarated voice:

"Loi needs one who shares his blood...I still don't understand why. Not because he can only possess such a relative. No, but because he needs a god of comparable strength to she whom he seeks to kill. It is not the strength of Ephielipax that Loi desires in me, only the blood...the blood of Anama," he deduced. "Tell me, am I wrong? We are all a family, albeit distantly and only by divine blood in ghostly veins. It is a tangled web of bonds, but Loi is a brother to me and Anama is my...*aieis'itkaiana*? Both my sister and my daughter?"

Golgamet's stony features cracked and slanted in a solemn nod.

"It is so. Gods may falter and have their souls pushed into the aetherplane by many means, yet a god can only be wholly annihilated if killed by one of their own family; a soul that shares their likeness and so can completely consume it. As mortals slew one another to rise to godhood, so the divergent families of the divine both protected themselves from their peers and made themselves vulnerable to their children...and their ancestors."

"Prophet, you have offered to give me all that I asked for in Loi's name. I will do the same. For him, my wellbeing is immaterial. I deal only for my wife's safety. If she will live, then I will give my body to Loi."

"Swear to me now, man," Golgamet charged, "That you will forsake your flesh to the will of god and leave your soul here within these walls."

A deep breath for Keimas, not from fear but at the magnitude of this decision, kept his resolve before committing himself.

"On Loi's name, and my own," he said at last.

Golgamet's mouth gaped, and the forceful wind arose again to pull at Keimas from behind. The gravelly voice continued to emanate from the void therein as Golgamet's jaw dropped to nearly mesh with the floor in a grotesque transmutation.

"Then enter, hand of god, and become the executioner of this evil," several of the smaller mask around invited at once. Keimas turned, faced the emptiness and shuffled forward, tucking in his wings against the mounting gale and ignoring the inner monologue that begged him to rethink this insanity. It required only a few diligent steps and one most bold into the swirling maw, then another into darkness. As his wingtips passed beyond the periphery of the wall he felt a striking heat follow behind the wind. The fire from the ring above followed him and poured over his skin, drawing him further into the cavernous hold. The rock above and below him compressed a bit and in a belated panic begat by the leaping flames, he thrust his palms overhead and tried to turn back. It was too late for that. He was too deep to flee and too overcome by the collapse of the stone. As the scorching wind ripped him back, he felt his footing give way, grasping noiselessly for rock that was no longer there as he fell beyond earthplane and into the embrace of the Veil. He stared down at himself as he fell, yet upward as well, both feeling and seeing a thin smile creep over the face of his former self as the latter was abandoned to the dark.

CHAPTER 27: SISTERS FOUND

anging Gate had become a boiling cauldron of sweat and screams, the forces of Gazan ushering forth to pile against the palisade doors of Nesh to keep the nightmare inside from breaking out. Every time its doors were struck from within, they bowed outward from their pegs and effused freezing smog that crept down around the ankles of the twenty-some soldiers that strained bodily against them. Among them, having left Gazan for the first time in several seasons, was its commandant.

Commandant Schaleikin was a scarred and battle worn Kubernu, one of the first to defend the city against incursion from the West. As first of the militia and principal regimental trainer of Gazan, she doled out orders, setting flanks and formations where they belonged while trying to support the team that braced Nesh. The thick furs she wore hung from belts, each decorated with morbid trophies of her countless kills; teeth and claws, skulls of smaller prey, vertebrae of giant schiis and their dried eyes which she claimed could see every mistake made by those under her command. She was a beacon of strength to her apprentices, yet continually refused a place on the council. She did not treasure pride or respect, prizing instead her dark charisma and sublime ability to instill absolute fear and obedience in all warriors of the preparation cadre. Perhaps the only person more intimidating in all of Hanging Gate was Artimecian, and Aroch the only one more respected. She had come with a rage upon hearing the sounds of futile panic of her own soldiers, first that they were losing a fight, now in seeing what fight they faced.

"Commandant, it's failing! HELP!" cried an exhausted Bakul as he repeatedly bounced off the bucking door.

"*Minta*! Grip the crossbeam, not the handles!" She commanded, about-facing another stocky Kubernu nearby as her knobby claws snapped back and forth, "New ranks, to the front and take up the door!" she shouted.

In this manner she rotated out the defense, giving rest to the relieved and buying more time for positioning, yet it was not the bodies that were weakening unto breakage. The dense wood of Nesh's access could neither be sealed nor blockaded against the advance of the grotesque behemoth so malformed that even those who knew Capheif saw nothing recognizeable. The pitching of timbers against the door bar had lasted long enough to get the battalion in order but even the most seasoned warriors turned pale at seeing the slats' fringes splintering out to reveal the massive claws within.

"Keep hands high!" Schaleikin barked, stoic and cold. "Whatever is in there will not find its freedom against us!"

"*Einla aiat*!" her troops rallied. "No escape!"

Rentish joined Schaleikin at the head of the army and pounded the ground beneath him brutishly with heavy Bakul fists.

"Commandant, bring up the third line to flanking positions! We need to soften the depth of the ranks. The Iron Sanctum arises at our back to fight this devil!"

"The time is right that they fall on what prey deserves them!" She cheered in response, looking over him at the young witchcrafters sprinting out of Ms'Egol.

She issued the order first. Then, by Rentish's side, took her stand atop a jutting boulder. Soon Simeyer and Liklita arrived as well, and the four grand masters of Gazan stood together to confront their fate.

Sky, being of another disposition, was in emotional collapse. Completely surrounded in the fields he was overwhelmed by the populace of Nesh as they surged in utter disarray and begged his guidance. The heads of the families fought them back and directed them to find shelter in the highest reaches of Ms'egol or Gazan while Sky blubbered and stammered beneath them. His instinct was to insist that there was no danger, that it would be handled by their warriors, though his own inability to cope with the threat undermined him. As it ever was, his only hope was that Artimecian would shoulder a burden he could not.

Lemalie, locking arms with her father and no less confused than the rest, stared at the scene unfolding before her and embraced deflective thoughts to curb fear's dreadful assault on her mind. She imagined what would be done if Keimas was here. How was she to defend her still hidden child without exposing it to harm? Threats such as this were why they had created Gazan and Ms'egol, the warpath and witchcraft. As she watched the barely contained carnage this fiend wrought she feared for the lives of the battalion that stood against it. Aroch began to pull her away and, acquiescing to his protection, she allowed herself to be steered to safety within the stronghold of Gazan with the rest of the young and precious. She wished to stay and fight, knew she could at least contest with the monster, yet it was no longer her life that needed guarding.

While death was a pervasive and stifling notion to most, Gazan's bloodthirsty lifestyle and contempt for their own mortality made many of its militia even more ardent when they believed it was near.

"Let it come," Schaleikin shouted to the ranks about her as one of the beams bracing Nesh snapped like a dry twig. She turned to face them, marching deliberately as if to impose her courage upon them. "Anama has made us worthy of this foe and you have made yourselves worthy of a good death! Where do we go today but unto Vaeba's black beach!? I cannot wait to feast with the gods that have fallen before me! Enter us today into the underhalls of the Veil, to die as we lived, in battle for all eternity! *Hawthen bolg'tsk rokhway! Bolganan khaaaa!*"

Her battle cry resounded as she bared her teeth and raced back to the front line, repeated by each row as she passed until the entire army roared at her back. As one they repeated the cry, again and again, soaking in the spirit of their brothers and sisters on either side and in turn building the others'.

"*Hawthen bolg'tsk rokhway! Bolganan kha!* Unto death and

beyond! A big death for all!"

The cliffs around the door cracked and, even with the immense Bakul still restraining its face, the door would not last long. Planks shattered and shrapnel flew outward, while through the holes there gleamed hideous popping eyes over a maliciously fanged smile.

"Big death comes! Big death for all the brave! *Hawthen bolg*!" Rentish bellowed, drawing a claw across his tongue and spitting blood into his hand. Liklita followed suit and they locked hands. Together they would carry the bonds of Gazan all the way to the next world.

Artimecian's acolytes caught back of the formation and worked their way through, though the arch-witchcrafter stood over them on a low ledge on the opposite cliff. He saw over all, eyes closed, heartbeat slowing, ignoring the seeping of pained tears on his chest and wringing his hands. His soul was restless, restraining the power in his flesh and smiling at the thought of at last giving his all against a deserving adversary.

"I'm coming my love, my family, my home," he whispered fatalistically. "Wait for me a moment longer."

With a final blow the great door went sailing over the hunkered militia. That which had been Capheif came roaring and cackling out into the dawn-flooded canyon in a plasmatic wave that blinded his opposition. He stood a giant, only vaguely resembling the man he had been. Every hair had elongated, turning rigid and sharp. His bones had reshaped themselves and his skin broke away like burning bark as ancient power boiled out of every crack and pore.

Gazan's frenzied horde advanced against him like a stampeding herd, easy prey that never made it to striking distance before gargantuan fists swept them away. The entire first wave was crippled, Schaleikin with it, as she reached the forefront and launched with swinging fists like hammers against him. Though smote hard, she shook herself out of a daze from the painful blow, looked blearily through bloodied corneas as the monstrosity descended on them. He reared back, standing three Kubernu tall and smashing down with a force that shook the city and drove four soldiers into the ground like stakes. He snapped horns and spines with his flailing, mutated limbs, untouched by claws and barely damaged by the spikes of the Bakul. Schaleikin's fear of the celestial beings was redoubled upon seeing this thing in the flesh.

An evil god walked among them, and they had no defense against it.

Her musings were blown away by a sweeping wind and the ominously cast shadow of massive wings that thundered overhead. The hunter-killers had arrived. Undetected by the great beast they dove onto its head, lashing at the back of his skull and neck in such rapid, brutal succession that, even with his huge mass, he was thrown face down in the dust. Zeniquorer's madness was unfocused and undisciplined but remained unstoppable. Pain was ignored and the damage discounted as Soto and the other hunts pursued, sliced and snapped at him until they were all firmly attached by serrated talons and straining in opposing directions to pull him into pieces. With strength born of lunacy he bucked some off, bleeding from only a single perforation where Bohg'thane, hunt of Govan, had found weak skin at the base of his neck. Though it was barely a hindrance, it earned punishment in the form of a slashing hand that connected squarely with Bogh'thane's torso and propelled him end over end into the cliffs. Within Govan burned a vengeance that hardened his muscles as he plunged against the mutant Kubernu with an ear-splitting screech. Both his talons sank into one glowing eye, ripped it in half in a spray of blood as Zeniquorer's unnatural cries of agony revealed that he was not invulnerable. The army rallied with fresh fury, yet the beast grew bigger to match them. One eye marred and oozing and the other a hating jewel that swam with light, he leered hungrily at the beleaguered face of Raphenie as she looked back, she and her protectors disappearing into the depths of Gazan. He pounded the ground in a fit, dove forward and stole along the ground to hunt her with disturbing and unhindered speed, bullying mortals apart like water and wailing like a feverish child.

"No! No, no, I want her! She's mine! MINE MINE MINE MIIIIINE!"

The Kutu were distracted from their attack as their comrades were tossed into the air, catching those they could and sparing them long drops. Warriors on foot could not hope to keep up, though a few late arrivals of the Sanctum already waited between Zeniquorer and the object of his lust. One witchcrafter knelt, her sister vaulting from her hunched back and sailing over the monster.

"Zeulipendi - Iron Finger!" shouted Ms'egol Aia Minciel as she

willed the energies of distant volcanic rock to pass through the Veil and into her body. Streams of molten metal sprang out of her and down onto Zeniquorer's head and neck like chains, burning into him as they hardened and fixed inside. Like the acrobatic Boroo she was she swung between the barbs and hauled on the last with her flying weight. Weighted down by the burning slag and sudden jerk the panicked god convulsed and stumbled as another voice rang above.

"*Zeulimagun* - Iron Hand!" Howled the sister, Ms'egol Aia Aten. As she leapt up and swung by her tail from one of the spears to go airborne she conjured her own strands of fiery stone from the ground to encase her glowing body. Superheated to fluidity, they banded around her in a shell of cerrubite, nickel and copper. Erratic, Zeniquorer reared and Aten's husk erupted from within as she landed squarely between his shoulders and drove her sister's weapons deeper, skewering the prey and splintering his bones.

Pain beyond anything he had felt since his ancient form was destroyed by Oorghunak shook the monster. The metallic discharge pushed him down again and stalled his every move such that Minciel could turn back on him from the ground, her igneous flesh drinking metal and rock with each footfall and her fingers slinging volleys of molten metal into his gut. The assault was too much to recover from quickly, yet every drop of blood he lost and every thorn cut away only filled him with greater fury and fed his growing body.

With disciplined calm, another challenger sped along the terrace near Gazan and readied himself to take on the god of corruption. They were too close to the Hall. Artimecian knew time was running out. He slid to a halt overhead, holding his hands together at his neck and calling his light to emerge. All the spirit he possessed rose from his deepest place and poured into a white spark that danced between his heart and trembling fingers. His eyes snapped open as he knelt over the edge nearly to falling and sneered down at the insidious creature. Then, with pride and gratitude, beamed at the enchanters who joined his own witchcrafters and summoned oppressive glyphs beneath Zeniquorer that intensified the pull of earthplane to hold him in place. They raised walls, chained him down, turned every element around them into a cage that would buy him a moment more.

Mani saw Artimecian above and frantically called retreat. Enchanters gathered in groups, surrounded themselves in what shields they could muster as the brute soldiers on the ground dove into alcoves or leapt into the river to escape the attack of the arch-witchcrafter. Zeniquorer heaved himself up with a mighty howl, breaking shackles one by one and clawing against the enchantments, only to be blinded by the incredible light of Artimecian's soul as it came.

Artimecian held his fire close as his lifetime of suffering, the source of every drop of essence he had ever accumulated, flowed like a waterfall from memory into passion, passion into fury, and fury into that single drop of light, then overturned his hands and let it fall with meteoric power.

There was no struggle for Zeniquorer, for before his next breath he felt himself struck. He was trapped by the explosive force that rushed through his stolen host and drowned his own body out. It burned, fragmented him from within and he could hardly hear his own screams as the dawn broke inside him, casting him out once and for all.

Thetrulengo speaks,

Mortality doesn't understand what it's vulnerable to simply by being so close to the Nhi'Thaun. Things such as this; they were destined to happen I suppose, and they will again. There can be no true destruction of a thing, only the reshaping of its essence into something else. Does this mean creation as well was merely a reshaping? All creation? If so, I wonder what came before Az'Rech, before Escharka...before me. Of course, I have wondered before and often, though it seems to me the simplest of truths that I simply am, born of I know not what.

Let me say now not that I am no longer a passive observer of this world but an advocate of fate and a believer that it can be changed. For in the beginning, I saw death and thought little of it, yet on the day I witnessed the murder of someone who was the very name of purity I felt regret that she was lost. I will never let such a thing happen again. The sons and daughters of the fallen will

293

avenge the wrongdoings against their parent souls.

I realized when I saw the suffering of the virgin goddess and could not raise a hand to her nemesis that I was not capable of enacting my own justice. I cannot kill, cannot take a soul away from that which possesses it. I have no soul just as I have no body. Why then do I exist? I am formless and yet, when I witness the strengths and weaknesses of mortality, they become my own. What could I be, that I may loath a wicked soul but be unable to bring myself to destroy it? It is not a matter of potential, only one of will. I will death upon Zeniquorer, yet I cannot act against him. The last time I tried such a thing...it seems like no matter what I do, when I involve myself in anything, creatures die. Continents die. Everyone dies. A goddess's corpse falls on Ellel and destroys it. A god touches a star and consumes it. I touch anything and...I won't ever forget the girl I allowed to die, neither will I forget the continent I mistakenly crushed and sank. Saving the world of the mortal is best left to their own kind. We divine creatures cannot save what we do not understand. Most can't even save themselves. Perhaps I myself am lost, fated for something terrible which will come in its own time.

~Chronicle of Wonders, the Edge of Reasonable Doubt

The terrorized Mantichaena emerged from hiding. Thinking the horrific foe defeated, they cheered over Capheif's maimed and bloodied body, now reduced to its normal size. Their joy would not be a lasting one, for there a cloud of darkness seethed with the last flicker of purple light. The effervescing seemed only a last gasp of the defeated soul's death and many began to discount it as such until bolts of precipitant shadow began to congeal and rose ominously up along the walls of Gazan. The crowd watched in amazement as it moved slowly, travelling in silence and rising to hover above Artimecian where he knelt in pain, nearly unconscious as the last flicker of essence within him struggled to rebuild itself. The purple light crackled at the core of the stream and the chilling visage of Zeniquorer appeared again as it had inside Raphenie's mind. He slipped past Artimecian, as if the mighty attack was not worthy of acknowledging. Vengeance was not required. His only thoughts were of his child, consuming him and driving him to her.

As he entered the eighth level of Gazan, pandemonium ensued. Mantichaena thronged in search of weapons to combat this new manifestation of evil. Eerily the cloud drifted through the air to the place where Raphenie lay under Khurk's care. Like a coiled schiis it spun and turned upright. Freakishly long legs and arms sprang from an amorphous torso. The empty eyes emerged from a hanging head and, with odious resolution, the whole plodded toward her on the slothfully scraping limbs.

Gazan's lower floors trembled as the army stampeded upward, too late to make it in time, yet Zeniquorer's advance slowed almost to a halt when the feeble, elderly mortals between him and his meal did not flee at his mere presence. Not only did they stand their ground but more came from all around. They joined to defend Raphenie, their children, elders, the sick and injured who had been sheltered there. Khurk was stone-faced as he took the front of a mob, their feet firmly planted in defiance. Nothing was said for a tense moment. Zeniquorer stared, and they stared back.

Unable to grasp the sheer idiocy driving their continued interference, Zeniquorer seethed and demanded in his caustic voice, **"Audacious morsels. Do you not know me!?"**

The volume of his high-pitched words was overwhelming, but Khurk gritted his teeth and bore it. No other that stood with him would retreat from the repulsive threat.

"*Minuein*, who you are matters none. You are evil and you will not touch our daughter," Khurk growled.

"My daughter! MINE!" The fallen god squealed, drooling and stomping.

"Not anymore," The smooth voice of Lemalie challenged as she gripped Khurk's shoulder and stepped up beside him. "Ms'Egol Aia Raphenie is Mantichaena. Our soul, OUR daughter! Whatever dark star you draw your power from, you have no authority here. Not over us, and not over her."

Zeniquorer seemed to hesitate. They really seemed unafraid. He clumsily sniffed around Lemalie, sensing something familiar about her, something reminiscent of himself, of Miohaelia, of Kulibreal and Raphenie.

"My Star...my star draws near, little grub. Soon it will be upon you, and you will drown in me."

"She will not give another warning," Khurk said sharply, looking aside at the young woman whose secreted power was unseen by himself, yet known by all to exist. He gave her a forlorn smile, hopeful but final, then stepped right up to the god's hideous face. "You are not the only god, certainly not the greatest. Your betters walk among us. Your enemies protect us. It is these who you test, not I."

Lemalie used all the time he gave her. Though her eyes were fixed on a god her mind was elsewhere, feeling through the vapor in the air to find where the waterfall flowed from the cliff, chasing it to find its path through the walls. She felt every drop, every current. It would terrify those who stood outside to see the falls suddenly cease to flow. The water went still as though frozen, held in place as she took hold of it. Then, with a growing rumble, it withdrew into the cliffs and sought its mistress.

Zeniquorer sneered viciously, his attention briefly diverted by the arrival of Schaleikin and her soldiers from the nearby stair before returning to Khurk's unwavering gaze.

"*Udaiiltmaeng*, you are brave...I like killing brave things."

"And your own children!?" Khurk shouted scornfully.

The horror said nothing, merely flipped his fingers at Khurk and, with a whiplash of smoke, hurled him upward into the ceiling with a sickening crunch. Children screamed and the elders parted as the lifeless corpse flopped down between them.

From behind Zeniquorer came a rallying shout as five bloodied Kulo and Kubernu launched themselves at him. With a lazy swing of his arm, an ashen wave reached out and swept them into the wall like dry leaves.

"Vermin! Filth! *Niklaul'tskaminla eihtya'maunwekti*!" he shrieked contemptuously.

Straining and grunting, Lemalie ordered Raphenie and her mob to make their escape. As fearful of her as they were of the monster, they scrambled to obey.

Zeniquorer smiled, his clunky teeth reeking of unimaginable rottenness as he licked them excitedly. "You never learn. Mortals never learn. I want her! I will have her! She is mine!"

Lemalie held one hand toward the back wall, tossing her hair over her shoulder to stare him down with a look of divine tranquility. The ground trembled, the ceiling seemed to rain, and a stinging cold gripped the air. Stones bounced from the floor as small cracks began to effuse a spray behind her, adding a hiss to her fiery scream:

"SHE IS HER OWN!"

Zeniquorer lunged as Lemalie's hand thrust against him, bringing with it the full force of the groundwater at her back. A lake upon the cliffs pressed down, its water surging through voids and its hammerlike strength tearing the stone to pound against him. Touched by her power, it carried the hidden light that she was born to. Though mere water would not bear against a fleshless creature, it instead became the strike of a living godlike that drove him back.

Sputtering and struggling, his skin hissing from the clash between his soul and hers, the aspect of the Bone Star bellowed and struck blindly, holding its ground but barely able to resist the torrent.

"It...cannot be. You have...stolen her power!" His hatred pushed him against her calm, giving him the strength to advance, never relenting. **"Thief! This power...is not yours!"**

Unshakably serene, Lemalie defied him to the end.

"You have no idea what power is mine."

Perhaps he was right. She was no true goddess, could not stop him, but it mattered not. Every moment she held him here was another moment of life for the rest of her kind, for Raphenie. Little did she know, a few moments was all that was needed. Fate could not be realized until the time came. Now, while eager stars looked down on them, this god's time had finally come.

Zeniquorer took one more step; the last step he would ever take. In the blink of an eye the intruding rays of daylight were broken as another shadow rushed in from the terraces, as haunting in its appearance as his own. He felt its presence, feared it, panicked and lost his resolve as he was swept back on his heels by the flying river. Staggered and terrified, he was blindsided by the avenging gal'tskhain, Naguza, descending upon him with an acidic hiss. The spindly talons of the atrocious Ennedeghe, the tines all across his hundred-foot segmented carapace and his curved fangs all sank into the weakened god's phantasmal half-body, coiled around him and constricted, the two of them tumbling over one another until they struck the wall and cracked it like an egg. Many saw the blow, both dreading and revering Naguza as his body slowly unwound from Zeniquorer.

What remained of the god was a lump of shriveled meat and crumbling light as the white glow of his eyes flickered out. Though barely manifesting a physical form, he had been dead the moment Naguza's needles touched him, every fiber of his being instantly and agonizingly stricken dead as the venom of Oorghunak eroded him into nothing. Ash was Zeniquorer's only body now; dusty limbs and a fractured head that would scatter into the breeze.

Thetrulengo speaks,

I'm a fool, forgetting that I was not the only one who cared for this woman or the goddess above her. Oorghunak did not pass on his power to this man by chance. It was his plan. Even I knew nothing of Zeniquorer hiding a part of himself inside Miohaelia's daughter, yet Oorghunak did. If I had been more alert, I would have noticed the connection; how Naguza began to show the very first signs of change the day the Mantichaena found Raphenie washed ashore. Oorghunak saw the soul of his enemy abiding in her, saw in Naguza a spirit of his own kind. That was it, wasn't it? The moment Naguza was chosen to be Oorghunak's child was that in which he lifted Raphenie's head from the sand. My heart breaks to think of him realizing he would be called a monster, feared and hated for what he was becoming. He had no choice but to hide away, yet clearly his love persisted. Let fate see such a thing undone. I am truly grateful to have found the strength to break free of my indifference, grateful for the wisdom to realize that it was he who was born to slay the Bone Star...proud that I could be the one to reach him when no one else could and bring him to face his destiny.

When will I see such a rare and powerful moment as this again? The last living remains of the needful god are destroyed and returned to their whole in the heart of the Bone Star. This is likely the end for Zeniquorer. It will be many, many seasons before he can manifest, or even achieve thought again. Without having preemptively laid a seed to bind himself to a host...who can say if he will ever resurface. Perhaps after this he is diminished enough for the House to take him at last, leaving behind only the memory of an unfulfilled hatred, what reign he possessed finally ended by the children of great Miohaelia and her beloved Oorghunak.

~Chronicle of Wonders, Love Beyond Life

The silence of a captive audience was as uncomfortable to Naguza as it was to those he had just saved. No one but Aroch had seen him since his exile, when he had still appeared something resembling Galaila. In his fully developed Ennedeghe form he was more monster than man and knew it without having to suffer the frightened stares of a people he hardly considered his own anymore. He held his bladed hands out a bit to show he was a friend but as one they retreated like a herd at the gesture. Beneath the prickly exterior was a heart more easily injured, and he felt shame as he was reminded once again that old friends had forgotten he was more than his appearance. His former life was too far gone.

Some of the more fearful fled the scene while others continued to hide. Others knelt, mourning Khurk inconsolably.

Naguza's long body contracted, bunched up against the wall and his partially recognizable upper half followed, not in fear of Sky's wrath but repulsed by the notion of defending himself against innocents. He could not fight against the city he still loved. As emotions calmed and reason returned, a murmur passed through the crowd, softening the ambiance as it praised Naguza. This great creature had come into their midst not to harm but to slay the one that had so terrorized them. He was a miracle, savior to each of them. One by one their hearts went out to him, changed by the woeful glint in his eyes and the corpse at his feet.

This did not include Sky, who elbowed his way up the stairs, shouting all the way and demanding an explanation as to what had become of their foe. He broke through the crowd, pushing between Rentish and Liklita, whose heads had been bowed solemnly until his intrusion and had no sooner caught sight of Naguza than boomed for Artimecian to attend him.

Artimecian shambled in from the tunnel near Naguza shortly after, huddled groups dividing and allowing him to approach the

Primarch. He was greeted by two of his students who hurried to his aid, talking over the top of each other in rapid succession as they carried on one another's thoughts. Aten spoke first, Minciel interrupting enthusiastically.

"*Bethir la!* See it, Father! It is Naguza again!"

"He killed it! He saved us!"

"See and know, he has done no harm!"

"*Ein la*! It's just as you said!"

Artimecian ogled Naguza, slack jawed at what he had become.

Sky circled around his minion, waving his arms in a fit to fend off the lesser witchcrafters as he leaned into Artimecian's face with desperate pomp.

"Quiet, you two! The insolence of... this is an outrage! Father Artimecian, I command you to drive this ghastly *gal'tskhain* back to whatever hole he crawled out of!"

Artimecian's eyes never left Naguza's. For the man to return to the city should have meant death, yet in his defiance Artimecian saw no sign of fear, only strength. As if woken from a dream, Artimecian's patience for Sky's abuse finally ran dry, his belief in the man's right to rule crashing to the ground. Without warning, he turned and deftly swung his taut knuckles into the Primarch's jaw, laying him across the ground.

"For once in your life, shut your dribbling mouth," Artimecian said coolly. Sky grunted and fumbled to rise but, seeing no more fight in him, the arch-witchcrafter turned unconcernedly away and attended Naguza, carefully approached him.

"*Utan* Ennedeghe," he whispered. "You've...you're so big!"

Naguza's weird mouth smiled wryly, and he scraped a bit closer.

"Tss...yessst, my friendt," came the anxious reply.

Artimecian held out a hand, Naguza as well, such that their fingers barely touched. At that simple gesture, the tension in the crowd melted away.

"*Einla*, it's been so long. I'd glimpsed Aroch climbing to you on occasion, but I never had the courage to inquire as to your condition."

"He didt thissst, *la*. Hissst friendst are mine but-t without-t him thissst people is ssstill mine...assst I am theirssst."

Sky's wide-eyed glare darted between the gathered archons,

300

more of whom were joining the growing crowd. His one powerful ally on the council had betrayed him and even now turned to the room with a remorseful face and drooping shoulders.

Artimecian contemplated as he faced each of his counterparts, thinking back on how they had come to this moment, not just as a governing force but as people. His gaze fell then to Raphenie, shivering and bloody from her ordeal. Several archons hung over Khurk's lifeless form and wept for his loss. Warriors of Gazan and the people they had boldly defended stood mutely together. Finally he faced Sky, who spoke derisively of these people, called them helpless, dumb beasts. Here they still stood, a wall around Raphenie and Khurk. It was they who protected the tribe, they heroes who kept hope alive.

Shame arose within him, the furthest roots of his younger and more hopeful self resurfacing. He had left so much behind when he founded the Iron Sanctum, swore their absolute allegiance to Sky, all because of the leader he remembered in Tieg Raev. Savory memories flashed through his mind: the choir in which he had performed as a boy, standing beside Tieg Udai Aroch and Tieg Udai Naguza, singing the music of their greatest generations in the first temple of Loi. Naguza, so handsome a child, had led him by the hand the first time they had all gone out together to seek adventure in the wilds of Ellel. Artimecian's father had forbidden it, but Naguza had pulled him along, not harshly but reassuringly. He remembered looking down the dark paths of the forests and complaining that it was not safe for a sculptor's son. Naguza's only reply was 'Do not let another man's fears become your own, or you will go to the same grave as he.' A child had said this and, while it was the very words that had shaped his life, he had somehow lost their meaning.

"Patriarch Aroch!" Artimecian barked for his attention.

Aroch emerged warily, though he could not suppress pride at Naguza's great feat. He said nothing, only waited.

Artimecian's face lightened for an instant when he saw Lemalie behind Aroch; youthful, powerful, mourning. She reminded him of the family he had loved. They were the missing piece of his life, the loss of which had driven him into servitude of the Primarch. Sky had delivered on his promise to punish the tribe that stole Artimecian's family from him, though only now did the wayward witchcrafter realize it was never for his sake or theirs. As Sky could use fear to chain the obstinate, so did he inspire loyalty to chain the powerful. Artimecian started to tear up as he fell to both knees penitently before Aroch and the council and raised his voice so that all could hear.

"I surrender myself for punishment by the Council of Archons. I am guilty of conspiracy against the safety of this city, fraudulence in enforcing the laws of the people and the attempted murder of the hunter-killer Nesh Udai Keimas!"

Sky came at him like a wild animal.

"NO! *Baen'sacht*! Coward!" he screamed.

Aten and Minciel intercepted Sky and locked their arms with his to throw him to the ground, securing his limbs while gawking in disbelief at their grand master. Weeping uncontrollably Artimecian extended both hands to Aroch, head bent in shame.

"And," he confessed painfully, "The murder of Patriarch Ms'egol *Utan* Raru, with him four academy classicists and…and the destruction of the high gate Tau." His words could barely be understood through his quivering gut and raspy breaths.

Aroch marched up to him, stood adjunctively at his side, calmly and quietly interrogated him while staring Sky down.

"As your arbiter confessor and speaker for the council, I accept your submission. Were you alone in these actions?" The crowd stood silently watching as he guided his prisoner's admission.

Sky watched helplessly, his ears pounding with his own heartbeat as his only weapon turned traitor with confession after tearful confession.

"No, Father," Artimecian said. "All of this and more I have done under the orders of Nesh *Utan* Rogan, Primarch Sky *Hauan Etainilt*."

The Division Age – A Historic Record
Article 63
Longhand Star rises, Windsong Star remains.

Today was a day that will live in infamy, told until the tribe is dust. Where do I even begin? A vast and long-growing betrayal of our people by the very man who leads us was finally revealed, by his own right hand no less. It could not have come at a better time, I think. We needed revelation, an explanation at least, but a victory most of all. Without something to bring our city together we were soon to fall to pieces. I am glad that such a terrible thing could be ended while simultaneously lifting my good friend Lemalie and her father as well, from the quagmire of distrust that Primarch Sky would have had them steeped in.

I suppose he is not Sky anymore, only Rogan. He and Artimecian were stripped of their titles. Artimecian went willingly but Rogan fought even after he was shackled. Liklita's men saw them both caged in Voddace for the duration of that day and the night that followed. I'm told Rogan never stopped beating on the bars, screaming and cursing Artimecian's name until only exhaustion brought him sleep.

He was not the only hidden infection. A demon walked among us, hidden in the most unlikely of places and full of a detestation I have never experienced. It killed many of us, including one of the archons. Hanging Gate gathered at the first light of Lindu to bid farewell to Patriarch Khurk and those who died with him. They fought honorably against an unthinkable adversary and contributed greatly to its ultimate demise. For that, they have earned a peaceful rest. Though no new Primarch has been chosen, the council as a whole decided that a new crypt would be built in Voddace, separate from those that represent the houses. This one will be reserved for the most valiant of our heroes who gave their lives here today. At its pinnacle will be mounted a statue commemorating father Khurk's final stand against the demon, and inscribed at its base the words 'Stood there the man, and to the beast he proclaimed that no evil would take our children. We live in his promise.'

Not all the workings of the council were so destined for fond memory. There was some deliberation about accusations from Patriarch Mani that young Raphenie had attacked him in some way, but apparently he himself refuted them and claimed it was a misunderstanding, that the specter had taken her as it had Capheif. His testimony was unrelenting until the innocence of the maiden was well known. If anyone was turned by that darkness it was Utan Capheif. I don't know how Artimecian was able to injure the horrid ghost inside him without destroying his body, but it may not matter. The man suffers a grave illness as a result of his possession.

A decision has been made on this, the dawn following our second great suffering. It concerns the fate of Rogan and is soon to be carried out. His life ends today.

Praise the sky, this life ends for me today as well. This will be my final entry before returning to my research.

~Ms'egol Aia Cisiveo
Physic, not scribe.

Very few were present for the dismal occasion of Rogan's sentencing. Only those who were directly involved in the incidents for which Artimecian and Rogan were responsible and those who sought justice against him on a personal level. While most families cherished the memories of fallen members or kept busy by beginning work on Voddace's new ossuary, Aroch presided over the remaining archons in a semicircle atop the pyre. The proud structure built by Rogan would now be used to deliver his punishment. The former Primarch was brought out at first light, his arms both stretched across a heavy wooden stay and his mouth tightly gagged. Aroch spoke for the council, not yet the Primarch but unanimously elected as the voice of their collective will for the present. As he spoke, so did a young apprentice of Ms'egol scribble his dictation:

"We gather to ordain the fate of Nesh Udai Rogan, Ms'egol Udai Artimecian, Ms'egol Udai Haerulf, Ms'egol Udai Gogol; murderers or collaborators thereof, as defined by the slaughter of Galaila and Mantichaena, this day amended to include any living breed associated with this tribe or any of similar kind or origin. Let it be written that this shall encompass natural-born Galaila and taken Mantichaena, both familiar and unfamiliar, to include all variations previously identified in all written records as *gal'tskhain*. Let this word become infamous as a curse, never again to be adopted for use against either individual or numerous class of the tribe as it has been described here…" He hesitated, then cruelly finished "Except it's owner."

Rogan was too weary, too pained by hunger and thirst to show any resistance after a two-day captivity in Voddace. The indomitable gaze that had defined his reign was now replaced by the glaze of utter despair. As he was brought before the council he fell to the ground and there remained motionless, face in the dirt as he waited for the verdict.

"Punishment for these most heinous transgressions," Aroch continued, "has been chosen for each perpetrator according to the severity of their involvement. As the paired witchcrafters known as the Iron Wind have not yet reappeared, the nature of their assignment forces this council to consider them a lethal threat to be handled with extreme prejudice. Should they surrender willingly upon their return, they will be treated as traitors to the tribe and interrogated prior to determining their sentence." He paused for a moment as murmurs rippled through the crowd. "For issuing the murder of a countryman and hunter-killer, as well as a Patriarch of this council and, furthermore, the destruction of this city's most hallowed relic, Ms'egol Udai Artimecian has been removed from this council and consigned to indefinite imprisonment in Voddace Hall."

No protest arose, though a few grunts and crossed arms made it clear that a harsher punishment was expected.

With a pained grimace, Aroch drew a breath before pronouncing the decision concerning Rogan. Though he had long wished he could be in this very position, he now found it to be one of the most excruciating of his life.

"As the architect of all these deeds, and for systematically undermining the collective community of Hanging Gate by the repeated, unwarranted exile of our men and women and the propagation of animosity against them: Nesh Udai Rogan, you are to be punished in kind with those you have failed as Primarch and protector." The collective rumble of agreement rose from the congregation. "You are hereby exiled from this tribe and this city to the mercy of the Thonsfa Tau. From this day forward you will live as the one *gal'tskhain,* without the possibility of return. Should you be seen again, you will be executed."

As Aroch spoke, one of Raru's remaining pupils stood by, vehement and tense as he impatiently awaited his chance to make this first of two men pay for his mentor's demise. Artimecian's time would come soon enough. For now, appreciated the opportunity given to him by Aroch. At the council's beckon he stepped forward and slowly pushed the tip of one claw into the skin of Rogan's forehead, held his neck and carved characters dictating his new title into it.

"Living trash," he whispered, then spat on the bloody mark and pushed Rogan away. Sebashni ushered the boy aside and Aroch continued.

"The West wild is not for you to travel. All settlements of this land were raised by those you betrayed, called filth and drove out. You've nowhere to turn now, so I condemn you to die in the Tau at a time of your choosing or your natural ending." Rogan's blood-drenched face never left the ground. His defeat was completed and dispute was futile. Aroch's voice was neither haughty nor virtuous, only clear and resolute.

"As this is fairly an execution, it is custom that the doomed be given the right to utter his final words…" At last, Rogan looked up but, before he could speak, Aroch motioned for him to be taken away, glowering. "…a right you tread upon when you dishonored and subverted the very laws that protected it. You will perish with no home and no people. There will be no memory of you." To those that moved to bear the prisoner, Aroch gave the final order: "Cast him beyond the gate."

CHAPTER 28: A HABIT OF DECEPTION

Rogan's feet alternately dragged and plodded heavily as he was drug down the road where only his executioners and the guardian statues would witness his expulsion. Unbeknownst to both, another followed in secret, watching intently. Perched up high on the head of a Mearnum sculpture and peering down from his hiding place in the Veil, Tzychala the eyebeast cocked his head and analyzed every weary motion of the deposed leader, every line in his face. He tried to mimic it, tried to formulate the impressions of real pain on his own; a pain other than anger and emptiness. It was no use. Though his many eyes practiced a meticulously formed appearance of sadness there were no tears.

He had been examining as many faces as he could since Zeniquorer's slaying. It was hard to judge those as unique as Naguza's but he had tried for only so long before realizing that to mimic such an ugly and unsociable man was not what he wanted. It reminded him too much of himself. Instead he tied himself mostly to Lemalie, shadowing her wherever she went without leaving the comfort and safety of his secret plane. She had no longer appeared perturbed about Keimas, which must have been good for her as she had not stopped smiling the last two days.

Tzychala had learned, in the many dialogues she had with her father and their mutual friends, as well as those who supported Rogan in his rule and presented their apologies one by one, that Aroch was the only candidate anyone considered for Primarch. Whatever that meant, it brought the young woman happiness. Anything that made Lemalie happy was a good thing, Tzychala thought. Apart from her pleasant attitude, she reminded him of his own sister, perhaps not in personality but in her ability to help him see things that might otherwise go unnoticed: good deeds, fair treatment, blessings around every corner.

To personally value such things still eluded him. Only if he looked into mortal eyes did he know if something was worthy of the attempt to appreciate. He remained cautious of his own mind. Was he using this new woman as his one definition of goodness now? Was he using Rogan as his sole example of pain? It was likely just a reflex, not unlike the understanding of imprisonment that he and Loi shared, which he considered to be the root of his understanding of empathy. All of it was confusing, though that made it even more appealing. Above all else he desired to unravel the mystery of what made a soul so infinitely versatile and unequivocally vulnerable. He had already found a new scheme for claiming a soul but experimenting among mortals might help while he waited for word of Keimas' successful capture.

Then, a thought hit him: perhaps it was true that his dedication to the god of these people and the new captive of his prior prison stemmed only from guilt. He had been told before that he was feeling something called guilt, but how could he know what guilt was? In his experience it was rare to see a mortal suffer from complete and genuine guilt without any selfish influences. Perhaps there was one now whom he could study for that pure emotion: the master witchcrafter, Artimecian.

In the rust-hued darkness of Voddace's dungeon, firelight was limited. There was no reason to illuminate the damned in their repentance or lack thereof, especially those guilty of such wrongdoings as Artimecian. Every man wanted his own freedom and Artimecian was no exception but he knew that freedom in life would not free him from his own conscience, nor repay the great harm he had inflicted.

The Patriarch who had single-handedly built the Iron Sanctum was visited only by those he had trained. They brought him food and drink purely out of duty, not out of sympathy. In their eyes, for his abuse of their trust and using them as tools for such nefarious deeds, he was rightfully condemned. They came and went silently while refusing him so much as a glance, Minciel alone bringing anything but water to sip. He didn't know how she had gotten a cup of savory wine past the acolytes. Though they had no restriction to prevent her bringing it, they likely would not have allowed such a kindness. Still, there it was beyond the bars, spreading its lovely aroma about his cell. After two days rotting, barely sipping water, the wine was of special interest. He sniffed it deeply and paused to enjoy the subtle undertone with a smile. It was wine, but there was more within; a faint smell of a well-known herb masked by the sweetness of fruit. She had brought him the one thing he wished to drink.

"Thank you," he whispered softly. Then as he raised the cup to his lips, he heard a gritty and slurred voice from the shadows outside his cell.

"Why did you do it?" the voice scratched.

His nerves curled inward at the question. Doing his best to seem undaunted, he set the cup aside, stood up creakily to grip the bars and press his face into them.

"No need to hide, stranger," he said. "There is no shame in hating one such as me."

"I do not hate you."

Artimecian leapt up and spun around. The voice now came from within his cell, in the shrouded corner where he himself had just been sitting. It was impossible but he was certain it was there as it grumbled:

"Forgive me interrupting. I don't want to keep you from your...your business. I just need to know."

"W-who are you?" the witchcrafter asked.

"You first," the voice insisted.

Artimecian squinted and took a shaky step but was reasonably satisfied that he wasn't facing a ghost when a flat palm extended to halt him. It had the general, hairy and sharp appearance of a Kulo but with red fur that bristled between the knuckles, while the oily black slenderness of the claws said it was something else entirely.

"Artimecian, Ms'egol Udai," he disclosed flatly. "And you...you're not..."

"Galaila, Mantichaena, or anything else you know of," came the quiet response. The mysterious creature rose slowly and emerged far enough that the foremost portions of his body were discernible along with the multi-pronged tail that flicked back and forth by its feet. "But I want to be," it said.

"God's blood!" Artimecian exclaimed. "A-are you a *vaena*?"

"No!" Tzychala responded ferociously. "I..." He closed his many eyes and turned his head away a moment to gather his patience. "What does it matter?" he conceded at last, rhetorically. "I cannot pretend forever and you...you're a dead man anyway. Call me whatever you want. Demon will suffice."

"Are you here for me?" Artimecian stammered.

"*Quost*? No, *minta,* why should I care about you?" Tzychala was confused by his accusation. "Is that what your kind believe?"

"There are evils that exist to punish the wicked."

Tzychala was floored by the accusation.

"Is that a jest? You believe that some evils exist to punish other evils?" He mulled it over a moment. "Mother's malady, I suppose you're right. It's not like we can tell one another apart."

"I beg you, specter, return to Vaeba," Artimecian lamented quietly. "I'll be with you shortly, in the hell of murderers and cowards."

"Don't be so eager. You'll be going nowhere while I still have need of you."

"I did it because Sky commanded me," Artimecian confessed, returning to the original query.

Tzychala stared, his mouth hanging open a little as he hesitated to respond.

"I'm...sure you had your reasons for obeying him. I don't rightly care. I want to know why you betrayed him."

"Why I...truly?" Silence was affirmation and so Artimecian leaned back against the bars, crouched and slid one hand through to retrieve some crushed berries and bread to soak them into. The demon waited patiently, a quizzical gaze barely visible in the faint light.

"*Bprosenas*, take all the time you need," Tzychala grunted

listlessly.

"*Eina*," Artimecian began around a mouthful, "A long time ago, shortly after we arrived, we started to transform in the aura of the K'hizu. We all went through changes and some were fairly extreme. There was one who turned into something straight out of your nightmares, a close friend called Naguza. He, Aroch and I…we grew up together. We looked after each other. But when Naguza started to turn, Sky took advantage of the people's poor reaction to him. They feared him. As we escaped the thuell and made our way to the Gate, Sky turned on Naguza and ordered him to go straight back. Aroch tried to stand up for him but I…gods, I was weak. I didn't want to lose favor with the Primarch or the tribe, and many of them agreed that he should be gone. They called him awful things, worse things than *gal'tskhain*. Sky told him that if he didn't go willingly into exile he would have me and my gothics kill him."

"And you did not refute him," Tzychala interjected.

"I couldn't even look Naguza in the eye. I was arch-witchcrafter, a prodigy of gothic power, and I let Sky wear me like a trinket. I wanted to scream at him, hurt him, but I knew how people felt about the gothic practice. I was just as feared as Naguza, yet I was fortunate enough to become a more common caste. One much more pleasant to look at. I knew if I contested Sky he would have me cast out as well. No one would raise a finger to stop it. Not even Aroch would, after what I did or…didn't do. I hated him for a long time, perhaps for having the strength I never could."

"The father of Lemalie?" Tzychala asked.

"*La, uta*. Eventually I was accepted. As time went on and fear faded people began to reminisce about Naguza, not to mention others exiled after him. They regretted what they had done. Some were still afraid of him, afraid of all us strange ones, yet for most it had passed like a mild illness. They revered Aroch as a savior of sorts who fought for all Mantichaena, no matter what form took them. His place was secured because he had the love of the people. He and Sky had this in common, though it was earned by different means."

"Was that the first time the man had tried to use you?" asked Tzychala.

311

"Yes," Artimecian paused before admitting, "Though it was not the first time I had done something unspeakable in his name."

"What changed?" Tzychala demanded. "Yesterday you were not the man you've described."

Artimecian sank into the bars and sighed dejectedly, closed his eyes for a long while, trying to find the answer, if he even knew it. Tzychala was about to ask again when the witchcrafter roused himself to answer.

"I thought I knew his heart. It turns out I was wrong," he said at last. "I finally understood when I saw Naguza, the banished and forgotten, come down and fight that thing. I understood that my own heart was alien to me. Sky was a simple creature, but I became his hand because I..." His voice cracked and he sobbed into his arms, barely audible in his rapid, undulant confessions. "...I believed in him. I believed SO HARD that what he was doing was right, that the people needed a strong leader no matter what sacrifices had to be made. I wanted to believe in him so badly that I would not see the truth of all he is. Have you been here? Have you seen it?" he looked up at the creature. "Rogan is as a god of pride. He doesn't care about the people, or even his own family. He would kill them before losing control of them." Artimecian looked into eyes that sparkled darkly back at him and, to him, promised proper punishment for his transgressions. "I made that nightmare a reality, not him. I was so scared of being hated, scared to be alone." Shame colored his words as he admitted his own culpability. He had not been self-serving as Tzychala suspected, only blindly obeyed, willingly enslaved by the fear of loneliness.

Tzychala felt a real...something. It was one of the only base and bitter emotions he was capable of. He recognized it from the first betrayal he had ever known, which he himself had committed. He pondered it and absently grumbled in response to Artimecian, "Yes...loneliness. I understand this idea."

"I was so gifted, equally obsessed," the witchcrafter continued. "I could do things even my best students and peers could not. It consumed me both in youth and age. I wanted to see my true limits, even became a danger in the eyes of the people. Rogan did his work well in convincing them I was of value, and so a danger I became."

He shook his head at his own senselessness.

Tzychala was intrigued, desperately wanted to be touched by the solemnity of what this wretched man was feeling. It stank of guilt, regret, a fair amount of sadness and a sprinkling of anger. It was a delicious feast for the eyes but the hole in his heart was not satisfied by merely observing it. He shared the discomfort of the simple and bland feelings, yet saw in Artimecian what he could not connect with. He was sure that whatever it was it was the key to his own freedom, needed to know more while he had the chance.

"Man...*udai*, do you think, if you have done something so terrible, that by such a drastic turn of the heart you could be redeemed?"

"Certainly not a demon, are you then?" Artimecian said humorlessly.

"Answer me."

A hostile silence followed as Artimecian chewed upon the question. When he finally responded it was with a lighter tone.

"No. A man can only be redeemed until he dies."

"You still draw breath," Tzychala noted.

"A curse I grow tired of. If all the stars of Aurba wished me to live I would not heed them."

"What happiness will death bring you?"

"I do not need happiness," Artimecian huffed. "I have accepted myself, made peace with my past and choose to pay for it with what remains of my future."

"Why?" Tzychala's mind muddled.

"Because," Artimecian whispered with a smile, "A man's future is all he has. It is the only ransom I can offer to repay what I have taken."

Much more than curiosity now churned inside Tzychala, unfamiliar things that made him itch and tremble. He saw a glimmer of happiness in Artimecian's eyes as the man resigned himself to a life now engulfed by the damage he had done. In it he saw himself, a Tzychala that knelt on a decayed Maengir in some distant future after mortality's time was ended, finally able to feel sorrow and weep as his brother and sister did. He saw himself weeping only for the death of mortality, the end of them all after he had given them passage beyond the fate his creator had decided for them.

Artimecian again raised the wine and touched it to his lips.

Tzychala was barely able to mutter an agonized 'Wait' before the man drank deeply of it. Artimecian smiled gratefully at the taste of poison therein and thought a few last good thoughts before his body began to die.

Tzychala's submergence into the Veil through a black rip in the air was fluid and silent but delayed due to the startling suicide he had just witnessed. He dematerialized, loomed, pondered and doubted as Artimecian slowly slumped over. The prisoner foamed at the mouth as his fingers twitched and scratched at the floor. Only eyes that looked from the Veil could see it, as Tzychala's did; the soul of a man with barely any essence left in him as it effused from his corpse, briefly retained its figure and features before becoming little more than a mist. It descended, permeating the earthplane, drawn deep by the power of the hidden door through which souls entered the House. In the past, when he was the flesh that made the star function, he would have been able to see every memory this man possessed as they were torn away and turned to nothing. It was unlikely he would ever feel the touch of that inmost light again. To hear this one's parting confession was the closest he could come.

Tzychala stared from the Veil until Artimecian's body was discovered. He limply drifted straight through the agitated guardsmen and archons that came to see the sight, then through the walls of Voddace and its front gate without breaking his pensive trance. All his eyes were downcast in weighing the meaning of a man's self-inflicted death. Was that the proper price for all sin or just the irrational solution of the soul to end suffering? Was his sister right about him after all? He imagined himself capable of such wondrous feats if he possessed a soul; to feel, trust, love. What then could happen to him the moment he was capable of real guilt? Would the millions upon millions of deaths he had brought to Maengir, all the living things he had devoured to sustain his vile powers revisit him in a single, terrible wave of self-loathing? If this man ended himself over so few dead, then how could Tzychala bear his own crimes?

In that revelation he could only think of Mnavaelle. She had done it; coped with the burden all this time and, with or without a soul, she had been capable of deep feeling since time immemorial. Was she simply accustomed to it? Conditioned for it? No, it was worse than that. She was lying about the depths of pain she lived in, wanted to die but could not bring it on herself. He had never thought of death as a solution before. For his kind it would be an even greater crime. If they three would perish it would undo the curse they had placed on their home, actualize their purpose and break open the dark edge again. Their lives were the only thing that held their mother back. If they went to death, then Maengir went with them. Their only remaining duty was to never die, to live forever. As Artimecian had felt, this was the greatest curse of all.

He looked beyond his surroundings and saw the sky far above, toward the Dhai and near where the flat-cropped mountains South of the Gate descended into salty marshes and smoking chasms. His vision revealed the very winged man he had led away, alive and flying overhead, though the light within it was different. Bereft of Keimas' soul his body sailed aloft, now on wings of white with jewel-encrusted feathers as sharp as knives and purified by the presence of the sky's last supreme authority. It was Loi, the god himself, freed and dwelling in the flesh of a man descended from his father. His plan had worked, his prize won.

Tzychala's eyes narrowed furiously, the account of how Sky had used Artimecian fresh in his mind. The body was free already, yet where was the soul? Would Loi even uphold his part in their agreement now? Tzychala would ensure it, he thought determinedly. If used he was, he would avenge his loss. This moment of triumph was meant to be for him, not some paltry god. His throat and jaw tightened, then burst wide with a scream that fluctuated hauntingly with his strange voice. Deep yet pitched and vibrating with hate it broke across the Veil, struck out across every corner of Manti and warned that the killing was not yet done for that day.

The piercing north winds that hindered Loi's advance toward Ni'ivitnem deafened his ear but did not drown out Tzychala's cry. He turned his head aside, searching for a physical enemy, unprepared for the shadowy breach opening overhead from which his demon sprang. With deadly swiftness Tzychala struck between

Loi's pearlescent wings and dragged him down in a flare of red light and cinders, smashed him face-first into the wind-scarred crags below.

Grunting, gasping and swinging wildly, the flesh-entombed god staggered to his Kutu feet and leapt out of the gash he had torn in the rocks, swatting dust clouds away and scanning the area for his attacker. It did not occur to him that Tzychala might be that enemy until he heard his raspy voice and saw his grotesque silhouette through the haze.

Staring down this strange vessel, agitated by the thing inside, Tzychala couldn't help but taunt his co-conspirator.

"Are you there, tiny godking?"

Loi complained like any man, scarcely pleased to be back in the physical world. As he spoke Tzychala was unnerved by the perfect similarity to Keimas' own voice, though it carried a twinge of divine arrogance.

"I despise it in here, Brother Bone," Loi grumbled angrily. "Every bone and muscle pongs of my father's impotent presence...what a pity that my mother's heir has already passed beyond reach. He would have been a more fitting armor to wear, now he's just another obstacle in my path."

As the clouds cleared away Loi was revealed to Tzychala, already becoming more like his true form. His eyes and parts of his skin were translucent white, precisely carved as if they had become stone. Though his wings were wholly white the skin that remained mortal was flaking, discolored and porous, rotting from the immense power that burned inside it.

"Pity indeed," Tzychala agreed. "I see even the flesh of your father's chosen disagrees with the essence of your mother."

Loi spread his arms and spun slowly, showing off his new body and reveling in his freedom.

"No flesh could! She was absolute...until I came along. I was absolute and soon will be again."

No mention was made of the natural soul of his host, the soul that was to be given. Enraged, Tzychala lunged forward, catching Loi off guard and throwing him back into a teetering monolith, cracking it in half with the back of his head.

"Where is it?" he shouted irately. "You swore to me! You promised me his soul if I delivered him to you!"

Loi was completely unfazed and, with a small smile of amusement, regained his footing and raised one finger of each hand in a patronizing response to Tzychala's unrestrained rage.

"Now, blood god," he said derisively, "I, for one, have come to expect a bit more delicacy when speaking with you. Can we not have a respectful conversat..." His words were cut off as a blast of char and twisting crimson blew from Tzychala's mouth. The Vulgoli thrust forward and viciously battered Loi's head against the top of the shattered stone until it was reduced to rubble at his feet, unhinged and raving.

"YOU. PROMISED. ME. HIS. SOOOUL!" As he brought his gnarled fist down once more, Loi seized his wrists firmly and lifted his undamaged face, smiling widely now.

"If I learned anything from my mother's memories it's that the honest man dies first in a fight."

Tzychala leaned heavily on his grip, smoldering at Loi but unable to break free of his clutches. He was strong. All elder gods were but the Vulgoli wasn't expecting this kind of resistance.

"You! You..." speechless, Tzychala sputtered uselessly.

"Am my mother's child! Bahaha!"

Laughingly gleeful, Loi twisted and hurled Tzychala into the ground, landed on top of him, pinning his arms and exclaiming, "*Khainiltigoli!* You SAW my mother use the same trick on this bastard's elder father and still it snared you? *Minta, Nhi'Thaun vulip'eih*, what were you thinking? You are a demon! A DEEEEEMON!" This he yelled playfully, rocking back and forth on Tzychala's chest. "The fleshes of Escharka and Az'Rech cannot be joined, you daft abomination! How do you think all this light around us came to be? Even if you could ingest an entire soul at once it would annihilate you! Actually...that's not a bad idea."

Tzychala didn't know truth from lie anymore but Loi's surety was not out of arrogance or anger. His words held conviction.

"How...how do you know this?" he questioned.

Loi's exuberance disappeared as abruptly as it had appeared and in a huff he rose, keeping Tzychala firmly in place with a heel planted in his throat.

"I know all about the Age of Unravelling. I know where the gods first came from, about the endless; you, your sister...even little brother." Tzychala went pale as Loi extrapolated. "I know everything! All for the hubris of a peon of the lightful ancient who brought us the essence and made us strong. The messenger Deina who thought he could save the world...he spilled all the secrets of life's beginning to my father, pleaded with him to end his conquest and fight for peace. Those memories belonged to my mother when she took his life and when I swallowed her whole they became mine! I have known all along what the House of Az'Rech was meant for and I wanted it eradicated!" Out of remembered frustration, he kicked the support out from under a column and let it crumble around him. "But no one knew how, so...I tried to get inside."

Tzychala could not have anticipated such a plan, so much knowledge and preparation where he believed there was only greed and misguided conflict.

"You wanted to stop the flow, prevent souls from being cleansed...from going home..."

"And this I will do, one way or another. Oh, demon, if only you could see me now." Loi raised his hands and praised himself, dreaming of his true power. "You, such a dark creature, could only rip the souls from the dead. When I freed you I took all the grand designs of the Deina that created that awful place and I tore them all down! The House was built for one such as you; one that could not grow from the light. They never expected one akin to the light would manage to take your place. My body didn't just separate the souls of the dead from their dark essence, I drank every last drop into myself! Thousands, millions of souls are mine now! And when I set myself free I will unleash them all upon this world! Not even the Deina will..." His mounting excitement was disrupted by Tzychala chuckling to himself. Loi was confused, irritated at the disrespect. "What? What!? Stop that!" he ordered, stomping the demon's throat harder.

Tzychala was no longer violent. In fact, he was perfectly calm, save for the effort it took to hold Loi's foot from crushing his windpipe.

"You must know, godking," he said quietly, reflecting back on his encounter with Rogan and Artimecian, "I met a man just like you this day. Two, actually; one very nearly as feared as yourself and the other his servant. It was illuminating to learn which held true power."

Thinking Tzychala bragged of himself, Loi responded with a condescending laugh.

"You think you are the power among us? Exceeding ME!?"

Loi gripped his throat with strong talons and hauled him up into the air, grabbed him by his flying hair and returned his head to the ground, cackling with elation through the flying spittle and blood.

Tzychala grasped the arms that held him in a vain attempt to control the powerful force, wheezing in a desperate fight for breath.

"No, god...I do...not,"

"Then go back to rotting among your little people!" Loi stood with the demon's throat held fast, discarded like refuse. "You can die with them when I have amassed..."

"I want to tell you something," Tzychala gasped, rubbing his throat. Instantly he fell through the ground, disappearing into a churning of shadows and reappearing very near in front of Loi, nursing his dripping face and shaking his head. "It has been revealed to me that, when presented with an unwelcome truth, these 'Little' people have a tendency to react with a mighty vengeance, no matter the foe."

Loi retaliated, leaping forward with fists raised but Tzychala's quick retreats into the Veil warped him in and out of location so quickly Loi could barely keep track of him, taking blind swipes and hitting nothing.

"They are a waste of light! Parasites! What can they do against a god!?" Loi shouted.

Tzychala's bursts of reply when he appeared had no concern in them.

"That's what another god thought, what a man more powerful than even myself thought, even what the would-be *Jiou* thought. And today..."

Loi's barrage finally connected, though only with Tzychala's extended palm and fingers, which bound his fist even as it slid its target backward on heels, the demon's claws tilling the ground.

"...They all died!"

Another strike, another puff of blackness and Loi staggered to keep his footing while roaring back at Tzychala's heckling.

"I am Loi, siege of the sky, you insufferable weevil! You can elude me as you did the Deina but you cannot kill me!"

319

Tzychala partially emerged with his face over Loi's shoulder, teasingly whispered:

"Then count your mistakes and tell me who can,"

Loi knew what he spoke of but did not believe his bluff.

"You can never reach him. He is sealed too deep even for you."

"Can I not? Is he?" Tzychala persisted smugly, ducking Loi's swinging elbow and warping out of reach. "Do you truly know how much blood is left in me or only what I have shown you? How could you possibly know what I am capable of? You claim to know the Age of Unravelling, yet you forget how many of its dead were my feed."

Loi swallowed and leaned away, backed off with the threatening scowl of a cornered animal. Tzychala remained material and followed, stepping as he did though not attempting to subdue nor attack him.

"You may know secrets, my godking, but you do not know me. You know not what oceans of gore have been drunk by Sleep and her brothers before your miserable life ever began; before light itself existed in this world. This season I have seen a tyrant not so different from yourself defeated by the truth, a sorcerer defeated by a drink, Zeniquorer's afterling broken by the fang of Oorghunak's and, in a few short days, I will see your father's true child lock his jaw upon your skull!"

Loi struck out ferociously but caught only the stinging energy of Tzychala's warp and turned heel, beat his wings with all his might to escape.

"You'll never free him!" The godking shouted back as he ascended. "This is my time, my world!"

No one was there to hear him. The demon was gone and Loi feared it would make good on its threat. God or not, his only chance of fulfilling his destiny was to reach his quarry before having to answer to his father. It was not the infantile Kutudai Keimas he dreaded but the serpent's soul gestating within him, soon to wake if Tzychala's was indeed still with him.

CHAPTER 29: MASTER OF NONE

Thonsfa Tau. Eastern Dust. With nothing left in the East except what they had lost, that same loss was in Rogan's heart as he stumbled through its melancholy dunes, tangled with their vicious thi'zech. He was a practical man, a man of survival, of results. He was nearly incapable of accepting defeat or even death. At first he had clung to an innate belief that he would return to his city, stronger than ever, and show the usurpers what a terrible mistake they had made. Progression through the wasteland robbed him of those passions until all that remained was a bound husk of a man. Feeling nothing, only resorting to base mechanical thought to press onward, he began making choices only to live another day.

His knees trembled as he shuffled into the desperately feeble shade of the thickets. With the thick beam still across his back, he leaned it against the thicker trunks and rested, wrists worn and bleeding as they hung from their bindings. The relief was momentary. In no longer feeling the abuse of the light, he suddenly felt thirst. Hunger would follow soon after. His nose keenly sensed what little was to be had from these lignified shoots, but he was reluctant to think too much on getting to it. It was only rational to do whatever needs must in pursuit of water. A little pain would keep him alive, so he stared intently at the slight bulges among the rivulets of bark; thick-skinned nodules of sap protected by the threatening spines that dug into the beam. He scooted his face closer, wondering what strategies the gothics used to ignore pain as he bared his teeth. As a Kuolt he was not adept at this sort of work and he lamented his predatory stature as he tried to pick away the thorns with his teeth, felt them more than once pierce his lip and gums. It was tedious to the point of spending more energy than he regained, working his way up and down the vine until he could no longer tell what was sap and what was blood. It was a fool's errand.

The thorns were sharp, but not sturdy. Try as he did to cut away the ropes it made no noticeable progress. The fresh fibers of the rope were still pliable, several days of drying from becoming brittle enough that his plan might have worked. His skin would be flaking from his bones by then.

The meandering path through the dunes took all his focus, even when night fell. His body started to fail, and one misstep at a time he came to rest at the top of a long hill. The biting discomfort of his yolk kept any true sleep far from him, but once truly exhausted, he fell to his knees and remained there for a long while.

His mind drifted, seeking a problem to solve or a scheme to hatch. All it found was a twisting web of every choice that had led him here. He would not remember this moment, when he recalled a moment that likely started the chain leading to this one: the moment he bartered with the Abpaanik tribe to raid Artimecian's home. Those fools were supposed to steal his goods, not his family. In the end it evoked the loyalty of a useful tool, but what use was a dagger if it found its way to your back? He had miscalculated. That was all. It was just a small miscalculation.

A single sound brought him back to reality. Without knowing it's origin, it was a sound recognized and now hated above all else: wingbeats, long and powerful, though far overhead. Destitute, he rolled on his side and lay staring skyward, his eyes quivering at the sight of white wings flashing in the night glow of the stars. He could not reason their existence, had no clarity left to see them as anything but the Kutu whose treason had brought him to this lowly state. All he saw were wings. How he hated them.

He woke to a pain in the back of his neck. Wood, the beam of course, but jerking against him suddenly. He had not moved, and so his first thought was of its cause, cracked one dried eyelid and saw what he was entirely certain was a dream: a face. A man's face. A Mearnum.

"IT'M ALIVE!" its choppy, uncultured voice boomed, jarring Rogan to consciousness.

Little hands hauled him upright, shooting a pain down his arms and back the likes of which he could not have imagined. He tried to speak through the shock, unable to articulate anything but desperation.

"P-please he…help."

Rogan could not discern what else the man said as it shuffled about, seeming panicked and suddenly dropping him roughly into the sand. He felt affronted, sitting achily and rolling onto his stomach to find the vexing creature. As soon as he did, there was a whip of air and a dull thud and the Mearnum who had turned from him fell backward and landed with his head but a single breath from Rogan's. It was motionless, frozen in a look of sudden shock with a thin shaft of wood protruding from a blood-foaming hole where its eye had been. Instinct took hold and brought renewed vigor to the fallen Primarch, but even in the face of death had no strength to fight to his feet from the weight and bulk of his yolk. He could do nothing but wait bitterly as the sound of heavy, armored footfalls broke the gritty hillside. Rising over his view of the Mearnum's corpse, he saw thick leather clothes, and upon heavy zeulf plates covering the head and chest, stained with blood and soot. Both shoulders were adorned with pelts ripped from all manner of creatures, menacing spikes of bone protruding between them. It set one foot on the Mearnum, hands on hips, the fingers of one gripping a heavy metal bow, and he saw a flash of teeth smiling in the darkened face behind the helmet. At last, it roared triumphantly over its shoulder:

"*Bpetsaudi, inkm mit* governor! There's another over here, *ink'tskud* looks different from the others!" He stepped over the dead man, ripping the arrow from its head to stand over Rogan. "And someone packed him up for us already."

Rogan's mind ignited at the words, both familiar and unfamiliar. It could not be. It was impossible. He tried to lift his head further, and in the pale nightlight, the man met his gaze.

"Y-you're…" Rogan barely croaked, "…you're Galaila…"

The man laughed, tossed his helmet aside, drew and nocked an arrow, and placed its tip on Rogan's throat.

"Unlike you, monster," he grumbled haughtily.

For Rogan, it was a relief that he no longer had to walk and was given enough water to last. He didn't care how the rickety cart that bore him vaulted on every stone, or the stench of the other corpses around him. There were four he could see, more around them no doubt, and if there were any alive they showed no sign. There came a time when he could not tell whose blood was dripping down his face. He could think clearly again but did not despair. If his mind was awake it was scheming. If these people kept prey alive, they were not just going to play with him. They were trained, precise, well-equipped and disciplined. They didn't hoot or taunt him, barely even spoke to each other. He could hear at least ten distinct voices. This was a patrol, and a professional one. All facts led to one conclusion: they had a leader, and he was here. He was a man of power, and the functionality of his soldiers meant he was a man of good form. A man someone like Rogan understood and could bargain with.

Rogan tracked the waves of Laesis overhead as it started to rise, just in time to notice a change in direction. He still could not hear the sea when they suddenly turned North, and the journey thereafter was twice what they had undergone thus far. He spent the whole next day staring up into the sky, the lighter parts of his face blanching and flaking. All the while he thought about what he might say to whatever immovable object led these deadly new adversaries. He thought of them as future allies, people he could one day control as he had everyone else in his life. All it took was the right twist of one blade or another.

Night fell fast, and Rogan's mind still whirled with clever words and passable lies as the levered end of the cart slammed into the dirt and slid him forward, face first into the sucking chest wound of one of the dead Mearnum. A question formed in his mind for the first time, an obvious one obscured by his first meeting with the strange and dusty rodent who woke him: who were these other prey? He recognized none from what little he saw, and saw neither Gogol nor Haerulf was among them. These were not Gate-dwellers. So fully formed, they must have arrived shortly after the first flotilla, or perhaps been left behind when the Gate was raised.

Postulation waned as the bodies were dragged off the cart, and him with them. Stood on his feet and marched ahead, he could see little in the dark, though hundreds of oil-lamps flickered all around him. They hung from tents, lean-tos, and the occasional wood structure wrought from the twisted thi'zech. He was expecting a fortress, but this was little more than a camp. It was nestled against the northern cliffs, where still the land was flat and desolate, but an icy wind howled across the rocks overhead. It was calmer below, but equally cold, gripping his skin wherever it could and chilling his whole body. *Perhaps not so sophisticated*, he thought.

He was patient as they pushed, collected as they shouted, refused to show pain as they hurled him onto his face inside a larger tent. He landed on fur, which was surprisingly soft. It remained bitterly cold even in this abode and light remained limited. The only fire was small, for there was not much wood to be had. Beyond it, glowering over its crackling tongues, was a simple chair draped in still more furs. Upon it sat a woman, strong and silent. By her side was a stand that held some of the most beautifully ornate and polished armor he had ever seen; zeulf rubbed so vigorously he could see his reflection in what parts of it were not embossed with painstakingly detailed symbols, all of them identical. It was two stars, each with seven points, falling onto a patch of land where the only feature was the florid text of a single word: Gnosmeim – 'Remember us'.

On the other side was a heavy weapon unlike anything Rogan had ever seen, like a bow, but with a long handle at its center, all of it reinforced with metal.

Behind it was an attendant, a slave by the look of her. She was a malnourished girl, perhaps twenty seasons, trembling on thin legs as she held a heavy-looking metal bowl, occasionally glancing to her owner in the hopes she would take it for a moment.

The mistress, pure Galaila as he had expected, might easily have been confused for a slave herself, had it not been for her protrusively defined muscles and apparent position of honor. Her only clothes were a loincloth and a single length of fine silk wrapped numerous times about her breast. Her left eye had an unusual metal patch nailed into her skull, bearing the strange symbol as the armor. Wavy golden hair, finely brushed and well-tended, obscured the other. She said nothing, did nothing, only lifted her head ever-so-slightly to stare at Rogan.

Instinctively, he addressed her in what fine voice he could muster with his parched throat.

"My great and admirable warlord..."

As fast as thunder her right hand snatched up her weapon, aimed it as though it weighed nothing and took a precise shot to plant a thick arrow in the dirt between Rogan's legs. His wide eyes flashed down, confirming the sensation that the razor-sharp projectile could not possibly have been any closer to his testicles.

"You will not speak to me," the woman grumbled lazily, then convincingly angry as she eyed the placement of her bolt. "Shame. I thought they would have hung lower by now."

Rogan sensed something familiar in her words; the hardness of her tone masking a naturally lyrical voice. Before he could identify it, she set the weapon aside and sternly took the bowl from the slave, addressed the man who had captured Rogan.

"Why is he here? He looks different."

"*La,* my *Khanaiat,* we thought you would want to question him, especially in his current condition. Someone bound him thusly before we found him."

That piqued her interest enough for her to give Rogan the longest, most uncomfortable glare he had ever met. He did not appreciate the full extent of the warning behind it but recalculated his approach as she put the bowl to her lips and gulped gracelessly from it, deep red wine gushing around her mouth and down her chest. She was a 'Khanaiat'? Some sort of supreme leader indeed, he thought. Why then did she sit in rags, drinking so sloppily? Believing he could still outsmart her, he tried once more.

"*Jiaia,* I can help you. I beg you to hear me or your people..."

She leapt from her seat and slid through the dirt on her knees straight through the fire, scattering cinders and wood even as they burned into her skin. Rogan went stiff, aghast at how this ruler dirtied herself, ignoring pain and decorum, finally concerned for his life when she connected with him. One hand locked around his throat and wrenched it upward, the other seizing the bolt in the ground and pressing its edge up into his dangling genitals. He gasped sharply, sputtering through her fierce clutches and trying to meet her eyes. He stared, and she stared back. Up close, he could discern how her face and body were heavily scarred, even stitched in some places. The wounds completed the memory he had of her voice and his lips quivered pathetically as he looked into the one good eye. He knew its color, knew her hair, her voice, her hatred of him.

"M…Mitheyai?"

The woman sneered, twisting the bolt painfully against him.

"Hello, lover," she said, devious and pleased.

"How c-can you be…"

"This place has done wonders for you, husband. Now you're as monstrous on the skin as you are in the heart."

Rogan could not control himself anymore. These people made no sense. His wife even less.

"How are you not changing!?" He shouted without composure, "How are you even alive!? It is not possible!"

Mitheyai, his beaten and discarded bride and mother of his children, went to stand by her throne and kicked her bowl aside, unconcerned with the burns on her legs.

"Oh lovely, clever Rogan. You were always too busy trying to make things as you wished them to be to see what they were meant to become. Fear not. I will show you what is possible."

He shook his head incredulously as she motioned for him to be taken away and wasting no time barking orders at the guardsmen.

"You two, send a scouting party to the wake of where you found him. Report to me all there is to see. If there are more of these things, do not go noticed. We will no doubt require a greater force here. As for this one…take him aboard the Woken Widow and see him to the brig. He's coming home with us."

"Home…" Rogan's voice tightened. "…It is…"

"Ellel awaits, my sweet," she huffed menacingly, "As does my inquisitor. I'd like to know more about these…creatures that my perfect Galaila have become."

"Inquis…woman, is there no forgiveness in your heart!? I'll tell you anything! Everything!"

She smiled over her shoulder, darkly delighted as her crew

327

bustled in preparation to leave.
    "Oh yes, you will."

ABOUT THE AUTHOR

Originally from Arizona, Giggy has lived happily in Oregon since 1995. A modern Renaissance man by nature, he lives an autodidactic life with little interest in scholastic education subjects despite an innate aptitude for learning.

After discovering a passion for poetry, ethics, Chinese and Greek philosophy at a young age, these influences became the voice of a budding interest in writing as a career. He continues to seek new adventures and inspirations in the mountains of central Oregon, down the west coast and in any country there is a unique opportunity to visit.

Written and edited while at home by the fire, travelling overseas or in active combat zones, the creation of *House of the Living Sky* began in 2003 and was not complete until 2019. Giggy claims the story was never meant to be published. The journey was instead intended as a form of self-reflection, taking personal attributes and conflicting thoughts then turn them into characters with their own voice and motivation.

Then, in the laboratory of the growing series, they would clash to resolve their incompatibility. The result of this experiment, as Giggy explains it, is the realization that the good and evil of any character is subjective and liable to criticism. This duality of heroic and villainous archetypes has come to be the very heart of *House of the Living Sky*.

www.ingramcontent.com/pod-product-compliance
Lightning Source LLC
Chambersburg PA
CBHW051937220626
47052CB00004B/692